THE HUNTING LODGE

The outside door opened easily enough; the electrolocks were dead. I was still surrounded by walls; the nearest exit was nearly half a mile away. That didn't bother me; I wasn't going to have to use it. There was a high-speed flitter waiting for me above the clouds.

I could hear it humming down toward me. Then I could see it, drifting down in a fast spiral.

Whoom!

I was startled for a timeless instant as I saw the flitter dissolve in a blossom of yellow-orange flame. The flare, marking the end of my escape craft, hung in the air for an endless second and then died slowly.

I realized then that the heavy defenses of the Lodge had come to life. . . .

THE BEST OF
RANDALL GARRETT

Edited by Robert Silverberg

A TIMESCAPE BOOK
PUBLISHED BY POCKET BOOKS NEW YORK

This collection is comprised of works of fiction. Names, characters, places and incidents are either the product of the author's imagination or are used fictitiously, and any resemblance to actual persons, living or dead, events or locales is entirely coincidental.

A Timescape Book published by
POCKET BOOKS, a Simon & Schuster division of
GULF & WESTERN CORPORATION
1230 Avenue of the Americas, New York, N.Y. 10020

ISBN: 0-671-83574-2

First Timescape Books printing January, 1982

10 9 8 7 6 5 4 3 2 1

POCKET and colophon are trademarks of Simon & Schuster.

Use of the TIMESCAPE trademark is by exclusive license
from Gregory Benford, the trademark owner.

Printed in the U.S.A.

ACKNOWLEDGMENTS

"The Hunting Lodge" Copyright 1954 by Street and Smith Publications, Inc. Originally appeared in *Astounding Science Fiction*, July 1954. Used by permission of the author.

"The Waiting Game" Copyright 1951 by Street and Smith Publications, Inc. Originally appeared in *Astounding Science Fiction*, January 1951. Used by permission of the author.

"Alfred Bester's *The Demolished Man*" Copyright © 1956 by Columbia Publications, Inc. Originally appeared in *Science Fiction Stories*, January 1956. Used by permission of the author.

"Isaac Asimov's *The Caves of Steel*" Copyright © 1956 by Columbia Publications, Inc. Originally appeared in *Science Fiction Stories*, March 1956. Used by permission of the author.

"Poul Anderson's *Three Hearts and Three Lions*" Copyright © 1978 by Randall Garrett and Vicki Ann Heydron. Originally appeared in *Takeoff* (The Donning Company/Publishers, 1979). Used by permission of the author.

"No Connections" Copyright © 1958 by Street and Smith Publications, Inc. Originally appeared in *Astounding Science Fiction*, June 1958. Used by permission of the author.

"The Best Policy" Copyright © 1957 by Street and Smith Publications, Inc. Originally appeared as "David Gordon" in *Astounding Science Fiction*, July 1957. Used by permission of the author.

"Time Fuze" Copyright 1954 by Quinn Publishing Company. Originally appeared in *If Worlds of Science Fiction*, March 1954. Used by permission of the author.

"A Little Intelligence" Copyright © 1958 by Columbia Publications, Inc. Originally appeared in *Future Science Fiction*, October 1958. Used by permission of the author.

"The Eyes Have It" Copyright © 1964 by The Condé Nast Publications, Inc. Originally appeared in *Analog*, January 1964. Used by permission of the author.

"The Spell of War" Copyright © 1978 by Randall Garrett. Originally appeared in *The Future at War 1: Thor's Hammer* (Ace Books, 1979). Used by permission of the author.

"Frost and Thunder" Copyright © 1979 by Davis Publications, Inc. Originally appeared in *Asimov's Science Fiction Adventure Magazine*, Summer 1979. Used by permission of the author.

CONTENTS

THE BEST OF
RANDALL GARRETT

INTRODUCTION

RANDALL GARRETT AND I HAD OUR FIRST ENcounter at the 1953 World Science Fiction Convention in Philadelphia, and it was not an auspicious one. I was just a young fan then, although I had actually made one professional sale and in fact would collect my payment for it right at that convention, which was the first big sciencefiction gathering I had ever attended. I was a college sophomore, then, in my late teens, and I was doing the convention in style, occupying a huge suite at the opulent Bellevue-Stratford Hotel. Of course, I couldn't afford a suite all by myself—the rent must have been at least $30 a night, maybe even more—so I went into partnership with a bunch of other fans of about my own age and we ran the place as a kind of dormitory. I can't remember at this late date how many of us there were, but some of their names still stick in my memory, obscure though they now may be to the general public: David Ish, Ian Macauley, Karl Olsen, Norman G. Browne and a certain Harlan Ellison.

Anyway, life in our suite was something of a perpetual party throughout the weekend, and a good many professionals actually wandered in—my first meetings with such good friends as Frank M. Robinson, Larry Shaw and Robert Sheckley took place at that convention. But although the suite's social life was active and hectic, we didn't intend to run a mere open house there. And so, one evening when I heard formidable knocks at our door and opened it to find a large and rowdy-looking stranger standing there, I shrugged and said, "Sorry, private party," and closed the door in his face.

"Jeez," Harlan said, "that was *Randall Garrett*."

"So?"

"He's had stories published!"

1

"So?"

"In *Astounding*," Harlan said.

"I don't care," I replied. "He looked drunk. And he was making too much noise."

"Would you shut the door in John Campbell's face if you thought he was too noisy?" somebody asked. "Heinlein's? Asimov's?"

I was imperturbable. "This is a classy party," I said. "We let only classy people in."

The next thing I knew, it was 1955 and Randall Garrett was living next door to me in a Manhattan boarding house.

Ellison gets the blame for that. I lived in the place—it was 611 West 114th Street, near Riverside Drive—because I was an undergraduate at Columbia. Harlan showed up in New York some time in 1954, with some notion of starting a career as a writer, and needed a place to live, so he phoned me and I found him a room in my building. When Garrett, who had been living in Illinois, moved to New York a few months later, he phoned Ellison, who got *him* a room there. I remembered the 1953 incident (Garrett didn't) and was a little troubled about it, because in the interim I had read a good many of his stories and had developed considerable respect for his work, whereas at the time of the door-closing I had hardly known who he was. By this time I had already launched my own career, selling four or five mediocre short stories and a novel, but the notion that I had a real professional writer living next door, one who had actually sold stories to John Campbell's legendary magazine *Astounding Science Fiction,* awed me a lot more than it had when he tried to crash my party at Philadelphia.

Garrett and I struck up a close friendship quickly—despite some profound differences in temperament and manner. I was then and am now slender, quiet, sardonic, temperate, an early-to-bed and early-to-rise type who enjoys an orderly, disciplined life. Garrett was then, although he went through some changes later, plump, boisterous, untidy, a hard drinker and heavy smoker who rarely surfaced by daylight and who did his best work, when he could bring himself to work at all, between midnight and dawn. Despite these grave disparities, or maybe because of them, we launched almost immediately into partnership. It was, indeed, a true symbiosis. Garrett was outgoing and exuberant; he knew all the New York magazine editors and visited their offices frequently. I, aloof and even shy,

2

had never met any of them, although I lived just a few miles from their headquarters. He took me downtown and introduced me to everyone as an up-and-coming star. Then, too, Garrett had a strong scientific background, with a technical education and a career as a chemist in his past; my own inclinations were toward literature and philosophy. As science-fiction writers, we complemented one another, each providing the skills and knowledge the other lacked. And I enjoyed working—I brimmed with ambition and drive—whereas Randall, left to his own devices, tended to write only when his last check was spent. So we were a perfect match. He used his hearty extroverted nature to make professional contacts for us; we plotted stories together, he contributing the technical aspects and I the character development and narrative format; then he (usually) wrote a quick first draft, working through the night while I slept; by day I took his chaotic manuscript and revised it into something fit to submit to a magazine, polishing the style and enlarging the characterization, and finally we went downtown together to make the sale. All through the second half of 1955 and the first part of 1956 we were a gloriously successful fiction factory. We sold so many stories that it became necessary to work under a host of pseudonyms, of which the best known was "Robert Randall."

I took my degree from Columbia in 1956, and after my marriage a little later that year I left the rooming house on 114th Street for an apartment of surprising luxury on West End Avenue. We continued our collaboration on an increasingly sporadic basis for a couple of years after that, but it became more difficult to work together as the rhythms of our lives changed, and in any event our separate careers were doing so well that the collaborations (and the division of earnings) become unnecessary. Garrett was now a major contributor to Campbell's *Astounding,* one of the two or three mainstays of the magazine, and I was hard at work producing fiction for the editors I had met under his auspices. With his help in making introductions for me, I had jumped years forward along the career track, and at the age of 23 or so had agreements for the purchase of fiction stretching far into the future.

Our ways parted in the 1960s. He inherited property in Texas and went down there to live; later, I heard, he had moved to Southern California. We saw each other rarely, with gaps of four or five years between our meetings.

3

Whenever we met, we ran through an obligatory set of reminiscences of our gaudy days in the mid-50s, but there wasn't much to say about the present time. My own career was going from strength to strength, but he had virtually given up writing several times in the 1960s. His main interest now seemed to be religion—nothing new, for he had been an active churchgoer even in his bawdiest days, and had talked often of entering the priesthood. But I think he spent much of his time in the late 1960s in monastic activities and very little of it writing. And if it sounds odd that a man so worldly and Falstaffian should have hovered most of his adult life on the edge of taking holy orders, so be it: he is a complex man full of fascinating contradictions, an interesting mix of sinner and saint, although the consensus is that there's rather more sinner than saint in him.

The upheavals of life eventually carried me 3000 miles westward to the San Francisco Bay Area, and lo! Randall Garrett had wandered that way too, so we became neighbors again. We even talked vaguely of collaborating, though not very seriously, and we never did. We continued to reminisce about the old days and to keep an eye on each other's careers—for Randall had begun writing again, his work centering around the parallel-world series featuring the detective Lord Darcy, and suddenly he was famous once more in the science-fiction world after long years of obscurity. All during the 1970s the Lord Darcy stories appeared, and he developed a loyal and eager following for them, eventually even a fan club. The Darcy stories brought together Garrett's interests in medieval history and religion, his love of speculative thinking and a gift for mystery-story writing that may be greater even than his knack for science fiction: they were the perfect summation of all his experience, and the love and intensity that went into them brought repayment in reader attention.

Irony is a writer's stock-in-trade, and so I appreciate gloomily the irony that handed Randall Garrett a serious, even a debilitating, illness just as he belatedly reached the peak of his career. In the summer of 1979, as he was in the midst of a host of writing projects both in the Lord Darcy series and otherwise, as he was finally achieving the kind of professional discipline and personal stability that would allow him to make the fullest use of his talents, he was invaded by an alien organism, a virus that for a time threatened his life and for a much longer time has made

4

it impossible for him to work. He is now fighting his way back to full recovery, but it will be some time yet before the next Lord Darcy story leaves his typewriter.

And so, in partial atonement for slamming that door on him in 1953, and in partial repayment for the help he gave me in launching my career two years later, I have assembled this collection of some of Randall Garrett's best science-fiction stories, and I have asked a dozen or so of his friends to contribute anecdotal accounts of the man, by way of providing an unexpurgated and many-dimensional view of him. And we offer this book now to Randall Garrett, to cheer him along the road to recovery, and to the readers who for the first time will discover his skills as a storyteller.

—Robert Silverberg.

THE MAN WHO CAME FOR CHRISTMAS

Philip José Farmer

RANDALL GARRETT INTRODUCED HIMSELF TO my wife Bette and me in Chicago in 1952 at the first science-fiction convention she and I attended. The tall handsome Robin Redbreastish fellow (who'd been published in *Astounding!*) overwhelmed us with his charm, anecdotes, jokes, puns, ribald ballads, limericks, parody-verses and Gilbert-and-Sullivan lyrics. We laughed until we wept.

After the con, Bette and I returned to Peoria; he, to Cincinnati. During his frequent and hours-long phone calls, he often sang the old classic, "How I Wish't I Was in Peoria!". When Bette found out he'd be alone on Christmas, she invited him to our house for the holidays.

Three years later, he left for New York.

Our children, all the neighborhood children, thought he was the best thing to come along since Santa Claus. Our daughter Kristen, 34 now, has very fond memories of "Uncle Randy." But Bette and I and our friends came to think of him as a combination of Falstaff and Henry Miller. In many ways, however, as time would reveal, he was then a sort of preconversion St. Augustine.

In 1953 we three went to an Ohio con with Beverly, his wife, who'd come from New Mexico for a final try at reconciliation. The con hotel was Beatley's-at-the-Lake, which we called Beastley's. We shared a single large room to save money for such necessities as beer and booze. It was in this room that five-foot 90-pound Beverly floored six-foot 190-pound Randall with a single blow of her fist. Why? Because he couldn't explain the lace panties sticking out from his coat pocket. He got up and reeled off, and, after he hadn't shown for several hours, I went out to find him. Wandering down Beastley's corridors, I heard a terrible commotion around the corner.

I turned it just as a young woman, naked, all her clothes under one arm, and screaming, ran past me. Then Randall, all his garments clutched to his chest, sped by me. Behind him came the manager's son and the hotel dick, their faces scarlet with rage. Randall was in trouble again.

When I got back to our room, I found him, now fully dressed except for one shoe, enduring a chewing out from Beverly and sporting a red eye that'd soon become black and blue. He finally confessed that he'd met an old flame in the bar, and, after many drinks, they'd gone to her room—they thought. But it was the room next to hers, which was unlocked, and Randall had bolted the door. Some time later, the legal occupant had tried to get in but was told by Randall to beat it.

The hotel dick and the manager's son were summoned. Randall told them to fuck off; he was busy fucking. They broke the door down, and in the ensuing argument the son hit Randall in the eye and chased the two culprits down the hall but failed to catch them.

After not having seen him for more than 20 years, I ran into Randall at a party in Santa Maria, California. He was in clerical garb and informed me that he was an ordained minister. I thought it'd be indiscreet under the circumstances to mention any Beastley-like incidents. Or the time in Peoria when he was to join the Anglican church but failed to show up because he'd gotten drunk in a barber shop. However, he claimed to be cured of alcoholism, so I asked him why he was dipping so heavily into the rum-punch bowl. He said his psychiatrist had assured him that he was the only alcoholic in the world who could be allowed to drink. This remark was so typically Garrettian that I broke up.

"So," I said, "the Hound of Heaven finally caught you?"

"Yes. His bite is painful, but it hurts so good."

Though he continued to drink, he behaved like the very model of a priest. There were no loud burstings into Gilbert and Sullivan, no dirty jokes or limericks, no insults, no kissing and fondling of all women within reach, no passing out on the floor, no need for anyone to give him a shiner.

I was so impressed that I got loaded.

This taut, tense story, published in *Astounding Science Fiction* in 1954, was the one that established Randall Garrett's popularity as a science-fiction writer. He had been appearing sporadically in the magazines for three or four years, but this time he had his name on the front cover and the story had the lead position inside. The regular readers' poll voted it the best in the issue and it has rarely been out of print ever since—a swift-paced tale that anticipates much of today's computerized society.

It exemplifies, also, one of Garrett's most persistent traits—the habit of selecting titles for his stories that carry some hidden punning connotation.

THE HUNTING LODGE

"WE'LL HELP ALL WE CAN," THE DIRECTOR said, "but if you're caught, that's all there is to it."

I nodded. It was the age-old warning: *If you're caught, we disown you.* I wondered, fleetingly, how many men had heard that warning during the long centuries of human history, and I wondered how many of them had asked themselves the same question I was asking:

Why am *I* risking *my* neck?

And I wondered how many of them had had an answer.

"Ready, then?" the Director asked, glancing at his watch. I nodded and looked at my own. The shadow hands pointed to 2250.

"Here's the gun."

I took it and checked its loading. "Untraceable, I suppose?"

He shook his head. "It can be traced, all right, but it won't lead to us. A gun which couldn't be traced almost certainly would be associated with us. But the best thing to do would be to bring the gun back with you; that way, it's in no danger of being traced."

The way he said it gave me a chill. He wanted me back alive, right enough, but only so there would be no evidence.

"OK," I said. "Let's go."

I put a nice, big, friendly grin on my face. After all, there was no use making him feel worse than necessary. I knew he didn't like sending men out to be killed. I slipped the sleeve gun into its holster and then faced him.

"Blaze away!"

He looked me over, then touched the hypno controls. A light hit my eyes.

I was walking along the street when I came out of it, heading toward a flitter stand. An empty flitter was sitting there waiting, so I climbed in and sat down.

Senator Rowley's number was ORdway 63–911. I dialed it and leaned back, just as though I had every right to go there.

The flitter lifted perfectly and headed northwest, but I knew perfectly well that the scanners were going full blast, sorting through their information banks to find me.

A mile or so out of the city, the flitter veered to the right, locked its controls, and began to go around in a tight circle.

The viewphone lit up, but the screen stayed blank. A voice said: "Routine check. Identify yourself, please."

Routine! I knew better. But I just looked blank and stuck my right forearm into the checker. There was a short hum while the ultrasonic scanners looked at the tantalum identity plate riveted to the bone.

"Thank you, Mr. Gifford," said the voice. The phone cut off, but the flitter was still going in circles.

Then the phone lit again, and Senator Rowley's face— thin, dark and bright-eyed—came on the screen.

"Gifford! Did you get it?"

"I got it, sir," I answered quietly.

He nodded, pleased. "Good! I'll be waiting for you."

Again the screen went dark, and this time the flitter straightened out and headed northwest once more.

I tried not to feel too jittery, but I had to admit to myself that I was scared. The senator was dangerous. If he could get a finger into the robot central office of the flitters, there was no way of knowing how far his control went.

10

He wasn't supposed to be able to tap a flitter any more than he was supposed to be able to tap a phone. But neither one was safe now.

Only a few miles ahead of me was the Lodge, probably the most tightly guarded home in the world.

I knew I might not get in, of course. Senator Anthony Rowley was no fool, by a long shot. He placed his faith in robots. A machine might fail, but it would never be treacherous.

I could see the walls of the Lodge ahead as the flitter began to lose altitude. I could almost feel the watching radar eyes that followed the craft down, and it made me nervous to realize that a set of high-cycle guns were following the instructions of those eyes.

And, all alone in that big mansion—or fortress—sat Senator Rowley like a spider in the middle of an intangible web.

The public flitter, with me in it, lit like a fly on the roof of the mansion. I took a deep breath and stepped out. The multiple eyes of the robot defenses watched me closely as I got into the waiting elevator.

The hard plastic of the little sleeve gun was supposed to be transparent to X rays and sonics, but I kept praying anyway. Suddenly I felt a tingle in my arm. I knew what it was: a checker to see if the molecular structure of the tantalum identity plate was according to government specifications in every respect.

Identity plates were furnished only by the Federal government, but they were also supposed to be the only ones with analyzers. Even the senator shouldn't have had an unregistered job.

To play safe, I rubbed at the arm absently. I didn't knew whether Gifford had ever felt that tingle before or not. If he had, he might ignore it, but he wouldn't let it startle him. If he hadn't, he might not be startled, but he wouldn't ignore it. Rubbing seemed the safest course.

The thing that kept running through my mind was *How much did Rowley trust psychoimpressing?*

He had last seen Gifford four days ago, and at that time Gifford could no more have betrayed the senator than one of the robots could. Because, psychologically speaking, that's exactly what Gifford had been—a robot. Theoretically, it is impossible to remove a competent psychoimpressing job in less than six weeks of steady therapy. It

11

could be done in a little less time, but it didn't leave the patient in an ambient condition. And it couldn't, under any circumstances, be done in four days.

If Senator Rowley was thoroughly convinced I was Gifford, and if he trusted psychoimpression, I was in easy.

I looked at my watch again. 2250. Exactly an hour since I had left. The change in time zones had occurred while I was in the flitter, and the shadow hands had shifted back to accommodate.

It seemed to be taking a long time for the elevator to drop; I could just barely feel the movement. The robots were giving me a very thorough going over.

Finally, the door slid open and I stepped out into the lounge. For the first time in my life, I saw the living face of Senator Anthony Rowley.

The filters built into his phone pickup did a lot for him. They softened the fine wrinkles that made his face look like a piece of old leather. They added color to his grayish skin. They removed the yellowishness from his eyes. In short, the senator's pickup filters took two centuries off his age.

Longevity can't do everything for you, I thought. But I could see what it *could* do, too, if you were smart and had plenty of time. And those who had plenty of time were automatically the smart ones.

The senator extended a hand: "Give me the briefcase, Gifford."

"Yes, sir." As I held out the small blue case, I glanced at my watch. 2255. And, as I watched, the last five became a six.

Four minutes to go.

"Sit down, Gifford." The senator waved me to a chair. I sat and watched him while he leafed through the supposedly secret papers.

Oh, they were real enough, all right, but they didn't contain any information that would be of value to him. He would be too dead for that.

He ignored me as he read. There was no need to watch Gifford. Even if Gifford had tried anything, the robotic brain in the basement of the house would have detected it with at least one of its numerous sensory devices and acted to prevent the senator's death long before any mere human could complete any action.

I knew that, and the senator knew it.

12

We sat.

2257.

The senator frowned. "This is all, Gifford?"

"I can't be sure, of course, sir. But I will say that any further information on the subject is buried pretty deeply. So well hidden, in fact, that even the government couldn't find it in time to use against you."

"Mmmmmm."

2258.

The senator grinned. "This is it," he said through his tight, thin, old lips. "We'll be in complete control within a year, Gifford."

"That's good, sir. Very good."

It doesn't take much to play the part of a man who's been psychoimpressed as thoroughly as Gifford had been.

2259.

The senator smiled softly and said nothing. I waited tensely, hoping that the darkness would be neither too long nor too short. I made no move toward the sleeve gun, but I was ready to grab it as soon as—

2300!

The lights went out—and came on again.

The senator had time to look both startled and frightened before I shot him through the heart.

I didn't waste any time. The power had been cut off from the Great Northwestern Reactor, which supplied all the juice for the whole area, but the senator had provided wisely for that. He had a reactor of his own built in for emergencies; it had cut in as soon as the Great Northwestern had gone out.

But cutting off the power to a robot brain is the equivalent of hitting a man over the head with a blackjack; it takes time to recover. It was that time lapse which had permitted me to kill Rowley and which would, if I moved fast enough, permit me to escape before its deadly defenses could be rallied against me.

I ran toward a door and almost collided with it before I realized that it wasn't going to open for me. I had to push it aside. I kept on running, heading for an outside entrance. There was no way of knowing how long the robot would remain stunned.

Rowley had figured he was being smart when he built a single centralized computer to take over all the defenses of the house instead of having a series of simple brains,

13

one for each function. And, in a way, I guess he was right; the Lodge could act as a single unit that way.

But Rowley had died because he insisted on that complication; the simpler the brain, the quicker the recovery.

The outside door opened easily enough; the electrolocks were dead. I was still surrounded by walls; the nearest exit was nearly half a mile away. That didn't bother me; I wasn't going to have to use it. There was a high-speed flitter waiting for me above the clouds.

I could hear it humming down toward me. Then I could see it, drifting down in a fast spiral.

Whoom!

I was startled for a timeless instant as I saw the flitter dissolve in a blossom of yellow-orange flame. This flare, marking the end of my escape craft, hung in the air for an endless second and then died slowly.

I realized then that the heavy defenses of the Lodge had come to life.

I didn't even stop to think. The glowing red of the fading explosion was still lighting the ground as I turned and sprinted toward the garage. One thing I knew: the robot would not shoot down one of the senator's own machines unless ordered to do so.

The robot was still not fully awake. It had reacted to the approach of a big, fast-moving object, but it still couldn't see a running man. Its scanners wouldn't track yet.

I shoved the garage doors open and looked inside. The bright lights disclosed ground vehicles and nothing more. The flitters were all on the roof.

I hadn't any choice; I had to get out of there, and fast!

The senator had placed a lot of faith in the machines that guarded the Lodge. The keys were in the lock of one big Ford-Studebaker. I shoved the control from auto to manual, turned the key and started the engines.

As soon as they were humming, I started the car moving. And none too soon, either. The doors of the garage slammed after me like the jaws of a man trap. I gunned the car for the nearest gate, hoping that this one last effort would be successful. If I didn't make it through the outer gate, I might as well give up.

As I approached the heavy outer gates, I could see that they were functioning; I'd never get them open by hand. But the robot was still a little confused. It recognized the car and didn't recognize me. The gates dropped, so I didn't even slow the car. Pure luck again.

And close luck, at that. The gates tried to come back up out of the ground even as the heavy vehicle went over them; there was a loud bump as the rear wheels hit the top of the rising gate. But again the robot was too late.

I took a deep breath and aimed the car toward the city. So far, so good. A clean getaway.

Another of the Immortals was dead. Senator Rowley's political machine would never again force through a vote to give him another longevity treatment, because the senator's political force had been cut off at the head, and the target was gone. Pardon the mixed metaphor.

Longevity treatments are like a drug; the more you have, the more you want. I suppose it had been a good idea a few centuries ago to restrict their use to men who were of such use to the race that they deserved to live longer than the average. But the mistake was made in putting it up to the voting public who should get the treatments.

Of course, they'd had a right to have a voice in it; at the beginning, the cost of a single treatment had been too high for any individual to pay for it. And, in addition, it had been a government monopoly, since the government had paid for the research. So, if the taxpayer's money was to be spent, the taxpayer had a right to say who it was to be spent on.

But if a man's life hangs on his ability to control the public, what other out does he have?

And the longer he lives, the greater his control. A man can become an institution if he lives long enough. And Senator Rowley had lived long enough; he—

Something snickered on the instrument panel. I looked, but I couldn't see anything. Then something moved under my foot. It was the accelerator. The car was slowing.

I didn't waste any time guessing; I knew what was happening. I opened the door just as the car stopped. Fortunately, the doors had only manual controls: simple mechanical locks.

I jumped out of the car's way and watched it as it backed up, turned around, and drove off in the direction of the Lodge. The robot was fully awake now; it had recalled the car. I hadn't realized that the senator had set up the controls in his vehicles so that the master robot could take control away from a human being.

15

I thanked various and sundry deities that I had not climbed into one of the flitters. It's hard to get out of an aircraft when it's a few thousand feet above the earth.

Well, there was nothing to do but walk. So I walked.

It wasn't more than ten minutes before I heard the buzzing behind me. Something was coming over the road at a good clip, but without headlights. In the darkness, I couldn't see a thing, but I knew it wasn't an ordinary car. Not coming from the Lodge.

I ran for the nearest tree, a big monster at least three feet thick and 50 or 60 feet high. The lowest branch was a heavy one about seven feet from the ground. I grabbed it and swung myself up and kept on climbing until I was a good 20 feet off the ground. Then I waited.

The whine stopped down the road about half a mile, about where I'd left the Ford-Studebaker. Whatever it was prowled around for a minute or two, then started coming on down the road.

When it finally came close enough for me to see it in the moonlight, I recognized it for what it was. A patrol robot. It was looking for me.

Then I heard another whine. But this one was different; it was a siren coming from the main highway.

Overhead, I heard a flitter whistling through the sky.

The police.

The patrol robot buzzed around on its six wheels, turning its search-turret this way and that, trying to spot me.

The siren grew louder, and I saw the headlights in the distance. In less than a minute, the lights struck the patrol robot, outlining every detail of the squat, ugly silhouette. It stopped, swiveling its turret toward the police car. The warning light on the turret came on, glowing a bright red.

The cops slowed down and stopped. One of the men in the car called out: "Senator? Are you on the other end of that thing?"

No answer from the robot.

"I guess he's really dead," said another officer in a low, awed voice.

"It don't seem possible," the first voice said. Then he called again to the patrol robot. "We're police officers. Will you permit us to show our identification?"

The patrol robot clicked a little as the information was

16

relayed back to the Lodge and the answer given. The red warning light turned green, indicating that the guns were not going to fire.

About that time, I decided that my only chance was to move around so that the trunk of the tree was between me and the road. I had to move slowly so they wouldn't hear me, but I finally made it.

I could hear the policeman saying: "According to the information we received, Senator Rowley was shot by his secretary, Edgar Gifford. This patrol job must be hunting him."

"Hey!" said another voice. "Here comes another one! He must be in the area somewhere!"

I could hear the whining of a second patrol robot approaching from the Lodge. It was still about a mile away, judging from the sound.

I couldn't see what happening next, but I could hear the first robot moving, and it must have found me, even though I was out of sight. Directional heat detector, probably.

"In the tree, eh?" said a cop.

Another called: "All right, Gifford! Come on down!"

Well, that was it. I was caught. But I wasn't going to be taken alive. I eased out the sleeve gun and sneaked a peek around the tree. *No use killing a cop,* I thought, *he's just doing his job.*

So I fired at the car, which didn't hurt a thing.

"Look out!"

"Duck!"

"Get that blaster going!"

Good. It was going to be a blaster. It would take off the tree top and me with it. I'd die quickly.

There was a sudden flurry of shots, and then silence.

I took another quick peek and got the shock of my life.

The four police officers were crumpled on the ground, shot down by the patrol robot from the Lodge. One of them—the one holding the blaster—wasn't quite dead yet. He gasped something obscene and fired the weapon just as two more slugs from the robot's turret hit him in the chest.

The turret exploded in a gout of fire.

I didn't get it, but I didn't have time to wonder what was going on. I know a chance when I see one. I swung

17

from the branch I was on and dropped to the ground, rolling over in a bed of old leaves to take up the shock. Then I made a beeline for the police car.

On the way, I grabbed one of the helmets from a uniformed corpse, hoping that my own tunic was close enough to the same shade of scarlet to get me by. I climbed in and got the machine turned around just as the second patrol robot came into sight. It fired a couple of shots after me, but those patrol jobs don't have enough armament to shoot down a police car; they're strictly for hunting unarmed and unprotected pedestrians.

Behind me there were a couple of flares in the sky that reminded me of my own exploding flitter, but I didn't worry about what they could be.

I was still puzzled about the robot's shooting down the police. It didn't make sense.

Oh, well, it had saved my neck, and I wasn't going to pinch a gift melon.

The police car I was in had evidently been the only ground vehicle dispatched toward the Lodge—possibly because it happened to be nearby. It was a traffic-control car; the regular homicide squad was probably using flitters.

I turned off the private road and onto the highway, easing into the traffic control pattern and letting the car drift along with the other vehicles. But I didn't shove it into automatic. I didn't like robots just then. Besides, if I let the main control panels take over the guiding of the car, someone at headquarters might wonder why car such-and-such wasn't at the Lodge as ordered; they might wonder why it was going down the highway so unconcernedly.

There was only one drawback. I wasn't used to handling a car at 150 to 200 miles an hour. If something should happen to the traffic pattern, I'd have to depend on my own reflexes. And they might not be fast enough.

I decided I'd have to ditch the police car as soon as I could. It was too much trouble and too easy to spot.

I had an idea. I turned off the highway again at the next break, a few miles farther on. There wasn't much side traffic at that time of night, so I had to wait several minutes before the pattern broke again and a private car pulled out and headed down the side road.

I hit the siren and pulled him over to the side.

18

He was an average-sized character with a belligerent attitude and a fat face.

"What's the matter, officer? There was nothing wrong with that break. I didn't cut out of the pattern on manual, you know. I was—" He stopped when he realized that my tunic was not that of a policeman. "Why, you're not—"

By then, I'd already cut him down with a stun gun I'd found in the arms compartment of the police car. I hauled him out and changed tunics with him. His was a little loose, but not so much that it would be noticeable. Then I put the helmet on his head and strapped him into the front seat of the police vehicle with the safety belt.

After being hit with a stun gun, he'd be out for a good hour. That would be plenty of time as far as I was concerned.

I transferred as much of the police armory as I thought I'd need into the fat-faced fellow's machine and then I climbed into the police car with him. I pulled the car around and headed back toward the highway.

Just before we reached the control area, I set the instruments for the Coast and headed him west, back the way I had come.

I jumped out and slammed the door behind me as the automatic controls took over and put him in the traffic pattern.

Then I walked back to Fatty's car, got in, and drove back to the highway. I figured I could trust the controls of a private vehicle, so I set them and headed east, toward the city. Once I was there, I'd have to get a flitter, somehow.

I spent the next 20 minutes changing my face. I couldn't do anything about the basic structure; that would have to wait until I got back. Nor could I do anything about the ID plate that was bolted to my left ulna; that, too, would have to wait.

I changed the color of my hair, darkening it from Gifford's gray to a mousy brown, and I took a patch of hair out above my forehead to give me a balding look. The mustache went, and the sides of the beard, giving me a goatee effect. I trimmed down the brows and the hair, and put a couple of tubes in my nostrils to widen my nose.

I couldn't do much about the eyes; my little pocket kit didn't carry them. But, all in all, I looked a great deal less like Gifford than I had before.

Then I proceeded to stow a few weapons on and about my person. I had taken the sleeve gun out of the scarlet tunic when I'd put it on the fat-faced man, but his own chartreuse tunic didn't have a sleeve holster, so I had to put the gun in a hip pocket. But the tunic was a godsend in another way; it was loose enough to carry a few guns easily.

The car speaker said: "Attention! You are now approaching Groverton, the last suburb before the city limits. Private automobiles may not be taken beyond this point. If you wish to bypass the city, please indicate. If not, please go to the free storage lot in Groverton."

I decided I'd do neither. I might as well make the car as hard to find as possible. I took it to an all-night repair technician in Groverton.

"Something wrong with the turbos," I told him. "Give her a complete overhaul."

He was very happy to do so. He'd be mighty unhappy when the cops took the car away without paying him for it, but he didn't look as though he'd go broke from the loss. Besides, I thought it would be a good way to repay Fat-Face for borrowing his car.

I had purposely kept the hood of my tunic up while I was talking to the auto technician so he wouldn't remember my new face later, but I dropped the hood as soon as I got to the main street of Groverton. I didn't want to attract too much attention.

I looked at my watch. 0111. I'd passed back through the time change again, so it had been an hour and ten minutes since I'd left the lodge. I decided I needed something to eat.

Groverton was one of those old-fashioned suburbs built during the latter half of the 20th century—sponge-glass streets and sidewalks, aluminum siding on the houses, shiny chrome-and-lucite business buildings. Real quaint.

I found an automat and went in. There were only a few people on the streets, but the automat wasn't empty by a long shot. Most of the crowd seemed to be teen-age kids getting looped up after a dance. One booth was empty, so I sat down in it, dialed for coffee and ham and eggs and dropped in the indicated change.

Shapeless little blobs of color were bouncing around in the tri-di tank in the wall, giving a surrealistic dance accompaniment to "Anna From Texarkana":

You should have seen the way she ate!
  Her appetite insatiate
Was quite enough to break your pocketbook!
  But with a yeast-digamma steak,
  She never made a damn mistake—
What tasty synthefoods that gal could cook!
  Oh, my Anna! Her algae Manna
  Was tasty as a Manna-cake could be!
  Oh, my Anna—from Texarkana!
  Oh, Anna, baby, you're the gal for me!

I sipped coffee while the thing went through the third and fourth verses, trying to figure a way to get into the city without having to show the telltale ID plate in my arm.

"Anna" was cut off in the middle of the fifth verse. The blobs changed color and coalesced into the face of Quinby Lester, news analyst.

"Good morning, free citizens! We are interrupting this program to bring you an announcement of special importance."

He looked very serious, very concerned, and, I thought, just a little bit puzzled. "At approximately midnight last night, there was a disturbance at the Lodge. Four police officers who were summoned to the Lodge were shot and killed by Mr. Edgar Gifford, the creator of the disturbance. This man is now at large in the vicinity. Police are making an extensive search within a 500-mile radius of the Lodge.

"Have you seen this man?"

A tri-di of Gifford appeared in place of Lester's features.

"This man is armed and dangerous. If you see him, report immediately to MONmouth 6-666-666. If your information leads to the capture of Edgar Gifford, you will receive a reward of $10,000. Look around you! He may be near you now!"

Everybody in the automat looked apprehensively at everybody else. I joined them. I wasn't much worried about being spotted. When everybody wears beards, it's hard to spot a man under a handful of face foliage. I was willing to bet that within the next half hour the police would be deluged with calls from a thousand people who honestly thought they had seen Edgar Gifford.

The cops knew that. They were simply trying to scare me into doing something foolish.

They needn't have done that; I was perfectly capable of doing something foolish without their help.

I thought carefully about my position. I was about 15 miles from safety. Question: Could I call for help? Answer: No. Because I didn't know the number. I didn't even know who was waiting for me. All that had been erased from my mind when the Director hypnoed me. I couldn't even remember who I was working for or why!

My only chance was to get to 14th and Riverside Drive. They'd pick me up there.

Oh, well, if I didn't make it, I wasn't fit to be an assassin, anyway.

I polished off the breakfast and took another look at my watch. 0147. I might as well get started; I had 15 miles to walk.

Outside, the streets were fairly quiet. The old-fashioned streets hadn't been built to clean themselves; a robot sweeper was prowling softly along the curb, sucking up the day's debris, pausing at every cross street to funnel the stuff into the disposal drains to be carried to the processing plant.

A few people were walking the streets. Ahead of me, a drunk was sitting on the curb sucking at a bottle that had collapsed long ago, hoping to get one last drop out of it.

I decided the best way to get to my destination was to take Bradley to Macmillan, follow Macmillan to 14th, then stay on 14th until I got to Riverside Drive.

But no free citizen would walk that far. I'd better not look like one. I walked up to the swiller.

"Hey, Joe, how'd you like to make five?"

He looked up at me, trying to focus. "Sure, Sid, sure. Whatta gotta do?"

"Sell me your tunic."

He blinked. "Zissa gag? Ya get 'em free."

"No gag. I want your tunic."

"Sure. Fine. Gimme that five."

He peeled off the charity brown tunic and I handed him the five note. If I had him doped out right, he'd be too drunk to remember what had happened to his tunic. He'd be even drunker when he started on that five note.

I pulled the brown on over the chartreuse tunic. I might want to get into a first-class installation, and I couldn't do it wearing charity brown.

22

"LOOK OUT!"
CLIKLIKLIKLIKLIKLIKLIK!

I felt something grab my ankle and I turned fast. It was the street cleaner! It had reached out a retractable picker and was trying to lift me into its hopper!

The drunk, who had done the yelling, tried to back away, but he stumbled and banged his head on the soft sidewalk. He stayed down—not out, but scared.

Another claw came out of the cleaner and grabbed my shoulder. The two of them together lifted me off the ground and pulled me toward the open hopper. I managed to get my gun out. These cleaners weren't armored; if I could only get in a good shot—

I fired three times, blowing the pickup antenna off the control dome. When the claws opened, I dropped to the sidewalk and ran. Behind me, the robot, no longer under the directions of the central office, began to flick its claws in and out and run around in circles. The drunk didn't manage to get out from under the treads in time.

A lot of people had stopped to watch the brief tussle, a few of them pretty scared. It was unheard of for a street cleaner to go berserk like that.

I dodged into an alleyway and headed for the second level. I was galloping up the escalator full tilt when the cop saw me. He was on the other escalator, going down, but he didn't stay there long.

"Halt!" he yelled, as he vaulted over the waist-high partition and landed on the UP escalator. By that time, I was already on the second level and running like mad.

"Halt or I fire!" he yelled.

I ducked into a doorway and pulled out the stun gun. I turned just in time to see one of the most amazing sights I have ever been privileged to witness. The cop was running toward me, his gun out, when he passed in front of a bottled-goods vendor. At that instant, the vendor opened up, delivering a veritable avalanche of bottles into the corridor. The policeman's foot hit one of the rubbery, bouncing cylinders and slipped just as he pulled the trigger.

His shot went wild, and I fired with the stun gun before the cop could hit the floor. He lay still, bottles rolling all around him.

I turned and ran again. I hadn't gone far before another cop showed up, running toward me. I made a quick turn toward the escalators and went down again toward street level.

The cop wasn't prepared for what happened to him when he stepped on the escalator. He was about halfway down, running, when the belt suddenly stopped and reversed itself. The policeman pitched forward on his face and tumbled down the stair.

I didn't wait to see what happened next. I turned the corner, slowed down and walked into a bar. I tried to walk slowly enough so that I wouldn't attract attention and headed for the rest room.

I went in, locked the door behind me and looked around.

As far as I could tell, there were no sensory devices in the place, so I pulled the last of my make-up kit out and went to work. This time, I went whole hog. Most of the hair went from the top of my head, and what was left became pure white. I didn't take off the goatee; a beardless man would stand out. But the goatee went white, too.

Then a fine layer of plastic sprayed on my face and hands gave me an elderly network of wrinkles.

All the time I was doing this, I was wondering what was going on with the robots. It was obvious to me that the Lodge was connected illegally with every robot service in the city—possibly in the whole sector.

The street sweeper had recognized me and tried to get me; that was clear enough. But what about the vending machine and the escalator? Was the Lodge's master computer still foggy from the power cutoff? It shouldn't be; not after two hours. Then why had the responses been so slow? Why had they tripped the cops instead of me? It didn't make sense.

That's when it hit me. *Was Rowley really dead?*

I couldn't be absolutely sure, could I? And the police hadn't said anything about a murder. Just a "disturbance." No, wait. The first cops, the ones whose car I'd taken. What had they said the robot reported? I couldn't remember the exact words.

It still didn't settle the question.

For a moment, I found myself wishing we had a government like the United States had had back in the third quarter of the 20th century, back in the days of strong central government, before everybody started screaming about Citizen's Rights and the preservation of the *status quo*. There wouldn't be any of this kind of trouble now—maybe.

But they had other kinds just as bad.

This wasn't the best of all possible worlds, but I was living in it. Of course, I didn't know how long that happy situation would exist just then.

Somebody rapped on the door.

I didn't know who it was, but I wasn't taking any chances. Maybe it was a cop. I climbed out the back window and headed down the alley toward Bradley Avenue.

If only I could get rid of that plate in my arm! The average citizen doesn't know it, but it isn't really necessary to put your arm in an ID slot to be identified. A sonobeam can pick up a reflected recording from your plate at 20 feet if there's a scanner nearby to direct it.

I walked slowly after running the length of the alley, staying in the shadows as much as possible, trying to keep out of the way of anyone and everyone.

For six blocks or so, I didn't see a soul. Then, just as I turned onto West Bradley, I came face to face with a police car. I froze.

I was ready to pull and shoot; I wanted the cop to kill me before he picked me up.

He slowed up, looked at me sharply, looked at his instrument panel, then drove on. I just stood there, flabbergasted. I knew as well as I knew anything that he'd beamed that plate in my arm!

As the car turned at the next corner, I backed into a nearby doorway, trying to figure out what I should do next. Frankly, I was jumpy and scared; I didn't know what they were up to.

I got even more jumpy when the door behind me gave. I turned fast and made a grab for my gun. But I didn't take it out.

The smoothly dressed girl said: "What's the matter, Grandfather?"

It wasn't until then that I realized how rattled I was. I looked like a very old man, but I wasn't acting like one. I paused to force my mind to adjust.

The girl was in green. The one-piece shortsuit, the sandals, the toenails, fingernails, lips, eyes and hair. All green. The rest of her was a smooth, even shade of pink.

She said: "You needn't be afraid that anyone will see you. We arrange—Oh!"

I knew what she was *oh*ing about. The charity brown of my tunic.

25

"I'm sorry," she said, frowning. "We can't—"

I cut her off this time. "I have money, my dear," I smiled. "And I'm wearing my own tunic." I flashed the chartreuse on her by opening the collar.

"I see, Grandfather. Won't you come in?"

I followed the green girl in to the desk of the Program Planner, a girl who was a deep blue in the same way that the first girl was green. I outlined what I wanted in a reedy, anticipating voice and was taken to a private room.

I locked the door behind me. A plaque on the door was dated and sealed with the city stamp.

GUARANTEE OF PRIVACY

This room has been inspected and sealed against scanners, microphones and other devices permitting the observation or recording of actions within it, in accordance with the provisions of the Privacy Act.

That was all very fine, but I wouldn't put enough faith in it to trust my life to it. I relaxed in a soft, heavy lounge facing the one-way wall. The show was already going on. I wasn't particularly interested in the fertility rites of the worshipers of Mahrud—not because they weren't intrinsically interesting, but because I had to do some thinking to save my own skin.

Senator Rowley, in order to keep his section under control, had coupled in his own robot's sensory organs with those of the city's Public Services Department and those of various business concerns, most of which were either owned outright or subsidized by the senator.

But something had happened to that computer; for some reason, its actions had become illogical and inefficient. When the patrol car had spotted me on the street, for instance, the sonobeam, which had penetrated the flesh of my arm and bounced off the tantalum plate back to the pickup, had relayed the modified vibrations back to the Central Files for identification. And the Files had obviously given back the wrong information.

What had gone wrong? Was the senator still alive, keeping his mouth shut and his eyes open? If so, what sort of orders was he giving to the robot? I didn't get many answers, and the ones I did get were mutually contradictory.

I was supposed to be back before dawn, but I could see now that I'd never make it. Here in Groverton, there weren't many connections with Public Services; the robot couldn't keep me under observation all the time. But the deeper into the city I penetrated, the more scanners there would be. I couldn't take a private car in, and I didn't dare take a flitter or a ground taxi. I'd be spotted in the subways as soon as I walked in. I was in a fix, and I'd have to think my way out.

I don't know whether it was the music or the soft lights or my lack of sleep or the simple fact that intense concentration is often autohypnotic. At any rate, I doped off, and the next thing I remember is the girl bringing in the papers.

This gal was silver. I don't know how the cosmeticians had done it, but looking into her eyes was like looking into a mirror; the irises were a glittering silver halo surrounding the dark pupil. Her hair was the same way; not white, but silver.

"Good morning, Grandfather," she said softly. "Here are the newspapers you asked for."

I was thankful for that "Grandfather"; it reminded me that I was an old man before I had a chance to say anything.

"Thank you, my dear, thank you. Just put them here."

"Your coffee will be in in a moment." She moved out as quietly as she had come in.

Something was gnawing at the back of my brain; something like a dream you know you've had but forgotten completely. I concentrated on it a moment, trying to bring it out into the open, but it wouldn't come, so I gave it up and turned to the paper, still warm from the reproducer.

It was splattered all over the front page.

MYSTERIOUS TROUBLE AT THE LODGE

Police Unable to Enter

The Police Department announced this morning that they have been unable, thus far, to pass the defenses of the Lodge after receiving a call last night that Senator Rowley had been shot by his secretary, Mr. Edgar Gifford.

Repeated attempts to contact the senator have resulted in failure, says a Department spokesman.

Thus far, three police flitters under robot control have been shot down in attempting to land at the Lodge, and one ground car has been blown up. Another ground car, the first to respond to the automatic call for help, was stolen by the fleeing Gifford after killing the four officers in the car. The stolen vehicle was recovered early this morning several hundred miles from here, having been reported by a Mr.—

It went on with the usual statement that the police expected to apprehend the murderous Mr. Gifford at any moment.

Another small item in the lower left-hand corner registered the fact that two men had been accidentally caught by a street cleaner and had proceeded to damage it. One of the men was killed by the damaged machine, but the other managed to escape. The dead man was a charity case, named Brodwick, and his associates were being checked.

So much for 'that. But the piece that really interested me was the one that said:

SENATOR LUTHER GRENDON OFFERS AID

"Federal Government Should Keep Hands Off," says Grendon.

Eastern Sector Senator Grendon said early this morning that he would do all in his power to aid Northwestern Sector in "apprehending the murderer of my colleague and bring to justice the organization behind him."

"There is," he said, "no need to call in the Federal Government at this time. The citizens of an independent sector are quite capable of dealing with crime within their own boundaries."

Interviewed later, Senator Quintell of Southwestern Sector agreed that there was no need to call in the FBI or "any other Federal Agency."

The other senators were coming in for the kill, even before it was definitely established that the senator was dead.

Well, that was that. I decided I'd better get going. It would be better to travel during the daytime: it's hard for a beam to be focused on an individual citizen in a crowd.

While the other Immortals were foreclosing on Senator Rowley's private property, there might be time for me to get back safely.

The silver girl was waiting for me as I stepped out the door to the private room.

28

"This way, Grandfather," she said, the ever-present smile on her glittering lips. She started down the corridor.

"This isn't the way out," I said, frowning.

She paused, still smiling. "No, sir, it isn't the way you came in, but, you see, our number has come up. The Medical Board has sent down a checker."

That almost floored me. Somehow, the Lodge had known where I was and had instituted a check against this particular house. That meant that every door was sealed except the one where the robot Medical checker was waiting.

The perfect trap. The checker was armed and armored, naturally; there were often people who did not want to be detained at the hospital—and at their own expense, if they were free citizens.

I walked slowly, as an old man should, stalling for time. The only armament a checker had was a stun gun; that was a point in my favor. But I needed more information.

"My goodness," I said, "you should have called me earlier, my dear, as soon as the checker came."

"It's only been here 15 minutes, Grandfather," the silver girl answered.

Then there were still plenty of customers in the building!

The girl was just ahead of me in the corridor. I beamed her down with the stun gun and caught her before she hit the floor. I carried her back into the private room I had just left and laid her on the couch.

Then I started pulling down draperies. They were all heavy synthetic stuff that wouldn't burn unless they were really hot. I got a good armful, went back into the corridor, and headed for the opposite end of the building. Nobody bothered me on the way; everybody was still occupied.

At the end of the hall, I piled the stuff on the floor beneath some other hangings. Then I took two of the power cartridges from the stun gun and pried them open. The powder inside ought to burn nicely. It wouldn't explode unless it was sealed inside the gun, where the explosion was channeled through the supersonic whistle in the barrel to form the beam.

I took out my lighter and applied the flame to a sheet of the newspaper I had brought along, then I laid the paper on top of the opened cartridges. I got well back and waited.

It didn't take more than a second or two to ignite the

29

powder. It hissed and went up in a wave of white heat. The plastic curtains started to smolder. Within less than a minute, the hallway was full of thick, acrid smoke.

I knew the building wouldn't burn, but I was hoping none of the other customers was as positive as I.

I yelled "Fire!" at the top of my lungs, then headed for the stairway and ran to the bottom. I waited just inside the street door for action.

Outside, I could hear the soft humming of a guard robot, stationed there by the checker to make sure no one left through that door.

The smoldering of the curtains put out plenty of smoke before they got hot enough to turn in the fire alarm and bring out the fire-fighter robots stationed in the walls. The little terrier-sized mechanisms scurried all over the place, looking for heat sources to squirt at. Upstairs, a heavy CO_2 blanket began to drift down.

I wasn't worried about the fire robots; they didn't have the sensory apparatus to spot me. All they could find was fire. They would find it and smother it, but the place was already full of smoke, which was all I wanted.

It was the smoke that did the job, really. People don't like to stay in buildings that appear to be burning down, no matter how safe they think they are. Customers came pouring down the stairway and out the door like angry wasps out of a disturbed hive. I went with them.

I knew that a fire signal would change the checker's orders. It couldn't keep people inside a burning building. Unfortunately, I hadn't realized to what extent the Lodge would go to get me, or to what extent it was capable of countermanding normal orders.

The guard robot at the door started beaming down everybody as they came out, firing as fast as it could scan and direct. It couldn't distinguish me from the others, of course; not in that mob. But it was hitting everything that moved with its stun beam. Luckily, it couldn't scan and direct fast enough to get everybody; there were too many. I watched and waited for a second or two until the turret was facing away from the corner, then I ran like the very devil, dodging as I ran.

A stun beam hit the fingers of my left hand, and my arm went dead to the elbow. The guard robot had spotted me! I made it around the corner and ducked into a crowd of people who were idly watching the smoke billowing from the upper windows.

I kept moving through the crowd, trying to put as much distance between myself and the checker's guards as possible. The guard evidently hadn't recognized me, personally, as Gifford, because it realized the futility of trying to cut down everyone in Groverton to find me and gave up on the crowd outside. But it kept hitting the ones who came out the door.

I got away fast. The thing really had me worried. I had no desire whatever to get myself mixed up with a nutty robot, but, seemingly, there was no way to avoid it.

I circled around and went down to Corliss Avenue, parallel to Bradley, for about seven blocks before I finally walked back over to Bradley again. Two or three times, police cars came by, but either they didn't test me with their beams or the answers they got weren't incriminating.

I was less than a block from the city limits when something hard and hot and tingling burned through my nerves like acid and I blacked out.

Maybe you've never been hit by a stun beam, but if you've ever had your leg go to sleep, you know what it feels like. And you know what it feels like when you wake up; that painful tingling all over that hurts even worse if you try to move.

I knew better than to try to move. I just lay still, waiting for the terrible tingling to subside. I had been out, I knew, a little less than an hour. I knew, because I'd been hit by stunners before, and I know how long it takes my body to throw off the paralysis.

Somebody's voice said: "He'll be coming out of it anytime now. Shake him and see."

A hand shook me, and I gasped. I couldn't help it; with my nerves still raw from the stunner, it hurt to be shaken that way.

"Sorry, Gifford," said another voice, different from the first. "Just wanted to see. Wanted to see if you were with us."

"Leave him alone a few minutes," the first voice said. "That hurts. It'll wear off quickly."

It was wearing off already. I opened my eyes and tried to see what was going on. At first, the visual pattern was a blithering swirl of meaningless shapes and crackling colors, but it finally settled down to a normal ceiling with a normal light panel in it. I managed to turn my head, in

31

spite of the nerve-shocks, and saw two men sitting in chairs beside the bed.

One of them was short, round and blond, with a full set of mutton chops, a heavy mustache and a clean-shaven, firm chin. The other man was taller, muscular, with a full Imperial and smooth cheeks.

The one with the Imperial said: "Sorry we had to shoot you down that way, Gifford. But we didn't want to attract too much attention that close to the city limits."

They weren't cops, then. Of that much, I could be certain. At least they weren't the police of this sector. So they were working for one of the other Immortals.

"Whose little boys are you?" I asked, trying to grin.

Evidently I did grin, because they grinned back. "Funny," said the one with the mutton chops, "but that's exactly what we were going to ask you."

I turned my head back again and stared at the ceiling. "I'm an orphan," I said.

The guy with the mutton chops chuckled. "Well," he grinned at the other man, "what do you think of that, colonel?"

The colonel (*Of what?* I wondered) frowned, pulling heavy brows deep over his gray eyes. His voice came from deep in his chest and seemed to be muffled by the heavy beard.

"We'll level with you, Gifford. Mainly because we aren't sure. Mainly because of that. We aren't sure even you know the truth. So we'll level."

"Your blast," I said.

"O.K., here's how it looks from our side of the fence. It looks like this. You killed Rowley. After 15 years of faithful service, you killed him. Now we know—even if you don't—that Rowley had you psychoimpressed every six months for 15 years. Or at least he thought he did."

"He *thought* he did?" I asked, just to show I was interested.

"Well, yes. He couldn't have, really, you see. He couldn't have. Or at least not lately. A psychoimpressed person can't do things like that. Also, we know that nobody broke it, because it takes six weeks of steady, hard therapy to pull a man out of it. And a man's no good after that for a couple more weeks. You weren't out of Rowley's sight for more than four days." He shrugged. "You see?"

"I see," I said. The guy was a little irritating in his manner. I didn't like the choppy way he talked.

"For a while," he said, "we thought it might be an impersonation. But we checked your plate"—he gestured at my arm—"and it's OK. The genuine article. So it's Gifford's plate, all right. And we know it couldn't have been taken out of Gifford's arm and transferred to another arm in four days.

"If there were any way to check fingerprints and eye patterns, we might be able to be absolutely sure, but the Privacy Act forbids that, so we have to go on what evidence we have in our possession now.

"Anyway, we're convinced that you are Gifford. So that means somebody has been tampering with your mind. We want to know who it is. Do you know?"

"No," I said, quite honestly.

"You didn't do it yourself, did you?"

"No."

"Somebody's behind you?"

"Yes."

"Do you know who?"

"No. And hold those questions a minute. You said you'd level with me. Who are *you* working for?"

The two of them looked at each other for a second, then the colonel said: "Senator Quintell."

I propped myself up on one elbow and held out the other hand, fingers extended. "All right, figure for yourself. Rowley's out of the picture; that eliminates him." I pulled my thumb in. "You work for Quintell; that eliminates him." I dropped my little finger and held it with my thumb. "That leaves three Immortals. Grendon, Lasser and Waterford. Lasser has the Western Sector; Waterford, the Southern. Neither borders on Northwestern, so that eliminates them. Not definitely, but probably. They wouldn't be tempted to get rid of Rowley as much as they would Quintell.

"So that leaves Grendon. And if you read the papers, you'll know that he's pushing in already."

They looked at each other again. I knew they weren't necessarily working for Quintell; I was pretty sure it was Grendon. On the other hand, they might have told the truth so that I'd be sure to think it *was* Grendon. I didn't know how deep their subtlety went, and I didn't care. It didn't matter to me who they were working for.

"That sounds logical," said the colonel. "Very logical."

"But we have to know," added Mutton Chops. "We

33

were fairly sure you'd head back toward the city; that's why we set up guards at the various street entrances. Since that part of our prediction worked out, we want to see if the rest of it will."

"The rest of it?"

"Yeah. You're expendable. We know that. The organization that sent you doesn't care what happens to you now, otherwise they wouldn't have let you loose like that. They don't care what happens to Eddie Gifford.

"So they must have known you'd get caught. Therefore, they've got you hypnoed to a fare-thee-well. And we probably won't find anything under the hypno, either. But we've got to look; there may be some little thing you'll remember. Some little thing that will give us the key to the whole organization."

I nodded. That was logical, very logical, as the colonel had said. They were going to break me. They could have done it gently, removed every bit of blocking and covering that the hypnoes had put in without hurting me a bit. But that would take time; I knew better than to think they were going to be gentle. They were going to peel my mind like a banana and then slice it up and look at it.

And if they were working for any of the Immortals, I had no doubt that they could do what they were planning. It took equipment, and it took an expert psychometrician and a couple of good therapists—but that was no job at all if you had money.

The only trouble was that I had a few little hidden tricks that they'd never get around. If they started fiddling too much with my mind, a nice little psychosomatic heart condition would suddenly manifest itself. I'd be dead before they could do anything about it. Oh, I was expendable, all right.

"Do you want to say anything before we start?" the colonel asked.

"No." I didn't see any reason for giving them information they didn't earn.

"OK." He stood up, and so did the mutton-chopper. "I'm sorry we have to do this, Gifford. It'll be hard on you, but you'll be in good condition inside of six or eight months. So long."

They walked out and carefully locked the door behind them.

* * *

I sat up for the first time and looked around. I didn't know where I was; in an hour, I could have been taken a long ways away from the city.

I hadn't been, though. The engraving on the bed said:

DELLFIELD SANATORIUM

I was on Riverside Drive, less than eight blocks from the rendezvous spot.

I walked over to the window and looked out. I could see the roof of the tenth level about eight floors beneath me. The window itself was a heavy sheet of transite welded into the wall. There was a polarizer control to the left to shut out the light, but there was no way to open the window. The door was sealed, too. When a patient got violent, they could pump gas in through the ventilators without getting it into the corridor.

They'd taken all my armament away, and, incidentally, washed off the thin plastic film on my hands and face. I didn't look so old any more. I walked over to the mirror in the wall, another sheet of transite with a reflecting back, and looked at myself. I was a sad-looking sight. The white hair was all scraggly, the whiskers were ditto, and my face looked worried. Small wonder.

I sat back down on the bed and started to think.

It must have been a good two hours later when the therapist came in. She entered by herself, but I noticed that the colonel was standing outside the door.

She was in her mid-30s, a calm-faced, determined-looking woman. She started off with the usual questions.

"You have been told you are under some form of hypnotic compulsion. Do you consciously believe this?"

I told her I did. There was no sense in resisting.

"Do you have any conscious memory of the process?"

"No."

"Do you have any conscious knowledge of the identity of the therapist?"

I didn't and told her so. She asked a dozen other questions, all standard buildup. When she was through, I tried to ask her a couple of questions, but she cut me off and walked out of the room before I could more than open my yap.

The whole sanatorium was, and probably had been for a long time, in the pay of Quintell or Grendon—or, possibly, one of the other Immortals. It had been here for years, a neat little spy setup nestled deep in the heart of Rowley's territory.

Leaving the hospital without outside help was strictly out. I'd seen the inside of these places before, and I had a healthy respect for their impregnability. An unarmed man was in to stay.

Still, I decided that since something *had* to be done, something *would* be done.

My major worry was the question of whether or not the room was monitored. There was a single scanner pickup in the ceiling with a fairly narrow angle lens in it. That was interesting. It was enclosed in an unbreakable transite hemisphere and was geared to look around the room for the patient. But it was *not* robot controlled. There was evidently a nurse or therapist at the other end who checked on the patients every so often.

But how often?

From the window I could see the big, old-fashioned 12-hour clock on the Barton Building. I used that to time the monitoring. The scanner was aimed at the bed. That meant it had looked at me last when I was on the bed. I walked over to the other side of the room and watched the scanner without looking at it directly.

It was nearly three-quarters of an hour later that the little eye swiveled around the room and came to a halt on me. I ignored it for about 30 seconds, then walked deliberately across the room. The eye didn't follow.

Fine. This was an old-fashioned hospital; I had known that much. Evidently there hadn't been any new equipment installed in 30 years. Whoever operated the scanner simply looked around to see what the patient was doing and then went on to the next one. Hi ho.

I watched the scanner for the rest of the afternoon, timing it. Every hour at about four minutes after the hour. It was nice to know.

They brought me my dinner at 1830. I watched the scanner, but there was no special activity before they opened the door.

They simply swung the door outward; one man stood with a stun gun, ready for any funny business, while another brought in the food.

At 2130, the lights went out, except for a small lamp over the bed. That was fine; it meant that the scanner probably wasn't equipped for infrared. If I stayed in bed

36

like a good boy, that one small light was all they'd need. If not, they turned on the main lights again.

I didn't assume that the watching would be regular, every hour, as it had been during the day. Plots are usually hatched at night, so it's best to keep a closer watch then. Their only mistake was that they were going to watch *me*. And that was perfectly OK as far as I was concerned.

I lay in bed until 2204. Sure enough, the scanner turned around and looked at me. I waited a couple of minutes and then got up as though to get a drink at the wash basin. The scanner didn't follow, so I went to work.

I pulled a light blanket off my bed and stuffed a corner of it into the basin's drain, letting the rest of it trail to the floor. Then I turned the water on and went back to bed.

It didn't take long for the basin to fill and overflow. It climbed over the edge and ran silently down the blanket to the floor.

Filling the room would take hours, but I didn't dare go to sleep. I'd have to wake up before dawn, and I wasn't sure I could do that. It was even harder to lie quietly and pretend I was asleep, but I fought it by counting to 50 and then turning over violently to wake myself again. If anyone was watching, they would simply think I was restless.

I needn't have bothered. I doped off—sound asleep. The next thing I knew, I was gagging. I almost drowned; the water had come up to bed level and had flowed into my mouth. I shot up in bed, coughing and spitting.

Fully awake, I moved fast. I pulled off the other blanket and tied it around the pickup in the ceiling. Then I got off the bed and waded in waist-deep water to the door. I grabbed a good hold on the metal dresser and waited.

It must have been all of half an hour before the lights came on. A voice came from the speaker: "Have you tampered with the TV pickup?"

"Huh? Wuzzat?" I said, trying to sound sleepy. "No. I haven't done anything."

"We are coming in. Stand back from the door or you will be shot."

I had no intention of being that close to the door.

When the attendant opened the door, it slammed him in the face as a good many tons of water cascaded onto him. There were two armed men with him, but they both went down in the flood, coughing and gurgling.

Judging very carefully, I let go the dresser and let the

swirling water carry me into the hall. I had been prepared and I knew what I was doing; the guards didn't. By turning a little, I managed to hit one of them who was trying to get up and get his stunner into action. He went over, and I got the stunner.

It only lasted a few seconds. The water had been deep in the confines of the little room, but when allowed to expand into the hall, it merely made the floor wet.

I dispatched the guards with the stunner and ran for the nurse's desk, which, I knew, was just around the corner, near the elevators. I aimed quick and let the nurse have it; he fell over, and I was at the desk before he had finished collapsing.

I grabbed the phone. There wouldn't be much time now. I dialed. I said: "This is Gifford. I'm in Dellfield Sanatorium, Room 1808."

That was all I needed. I tossed the stunner into the water that trickled slowly toward the elevators and walked back toward my room with my hands up.

I'll say this for the staff at Dellfield; they don't get sore when a patient tries to escape. When five more guards came down the hall, they saw my raised hands and simply herded me into the room. Then they watched me until the colonel came.

"Well," he said, looking things over. "Well. Neat. Very neat. Have to remember that one. Didn't do much good, though. Did it? Got out of the room, couldn't get downstairs. Elevators don't come up."

I shrugged. "Can't blame me for trying."

The colonel grinned for the first time. "I don't. Hate a man who'd give up—at any time." He lit a cigarette, his gun still not wavering. "Call didn't do you any good, either. This is a hospital. Patients have reached phones before. Robot identifies patient, refuses to relay call. Tough."

I didn't say anything or look anything; no use letting him think he had touched me.

The colonel shrugged. "All right. Strap him."

The attendants were efficient about it. They changed the wet bedclothes and strapped me in. I couldn't move my head far enough to see my hands.

The colonel looked me over and nodded. "You may get out of this. OK by me if you try. Next time, though, we'll give you a spinal freeze."

He left and the door clicked shut.

Well, I'd had my fun; it was out of my hands now. I decided I might as well get some sleep.

I didn't hear any commotion, of course; the room was soundproof. The next thing I knew, there was a Decon robot standing in the open door. It rolled over to the bed.

"Can you get up?"

These Decontamination robots aren't stupid, by any means.

"No," I said. "Cut these straps."

A big pair of nippers came out and began scissoring through the plastic webbing with ease. When the job was through, the Decon opened up the safety chamber in its body.

"Get in."

I didn't argue; the Decon had a stun gun pointed at me.

That was the last I saw of Dellfield Sanatorium, but I had a pretty good idea of what had happened. The Decontamination Squad is called in when something goes wrong with an atomic generator. The Lodge had simply turned in a phony report that there was generator trouble at Dellfield. Nothing to it.

I had seen Decons go to work before; they're smart, efficient and quick. Each one has a small chamber inside it, radiation shielded to carry humans out of contaminated areas. They're small and crowded, but I didn't mind. It was better than conking out from a psychosomatic heart ailment when the therapists started to fiddle with me.

I smelled something sweetish then, and I realized I was getting a dose of gas. I went bye-bye.

When I woke up again, I was sick. I'd been hit with a stun beam yesterday and gassed today. I felt as though I was wasting all my life sleeping. I could still smell the gas.

No. It wasn't gas. The odor was definitely different. I turned my head and looked around. I was in the lounge of Senator Anthony Rowley's Lodge. On the floor. And next to me was Senator Anthony Rowley.

I crawled away from him, and then I was *really* sick.

I managed to get to the bathroom. It was a good 20 minutes before I worked up nerve enough to come out again.

Rowley had moved, all right. He had pulled himself all of six feet from the spot where I had shot him.

My hunch had been right.

The senator's dead hand was still holding down the

programming button on the control panel he had dragged himself to. The robot had gone on protecting the senator because it thought—as it was supposed to—that the senator was still alive as long as he was holding the ORDERS circuit open.

I leaned over and spoke into the microphone. "I will take a flitter from the roof. I want guidance and protection from here to the city. There, I will take over manual control. When I do, you will immediately pull all dampers on your generator.

"Recheck."

The robot dutifully repeated the orders.

After that, everything was simple. I took the flitter to the rendezvous spot, was picked up and, 20 minutes after I left the Lodge, I was in the Director's office.

He kicked in the hypnoes, and when I came out of it, my arm was strapped down while a surgeon took out the Gifford ID plate.

The Director of the FBI looked at me, grinning. "You took your time, son."

"What's the news?"

His grin widened. "You played hob with everything. The Lodge held off all investigation forces for 30-odd hours after reporting Rowley's death. The Sector police couldn't come anywhere near it.

"Meanwhile, funny things have happened. Robot in Groverton kills a man. Medic guard shoots down 18 men coming out of a burning house. Decon Squad invades Dellfield when there's nothing wrong with the generator.

"Now all hell has busted loose. The Lodge went up in a flare of radiation an hour ago, and since then all robot services in the city have gone phooey. It looks to the citizens as though the senator had an illegal hand in too many pies. They're suspicious.

"Good work, boy."

"Thanks," I said, trying to keep from looking at my arm, where the doctor was peeling back flesh.

The Director lifted a white eyebrow. "Something?"

I looked at the wall. "I'm just burned up, that's all. Not at you; at the whole mess. How did a nasty slug like Rowley get elected in the first place? And what right did he have to stay in such an important job?"

"I know," the director said somberly. "And that's our job. Immortality is something the human race isn't ready for yet. The masses can't handle it, and the individual can't handle it. And, since we can't get rid of them legally, we have to do it this way. Assassination. But it can't be done overnight."

"*You've* handled immortality," I pointed out.

"Have I?" he asked softly. "No. No, son, I haven't; I'm using it the same way they are. For power. The Federal government doesn't have any power anymore. I have it.

"I'm using it in a different way, granted. Once there were over 100 Immortals. Last week there were six. Today there are five. One by one, over the years, we have picked them off, and they are never replaced. The rest simply gobble up the territory and the power and split it between them rather than let a newcomer get into their tight little circle.

"But I'm just as dictatorial in my way as they are in theirs. And when the *status quo* is broken, and civilization begins to go ahead again, I'll have to die with the rest of them.

"But never mind that. What about you? I got most of the story from you under the hypno. That was a beautiful piece of deduction."

I took the cigarette he offered me and took a deep lungful of smoke. "How else could it be? The robot was trying to capture me. But also it was trying to keep anyone else from killing me. As a matter of fact, it passed up several chances to get me in order to keep others from killing me.

"It had to be the senator's last order. The old boy had lived so long that he still wasn't convinced he was dying. So he gave one last order to the robot:

" '*Get Gifford back here—ALIVE!*'

"And then there was the queer fact that the robot never reported that the senator was dead, but kept right on defending the Lodge as though he were alive. That could only mean the ORDERS circuits were still open. As long as they were, the robot thought the senator was still alive.

"So the only way I could get out of the mess was to let the Lodge take me. I knew the phone at Dellfield would connect me with the Lodge—at least indirectly. I called it and waited.

"Then, when I started giving orders, the Lodge accepted me as the senator. That was all there was to it."

The Director nodded. "A good job, son. A good job."

41

RANDALL

Marion Zimmer Bradley

I'VE BEEN A SCIENCE-FICTION FAN SINCE 1946, and a science-fiction pro writer since 1952, and in the course of that time, I've gone to a lot of science-fiction conventions and met a lot of strange people. But in those 30-odd years in science fiction, some of them very odd indeed, I don't think I was ever taken more aback by any meeting than by the meeting with Randall Garrett.

It was some time in the late '50s, and in Cleveland or Cincinnati or someplace like that—I can't tab it any closer. I walked into a party, and this big, overpowering, *huge* man walked up, loomed over me and intoned "*Coito, ergo sum.*"

For once in my life, (and I've been called one of the talkiest people in science fiction) I was struck speechless. Literally speechless. In fact, even after 20 years or so, I can't think of the *mot juste* to reply to such an opening.

And certainly I couldn't then. Years later, when I knew Randall much, much better, he told me that he had thought that I was offended by the remark; that he'd said so to Tony Boucher, and that Tony's answer had been, "If she'd be offended by that, she's not worth worrying about." I wasn't offended—simply stricken mute. At that time, though, I was in my middle 20s, I had been living since my late teens in a Texas town of 650 people or so, and I was a shy little Texas housewife who had never been anywhere or done anything or met anybody. I thought at first that Randall had greeted me with the Descartes epigram; but I did know enough Latin to puzzle it out, and I didn't know whether to blush, giggle or think of some snappy remark to make; and so I said nothing at all, and felt like a goop.

42

But I did get to know Randall better—much better. When I moved to the Bay Area in the '60s, I used to meet him at Mystery Writers of America meetings, and discovered that he was one of the few people in the universe whom I could tolerate when drunk. (I grew up in the house with a *real* drunk, and normally I can't stand drunks.) But Randall, like the late Tony Boucher, when drunk grows only more affable and talkative, and I credit Randall with the change in my attitude which made it possible to join in social drinking. I've never been much of a drinker—I get sick or fall asleep before most people would think I was drunk at all. But until I got to know Randall, I was scared to death by drunks, and although I was never a Carrie Nation abolitionist—I couldn't swing a hatchet without cutting off my own finger—I was always scared to drink at all for fear I'd wind up like my father. Randall convinced me that one drink doesn't always make a drunk, and I'll always be grateful.

Later I discovered that Randall was even more enchanting as a sober companion than as a drinking buddy. And when—after a long hiatus in exile in New York (the cancer on the bosom of America)—I moved back to the Bay Area, I found Randall already a close family friend. I was moved by the knowledge—which has never been shared before—that while my mother was very hard up, in my absence he had been providing her with candy and wine and other little comforts to make her life easier. People who think of Randall as a noisy, humorous "funny man" would never imagine that side of him, the side that would bother to do small kindnesses to an elderly lady. It's easy to do big heroic public things; but to take time off, quietly, to visit and run errands for and bring small gifts to an old woman who doesn't get around much—that's Randall.

Over the years I came to depend on Randall more than I knew, as the person whose brains I picked when I needed some hard science in my science fiction. I have considerable knowledge of medicine, biology and psychology and the social sciences. But my knowledge of mathematics, chemistry and physics is almost a minus quantity; and Randall (who has a degree in chemical engineering) was the person I'd call up when I had a good idea for a story, and ask whether the science would work. For instance, in writing *Endless Universe,* he helped me work out the subsonics and supersonics in the "Hellworld" sequence—though one goof I made got by him; I had believed that diamonds and rubies were similar in chemical structure, and he didn't catch it till the book was in print; actually one is carbon and one is, I think, aluminum. He worked out for me, too, the "energy eater" heat-trope in the "Cold Death" sequence.

I hadn't realized how very much I'd come to depend on him as my science resource person until I had to work out the mathematics of the space probe in *Survey Ship,* which was written during his serious illness. I finally had to ask Elisabeth Waters to program the problem and run it off on the public computer in the Lawrence Hall of Science— how long it would take a space ship accelerating at one gravity to reach Mars, the Asteroid Belt and the orbit of Pluto. I'm perfectly sure I could have called up Randall, or gone to visit him, and he would have had the answer for me right away on his pocket calculator (with which he struggled for many valiant hours trying to teach me to read algebraic formulas, a task as hopeless as the proverbial shampooing of a donkey!).

I also came to depend on Randall for an unfailing critic of the best kind—the one who can read your story and give you a straight answer without pulling any punches. I remember being stuck, once, in the middle of a book. A hundred and fifty pages which should have been good were sitting in a box on my desk; I *knew,* in the despairing way one always knows, that the damn thing wasn't going right, but I couldn't figure out just *why* five chapters of very good prose were just lying there like a lump. I kept telling myself, "Go ahead, finish it anyhow, nobody will know the difference anyway," but it was wrong, wrong, *wrong,* and I couldn't put my finger on *what* was wrong with it.

So I drove out to Castro Valley, where Randall was living with his friend Vicki, and plonked the damn thing, despairingly, on his desk. "Randall," I entreated, "What the *hell* is wrong with this book so far?" He read it through, while I prowled around his office, reading old magazines and chewing my nails till I felt like the Venus de Milo. Finally he lifted his head, plunked the manuscript down, sighed and said, "Honey, you know what's wrong with this book? It's written very well and it's a nice idea. But your hero is a klutz. Nobody wants to read about a klutz."

And the minute he said it, I knew he was right. So back I went to the beginning and examined the whole structure of Cameron Fenton in *The House Between the Worlds,* making him—as Randall put it—more definite in doing instead of being done by. And when I had rewritten up to that point, I kept on going and never stopped again. That point—the klutziness and passiveness of my hero—was what had been holding me back; I'd known, instinctively, that *something* was wrong. Only it took Randall to tell me what.

He did that for me two or three times. But on the other hand, it wasn't all one way. He'd send me an SOS sometimes, and when I got out to Castro Valley and climbed up to Number 6 where they lived then, he'd greet me at the door in his working costume of skivvy briefs and socks, and hand me a thick chunk of manuscript, commanding: "Read that out loud to me." Hearing it in someone else's voice seemed to clarify, for him, whatever had gone wrong in his work.

This sort of thing had its frustrations. One was apt to read halfway through an exciting, suspenseful detective-style story—*The Napoli Express,* for instance—and ten pages short of the end, when Lord Darcy was about to proclaim the identity of the murderer, suddenly find that the story had come to an end in the very middle of a paragraph. I would be left chewing on what was left of my fingernails. He would never tell me. He said the question was had I, in reading that far, been seized with an insatiable desire to know who the murderer was. Once or twice I said "No, I find I really don't care—" at which point he'd try to find out why I had lost interest. Or I would guess, and if I guessed too easily, or too far wrong, he'd bite his lip, sulk, scowl and start picking over what he had done.

And once he gave me an idea for a story by what he didn't write. His short story "Lauralyn," which was nominated for a Hugo (and didn't get it), was read aloud by me in incomplete form, some months before publication, and I thought, *Aha, I bet I know the gimmick!* Weeks later, at a reading party given by the Blackstone Agency, which handles Randall's work, (Tracy Blackstone is married to my brother Paul) I heard the entire story read aloud, and discovered that I had been *wildly* wrong about the gimmick. So I decided: Yes, but my version of the gimmick would make a marvelous story! So I sat down and wrote "Elbow Room," which Judy-Lynn Del Rey bought for an anthology.

Randall may have given me a story idea, but I introduced him to his wife. Vicki Ann Heydron (then Horne) was a fan I met en route to the Fantasy Faire; we found ourselves on the curbside together at the bus station into Los Angeles from the airport, and, finding out that we were bound for the same destination, agreed to share a cab. She had never met a fan before, and when she found out that I was the guest of honor, as I was that year, she tended to be a mite over-awed; but after I introduced her to other writers, including Randall and my brother Paul, she quickly got into the stream of things, and the next thing I knew, there she was with Randall. Randall had been through two marriages, neither of them very successful, though he remained friendly with his ex-wives. He fell hard for Vicki, and mine was the big-sisterly bosom to whom he confided his infatuation. To one who had known Randall as a great womanizer (and everyone who has met Randall has heard his standard greeting to a new face: "Hey, my name's Garrett, let's fuck"), it was touching to hear him say that he felt like a teenager; that never before in his life had he thought he would ever want to spend the rest of his life with one woman. I think all of Randall's lady friends were a little sad to be out of the center of his attention, but we rejoiced for him, because Vicki was so definitely the *right* person for him. It was during this time that he made the heroic effort of sobering up *completely;* for months he did not take a single drink, and even after that would confine himself to a glass of white wine, sometimes mixed with diet soda. He became slender and handsome, and his work output went up amazingly. At that time he discovered that he and Vicki could write together in the same way that the late Hank Kuttner and C. L. Moore managed—a story which they wrote together could be read without any of the seams showing, so that not even those who knew Randall well could see where his work stopped and Vicki's began.

I remember that he called me, and that we cried together over the phone for nearly an hour, when the first report of Leigh Brackett's death was circulated. Later it was discovered that this report had been premature, and some people got very angry at Randall, thinking he had played a cruel hoax. But I had heard his tears; I knew he had only wanted to share his grief, and I had also shared his relief and elation when he found out that the report was false, that he had actually talked to her.

And the last time I actually saw Leigh is indissolubly

associated in my mind with Randall. She and I, with C. L. Moore and, I think, Alva Rogers and Andi Shechter, had breakfast together at the World Fantasy Con in Los Angeles. As everyone who actually knows Randall will know without being told, many of Randall's jokes and sight gags are unprintable—or at least unsuitable for a family magazine. The day before, he had told me one such joke, asking me if I knew the difference between pussy and parsley. I said no, and he replied, "Nobody eats parsley."

Well, you can take the woman out of the boondocks, but you can't take the boondocks out of the woman, and such was my naiveté that for a minute I didn't get it!

Next morning, at the breakfast table, as we ate our eggs and bacon and other goodies, I noticed that Leigh, like a conscientious vitamin-C lover, was chomping up the little sprig of parsley adorning her fried eggs. I said "Randall, look, damnit!" And he cracked up. And I cracked up. And Leigh wanted to know what the joke was.

But Randall shared one other thing with me. He had been writing since 1943—but he was still in absolute awe of the other person at our table, the First Lady of Science Fiction, the wonderful—and elegant, and charming, and above all, ladylike—Cathy Moore. And so neither he nor I was about to tell a dirty joke in Catherine's presence; so we sat there and howled and I blushed and nobody ever found out why we were behaving like such absolute idiots.

But the best joke I ever heard Randall tell was completely clean. It was on New Year's Eve, at Greyhaven, at the party given every New Year's for Blackstone Agency clients and family friends. About midnight, he and Vicki got up and announced what every one of us had been hoping to hear: that he and Vicki had gone away and gotten themselves married that day.

"But I want to tell you," Randall said solemnly, "that I will continue to write under my maiden name."

This was Randall Garrett's first published story—it appeared in the January 1951 issue of *Astounding*. Many science-fiction writers begin clumsily, a notch above the amateur level, and find their stride a few years later; but this was an impressive debut, traditional *Astounding*-type themes handled in a smooth, fully professional manner.

THE WAITING GAME

"During the early years of its expansion, the Solar Federation discovered only two races of beings who had mastered the science of interstellar travel: the decadent remnants of the long-dead Grand Empire of Lilaar, and the savagely nonhuman race of the Thassela."
—JASIN BRONE, YF 402
The Biology of Intelligent Races

MAJOR KARL GORMAN LOOKED GLOOMILY OUT of the main port of the forward observation deck at the pinhead disk of light far ahead. Sol, and bright blue Earth swinging around it, though the ship was as yet too far away for him to see the planet.

Would it, he wondered, *be the same as the rest?* The closer he had come to the Federation capital, the worse it had become, until now, after Procyon, he was almost sick. He had thought of making the dog-leg jump to Sirius, but had decided against it. He might as well jump right into the middle of the whole mess!

He turned away from the starry view before him and walked back toward the bar, feeling the eyes of the crowd on his uniform.

They weren't all looking at him, of course; a Spacefleet major wasn't that unusual. But a few of them had noticed the tiny silver spearhead on his shoulder, and knew it for what it was.

And men from the Federation Outposts *were* rare.

Gorman bought his drink and stared angrily at the hard, dark, blocky face that was reflected in the bar's shining surface. He'd been on the ship for more than three days, now, and this was the first time he had felt the necessity of leaving his cabin. He didn't feel like talking to anyone around him; they just weren't his kind of people.

A low, resonant voice next to him jarred his train of thought, and he turned his head with a jerk.

"Ah, home from the wars, major?" the tall, hairless, pleasantly smiling being beside him asked.

Gorman silenced his biting request to be left alone before it began; after all, there wasn't any reason not to be civil.

"No, my home is on Ferridel III. This is the first time I've ever been to Earth."

"Not surprising," commented the other. "There aren't very many outpost officers from Earth. After all, two years is a long time to spend just traveling."

Gorman finished his drink and ordered another. "It sure is."

"If I am not being too personal, major, may I ask why you are making the trip?"

Major Gorman looked up at the being's face. He knew what he was, of course; a Lilaarian. But this was the first time he had ever talked to one.

"Not at all. I suffer from a disease known as Utter Boredom. All my life, sir, I have been either fighting or getting ready to fight the Thassela. The war has been going on for more than 200 years, and, as my home was right in the thick of it, I have been bred and trained in its atmosphere.

"Now, however, the war in my sector is nearly over; it has reduced itself to mopping-up operations on whatever of the Thassela are left. Therefore"—he paused to finish his second drink and order a third by a gesture to the steward—"I, a professional Thassela-killer, having no more Thassela to kill, have nothing to do but kill time."

"Please, major! This talk of . . . ah . . . such things distresses me," the pleasant bass voice admonished.

"Oh." Gorman looked at him. "I . . . I'm sorry. I forgot." He remembered now what he had heard of the Lilaar. Their religion, or something, forbade talk of death.

"You see, your race is not too well represented in my

part of the Federation, and it is only in the past few months that I have seen any of your people. In fact, you are the first I have ever spoken to."

"Quite all right. The error was mine. Please go on."

"Oh, there's nothing much more. I decided to come to Sol and Earth in search of high adventure—pretty girls to be rescued from evil, villains to ki . . . er . . . punish, and all that sort of thing."

"You sound bitter, Major," the Lilaarian commented analytically.

"I am, sir, I am. What do I find? I find people tending flower gardens, listening to soft music and admiring fine *objets d'art*, that's what I find!"

"And you find this distasteful?" the other asked, somewhat surprised.

Hastily, Gorman covered his tracks. "Why . . . no-o-o, it's just that it's not what I was looking for, you understand."

He had remembered another thing he had heard about the Lilaar—they were not in the least mechanically or scientifically minded. Instead, they were the masters of the very music and art which he had just been on the verge of denouncing. He decided to change the subject.

"By the way, my name is Gorman, Karl Gorman." He held out his hand, and tried not to show his surprise at the unusual touch of the six-digited hand with the double-opposed thumbs, one on either side.

"Sarth Gell. May I buy you another drink?"

Gorman accepted, then, waxing warm inside, asked a question.

"Sarth, do you mind if I ask you something? As I say, I have always been a fighting man; I never had much time for history. When did the Federation contact your race?"

Sarth Gell leaned back, smoothed a hand over his hairless skull and said:

"It was some 300 years ago, in the Year of the Federation 313, to be exact, that one of the exploratory ships first contacted us."

Gorman nodded. "That region is almost straight out beyond Altair, isn't it?"

"Yes. About eleven hundred light-years."

"So?" Gorman raised an eyebrow. "You must be a long way from home, too."

"Oh, no," chuckled Gell. "Not at all. I was born and

raised on Tridel of Sirius. I am no more a Lilaar than you are of Earth."

Gorman signaled, and the steward brought more drinks. The conversation went on.

The huge passenger vessel bored on through the emptiness. Or perhaps that isn't the right term. Around? Past? Between, maybe? However she did it, at top speed she could make nearly 1,000 light-speeds, although she wasn't doing that now. Her engines cut down and down as she approached Earth, until, finally, at one light, there was the familiar buzzy shiver as the ship passed into a more normal existence, although the accelerator field didn't cut itself out until the velocity dropped far below even that relatively low figure.

When the field cut, Major Gorman didn't even feel it. He was boiled to the ears.

He woke up in the hotel near the spaceport feeling just as he should feel, and lifted his head from his pillow with the care usually observed in such cases.

That sweet liquor! he thought. *I ought to have more sense than to drink stuff with so much junk in it! I wonder how many of the higher alcohols it's loaded with?*

Edging himself off the bed, he reached into his uniform pocket and got the box of small blue capsules he carried for such emergencies, swallowed one and waited. When it had taken effect, he decided that all he'd need to feel perfect again was enough water to cancel the dehydration brought on by the liquor, and some breakfast to take the dark-brown taste out of his mouth.

The breakfast helped, but by noon he felt ill again. Not from liquor, but from the same thing that had made him so sick all the way from Ferridel.

Oh, Earth was beautiful, all right. All green and parklike, with tall trees, pretty flowers, tinkling fountains, and fairy buildings. All very lovely. And dull as the very devil!

He prowled around the city all the rest of the day, and by nightfall, he was ready to call it quits.

He'd gone into three or four of the establishments that purported to be bars, and found that no one drank anything but the sweet and aromatic synthetics, all of which would have made his stomach uneasy. He'd tried to talk to two or three of the girls, but they didn't seem to want to talk about anything but the soft strains of some melody or other that whispered through the late afternoon air. If he'd known the phrase, he would have called them mid-Victorian, although they possessed none of the hypocrisy of that long-forgotten age, and absolutely none of its sense of humor.

It was, he decided, even worse than Procyon; at least he'd been able to buy some decent liquor there.

When he got back to his hotel, Sarth Gell was waiting for him.

"Good evening, Karl, I see you've been out. How do you like our lovely city?"

"Oh, fine, Sarth, just fine," lied Gorman. "Very nice. Of course, I'm used to the Outposts, but I think I'll get used to this pretty quick." But he knew better. He knew he couldn't spend 36 years of his life smashing the onslaught of the evilly monstrous Thassela and then settle down to music.

"I'm glad to hear that," Gell smiled. "I wanted to ask you to accompany me to the concert tonight. I have a special seat."

Oh, great, moaned Gorman inwardly, *just great! I'm so happy I could simply die!*

The concert hall was filled with people, all beautifully dressed to set off the softly shifting pastel colors of the walls and floor. There was no ceiling; just the sighing breeze pushing fluffy little clouds across the face of the planet's one white satellite.

He watched as the great curtains drifted silently away, disclosing the musicians. Each was seated before the multi-keyed control board at his own panel; 100 of them poised motionless, waiting for their signal.

Then the control master came out, sat down at the master panel and flexed his fingers.

Gorman looked closer. Six fingers! He hadn't noticed it at this distance, but now he could see that every one of those musicians was a Lilaarian. He glanced sideways at Gell, but his companion was looking straight at the orchestra.

Somewhere, from deep within his brain, a soft murmuring note sounded. It became a chord. It grew louder, and he actually did not realize until it grew fairly loud that it had come, not from his own mind, but from the orchestra before him.

As the music grew louder and wove in and out of itself, it became definitely apparent that the people of Lilaar

52

were really master musicians. The shifting colors of the walls swirled in time to the undulating harmony of the orchestra.

He listened, and, after a little while, the music faded as it had begun, in a single note, dying in his brain.

He waited for the second composition, and was disturbed by Sarth Gell's touch upon his arm. He turned and noticed that everyone else was quietly leaving. Startled, he glanced at his wrist watch. Three hours! And he hadn't even realized it!

The next day, he went to the Great Library and began a search through the history section. Nothing too new, he decided. Something written back in the late Four or early Five Hundreds, at least a century old.

He finally found what he was looking for, selected two chapters for the reader, and flipped the switch.

"As has been related in previous chapters," it began, *"several nonhuman races of fair intelligence were discovered, but it was not until YF 313 that any race was found which had ever had interstellar travel.*

"In that year, Expedition Ship 983, commanded by Colonel Rupert Forbes, discovered—"

The great ship hung high above the atmosphere of the planet, the engines quiescent. Colonel Forbes waited impatiently for the arrival of the scout ship. When it finally came, he ordered Lieutenant Parlan to report immediately, in person.

"I don't want anything formal, lieutenant," he said. "Just tell me what you found."

"Well, sir, the planet is inhabited all right, and they're almost human." He handed a sheaf of photographs to the colonel and went on. "You can see for yourself. They live in huge cities that look as if at one time they'd been really something, but now they're falling to pieces; they look *old,* old as the mountains—weatherbeaten, if you know what I mean, sir.

"Anyway, these people just live in them, they don't build them. And they don't use any kind of power. They light the buildings with lamps that burn some kind of oil, and they do their work by hand."

"I see," nodded Colonel Forbes, "backward and ignorant, eh?"

"Yes, sir, in a way. Though they must have had quite a civilization at one time, from the looks of things."

"I think I'll get Philology busy on the language right away, and—"

"A thorough study of the language took the better part of a year, and by that time, several other facts made themselves apparent. First, that the natives had no knowledge whatever of science; second—"

"A funny bunch of people, colonel," commented Lieutenant Parlan. "They believe that they are a part of what might be translated roughly as 'The Great Empire of Heaven'. Their word for themselves is 'Lilaar,' but that also means 'sky' or 'universe.' The birth rate is appallingly low; only one child per couple every fifteen or twenty years. I don't see how they kept themselves from extinction this long."

Colonel Forbes rubbed a thumb across his chin, "How do you think they'll react to Federation rule?"

"Duck soup. They have absolutely no weapons; they are strict vegetarians; they're the laziest and most sheeplike, peaceful people I ever saw."

"Very well, I'll send my report in."

The report went in by subspace radio, propagated at a velocity which, though finite, is so great that the means of measuring it is unknown—the distance required is too great.

Expedition Ship 968 shot off toward her next target, a sun some 3.2 light-years distant.

Colonel Forbes addressed his staff: "Gentlemen, we have been away from Earth for better than two years. This is the last stop on our cruise. From here we return home!" There were general smiles and pleased murmurings all around.

"We have done well," Forbes continued. "We have discovered twelve planets which humanity can colonize, and more than that, one planet inhabited by intelligent beings, a discovery which is extremely rare among ships of the Exploratory Forces.

"Lieutenant Parlan, our contact officer, is, at this momoment, exploring the 13th and last planet. When he reports back—I expect him any minute—I hope we shall be able to report that we have discovered 13 habitable worlds on our outward trip; more than any other ship has so far found. To that, we can add the discovery of an alien race on one of the few—"

"Two," came the voice of Lieutenant Parlan from the door.

"I beg your pardon?" blinked Forbes, startled at the interruption.

"I said two, sir. We have found two planets inhabited by nonhuman races—or rather race."

"Please be more explicit, lieutenant," the colonel said sharply.

"The planet below us, sir, is populated by the Lilaar!"

"All in all, the next 70 years of exploration in that region uncovered 71 planets of the Grand Empire of Lilaar, all of which—"

Gorman snapped it off. That was enough. It tallied. He set the other chapter he had selected, and started the reader again.

"Beginning in YF 380, several Expeditionary ships stopped sending in their reports abruptly, and were never heard of again. Because of the obvious dangers inherent in interstellar exploration, not too much significance was attached to these disappearances, although it was noticed that the incidents all took place in one section of the outermost fringes of the Federation. It was not until early in 384 that the truth became known.

"In that year, Expedition Ship 770 reported that it was being attacked by alien forces. They subsequently ceased to report.

"Federal Security forces immediately went into action. The Biomathematical Section had long warned of the probability of inimical alien life, and thus the Government was prepared. The cry of 'Remember the Seven Seven Oh!' became the battle cry of the Federation. The Interstellar Secrecy and Security Act went into effect and—"

Again Gorman cut the reader off. One more check and he would have what he wanted.

He and the librarian went through the Laws of the Federation for several minutes until he found the original draft of the Act.

It read: "For the security of the Solar Federation . . .

no person, corporation, planetary or system government . . . shall build or construct . . . any interstellar vessel, for any use whatsoever, except upon explicit contract with the Federal Government.

"All such now in use shall be . . . turned over to the Federal Government without delay.

"No subspace radio shall . . . operate or be operated . . . without explicit instructions from the Federal Government."

There was more, but that was all that interested Gorman. He was sure, now. Here was what he was looking for.

He had had a small smile at the part that stated that no "person or corporation" would build a spaceship. Any "person or corporation" wealthy and powerful enough to construct one would have long since ceased to be a "person or corporation" as such—they would have become a government.

Then he went out to the Federal Radio Office, sent an Interstellar 'gram—three eighty-five a letter for 19 letters —paid, and left for dinner. After dinner, he poked around until he found a bar near the spaceport which sold a concoction that wasn't so ungodly sweet, had three drinks, and went to bed.

Next morning, he had company.

"Fleet Intelligence," said the smartly uniformed captain who stood in the doorway as Gorman opened it. His credentials were in his hand, but Gorman just gave them a quick glance.

"Come in," he said, mentally parenthesizing that for an Intelligence man, the guy didn't look too intelligent. Soft, bland face, wide-open eyes that kept blinking like a couple of synchronized camera shutters, and a prim mouth. Behind him were two more nonentities just like him in lieutenant's uniforms. They all trooped into the room, one right after the other.

"May I see your papers, Major?" asked the captain.

"Certainly, captain." He handed over the thick sheaf of folded papers in their heavy official envelope. The Intelligence man scrutinized them for the better part of ten minutes, moving his lips in a not-quite-inaudible whisper as he did so.

"They seem to be quite in order, sir," he said when he finished. "They seem to be quite in order."

"May I ask what the trouble is, captain?"

"Well, to be frank, there were quite a few people who wondered just how a Spacefleet major, wearing an Outpost Spearhead, happened to get the extended leave required to come to Earth, especially with a war on out there."

Gorman absorbed that statement for a full second before the full import struck him. The fathead actually did not know the war was over! And had been for better than two and a half years!

He worded his second question cautiously.

"Tell me, captain, isn't this stuff radioed into GHQ?"

The captain looked startled. "Why . . . ah . . . yes . . . yes, I believe it is. But after all, Major, you must realize that such things are merely for the record. Now that we have checked your papers, I have no doubt that my superiors will check them against the files to confirm them, but up to now, there has been no reason to look over those 'grams. They are simply received and filed until needed."

Gorman, still cautious, worded his next question a little more broadly. "But why? I should think you'd want to know what's going on in the Galaxy."

The captain's smile was a little superior. "My dear major, do you realize the immensity of correspondence that must come from better than 70,000 million cubic light-years of space filled with uncounted thousands of billions of living beings? Why, it couldn't possibly be all correlated! I'm afraid, major, that you are thinking in terms of planetary governments. The Federation simply couldn't be run that way."

Gorman realized then why no one knew the war was over. It wasn't, really; there were still a few mopping-up operations to be taken care of, still a few Thassela attempting to flee from the Federation Spacefleet. No one headquarters anywhere in the Outposts had sent the specific message: WAR OVER EXCEPT FOR MOP-UP. It would take a correlation of all the millions upon millions of reports from each of the widely scattered planets of the far-flung Outpost stars.

He chuckled mentally at the thought that several thousand of the clerks in the Federation offices each knew a tiny fraction of the fact that the Human-Thassela War was over. And who was he to tell them? After all, he was no official spokesman for the Outpost Fleet; he might not—he probably wouldn't—be believed.

"You're probably right, captain; I must seem a bit provincial to you. Well, if you're quite satisfied I—"

"Ah—one more question, major." He ruffled through a notebook. "What was the meaning of the 'gram you sent to a Major Mark Gorman on Kaibere IV last night? It reads: *Altair cap sppt six mos.* What does that mean?"

Gorman shrugged. "At three eighty-five, space rates, I saved a devil of a lot of money by not saying, 'Dear Mark, please meet me at the Altair capital spaceport six months from now.' O.K.?"

"Why say 'Altair capital'? 'Pelma' would have been a great deal shorter. Would've saved you fifteen-forty." The captain did not seem to be questioning in an official manner, now, he just seemed genuinely interested.

"I'm no stellographer. Neither is Mark. Tell me; what is the only planet of Meargrave?"

"I don't know."

"But you could get there?"

"Yes. Easily."

"What if I told you to go to Hell?"

"What?" The captain looked scandalized, shocked and insulted, all in one face.

"Hell, my dear captain, happens to be the only planet of Meargrave." Gorman particularly liked to use that example. It had a shock effect he was fond of.

"Oh." The face cleared, "I see what you mean. Well, sir, I think everything is in order. Thank you, Major, for your co-operation."

He saluted and left, the two lieutenants following silently after.

Gorman sat down on the bed, looked wonderingly after them for a moment, then grinned.

"What a bunch of fogheads. The Thassela could have battled their way clear in to Procyon before they'd know it."

He had six months to wait.

The first three he spent on Earth. He wanted to see the entire planet but he just didn't have the time; therefore a representative sample would have to do.

He noticed quite early that most of Earth's inhabitants, both Human and Lilaarian, avoided him after first contact, especially if he mentioned anything about the war, or if they happened to see and know the Silver Spearhead. He knew what they must be thinking:

Here is a soldier, a killer, back from his awful business. Here is a man who has been trained to murder other beings. What if he gets bored with us? What if we anger him somehow? What then? Would he not just as soon kill a Human or Lilaarian as a Thasselan? Perhaps. It would not be too wise to associate with him, at any rate.

They were polite, but evasive.

Not, he reflected, that he blamed them. He was probably the first real veteran they had ever seen. To them, the war had not been close. They had lived with it all their lives, as he had, but it was not the same. To them, it was a vague thing; something 2,000 light-years away that they heard of once in a great while and dismissed distastefully.

If a fully armed and armored Thasselan battle fleet had started for Earth yesterday, it would be a full two years at top speed before they would arrive. There would be plenty of time to prepare.

Even the planets near the periphery of the Federation shared, to some slight extent, the feeling Earthmen had toward the returned fighting man. He remembered Telsonn, two ship-months, 150 light-years, in from the front. They had had men, sons, fathers and husbands, who had fought in the war, although not actually as fighting men, and even they shied away from their homecoming relatives as though they were some other sort of life.

Here on Earth, of course, it was immensely worse. For the past century or more, no Earthman had volunteered for front duty, and it had not been necessary to order them there; the war had been going well, even then. The only duty imposed upon Spacefleet men of Earth was the Ferry Service; the duty of taking the fabulously expensive and highly necessary spaceships out for a month or two to some relay point where they would be picked up by another crew and taken a little farther, and so on until they reached their destination. The original crew would return by luxury liner to Earth for a leave, then pick up another ship.

After three months, Gorman grabbed the first available ship for Altair and—what was it?—Pelma, the System's capital.

The great automatic ship had only three passengers besides himself. No one did much traveling any more, and those who did weren't very interesting to talk to. Major Gorman kept to his cabin most of the time.

When he had begun his long journey in from Ferridel, now almost three years ago, he had been vastly interested in the liners, so different were they from the battleships he was used to. They were completely automatic, pursuing and correcting their courses through those immense distances with unerring precision, requiring no human hand at their control. Indeed, no human being could possibly move fast enough or think fast enough to control anything moving at nearly 200 million miles per second.

The ships were robots, and for that very reason they had been fascinating. But they were blind, reasonless robots, designed to take their course and return. They had no real intelligence, and they soon palled on him. He had come to ignore them completely.

The trip took only a few days, but he was heartily glad when it was over.

Pelma of Altair, he soon discovered, was a great deal like Earth. Too much, in fact. The one redeeming factor was that here there were fewer people who recognized the Spearhead on his shoulder. Several times, on Earth, he had been tempted to put on civilian clothes, and had even gone so far as to try a suit on, but in the first place, it was strictly against military law, and in the second, civvies didn't feel natural on his body.

After he had been there a few days, he received another visit from Intelligence, and they had evidently had no word from Earth that he was cleared there. The interview was shorter than the first had been, but the end result was the same. Major Gorman went on about his business.

Life suddenly became infinitely more bearable in the middle of the fourth week. She was sitting on a little grassy knoll in one of the innumerable parks, scattering food to a flock of the little bushy-tailed mammals that seemed to infest so many planets in this part of the Federation. Gorman watched her for a long time, trying to figure out an angle of approach that would work but wouldn't be too obvious.

She seemed to have some of the animals rather well-tamed; they would come right up to her with their funny scrambling gait, snatch the food right out of her fingers and then run off, nibbling it between their forepaws.

Suddenly, she screamed and jerked her hand away from one of the beasts. Gorman saw immediately what had happened: one of the little monsters had bitten her.

60

Arise, brave soul, and dash to her rescue, Gorman thought, and made motions to suit.

"What happened, Miss?" he asked, pretending a great worry over what he knew was an inconsequential wound.

She was crying and could hardly speak, but she held the injured and bleeding digit, out for his inspection.

"Hm-m-m," he hm-m-m'd. He took an ampoule out of the E-kit at his belt, aimed it at the tip of the finger he was holding, and squeezed the end. It spat a fine cloud of mist at the ragged little incision. Then he wrapped the finger.

"I think that'll do it. You can go to a physician if you want, but I don't believe it will be necessary."

She smiled prettily. "It doesn't hurt a bit, now. Thank you"—her gray eyes darted to his collar—"Major, thank you very much."

"Well, now, I wouldn't be in too much of a hurry to run off," cautioned Gorman. "You really ought to go somewhere and sit down for a while; animal bites can be poisonous sometimes, you know. Is there somewhere we can—"

She looked a little worried. "Why . . . why, yes, I know a diner down the parkway. Do you really think—?"

Gorman didn't know quite what to think. Was she taking him seriously, or did she think he wasn't quite bright? Who cared? Play it along, boy, play it along.

"I wasn't thinking of a diner, exactly. You see, it is a well-known fact that alcohol is just the thing for bites—provided that they're treated first, of course."

She brightened again. "Oh, really? I didn't know that. I suppose I had better have some, then."

They had some. The place labeled itself a "cocktail lounge," but it mixed drinks out of the assorted flavors and synthetics, then spiked them with a little bit of straight ethanol. It took quite a little talking to convince the steward that he should jigger up the mechanism so it would serve the ethanol with nothing but soda water and a dash of bitters, but Gorman finally did it. It took him almost as long to convince the girl that she should drink the stuff, but he finally did that, too.

Her name, it turned out, was Lanina Indar, and she was a music interpreter.

Upon questioning, Gorman discovered that a music interpreter interpreted music, a fact which he had already suspected. He asked her to explain further.

"Well, you see, it's this way. Lilaarian music all means something. It's very, very old music, most of it, dating back to the old Grand Empire itself. The Lilaarians know, or, rather, they *feel* exactly what the music means. It's really a language of sorts, you know, except that it expresses mood and emotion rather than ideas or anything like that. You see?"

Gorman did see, after a fashion. He waved a vague gesture into the air. "What is that saying?"

She listened for a moment to the soft pulsing rhythm, then closed her eyes. Her lips began to move softly.

"We dream of peace, to sleep and dream; to quietness and gentle sleep our goal; we rest forever—"

She went on like that for the better part of ten minutes, and Gorman was reminded, somehow, of an old poem he had read in one of the museums he had visited on Earth. Something about—

". . . To die, to sleep;
To sleep: perchance to dream: ay, there's the rub;
For in that sleep of death what dreams may come
When we have shuffled off this mortal coil
Must give us pause."

That, at least, was a rough translation. He wondered, fleetingly, what that ancient bard would have thought of Earth today. Then, his thoughts were broken by Lanina's voice.

"See? Isn't it beautiful? Of course, to really understand it, you have to listen closely and listen to a lot of it, but eventually, you really get the feel of the music; then it comes easily."

"It sounds a little morbid to me," Gorman murmured.

"Oh no it isn't, really; it isn't at all. It's sort of beautiful and peaceful."

"Are they all like that?"

"Oh, no. Some of them deal with pure beauty, others with light and color, and—"

Gorman listened for a long time, nodding his head occasionally, and sticking in an appropriate remark now and then, but his heart wasn't in it. He was thinking.

Here I am again, listening to a nice dissertation on Lilaarian music. Tomorrow night, it will be flowers, and the next night it will be statuary, and the night after that light symphonies of music again.

No! I'm going to get this piece of fluff to talk about something else if I have to completely re-educate her all by myself!

He knew from the beginning that such an education would have to be begun on her level. He began by painting word-pictures of the awful beauty of interstellar space, of the grandeur of the vast loneliness and emptiness between the stars; he went from there to the wonders of adventure, the desire to explore and see things that no man had ever seen before. He talked carefully, choosing each word for semantic content on the girl's own level, twisting the conversation back toward his own goal every time she tried to throw it off course.

In the end, he didn't think he had been too successful. After two months of education, it was a little disheartening to find that she didn't really seem to be interested in what he was saying. A blow to the ego, to say the least.

She was with him the day Mark arrived. They were eating dinner in the spaceport cafe, when the ship arrived. Lanina had kept nagging him to tell her who they were going to meet, but all he'd tell her was "a relative."

When Major Mark Gorman came in and sat down, she watched the back-slapping and greetings with slightly startled eyes.

"Why, you're twins!" she exclaimed, at last.

"Oh, no," laughed Karl. "Mark is older than I by several years. Right, Grampaw?"

"Right. But look, junior, where's your manners?"

"Oh. Sorry, Lanina, Mark Gorman."

Lanina searched Mark's face carefully. When he took off his cap she smiled. "You don't look any older, but I can see now that you aren't identical twins. Your hair is light-brown, almost the same color as mine, Karl's is almost black."

Mark rubbed his hands together briskly. "Well, son, what's on the agenda? How was Earth? I didn't come through there, so I figured you'd have to tell me all about it."

Gorman looked comically downcast. "We are the Forgotten Men. No one appreciates us around here. In fact, nobody even knows we exist."

"That's about the way I had it made out. Shame."

They eyed each other sadly for a moment, then broke out laughing. "Come on," said Gorman, "I know of a little place where the three of us can talk. I have bribed the automatics to make something that borders on being fit to drink. You have to watch those synthetics. They flavor them with some frightful messes."

The conversation that night was sometimes over Lanina's head. Most of the time the men talked to her, and the conversation was very stimulating, but every once in a while, they seemed to run across some private joke that she couldn't fathom, especially those about Lilaarians. Oh, well. She didn't understand Spacefleet men, anyway.

The next morning, they were in the Spaceport office quite early, poring over timetables, making calculations, checking back over old passenger lists, and looking up immigration and emigration statistics. It was nearly nighttime before Karl Gorman was able to place his hand over a section of the tank chart and say: "Here."

"Here *what?*" Lanina asked confusedly.

Mark smiled. "My friend, the idiot, may not have told you, my dear, but I am a man with itchy feet. We were just deciding on the proper spot for my vacation—for the next five or six years."

The girl turned pleading eyes on Karl. "You . . . you aren't going with him? Are you?"

"Nope. I have decided to become a homebody. I like Pelma."

"But won't you have to go back to duty?"

"Nope, again. I am on 'indefinite leave'; don't have to go back until they call me." To which he added mentally: *And I don't think they will.*

The years passed swiftly for Karl Gorman, and yet, in another way, they were easy-going and full. Before the end of the first year he had acquired an apartment, and the lettering on the door said: KARL GORMAN, THEORETICAL MATHEMATICIAN.

It was as good a title and profession as any, and quite true, although there was little call for his services. Nevertheless, he worked at it. He and Lanina set up a small calculator in one of the rooms, and he patiently taught her how to set up equations on it after he had written them out. She never really quite learned what she was doing, but after he showed her how the music of Lilaar could

64

be interpreted mathematically, she loved the work he gave her to do.

Meanwhile, the little, and highly illegal subspace radio began receiving reports from Mark's equally illegal set.

Karrvon; 300 light-years from Earth; Index .63.
Ressalin; 420 light-years; Index .50.
Mensidor; 690 light-years; Index .39.
Hessor-Del; 800 light-years; Index 21.
Thilia; 1,200 light-years; Index .08.

And Gorman carefully fed them all into the computer, came up with figures that were meaningless to anyone but himself, fed these back in and came up with figures that were even more meaningless, if possible.

At other times, he computed Lanina's music for her, although he told her not to tell anyone where she had obtained her results.

"Every other interpreter would want me to do it, and I haven't that much time," was the absolutely untruthful answer he gave her.

And, again, he would go out to art galleries and measure lines and curves and color wavelength and intensity. And these, too, went into the computer, and came out unrecognizable.

And one morning, when nearly six years had passed, Gorman and Lanina were eating breakfast when the door chime announced a visitor.

Mark Gorman was back again.

The Spacefleet Intelligence men and the CID were 45 minutes behind him. This time they hadn't delegated the duty to a mere captain; having evidently decided they should outrank their quarry, they had sent two colonels.

"Which one of you is Major Gorman?" asked the tough-looking CID man.

Two thumbs jerked simultaneously. Two voices said: "Him."

The colonel glared. "Let me see your papers!"

He looked them over, then looked back at the two who were standing at attention before him. "Very funny. And for that remark, I think we'll take both of you in."

"On what charge, sir?" asked Mark.

"Grand larceny and interstellar piracy. To be explicit, for feloniously disrupting the robot controls of, diverting the course of, and taking illegal possession of an interstellar passenger liner."

Karl gazed upon Mark with a mock glower. "Shame on you."

Mark tried to look innocent. "Well, nobody was using it."

"Enough!" barked the colonel savagely. "Let's go!"

Lanina said nothing, but her eyes were wide with terror. When they left, she was sobbing quietly.

An hour later, the Majors Gorman were sitting on a bench in a windowless cell, watching the door slide shut with a click.

"And now what?" asked Karl.

"And now, my boy, we are to be left for a time in order to thoroughly discuss our crime, so that concealed pickups can relay the complete details to our stuffy friend, the colonel."

Then the shock came. Energy rippled searingly through their bodies, and they sagged slowly to the floor.

When they opened their eyes, they were seated in a softly luxurious room in comfortable chairs, bound there by restraining, but not uncomfortable, straps. Before them was a large, finely paneled desk. Behind it was seated a Lilaarian. Karl recognized him. It was Sarth Gell.

"Ah, you are awake," said Gell.

"An astute observation, to say the least, Master Gell."

"Oh," said Mark. "You know this pleasant fellow?"

"Ah, yes. We got sotty together some years back."

"Permit me to correct your brother, Mark Gorman," Gell interjected softly. "*He* got sotty. Lilaarians, in case you didn't know, eschew intoxicants in any form."

"I didn't know," Mark murmured. "But it's fascinatin' information. Do go on."

"I shall. I am about to make a very long, but, I trust, not tiresome speech. I hope both of you can restrain your admittedly very witty remarks until I am through.

"To begin with, let me tell you that I know exactly what you two have been doing for the last several years, and have followed your progress with avid interest. You have discovered that we of the Lilaar have begun to, and eventually will, take over complete control of the Federation, although the Federation will not exist as such by that time.

"As you, Mark, have discovered in your wanderings in

66

that stolen spaceship, the regularly scheduled flights in that portion of the Galaxy are no longer being made. The planets there have not made any reports to Earth for some years, in some cases more than a century. Because of the very carefully planned decay of Earth's correlation system, they do not as yet know this, and by the time they do, it will be too late.

"And you, Karl, have discovered that our subtly hypnotic art forms are the means we use to further our purpose.

"Because you have discovered these things, I am sorry to say that I must forever prevent that information from reaching Earth. You will never report what you have found.

"Now as to why and how we have done this. To begin, I must go back a good many centuries; back to the first century of the Federation. And I must also explain exactly who and what the Lilaar are.

"We of the Lilaar, you see, are immortal."

Karl Gorman's eyes narrowed. "Precisely what do you mean by 'immortal,' Gell? That's a pretty broad term."

"By that, I mean that we do not suffer, as you do, from the racial disease known as 'old age.' Except for accidents and a few rare diseases, there is nothing to keep us from living forever. You must understand this in order to understand what you have seen.

"Our birth rate, as you know, has been referred to as being extremely low. Actually, quite the reverse is true. Each couple averages one birth every 30 years. That means that our population is *doubled every 60 Earth-years!*

"Of necessity, therefore, we had to expand. And in doing so we found that we had competition. You, of Earth, and the Thassela. We are not, however, fighters. Because of the vast value of life, we cannot, by our very nature, take the life of an intelligent living being." Gell's face twisted as he said this, as though he were going to be sick at the very thought of death.

He paused to relax for a moment, then went on.

"When your first ship found us, in YF 313, the Plan had already been in operation for some two hundred of your years. We pretended to be decadent. We made you believe that our glorious Grand Empire was dead. Neither is true.

"We knew in the beginning that your race, being inherently what it was, would eventually win the Thassela-Human war. Therefore, we are permitting you to do so. At the same time, we are completely undermining your once-tight and compact organization of government. The Federation should collapse in about one hundred fifty to two hundred years, at which time you will have won the war with the Thassela."

"It is obvious," remarked Mark calmly, "that you have, and can use, a space drive capable of much greater velocities than ours. Tell me, why don't you use it?"

Gell's brows lifted in surprise. "You are a very observant young man in some ways, but in others you are not. But"—he shrugged—"I will answer the question. Yes, we have had the infinity drive for many hundreds of years. We do not use it within the boundaries of the Federation unless absolutely necessary because it interferes with subspace radio, and is, therefore detectable.

"Our kidnapping you from under the noses of the Spacefleet CID was done only because of the extreme urgency of the situation. We could not permit you to return to Earth."

"May I ask why you are dooming the Federation?" Mark asked.

"We need the planets which you are using. Our population growth has required a tremendous amount of shifting about in the Federation, and a great deal of name-changing in order that your race may never discover the fact that we do not . . . ah . . . die." The last word was almost a whisper. "This is a nuisance and a bother. We are, however, eliminating it, since there will soon be no subspace report the fact that there are certain irregularities in our radios in operation near our portion of the Federation to life span."

Gell placed his fingertips together and smiled benevolently.

"Our plan, as you can see, is working well. The Thassela are too monstrously savage, too physically unlike us to have permitted our infiltration. The Humans, on the other hand, have proved themselves relatively easy to manage.

"And, if you will reason it out logically, you will see that it is all for the best. Both you humans and the Thassela are basically unfit for the role of Galactic rulers. You are basically killers; destroyers of life; diseases which should never have evolved!" His voice shook with loathing.

"Careful, Gell," Karl Gorman cut in. "You'll get high blood pressure." But Seth Gell was calm again.

"The disease will be permitted to run its course, but by isolating the colonies of infection we will be able to control and eventually eliminate it. The immortals must rule the galaxy."

"What about us? If you can't murder us in cold blood, what do you intend to do to put us permanently out of the way?" Mark was purposely gory for Gell's discomfort.

"We are leaving you here. The whole planet is yours. It will not be required by our race for another century. This house has been constructed for your comfort, but there is nothing else on this entire world in the way of civilized artifacts. You cannot build spaceships; on the nearer of the two satellites is a device which will prevent your sending a subspace message, even if you should be able to construct a radio. You will remain here for the rest of your lives."

"This planet? Where are we?" Mark's voice was cold.

"While you were unconscious, you were transported here by one of our infinity ships. When this sun sets, I rather imagine you will like the view; you are in the center of the vast star clouds beyond Sagittarius, 30,000 light-years from Earth. When I return, this planet will again be vacant and ready for our use. The Lilaar can afford to wait."

Sarth Gell, the Lilaarian, turned and left the room. In a few moments the ground quivered a little, and there was the distant buzz of a space vessel as it lifted, leaving the two behind to work their way out of the straps that bound them to the chairs, knowing they could never work their way out of the vaster bonds of space.

"Are they gone?" Karl asked after a moment.

Mark Gorman's brain reached out through the twists of spacetime and contacted that of the robot in the Lilaarian ship. And the stupid, unimaginative thing answered truthfully.

Mark smiled. "Yes, they're gone."

The two stood, the binding straps splitting and rending as they did so.

"Now what, Grandfather?" Karl asked.

"I have been sending in my reports regularly, ever since we were assigned to discover why the Federation Government had become so lax. Now we know. I'll finish my report so that you can send in the math involved."

"Check. I'll wait."

Mark Gorman lay on a soft couch in the Lilaar-provided room, and closed his eyes. Again his brain reached out, this time further, much further than before. Finally he contacted it, fitted himself in and took control.

And, more than 30,000 light-years away, on Ferridel III, a robot-controlled printer began to make impressions on a strand of ultrafine plastic, subtly altering its molecular structure.

A REPORT ON THE GRAND EMPIRE
OF THE LILAAR

From: Mark of Ferridel III; somewhere in the center of the Galaxy.
To: Commanding General, Outpost Spacefleet, Control Division.
Via: Interbrain Paracontrol beam.

From the above portions of this report, I believe it will be possible for our psychologists to find the precise stresses necessary to disrupt their Empire. These will, I believe, be slight, since it is my opinion that they are already psychotic to some degree in that they do not admit their position in the basic realities of the Universe.

I give as examples the references to their living "forever"; a self-obvious fallacy, and their so-called "infinity" drive, also as obvious. The long and boastful speech which Sarth Gell made just before he deserted us here is also significant. Their basic revulsion to death is another factor, in that it springs, not from a high moral code, but from fear.

It is because of this fear, I believe, that they, like Earth, do not know that the Thasselan war is over. They avoided the entire sector. It is also responsible for their ignorance of our existence.

Earth, because of the Lilaarian disruption of Federal Coordination and Correlation, has forgotten us.

My grandson, Karl, will send in the complete mathematical analysis through me as soon as he has incorporated the data just received, but for those not equipped with computer brains, I think the following will explain in some measure our position:

When, three centuries ago, it became obvious that no ordinary robot could control an interstellar battleship to the extent necessary to overwhelm the antlike coordination of the Thassela, Dr. Theodore Gorr was sent to the Outpost planets to build a robot which could do the job required.

At this time, the Lilaar were not as yet beginning their actual infiltration, since they had not been accepted as citizens of the Federation; therefore, they knew nothing of Dr. Gorr's highly secret mission. When Dr. Gorr produced the first Gorr-man on Ferridel III, he probably did not realize that the real enemy of Earth was attacking from far across the Federation, but nevertheless, as is well known, we were so equipped as to be able to ward off attack in almost any conceivable form.

The Lilaar, naturally, could know nothing of this, but they could have deduced it logically had not their fear of death kept them from the immediate area of the war. No human being is capable of computing the forces and the vectors thereof which obtain at ultralight velocities in interstellar space. Had the Lilaar known that our fighting ships do not have built-in control robots, they would have known that they were controlled by some other type, and thus would have known of our existence. My grandson, by the way, has shown that the probable deduction would have been wrong, insofar as our method of ship control would have been assumed to be by the so-called "subspace" radio, and not by the actual application of mental energy.

Our activities for the past ten years were so calculated as to be suspicious only to the Lilaar. This was necessary because Karl's equations showed that the final factors could only come from a Lilaarian speaking of his own free will.

Karl, therefore, stayed on Pelma of Altair after his preliminary reconnaissance, while I inspected the area already under the control of Lilaar. My grandson, as you know, while only 30 at the time—he was commissioned a major 12 years ago—is deserving of the rank in every way. He is, however, one of the new Type Beta Gorr-men, whose purpose is sociomathematical computation, and therefore is not telepathic

71

and cannot direct a ship as we of Type Alpha because of the extra brain capacity required for these forms of higher-stage computers.

On Pelma, he set up a "front" as a practical mathematician and actually bought himself an electric computer which he taught a young human girl to operate, in order to free his brain of the tiresome details of some of the simpler problems. He investigated Lilaarian art forms, computed their hypnotic qualities, figured in the indices of general effect which I gave him from space and entered all these into what he calls the Lilaarian Equations.

In general, these equations show the following:

A. The Lilaar, because their fear of death prevents them from practicing birth control, will so overpopulate their planets that they will starve, since they require as fuel the hard-to-synthesize carbohydrates, but cannot also utilize, as we do, the lower alcohols.

B. Even their so-called "infinity drive" cannot move them to new planets fast enough, as a little figuring with geometrical progression will show. Their population doubles every 60 years; therefore, their portion of the Galaxy can be shown to be an expanding sphere which must double in volume every second generation. The Lilaarians must, however, go to planets outside the "surface" of that sphere, a surface which is constantly decreasing in proportion to the total volume. Theoretically, this would reach a point where it would be physically impossible for them to be "emitted" from the "radiating surface" fast enough. Long before that point is reached, however, the area in the center of this sphere will begin to starve. The death of its inhabitants will start a mass psychosis of the entire race which will eventually destroy them.

C. The Lilaar will be unable to admit this, even to themselves, and will, therefore, do nothing to prevent it.

We will stay upon this planet until the scientists of Ferridel learn the secret of the Lilaar drive, which, it is estimated, will not take more than from 10 to 60 Earth-years.

We can well afford to wait.

Mark of Ferridel III
Major, Spacefleet Ship Control

72

RANDALL AND I

Isaac Asimov

I DON'T WASTE MUCH TIME ENVYING OTHER people their cleverness and wit. What with my own cheerful self-appreciation, I have the comfortable feeling that I have enough cleverness and wit to fill three of your average geniuses.

But I envy Randall.

I can perhaps match his science-fiction ability, but I can only distantly approach his knack at writing clever comic verse. And what really knocks me for a loop every time I remember them are the little ceramic three-dimensional versions he once manufactured of the characters in *Pogo Possum*. That's really piling on the talents to a prohibitive degree.

And I have to pant when it comes to keeping up with him in sheer madness.

When I think of science-fiction conventions, I think of Randall. There are two kinds of science-fiction conventions that I attend—those at which Randall is also present and those at which he is not. When he and I are there together—well, I think you've heard of welkins ringing? We're the guys who ring them.

We were at our peak, perhaps, at the 1955 World Science Fiction Convention at Cleveland (ah, youth, youth.) We reeled through halls of molten blue, so we did (drunk with carefree laughter, rather than alcohol), and leaned against the sun—outdoing it in brightness in our own minds.

That was the convention at which we sat up virtually all night in an all-night diner (where else?) with half a girl apiece—one girl, that is, seated on the counter stool between us, and perfectly safe. I don't say she would have been perfectly safe if either one or the other of us had been there alone—but with both of us present, we were far too busy being on display and topping each other's bon mots to be interested in anything as evanescent as sex.

That was the convention at which we revved each other up so high that Judy Merril emptied a full ashtray on our heads. I forget the reason but it was undoubtedly a good and sufficient one.

That was the convention at which Harlan Ellison referred to us as "Tweedledee and Tweedledum" and we raced each other to see which of us could say "I'm Dee" first.

That was the convention at which, when the morning program was late getting started and the troops were getting restless, Randall and I got up on the platform for a program of songs and snappy patter.

And you think it was all 1955? Not at all.

In December 1978, I was giving a talk at San Jose, California, (got there by train) and Randall was in the audience. Toward the end of the talk, he placed a piece of paper on the podium. It was a parody he had written to the tune of "Home on the Range." A parody on clones —clever and ribald and absolutely inoffensive.

I sang it and brought the house down. I've sung it on numerous occasions since, with added verses of my own, even on network television (always giving Randall due credit) and each time I do, I am young again and Randall and I are marching through a corridor arm in arm and all around us is the joyous hullabaloo of a science-fiction convention.

When Randall lived in the Cincinnati area, early in the 1950s, one of his good friends was the legendary and venerable Charles R. Tanner, author of some of the classic science-fiction stories of the Hugo Gernsback era. Tanner was a master of doggerel and had composed some splendidly funny verse versions of the novels of Edgar Rice Burroughs, E. E. Smith and others of the time. Randall committed these to memory and recited them to great effect—always with due credit—at almost any occasion. And in time he composed a good many of these affectionate comic pastiches himself. Herewith a selection of the most choice.

ISAAC ASIMOV'S *THE CAVES OF STEEL*: A REVIEW IN VERSE

In the future, when the towns are caves of steel
Clear from Boston, Massachusetts, to Mobile,
There's a cop, Elijah Baley, who's the hero of this tale. He
Has a Spacer robot helper named Daneel.

For it seems that there's some guys from Outer Space
(They're descendants of the Terran human race),
And all over Terra's globe, it seems they're giving jobs to robots,
Which are hated by the people they replace.

So a certain Spacer, Sarton, gets rubbed out,
And the Chief says to Elijah: "Be a scout;
Go and find out just whodunit, and, although it won't be fun, it
Will result in your promotion, without doubt!"

The assignment puts Elijah on the spot.
 He must do the job up right; if he does not,
It not only will disgrace him, but the robot will replace him
 If the robot is the first to solve the plot.

 In the city, there's a riot at a store.
 R. Daneel jumps on a counter, and before
Baley knows it, pulls his blaster. Then he bellows: "I'm the
 master
 Here, so stop it, or I'll blow you off the floor!"

 So the riot's busted up before it starts,
 And Elijah's wounded ego really smarts.
"Well," he says, "you quelled that riot, but a robot wouldn't try
 it!
 Dan, I think you've got a screw loose in your parts!"

 Baley doesn't see how R. Daneel could draw
 Out his blaster, for the First Robotic Law
Says: "No robot may, through action or inaction, harm a fraction
 Of a whisker on a human being's jaw."

 Since Daneel, the robot, has a human face,
 And he looks exactly like the guy from space
Who has been assassinated, Mr. Baley's quite elated,
 For he's positive he's solved the murder case!

 "The Commissioner," he says, "has been misled,
 'Cause there hasn't been a murder! No one's dead!
Why you did it, I don't know, but I don't think you are a robot!
 I am certain you are Sarton, sir, instead!"

 "Why, that's rather silly, partner," says Daneel,
 "And I'm awful sorry that's the way you feel."
Then, by peeling back his skin, he shows Elijah that, within, he
 Is constructed almost totally of steel!

 Well, of course, this gives Elijah quite a shock.
 So he thinks the whole thing over, taking stock
Of the clues in their relation to the total situation,
 Then he goes and calls a special robot doc.

 Says Elijah Baley: "Dr. Gerrigel,
 This here murder case is just about to jell!
And to bust it open wide, I'll prove this robot's homicidal!
 Look him over, doc, and see if you can tell."

So the doctor gives Daneel a thorough test
   While the robot sits there, calmly self-possessed.
After close examination, "His First Law's in operation,"
   Says the doctor, "You can set your mind at rest."

That leaves Baley feeling somewhat like a jerk,
   But Daneel is very difficult to irk;
He just says: "We can't stand still, or we will never find the
      killer.
   Come on, partner, let us buckle down to work."

Now the plot begins to thicken—as it should;
   It's the thickening in plots that makes 'em good.
The Police Chief's robot, Sammy, gives himself the double
      whammy,
   And the reason for it isn't understood.

The Commissioner says: "Baley, you're to blame!
   Robot Sammy burned his brain out, and I claim
That, from every single clue, it looks as though you made him do
      it!"
   Baley hollers: "No, I didn't! It's a frame!"

Then he says: "Commish, I think that you're the heel
   Who's the nasty little villain in this deal!
And I'll tell you to your face, I really think you killed the
      Spacer,
   'Cause you thought he was the robot, R. Daneel!"

The Commissioner breaks down and mumbles: "Yes—
   I'm the guy who did it, Baley—I confess!"
Baley says: "I knew in time you would confess this awful crime.
      You
   Understand, of course, you're in an awful mess!"

The Commissioner keels over on the floor.
   When he wakes up, R. Daneel says: "We're not sore;
Since the crime was accidental, we'll be merciful and gentle.
   Go," he says in solemn tones, "and sin no more!"

Then says Baley to the robot, with a grin:
   "It was nice of you to overlook his sin.
As a friend, I wouldn't trade you! By the Asimov who made you,
   You're a better man than I am, Hunka Tin!"

No one who was reading science fiction in the early 1950s will ever forget the impact Alfred Bester's astonishing novel *The Demolished Man* made—a diabolically ingenious thriller ornamented by the cleverest set of typographical gimmicks since Romulus was a rebus. In transforming Bester's classic novel to verse, Garrett reproduced most of the book's tricky typography, but threw in a dozen or two tricks of his own, of which the one in the final line is surely the finest. Here's an item that insists on being read aloud.

ALFRED BESTER'S *THE DEMOLISHED MAN*: A REVIEW IN VERSE

In the far & distant future—you can pick the d8 2 suit your-
Self, the author, Mr. Bester, doesn't specify the year—
There's a fellow named Ben Reich, a rich investor who's no
piker,
Who has dreams about a Faceless Man in nightmares odd &
queer.

Craye D'Courtney is his rival. Says Ben Reich: "While he's alive,
I'll
Never rest, so I must rub him out the best way th@ I can!"
But, according 2 report, neither Ben Reich nor old D'Courtney
Knows the other well enough 4 Ben 2 h8 the older man.

Now, despite his wealth & power, Ben Reich still does not see
how ar-
Ranging old D'Courtney's death can be achieved with grace &
ease.
If he gets in2 a mess, perception by an expert Esper
Will eventually happen, 4 these lads are thick as fleas.

But since Reich remains determined 2 extermin8 th@ vermin, d-
 Rastic action must be taken 2 make sure he won't get caught.
So he calls Augustus T8, a doctor who, we find, is r8ed
 As a 1st Class Esper Medic. Reich is sure he can be bought.

"Gus, D'Courtney is a bird I rather think I'd like 2 murder,
 & I'll pay an even million if you'll help me kill the slob!"
T8 says: "I don't like it, still you never know—an even million?
 Th@'s an awful lot of money, Ben; I think I'll take the job!"

Next he needs some brain protection from the Espers' keen
  detection;
 Just a song th@ he can think of so they cannot read his mind.
So he calls a gal named Duffy, who is just a bit of fluff he
 Knows, who has a music shop th@ carries songs of every
  kind.

"Just a song with rhythm in it?" Duffy frowns & thinks a
  minute.
 "Well, we have all kinds of songs, but if you simply must
  have 1
Th@ keeps running through your head, the best we have is
  '10ser, said the
 10sor, 10sion, apprehension & dis¢sion have begun!' "

Now the fireworks really start; he hears from T8 about a party
 At the Beaumonts'. Craye D'Courtney will be there without a
  doubt.
Ben Reich packs his g@ & goes there, smiles @ everyone he
  knows there,
 & sneaks up 2 old D'Courtney's room when all the lights are
  out.

Craye says: "Ben, I'm sick & feeble!" Says Ben Reich: "You
 can't make me bel-
 Ieve a word of all th@ guff!" & then he shoots Craye through
  the head.
But Ben's planning's all 4 naught; around comes old D'Courtney's
  daughter,
 & she grabs the g@ & runs off when she sees her father dead.

Now comes Powell, a detective, whose main job is 2 collect ev-
 Aders of the law, who ought 2 know th@ they can not
  succeed.
He's an Es% by the police 2 peep @ all the people
 @ the party 2 determine who has done this dreadful deed.

79

His Lieu10ant, known as $$son, is hot beneath the collar.
  "What's the motive? Where's the witness? Who's the killer?
    Where's the gun?
Ben Reich's mind cannot be read, the best I get is: '10ser, said
    the
    10sor, 10sion, apprehension & dis¢ion have begun!' "

"It's a tough 1," murmurs Powell, "& I really don't see how I'll
    Get the evidence I need 2 take this murder case 2 court.
& I may be wrong, but still, I really think Ben Reich's the killer.
    If he is, 2 take him in will prove 2 be a bit of sport."

Ben says: "This'll be a b@tle, & I'm much afraid the f@'ll
    Soon be in the fire unless I find the young D'Courtney dame."
Likewise, Powell's biggest worry is 2 get his hands on her, he
    Knows he'll really have 2 scurry, 4 Ben Reich's goal's just the
    same.

Babs D'Courtney is loc8ed by Ben Reich, but he's 2 l8, a d-
    Ame who's known 2 all as Chooka tells friend Powell where
    she's @.
Ben Reich's chances would be gone, except th@ Babs is
    c@@onic,
    & the 3rd° can't make her tell where she got Ben Reich's g@.

Powell still has 1 more chance. A Reich employee has the answer
    2 a note Ben sent D'Courtney 2 conclude a business deal.
Powell's sure th@ Ben Reich's motive 4 the murder's in this
    note, he v-
    Ows 2 get it from this Hassop, even if he has 2 steal.

Then, 2 Powell's consternation, Ben Reich goes 2 a space station
    Known as Ampro, a resort with tropic jungles grown inside.
Ben goes in with Hassop. "Now I'll have 2 find them," mutters
    Powell.
    "Mr. Hassop has gone in2 th@ mor* his hide!"

Since he knows th@ Ben won't pass up this big chance 2 murder
    Hassop,
    He & several other Pee%er Ampro 4 the search.
But when the note's collected, it's not what the cop expected,
    & the case just falls apart, which leaves poor Powell in the
    lurch.

Powell mutters: "I'll get dirty! Though Ben thinks he can't be
    hurt, he
    Still has dreams about a Faceless Man and wakes up screaming
        screams."
Espers of the 1st Class r8ing start their minds 2 con¢r8ing—
    Ben begins 2 see the Faceless Man come stalking from his
        dreams!

Powell has the famed "last laugh"; he drives poor Ben completely
    daffy,
    & they take him 2 a nuthouse, where he's out of Powell's hair.
Though they've gone and caught the villain, I'm inclined 2 think
    it's still un-
    Necessary 4 policemen 2 be quite so damned unfair.

There's a part of the plot I completely forgot;
    I'll insert it down here, if you like.
Craye D'Courtney & Barbara, respectively, are
    The (ter of Reich.

This tongue-in-cheek version of Poul Anderson's wonderful fantasy novel was first loosed on the world at the 1968 World Science Fiction Convention in Oakland, California, when Randall and his second wife Alison sang it in full medieval dress during the awards banquet. The room had horrendous acoustical problems, and those of us who were within close range (as toastmaster of that banquet, I stood five feet away) listened with delight while others farther out in the audience felt mainly bewilderment. Norman Spinrad, a few introductions further along in this book, describes vividly the somber effects on the entire course of history that ensued.

And herewith Poul Anderson describes his own response to Randall's versification of his novel—

OF PASTICHE AND PARODY

Poul Anderson

PARODY AND PASTICHE, TWO DISTINCT THOUGH related arts, are among those of which Randall Garrett is a master. You'd expect as much, from his sense of humor. Even his most serious works are often loaded with private jokes. For instance, "Olga Polofsky, the beautiful spy," who appears in the Lord Darcy stories, refers to a comic song of that title, composed (in English) by a Dane, which I once played for him. He has made more overt reference to the creations of other writers on numerous pleasurable occasions.

A parody is a mimicry of such a creation, with enough

exaggeration or distortion to produce a comic effect. While frequently done in order to ridicule, it need not be; some parodies are gentle in intent and effect, a gesture akin to that of a man addressing a friend as "you old so-and-so." Garrett's takeoff on E. E. Smith's Lensman saga is devastating in a way, but likewise affectionate. It draws nostalgia as well as laughter from those of us who grew up reading those tales.

A pastiche, at least in the current sense of the word, is always a tribute. It must be carefully distinguished from a plagiarism. The author of a pastiche writes, as nearly as he is able, in the manner of his original, about the same material and generally some of the same characters, but never claims to be doing anything else. Examples include various continuations or amplifications of the Sherlock Holmes and Conan series. Garrett has produced a few excellent items of this kind, notably one of Isaac Asimov's "Foundation" epic.*

He has managed to combine parody and pastiche in his verse redactions of certain science-fiction and fantasy stories, which have appeared over the years to the delight of readers and, even more so, authors. My own *Three Hearts and Three Lions* has been the subject of a special tour de force, it being a calypso song to boot. If you have read the book you will note how the ballad, while spinning the same yarn, carefully avoids touching on any of the more serious incidents or meanings: another demonstration of sheer skill in the writer's craft. If you have not read the book, I think you'll enjoy this lighthearted item anyway.

* See "No Connections" in this volume. —R.S.

POUL ANDERSON'S
THREE HEARTS AND THREE LIONS
A Calypso in Search of a Rhyme

Words and Music by
Randall Garrett

Arrangement by
Vicki Ann Heydron

Broad Calypso tempo

1. Here's a tale of knight-hood's flo-wer And of one man's fin-est ho-ur: The sto-ry of a most strange land Of Hol-ger Carl-sen's lit-tle band, Of fights with trolls and gi-ants, and The win-ning of a swan-may's hand. By one of Den-mark's nob-lest act-ons

CHORUS: THREE RED HEARTS AND THREE GOLD LI-ONS!

2. *last verse only*

THREE RED HEARTS AND THREE GOLD LI-ONS!

© Copyright 1978 by Randall Garrett and Vicki Ann Heydron

POUL ANDERSON'S *THREE HEARTS AND THREE LIONS*: A CALYPSO IN SEARCH OF A RHYME

Here's a tale of knighthood's flower
And of one man's finest hour:
  The story of a most strange land,
  Of Holger Carlsen's little band,
  Of fights with trolls and giants, and
  The winning of a swan-may's hand.
By one of Denmark's noblest scions.
(*Chorus*) Three Red Hearts and Three Gold Lions!

Holger Carlsen's fighting Nazis;
While he's dodging their potshots, he's
  Wounded badly in the head,
  But he does not fall down dead,
  Nor go to hospital bed,
  But to Middle World instead.
Magic here holds sway, not science.
(*Chorus*) Three Red Hearts and Three Gold Lience!

When he wake up, there beside him
Stands, for Carlsen to ride him,
  A horse with armor, shield and sword,
  Clothing and misericord,
  Fine enough for any lord;
  Holger Carlsen climb aboard.
Hungry, he must search for viands.
(*Chorus*) Three Red Hearts and Three Gold Liands!

Holger rides up to a cottage,
Where an old witch offers pottage.
  "How can I get home?" says he.

85

"Well," the witch says, "seems to me
That thou ought to go and see
Good Duke Alfric in Faerie.
He will aid in gaining thy ends."
(*Chorus*) Three Red Hearts and Three Gold Ly-ends!

Off he rides to land of Faerie
With Hugi, a dwarf who's very
Dour and speaks much like a Scot
(Which he may be, like as not),
Though ofttimes he talks a lot.
Next the sex come in the plot.
(*Please don't take offense at my hints.*)
(*Chorus*) Three Red Hearts and Three Gold Ly-hints!

Here she is, named Alianora;
Holger really does go for her.
She can change into a swan
And go flying on and on.
She make friends with doe and fawn;
He feel love about to dawn.
But he's pure, so pardon my yawns.
(*Chorus*) Three Red Hearts and Three Gold Ly-yawns!

Off to Faerie they go quickly,
Where the light is dim and sickly.
Alfric and Morgan-le'Fe
Ask Holger to spend the day
'Neath Elf Hill not far away;
He is saved by his swan-may.
Beneath that hill, one night is eons.
(*Chorus*) Three Red Hearts and Three Gold Leons!

Off they flee across the border;
Spooks pursue on every quarter;
First a dragon overhead—
Holger Carlsen kill him dead;
Next a giant huge and dread
Who is looking to be fed.
Holger holds him in abeyance.
(*Chorus*) Three Red Hearts and Three Gold Leyance!

"Fight with riddles," says the giant;
Holger Carlsen's quite compliant.
So they fight with quip and pun

Till the U-V of the sun
Hit that giant like a gun.
  "He's stoned!" says Holger, "Now let's run."
All the air is filled with ions.
(*Chorus*) Three Red Hearts and Three Gold Lions!

Next they ride into a village
Where a werewolf's bent on pillage.
  Who the warg is, folks can't guess.
  Holger Carlsen solves the mess,
  And he makes that warg confess
  She's the local young princess.
"Now," he says, "it's out of my hands."
(*Chorus*) Three Red Hearts and Three Gold Ly-hands!

When the village folk release 'em
On to Tarnberg go the threesome.
  By a good mage they are told
  They must find a very old
  Sword, that's worth its weight in gold
  At St. Grimmin's-in-the-Wold.
He found this out at a séance.
(*Chorus*) Three Red Hearts and Three Gold Léance!

Meanwhile, they have met a knightly
Saracen, with manners sprightly.
  Northward they all head apace,
  Searching for that dreadful place.
  But the swan-may's pretty face
  Is hurting Holger's state of grace.
"Should I," says he, "yield to my yens?"
(*Chorus*) Three Red Hearts and Three Gold Ly-yens!

Holger's kidnapped by a nixie
(*That's an underwater pixie*).
  Nixie, who is on the make,
  Drags Holger beneath the lake.
  "This is more than I can take!"
  Holger says, "I'll make a break.
Come on," says he, "let us flee hence!"
    (*Chorus, spoken*) Flee hence?
    (*Spoken*) Uh—fly hence?
(*Chorus*) Three Red Hearts and Three Gold Ly-hence!

Now to blast their hopes asunder,
They find that they must go under-
  Neath a mountain, where a troll
  Lurks in his disgusting hole.
  They kill him and head toward their goal;
  Holger says, "Now, bless my soul,
That was worse than fighting giants."
(*Chorus*) Three Red Hearts and Three Gold Liants!

Now, though it's no place for women,
They come to church of St. Grimmin.
  Round the altar they all flock;
  Holger pries up big stone block
  There is sword beneath the rock;
  Holger says, "Now, this I grok!
We found it, though surrounded by haunts."
(*Chorus*) Three Red Hearts and Three Gold Ly-haunts!

End of story! Jesu Christe!
Seems to me it's kind of misty.
  He should be belted and earled,
  But through space-time he is hurled,
  And, un-knighted and un-girled,
He ends up in our own dull world.
His future's vague as that of Zion's.
(*Chorus*) THREE RED HEARTS AND THREE GOLD LIONS!

HOW I STOLE THE BELT CIVILIZATION

Larry Niven

WELL, AFTER ALL, IT WAS JUST SITTING THERE waiting for anyone to come along and pick it up . . . nobody was around, so . . . no, no, it wasn't like that. It was like this:

I discovered science fiction through Robert Heinlein, at age 12, just like everybody. I played the glutton with Heinlein and del Ray and Leinster, and presently discovered the magazines. There was a used-book store in Pasadena, and I'd leave there with double armloads of used science-fiction magazines, and presently I flunked out of Cal Tech.

There was a magazine called *Astounding,* whose title gradually shifted to *Analog,* and whose size changed too. The (temporary) large format made the covers look better: more vivid. I remember *both* of the cover paintings for one of Randall Garrett's asteroid-civilization stories, a tale that featured the scoopship-mining of Jupiter's atmosphere. Randall Garrett appeared frequently in *Analog:* more frequently than I knew. Three or four of my favorite writers were Randall Garrett's pseudonyms. I wouldn't have noticed anyway. I didn't start remembering who wrote what until I was a selling writer myself, which was when my ego got involved.

At age 25 I was at work on a novella, *A Relic of Empire.* (Frederik Pohl changed it to *World of Ptavvs.* Later I recycled the title.) I've always been in love with ingenuity in science-fiction stories. *World of Ptavvs* was full of sparkling new ideas . . . new, if not especially probable. Pluto is unlikely to catch fire the first time a spacecraft tries to land on the surface. Kzanol's stasis field can't be made consistent with known physics.

But the Belters weren't new at all.

Randall Garrett's view of a developing asteroid belt civilization made so much *sense* to me. I just swallowed it whole . . . the Belters' self-reliance, the anarchism, the intolerance of fools, the wary respect for an unforgiving environment, the one-man ships, the political friction with Earth . . . even the stuff Randall called "thin edge", that I called "Sinclair molecule chain" and John Brunner called "monofilament." (There *were* ideas that hadn't been Randall's. Confinement Asteroid and the other bubble-worlds had been well-described in Cole's *The Challenge of the Planetoids,* and the picture of a crater-spattered Mars was hot from the presses.)

World of Ptavvs was published two or three years before I met Randall Garrett. But I'd heard stories . . . and he lived up to them. I met him at Poul and Karen Anderson's, the day after a Science Fiction Writers of America Nebula Awards banquet. He was witty, charming, energetic, bubbling with puns and stories. He'd read my stories, and he raised the subject of the Belters . . . diffidently, but with some amusement. *He* knew that the sincerest form of flattery is copyright violation.

Believe it or not, it had not occurred to me that the Belt civilization was Randall's. I didn't remember authors' names then, remember? On reflection it was perfectly obvious, and I admitted all.

But this is the first time I've put it in print.

Garrett in the pastiche mode again—this time in prose. The target again is Isaac Asimov, his epic *Foundation* series, and Garrett announces both his intentions and his victim in the opening sentence. (The astute reader of course observes the pun buried in the name "Ducem Palver.") From that point on the story proceeds serenely toward its terminal pun, scoring elegantly at every turn. But—and this is the true tour de force—"No Connections" is entertaining reading even to one who has never heard of Asimov's *Foundation*.

NO CONNECTIONS

"IMITATION," SAID DUCEM PALVER, "IS SUP-posed to be the sincerest form of flattery, isn't it?"

Dr. Nikol Buth inspected what was left of his cigar and decided that between the ash and the chewed stub there was not enough tobacco to make further puffing worth-while. He dropped it into the disposal and watched the bright flash of light that marked its passing before he answered the question that Palver had asked.

"In a way, I suppose—if you can call it imitation to take a hint from a myth and develop something from it."

Ducem Palver leaned back in his chair. His blue eyes seemed to twinkle beneath his slightly arched brows, although there was no obvious trace of a smile on his round face. "Then," he said, "you consider mathematical treatment of vast numbers of human beings to be a myth?"

Dr. Buth considered that for a moment. He hardly knew how to speak to his visitor. Palver, he knew, occupied some small post in the Imperium—Imperial Librarian, Third Class—but Buth wasn't sure just how important the man was nor exactly why he had come. Nor did he know how much Palver knew of archaeology.

Buth said: "I realize that people once believed in such a thing—seven or eight hundred years ago. But the barbaric period of the Interregnum, before the establishment of the Second Galactic Empire, was hardly a period of vast scientific knowledge." He gestured with one hand. "Oh, I'll grant you that there may just possibly be something to the old story that a mathematical treatment of the actions of vast masses of human beings was worked out by a scientist of the First Empire and then lost during the Interregnum—but I don't believe it."

"Oh?" Palver's face was bland. "Why not?"

"It's ridiculous on the face of it. Discoveries are never lost, really. We still have all the technological knowledge that the First Empire had, and much more; myths and legends, on the other hand, have no basis, except in easily explained exaggerations."

Palver looked the slightest bit defensive. "Why do you call them legends? It seems to me to be a bit too pat to say that those arts which were not lost were real and that those which *were* lost are legendary."

Dr. Nikol Buth had long since made up his mind that Ducem Palver was nothing but another small-time, officious bureaucrat who had decided, for some reason, to make a 30,000 light-year trip from the Imperial capital just to get in his, Buth's, hair. Inwardly, he sighed. He had walked on eggs before.

Outwardly, he was all smiles. "I'll admit it sounds odd when you put it that way. But look at it from another angle. We have fairly accurate information on the history of the First Empire; the last 10,000 years of its existence are very accurately documented, thanks to the information found in the old Imperial Library. And we have no mention of 'lost arts' or anything else like that. None of the records is in the least mysterious. We know that one nonhuman race was found, for instance. Nothing mysterious there; we know what happened to them, how they escaped the First Imperial Government, and their eventual fate."

Dr. Buth fished in his pocket for another cigar and found none. He got up and walked over to the humidor on his desk, saying: "On the other hand, the records of the Interregnum are scanty, inaccurate and, in some cases, patently falsified. And it is during the Interregnum that we find legends of supermen, of mental giants who can control the minds of others, and of 'lost' sciences which can do wonders."

Buth lit his cigar, and Ducem Palver nodded his head slowly.

"I see," the librarian said at last. "Then you don't believe that a mathematical treatment of the future actions of a mass of people could be formulated?"

"I didn't say that," Dr. Buth said, somewhat testily. "I said that I did not believe it was ever done in the past." Then he forced a smile back onto his face and into his voice. "Not having any such thing as a mathematical system of prediction, I can hardly predict what may be done in the future along those lines."

Ducem Palver steepled his hands pontifically. "I'm inclined to agree with you, Dr. Buth—however, I understood that you had evolved such a system."

Dr. Buth exhaled a cloud of smoke slowly. "Tell me, Mr. Palver, why is the Imperial Government interested in this?"

Palver chuckled deprecatingly. "I *am* sorry, Dr. Buth. I didn't intend to lead you to believe that the Imperium was interested. In so far as I know, they are not." He paused, and his blue eyes seemed to sparkle for a moment with an inner, barely hidden mirth. "Ah, I see that you're disappointed. I don't blame you; it would be quite a feather in your cap to have your work recognized by the Imperium, would it not? I'm truly sorry if I misled you."

Buth shook his head. "Think nothing of it. As a matter of fact, I should be . . . uh . . . rather embarrassed if my work came to Imperial notice at this time. But . . ."

". . . But, then, why am I here?" Palver finished for him. "Purely out of personal curiosity, my dear sir, nothing more. Naturally, the records of your published works are on file in the Imperial Library; my position at the Library is that of Keeper of the Files. Have you ever seen the Files?"

Dr. Buth shrugged. "No—but I've read descriptions."

"I'm sure you have. It's a vast operation to feed all the information of the galaxy into that one great machine to be correlated, cross-indexed, filtered, digested and abstracted so that it may be available at any time. Only about one billionth of the total information flowing into that machine ever comes to my direct notice, and even then it is fleetingly glanced over and forgotten.

"But my hobby, you see, is History." He pronounced the word with a respect touching on reverence. "I'm especially interested in the—as you pointed out—incomplete history of the Interregnum. Therefore, when your mathematical theories of archaeology came to my attention, I was interested. It happens that my vacation period came due some weeks ago, so I decided to come here, to Sol III, to . . . ah . . . have a chat, as it were."

Dr. Buth dropped some cigar ash into the dispenser and watched it flare into oblivion. "Well, I'm afraid you may find you've come for nothing, Mr. Palver. We're not investigating Interregnum history, you see."

Ducem Palver's blue eyes widened slightly and a faint look of puzzlement came over his cherubic face. "But I understood that you were working on pre-Imperial civilization."

Dr. Nikol Buth smiled tolerantly. "That's right, Mr. Palver. Pre-*First*-Imperial. We're digging back more than 30,000 years; we're looking for the origin of the human race."

Palver's face regained its pleasant impassivity. "I see. Hm-m-m."

"Do you know anything of the Origin Question, Mr. Palver?" Buth asked.

"Some," admitted Palver. "I believe there are two schools of thought, aren't there?"

Buth nodded. "The Merger Theory, and the Radiation Theory. According to the Merger Theory, mankind is the natural product of evolution on all worlds with a water-oxygen chemistry and the proper temperatures and gravitational intensities. But according to the Radiation Theory, mankind evolved on only one planet in the galaxy and spread out from that planet after the invention of the first crude hyperspace drive. I might point out that the Merger Theory has been all but abandoned by modern scholars."

"And yourself?" Palver asked.

"I agree. The Merger Theory is too improbable; it requires too many impossible coincidences. The Radiation Theory is the only probable—one might almost say the only possible—explanation for the existence of Man in the galaxy."

Palver leaned over and picked up the carrying case which he had placed beside his chair. "I transdeveloped a copy of your 'Transformations of Symbolic Psychology and Their Application to Human Migration.' It was, in fact, this particular work which decided me to come here to Sol III. I'm not much of a mathematician, myself, you understand, but this reminded me so much of the old legends that . . . well, I was interested."

Dr. Buth chuckled. "There have been, I recall, legends of invisibility, too—you know, devices which would render a human being invisible to the human eye so that he could go where he pleased, undetected. If you had heard that I had written a paper on the transparency of glass, would you be interested?"

"I see the connection, of course," said Ducem Palver. "Just how does it apply here?"

"The legend," Buth said, puffing vigorously on his cigar, "concerns a mathematical system which can predict the actions of vast masses of people—the entire population of the galaxy.

"My work has nothing to do with prediction whatever —unless you want to call it prediction in reverse. I evolved the system in order to work backwards, into the past; to discover, not what the human race was *going to do,* but what it *had done.* You see, there is one fatal flaw in any mathematical prediction system; if people know what they are supposed to do, they will invariably try to do something else, and that can't be taken into account in the system. It becomes a positive feedback which automatically destroys the system, you see."

Palver nodded wordlessly, waiting for Dr. Buth to continue.

"But that flaw doesn't apply to my work because there can't be any such feedback into the past. What I have done is trace the human race backwards in time—back more than 30 millennia, through the vast migrations, the movements through the galaxy from one star to another, taking every lead and tracing them all back to their single focal point."

"And have you found that focal point?" Palver asked.

"I have. It is here—Sol III. My system shows positively that this is—*must be*—the birthplace of the human race."

Ducem Palver looked out the transparent wall at one end of the room. "I understand that archaeologists have always supposed the Origin Planet to be somewhere here in the Sirius Sector, but I wouldn't have thought such a bleak planet as this would be the one. Still"—he laughed pleasantly—"perhaps that's why they left."

Dr. Buth allowed his gaze to follow that of his visitor to the wind-swept, snow-covered terrain outside. "It wasn't always like this," he said. "For reasons we haven't nailed down exactly as yet, this planet shows a definitely cyclic climate. There appear to be long ice ages, followed by short periods of warmth. Perhaps, in the long run, the cycle itself is cyclic; we're not too sure on that score. At any rate, we're quite sure that it was fairly warm here, thirty to fifty thousand years ago."

"And before that?" Palver asked.

Buth frowned. "Before that, another ice age, we think. We've just barely started, of course. There is a great deal of work yet to be done."

"No doubt. Ah—what have you uncovered, so far?"

Dr. Buth stood up from his chair. "Would you like to see? I'll show you the lab, if you'd like."

"Thank you," said Ducem Palver, rising. "I'd like very much to see it."

A well-equipped, operating archaeological laboratory is like no other laboratory in the galaxy. This one was, if the term can be used, more than typical. Huge radiodating machines lined one wall, and chemical analyzers filled another. Between them were other instruments of all sizes and shapes and purposes.

The place was busy; machines hummed with power, and some technicians labored over bits of material while others watched recorders attached to the machine in use.

Dr. Buth led his visitor through the room, explaining the function of each instrument briefly. At the end of the room, he opened a door marked: SPECIMEN CHAMBER and led Ducem Palver inside. He waved a hand. "Here are our specimens—the artifacts we've dug up."

The room looked, literally, like a junk bin, except that each bit of junk was carefully tagged and wrapped in a transparent film.

"All these things are artifacts of Man's pre-space days?" Palver asked.

Buth laughed shortly. "Hardly, Mr. Palver. This planet was a part of the First Empire, you know. These things date back only ten or eleven thousand years. They prove nothing. They are all from the upper layers of the planet's strata. They've been duly recorded and identified and will doubtlessly be forgotten.

"No, these are not important; it is only below the D-stratum that we'll find anything of interest."

"The D-stratum?"

"We call it that. D for Destruction. There is an almost continuous layer over the land of this planet, as far as we've tested it. It was caused, we believe, by atomic bombardment."

"Atomic bombardment? *All over the planet?*" Ducem Palver looked shocked.

"That's right. It looks as though uncontrolled atomic reactions were set off all over the planet at once. Why? We don't know. But we do know that the layer is nearly 25,000 years old, and that it does *not* antedate space travel."

"How so?"

"Obviously," Buth said dryly, "if such a thing had happened *before* mankind discovered the hyperspace drive, there would be no human race today. Man would have died right here and would never have been heard of again."

"Of course, of course. And what have you found below that . . . uh . . . D-statum?"

A frown came over the archeologist's dark eyes. "Hardly anything, as yet. Come over here."

Ducem Palver followed his host across the room to a pair of squat objects that reposed on the floor. They looked like pieces of grayish, pitted rock, crudely dome-shaped, sitting on their flat sides. From the top of the irregular dome projected a chimney of the same material. They were, Palver estimated, about 36 centimeters high, and not quite that big in diameter at their base.

"We haven't worked on these two yet," Dr. Buth said, "but they'll probably turn out the same as the one we've already sectioned."

"What are they?" Palver asked.

Buth shook his head slowly. "We don't know. We have no idea what their function might have been. They're hollow, you notice—you can see the clay in that chimney, which was deposited there during the millennia it lay in the ground.

"See this flange around the bottom? That's hollow, too. It's a channel that leads to the interior; it's connected with this hole back here." He pointed to another hole, about the same size as that in the top of the chimney, but located down near the base. It was perhaps seven centimeters in diameter.

"And you haven't any definite idea what they were used for?" Palver said.

Buth spread his hands in a gesture of temporary bafflement. "Not yet. Ober Sutt, one of my assistants, thinks it may have been some sort of combustion chamber. He thinks that gases—hydrogen and oxygen, for instance—might have been fed into it, and the heat utilized for something. Or perhaps they were used to synthesize some product at high temperatures—a rather crude method, but it might have been effective for making . . . oh, ammonia, maybe. I'm not a chemist, and Sutt knows more about that end of it than I do."

"Why does he think it's a high-temperature reaction chamber? I mean, why *high*-temperature, specifically?"

Dr. Buth waved his cigar at the objects. "They're made out of a very crude ceramic, a heavy mass of fired silicon and aluminum oxides, plus a few other things. They're eroded, of course, and rather fragile now, but to stand up under all the abuse of three or four hundred centuries, they must have been pretty strong when they were made."

"Perhaps the ceramic was used because of its structural strength?" Palver said, half questioningly.

"That's doubtful. We know they used metals; there are oxides of iron, copper, zinc, chromium and aluminum everywhere, in deposits that indicate the metals once formed artifacts of some kind. It wouldn't be logical to use a ceramic, brittle as it is, when metals were used."

"So you think the combustion chamber idea is the most likely?"

Dr. Buth took a long pull at his cigar and looked abstractedly at the glowing ash. "Well, Ober Sutt puts up a good argument for it, but I don't know . . ." He waved again with the cigar. "Those things don't have any bottom, either, and I don't think they ever did—not connected directly, at least. Sutt counters that by saying that they must have sat on a ceramic plate of some kind, but so far we haven't found any of those plates, if they exist."

Palver looked carefully at the two objects, then shrugged. "What else have you found?"

"Aside from a few shards," Dr. Buth said carefully,

"that's all we've found below the D-layer. However, as I said, we've just begun."

Back in Buth's office, Ducem Palver picked up his carrying case, snapped it shut. "Well, I'm sorry to have bothered you, Dr. Buth," he said. "I must admit, however, that the solution of the Origin Question holds little interest for me. The history of the latter part of the First Empire, and that of the Great Interregnum—ah, those are deeply interesting. But, as to how Man came to be spread throughout the galaxy—" He lifted his eyebrows and cocked his head to one side. His blue eyes seemed very deep for a moment. "Well, Man is here. I will leave it to others to find out how he got here, eh?"

Dr. Buth smiled tolerantly. "It's just as well that we're not all interested in the same thing, isn't it?" He walked over to the transparent wall and looked out at the bleak whiteness of the wind-swept snowscape. "But to me, the fascinating thing about Man is his peculiar drives. Imagine a time when men had no spaceships, no modern instruments of any kind. What must it have been like to look out at the stars and feel trapped on one single planet?"

Behind him, Ducem Palver's voice said: "Perhaps you could draw a parallel from the planet Kaldee. During the Interregnum, they were cut off from the rest of the galaxy; they lost all their history—everything. They knew nothing of the spaceship, nor of the stars themselves. They thought those lights in the sky were nothing more than bits of glass, reflecting the light of their sun. They believed the night sky was a black bowl a few miles above their heads, upon which these pieces of broken glass were fixed."

"Oh?" said Dr. Buth without turning. "And how did they feel about their isolation?"

"They didn't know they were isolated. They were quite happy, all things considered. They had no burning desire to leave their planet—indeed, they reserved that privilege for the dead."

Dr. Buth's brows drew together. "Then what made primitive Man want to leave? Why wasn't he happy on one planet? What happened?"

And suddenly, it seemed as if his whole mind came to a focus on that one question. *Why had they decided to conquer space? Why? What caused that odd drive in Man?*

"I've got to know," he said—aloud, but very softly.

Ducem Palver didn't even seem to hear.

After nearly a full minute, Ducem Palver said quietly, "I must be going now. I wish you success, Dr. Buth."

"Yes," said Buth, still looking at the icy plain outside. "Yes. Thank you very much, Mr. Palver. Very much. Good-bye . . ."

Ducem Palver left him that way, standing, staring at the whiteness of the landscape of Sol III.

It was an old planet, civilizationwise. Not, thought Dr. Nikol Buth, as old a planet in that respect as Sol III, but old, nonetheless. Before the Interregnum, it had served as the capital of the First Empire, and before that, as the nucleus from which the First Empire had grown. It had once been a mighty world, sheathed in metal and armed with the might of the Galactic Fleet, the center of strength of the First Galactic Empire. And then that Empire had fallen, collapsed in upon itself, and with it had collapsed its capital.

It had been great once. And now?

Now it was beautiful. The capital of the Second Empire was far away in space, and this old planet was of no consequence whatever. But it was beautiful.

It was a garden planet now, filled with green forests and broad sweeps of grass and fields of flowers. It was a place where a young man could relax for a few weeks before returning to the busy work of maintaining the Empire, a place where an old man, freed from the seemingly eternal grind, could find peace in doing other, less strenous work.

Dr. Nikol Buth was such a man. He was old now, and the years had not treated him kindly; now, after 30 years of driving himself toward an unattainable goal, he sought only peace. Here, on this garden world, he would find it.

It wasn't easy to become a permanent resident here. The planet was an Imperial Protectorate, the personal property of the Emperor himself, although His Imperial Majesty never visited it. Tourists were allowed access to certain parts of it, but there were vast estates reserved for those who had earned the right to spend their last years in quiet and solitude. The right to live here had to be earned, and it had to be granted by the Emperor in person. In his pocket, Dr. Nikol Buth carried a precious document—a signed, sealed Imperial Grant.

He had landed at the terminal—like all spaceport terminals, a busy place, even here—and had supervised the shipping of his personal effects to his new home at a little village called Mallow and then had taken an aircar there himself.

At the air depot at Mallow, he had been met by a pleasant young man who had introduced himself as Wilm Faloban—"General factotum and chief of police—for all the need they have of police here."

He had quietly checked Buth's identification papers and his Imperial Grant, then he'd said casually: "You haven't seen your home yet, I take it?"

Buth shook his head. "Not directly. Full stereos, of course; it's quite what I want. I—" He stopped, realizing that he wasn't making much sense to the young man. He started again: "I really don't see how I managed to get a place here; think how many must apply each year—hundreds of billions, I suppose."

"About that," agreed Faloban. He opened the door of his ground car. "Hop in," he said, "I'll drive you out to your place."

Buth nodded his thanks and stepped carefully inside the little machine. He had to move carefully these days, had to remember that old bones are brittle and old muscles tear easily. "And how many are accepted?" he continued. "Only a few."

Faloban slid into the driver's seat. "An average of 10,000 a year," he said. "Not many are chosen."

"I don't know what I ever did to deserve it," Buth said.

Faloban chuckled as he trod on the accelerator and the little vehicle slid smoothly out to the road. "You really great men are all like that. You never think you've done anything."

"No, no," said Dr. Buth, "it's not like that at all. I really never did do anything."

Faloban just chuckled again. "You'll have to talk to your neighbor old Ducem Palver, on that score. He's always saying he never did anything, either. Amazing, isn't it, how the Emperor never picks anyone but ne'er-do-wells?"

But Dr. Nikol Buth wasn't listening. *Ducem Palver,* he was thinking, *Ducem Palver. Where have I heard that name before?*

And then he remembered. Aloud, he said: "Yes, I will have to see Mr. Palver. He's a near neighbor, you say?"

"Just a kilometer away. We'll go right by his place on the way to your new home," Faloban said.

It was a woman who opened the door, a short, round, pleasant-faced woman whose halo of white hair seemed almost silvery. She was old, yes, but her face still held the beauty of her youth, modified by the decades of life so that it was changed into a graciousness—almost a regal queenliness.

"Yes?" Her voice was soft, and her smile kindly.

"I—" Buth felt the hesitation in his voice and tried to overcome it. "I'm looking for Mr. Ducem Palver. My name is Buth—Dr. Nikol Buth. I . . . I don't know if he remembers me, but—"

The woman stood aside. "Come in, Dr. Buth, come in. I'm Mrs. Palver; I'll see if my husband is busy."

She led him to a chair and made sure he was comfortable before she left to find her husband.

Queer, thought Buth, *I'd never thought of Palver's having a wife. Still, it's been 30 years; maybe he married after—*

"Ah! Dr. Buth! How good to see you again!"

Buth covered his slight start at hearing Palver's voice by rising quickly to greet his host. A slight twinge in his back warned him against moving quite so rapidly.

Palver himself had changed, of course. His hair, which had been thick and black, was now thin and gray. His face was still full and round, although it tended to sag a bit, and his eyes seemed to have faded somewhat. Buth had the feeling that they weren't quite the deep blue they had been three decades before.

But he showed that he still had the same brisk way about him as he extended his hand and said: "Am I the first to welcome you to Mallow and Forest Glade?"

Buth took his hand. "Except for a young chap named Faloban, yes. Thank you."

"You liked cigars, I think?" Palver went to a panel in the wall, slid it aside and took out a small cigar humidor. "I don't use them myself," he said, "but I like to keep them for friends."

Buth accepted the cigar, lit it carefully. "I have to limit myself on these," he told Palver. "I'm afraid I overdid it for too many years. My lungs aren't what they used to be."

"Well, well"—Palver pulled up a chair and sat down—"how have you been? I didn't think you'd even remember

102

me—a nobody. What did you ever find on Sol III? I haven't been following your work, I'm afraid. They kicked me upstairs to rot a while back, you know; haven't been able to keep up with anything, really."

"There wasn't much to keep up with," Buth said. "Sol III was a dead end. I couldn't prove a thing."

Palver looked blank. "I don't think I quite understand."

Dr. Buth settled himself more comfortably in his chair. "There's nothing to understand. I'm a failure, that's all. No joke, no false modesty—no, nor bitterness, either. I spent 30 years of my life looking for something that wasn't there to be found, trying to solve a problem that couldn't be solved."

Ducem Palver looked somewhat uncomfortable. Buth noticed it, and realized that it was perfectly possible that Palver didn't have even the foggiest notion of what he was talking about. Thirty years is a long time to remember a conversation that only lasted an hour. Even Buth himself hadn't remembered it until Faloban had mentioned Ducem Palver's name.

"If you recall," Buth said swiftly, "my group and I were digging on Sol III, searching beneath the D-layer for anything that might show us that Sol III was the original home of mankind. Above the Destruction Stratum, everything was post-spaceflight; it proved nothing. But we did have hopes for the artifacts below that layer."

"I see," said Palver. "It turned out that they, also, were post-spaceflight?"

There was a trace of bitterness in Buth's short laugh. "Oh, no. We didn't prove anything—not *anything*. We don't know, even now, whether those artifacts we found were pre- or post-spaceflight. We don't even know who made them or how or why."

"What about those ceramic things?" Palver asked. "Were those all you found?"

Buth laughed again, bitterly, almost angrily. "It depends on how you mean that question, 'Were those all you found?' If you mean, did we find any more, the answer is an emphatic *yes*. If you mean, did we find anything else, the answer is almost *no*. We found plenty of them—to be exact, in 30 years we uncovered 12,495 of them!"

He paused for breath while Palver blinked silently.

"After the first few thousand, we quit bothering with them. They got in the way. We had classified some 200

103

different varieties under about nine group headings. We were beginning to treat them as animals or something, classifying them according to individual and group characteristics." His voice became suddenly angry. "For 30 years, I worked, trying to find some clue to the mind of pre-spaceflight Man. It was my one drive, the one thing on my mind. I dedicated my life to it.

"And what did I find? Nothing but ceramic mysteries!"

He sat silently for a moment, his lips tight, his eyes focused on the hands in his lap.

Palver said smoothly: "You found nothing else at all?"

Buth looked up, and a wry smile came over his face. "Oh, yes, there were a few other things, of course, but they didn't make much sense, either. The trouble was, you see, that nothing but stones and ceramics survived. Metals corroded, plastics rotted. We did find a few bits of polyethylene tetrafluoride, but they had been pressed out of shape.

"We couldn't even date the stuff. It was at least 20,000 years old, and possibly as much as 150,000. But we had no standards—nothing to go by.

"We found bones, of course. They had 32 teeth in the skulls instead of 28, but that proved nothing. We found rubble that might have been buildings, but after all those thousands of years, we couldn't be sure. In one place, we found several tons of gold bricks; it was probably a warehouse of some kind. We deduced from that evidence that they must have had ordinary transmutation, because gold is pretty rare, and it has so few uses that it isn't worth mining.

"Obviously, then, they must have had atomic power, which implies spaceflight. But, again, we couldn't be sure.

"But, in the long run, the thing that really puzzled us was those ceramic domes. There were so *many* of them! What could they have been used for? Why were so many needed?" Buth rubbed the back of his neck with a broad palm and laughed a little to himself. "We never knew. Maybe we never will."

"But see here," said Palver, genuinely interested, "I thought you told me that one of your men—I forget his name—had decided they were used for high-temperature synthesis."

"Possibly," agreed Dr. Buth. "But synthesis of what?

Besides, there were samples which weren't badly damaged, and they didn't show any signs of prolonged exposure to high temperatures. They'd been fused over with a mixture of silicates, but the inside and the outside were the same."

"What else would you have to uncover to find out what they were?" Palver asked.

Buth puffed at his cigar a moment, considering his answer.

"The connections," he said at last.

"Eh?"

"They were obviously a part of some kind of apparatus," Buth explained. "There were orifices in them that led from some sort of metallic connection—we don't know what, because the metal had long ago dissolved into its compounds, gone beyond even the most careful electrolytic reconstruction. And there are holes in flanges at the top and bottom which—" He stopped for a moment and reached into his pocket. "Here . . . I've got a stereo of our prize specimen; I'll show you what I mean."

The small cube of transparency that he took from his pocket held a miniature reproduction of one of the enigmatic objects. He handed it to Ducem Palver. "Now that's the —No, turn it over; you've got it upside down."

"How do you know?" Palver asked, looking at the cube.

"What?"

"I said, how do you know it's upside down?" Palver repeated. "How can you tell?"

"Oh. Well, we can't, of course, but it stands to reason that the biggest part would be at the bottom. It would be unstable if you tried to set it on the small end, with the big opening up. Although"—he shrugged—"again, we can't be sure."

Palver looked the little duplicate over, turning it this way and that in his hands. It remained as puzzling as ever. "Maybe it's a decoration or something," he said at last.

"Could be. Ober Sutt, my assistant for 20 years, thought they might have been used for heating homes. That would account for their prevalence. But they don't show any signs of heat corrosion, and why should they have used such crude methods if they had atomic power?" Again he laughed his short, sharp laugh. "So, after 30 years, we wound up where we started. With nothing."

"It's too bad you didn't find traces of their writing," said Palver, handing the stereo crystal back to his visitor.

"We did, for all the good it did us. As a matter of fact, we found engraving on little tiles that we found near some of the domes. Several of the domes, you see, were surrounded by little square ceramic plates about so big." He held up his hands to indicate a square about eight centimeters on a side. "We thought they might have been used to line the chamber that the domes were in, to protect the rest of the building from the heat—at least, we thought that at first, but there weren't any signs of heat erosion on them, either.

"They must have been cemented together somehow, because we found engravings of several sets that matched. Here, I'll show you."

He took out his scriber and notebook and carefully drew lines on it. Then he handed it to Ducem Palver.

"Those lines were shallow scorings. We don't know whether that is printing—writing of some kind—or simply channels for some other purpose. But we're inclined to think that it's writing because of the way it's set down and because we did find other stones with the same sort of thing on them."

"These are the engravings you found near the mysterious domes?" Palver asked.

"That's right."

"They make no sense whatever."

"They don't. They probably never will, unless we can find some way of connecting them with our own language and our own methods of writing."

Palver was silent for several minutes, as was Dr. Buth, who sat staring at the glowing end of his cigar. Finally, Buth dropped the cigar into a nearby disposer, where it disappeared with a bright flash of molecular disintegration.

"Thirty years," said Buth. "And nothing to show for it. Oh, I enjoyed it—don't think I'm feeling sorry for myself. But it's funny how a man *can* enjoy himself doing profitless work. There was a time when *I* thought I might work on my mathematical theories—you remember?—and look how unprofitable that might have been."

"I suppose you're right," Palver said uncomfortably. He handed the notebook back to Dr. Buth.

"But still," Buth said, taking the notebook, "a man hates to think of wasting 30 years. And that's what it was."

He looked at the lines he had drawn. Meaningless lines that made a meaningless pattern:

EMPLOYEES MUST WASH
HANDS BEFORE LEAVING

"Waste," he said softly, "all waste."

RANDALL GARRETT—BIG-HEART

Ben Bova

IN MY MIND, RANDALL GARRETT IS INEXTRI-
cably linked with the limits of human endurance.

I have never been a science-fiction fan. (If that be
treason, make the most of it.) Oh, sure, I've *read* science
fiction since childhood. I've *written* science fiction for 30
years and more. I've even edited science fiction now and
then.

But I was never a fan, in the sense that I read or wrote
for fan magazines, or attended science-fiction conventions, or knew the difference between Forrest J Ackerman
and David P. Kyle.

My first experience with fans and fannishness was at
the 14th World Science Fiction Convention, NYCon, in
New York in 1956. I was a technical editor on Project
Vanguard; back in those days we still thought of Vanguard as "man's first artificial satellite." I had been invited to bring a couple of Vanguard engineers to the
convention to tell the palpitating multitudes about a *real*
outer-space project.

I did not meet Randall Garrett at that convention.

However, I did hear that Isaac Asimov and Randall
Garrett arrived at one of the convention's sessions at the
same time, wearing the same kind of charcoal gray suit,
white shirt and narrow bow tie that was in fashion in
those days. They were both about the same height. And
girth. So much so that a fan, upon spotting them standing
cheek by jowl, yelled loudly, "Tweedledum and Tweedledee!"

Isaac immediately snapped, "I'm Dee!"

It is the only time I've ever heard of Randall being
out-quipped.

I stayed at NYCon only for the one day it took my two engineering pals to work up their nerve and speak to the fans. But a few years later I worked up my own nerve and went down to Washington, D.C., to attend the 21st World Science Fiction Convention, Discon I, on my own.

You never saw anyone look more lost. Or feel it. The only person I really knew there was Isaac, because I had moved to the Boston area by then and met Isaac socially on a few occasions. But here at the convention, The Good Doctor was always surrounded by adoring fans. Through the first couple days of the convention I wandered through the rambling old hotel, hardly uttering a word, staring agape (or was it aghast) at the goings-on of the mightiest minds of the science-fiction universe.

Somehow this fellow Garrett saw that I was doing a fair imitation of wallpaper and took it upon himself to introduce me to everyone, shower me with puns and ethnic jokes and just generally jolly me out of my silence. I began to enjoy all the craziness swirling around me.

Finally we meandered down to the bar in the hotel lobby. I insisted on buying Randall a beer. He graciously accepted, and when the drinks came he offered a strange toast: *"Deo gratias,"* is what he said.

"Thank God?" I translated/queried.

"Yes," said Randall, quaffing his brew.

"Is that what you usually say when you drink?"

"No. Only when an Italian is picking up the check."

I uttered something eloquent, like, "Huh?"

Randall smiled benignly. "My dear old Pappy told me many years ago, 'Never let a day go by without thanking God.' "

It took me several moments to realize that what he was saying was, "Never let a Dago buy without thanking God."

We've been friends ever since. But just barely.

Middle-period Garrett, from *Astounding* as usual—a sly and eloquent explication of the value of the half-truth in intergalactic dealings. Or perhaps those are whole truths that Ed Magruder tells here with such devastating effect. Garrett, as I once had occasion to say elsewhere, is a man who has spent considerable time studying the art of creating confusion without exactly lying—and he puts those studies to good use here.

THE BEST POLICY

THAGOBAR LARNIMISCULUS VERF, BORGAX OF Fenigwisnok, had a long name and an important title, and he was proud of both. The title was roughly translatable as "High-Sheriff-Admiral of Fenigwisnok," and Fenigwisnok was a rich and important planet in the Dal Empire. Title and name looked very impressive together on documents, of which there were a great many to be signed.

Thagobar himself was a prime example of his race, a race of power and pride. Like the terrestrial turtles, he had both an exo- and an endoskeleton, although that was his closest resemblance to the *chelonia*. He was humanoid in general shape, looking something like a cross between a medieval knight in full armor and a husky football player clad for the gridiron. His overall color was similar to that of well-boiled lobster, fading to a darker purple at the joints of his exoskeleton. His clothing was sparse, consisting only of an abbreviated kilt embroidered with fanciful designs and emblazoned with a swirl of glittering gems. The emblem of his rank was engraved in gold on his plastron and again on his carapace, so that he would be recognizable both coming and going.

All in all, he made quite an impressive figure, in spite of his five feet two in height.

As commander of his own spaceship, the *Verf*, it was his duty to search out and explore planets which could be colonized by his race, the Dal. This he had done diligently for many years, following exactly his General Orders as a good commander should.

And it had paid off. He had found some nice planets in his time, and this one was the juiciest of the lot.

Gazing at the magniscreen, he rubbed his palms together in satisfaction. His ship was swinging smoothly in an orbit high above a newly-discovered planet, and the magniscreen was focused on the landscape below. No Dal ship had ever been in this part of the galaxy before, and it was comforting to have discovered a colonizable planet so quickly.

"A magnificent planet!" he said. "A wonderful planet! Look at that green! And the blue of those seas!" He turned to Lieutenant Pelquesh. "What do you think? Isn't it fine?"

"It certainly is, Your Splendor," said Pelquesh. "You should receive another citation for this one."

Thagobar started to say something, then suddenly cut it short. His hands flew out to the controls and slapped at switch plates; the ship's engines squealed with power as they brought the ship to a dead stop in relation to the planet below. In the magniscreen, the landscape became stationary.

He twisted the screen's magnification control up, and the scene beneath the ship ballooned outward, spilling off the edges as the surface came closer.

"There!" he said. "Pelquesh, what is that?"

It was a purely rhetorical question. The wavering currents of two hundred odd miles of atmosphere caused the image to shimmer uncertainly, but there was no doubt that it was a city of some kind. Lieutenant Pelquesh said as much.

"Plague take it!" Thagobar snarled. "An occupied planet! Only intelligent beings build cities."

"That's so," agreed Pelquesh.

Neither of them knew what to do. Only a few times in the long history of the Dal had other races been found—and under the rule of the Empire, they had all slowly become extinct. Besides, none of them had been very intelligent, anyway.

"We'll have to ask General Orders," Thagobar said at

last. He went over to another screen, turned it on, and began dialing code numbers into it.

Deep in the bowels of the huge ship, the General Orders robot came sluggishly to life. In its vast memory lay 10,000 years of accumulated and ordered facts, 10,000 years of the experiences of the Empire, 10,000 years of the final decisions on every subject ever considered by Thagobar's race. It was more than an encyclopedia—it was a way of life.

In a highly logical way, the robot sorted through its memory until it came to the information requested by Thagobar; then it relayed the data to the screen.

"Hm-m-m," said Thagobar. "Yes. General Order 333,-953,216-A-j, Chapter MMCMXLIX, Paragraph 402. 'First discovery of an intelligent or semi-intelligent species shall be followed by the taking of a specimen selected at random. No contact shall be made until the specimen has been examined according to Psychology Directive 659-B, Section 888,077-q, at the direction of the Chief Psychologist. The data will be correlated by General Orders. If contact has already been made inadvertently, refer to GO 472,678-R-s, Ch. MMMCCX, Par. 553. Specimens shall be taken according to . . .' "

He finished reading off the General Order and then turned to the lieutenant. "Pelquesh, you get a spaceboat ready to pick up a specimen. I'll notify psychologist Zandoplith to be ready for it."

Ed Magruder took a deep breath of spring air and closed his eyes. It was beautiful; it was filled with spicy aromas and tangy scents that, though alien, were somehow homelike—more homelike than Earth.

He was a tall, lanky man, all elbows and knees, with nondescript brown hair and bright hazel eyes that tended to crinkle with suppressed laughter.

He exhaled the breath and opened his eyes. The city was still awake, but darkness was coming fast. He liked his evening stroll, but it wasn't safe to be out after dark on New Hawaii, even yet. There were little night things that fluttered softly in the air, giving little warning of their poisonous bite, and there were still some of the larger predators in the neighborhood. He started walking back toward New Hilo, the little city that marked man's first foothold on the new planet.

Magruder was a biologist. In the past ten years, he had

prowled over half a dozen planets, collecting specimens, dissecting them with precision and entering the results in his notebooks. Slowly, bit by bit, he was putting together a pattern—a pattern of life itself. His predecessors stretched in a long line, clear back to Karl von Linné, but none of them had realized what was missing in their work. They had had only one type of life to deal with—terrestrial life. And all terrestrial life is, after all, homogeneous.

But, of all the planets he'd seen, he liked New Hawaii best. It was the only planet besides Earth where a man could walk around without a protective suit of some kind —at least, it was the only one discovered so far.

He heard a faint swishing in the air over his head and glanced up quickly. The night things shouldn't be out this early!

And then he saw that it wasn't a night thing; it was a metallic-looking globe of some kind, and—

There was a faint greenish glow that suddenly flashed from a spot on the side of the globe, and all went blank for Ed Magruder.

Thagobar Verf watched dispassionately as Lieutenant Pelquesh brought the unconscious specimen into the biological testing section. It was a queer-looking specimen; a soft-skinned, sluglike parody of a being, with a pale, pinkish-tan complexion and a repulsive, fungoidal growth on its head and various other areas.

The biologists took the specimen and started to work on it. They took nips of skin and samples of blood and various electrical readings from the muscles and nerves.

Zandoplith, the Chief Psychologist, stood by the commander, watching the various operations.

It was Standard Procedure for the biologists; they went about it as if they would with any other specimen that had been picked up. But Zandoplith was going to have to do a job he had never done before. He was going to have to work with the mind of an intelligent being.

He wasn't worried, of course; it was all down in the Handbook, every bit of Proper Procedure. There was nothing at all to worry about.

As with all other specimens, it was Zandoplith's job to discover the Basic Reaction Pattern. Any given organism could react only in a certain very large, but finite number of ways, and these ways could be reduced to a Basic Pattern. All that was necessary to destroy a race of crea-

113

tures was to get their Basic Pattern and then give them a problem that couldn't be solved by using that pattern. It was all very simple, and it was all down in the Handbook.

Thagobar turned his head from the operating table to look at Zandoplith. "Do you think it really will be possible to teach it our language?"

"The rudiments, Your Splendor," said the psychologist. "Ours is, after all, a very complex language. We'll give him all of it, of course, but it is doubtful whether he can assimilate more than a small portion of it. Our language is built upon logic, just as thought is built upon logic. Some of the lower animals are capable of the rudiments of logic, but most are unable to grasp it."

"Very well; we'll do the best we can. I, myself, will question it."

Zandoplith looked a little startled. "But, Your Splendor! The questions are all detailed in the Handbook!"

Thagobar Verf scowled. "I can read as well as you, Zandoplith. Since this is the first semi-intelligent life discovered in the past thousand years or so, I think the commander should be the one to do the questioning."

"As you say, Your Splendor," the psychologist agreed.

Ed Magruder was placed in the Language Tank when the biologists got through with him. Projectors of light were fastened over his eyes so that they focused directly on his retinas; sound units were inserted into his ears; various electrodes were fastened here and there; a tiny network of wires was attached to his skull. Then a special serum which the biologists had produced was injected into his bloodstream. It was all very efficient and very smoothly done. Then the Tank was closed, and a switch was thrown.

Magruder felt himself swim dizzily up out of the blackness. He saw odd-looking, lobster-colored things moving around while noises whispered and gurgled into his ears.

Gradually, he began to orient himself. He was being taught to associate sounds with actions and things.

Ed Magruder sat in a little four-by-six room, naked as a jay-bird, looking through a transparent wall at a sextet of the aliens he had seen so much of lately.

Of course, it wasn't these particular bogeys he'd been watching, but they looked so familiar that it was hard to believe they were here in the flesh. He had no idea how long he'd been learning the language; with no exterior references, he was lost.

Well, he thought, I've picked up a good many specimens, and here I am, a specimen myself. He thought of the treatment he'd given his own specimens and shuddered a little.

Oh, well. Here he was; might as well put on a good show—stiff upper lip, chin up and all that sort.

One of the creatures walked up to an array of buttons and pressed one. Immediately, Magruder could hear sounds from the room on the other side of the transparent wall.

Thagobar Verf looked at the specimen and then at the question sheet in his hand. "Our psychologists have taught you our language, have they not?" he asked coldly.

The specimen bobbled his head up and down. "Yup. And that's what I call real force-feeding, too."

"Very well; I have some questions to ask; you will answer them truthfully."

"Why, sure," Magruder said agreeably. "Fire away."

"We can tell if you are lying," Thagobar continued. "It will do you no good to tell us untruths. Now—what is your name?"

"Theophilus Q. Hassenpfeffer," Magruder said blandly.

Zandoplith looked at a quivering needle and then shook his head slowly as he looked up at Thagobar.

"That is a lie," said Thagobar.

The specimen nodded. "It sure is. That's quite a machine you've got there."

"It is good that you appreciate the superiority of our instruments," Thagobar said grimly. "Now—your name."

"Edwin Peter St. John Magruder."

Psychologist Zandoplith watched the needle and nodded.

"Excellent," said Thagobar. "Now, Edwin—"

"Ed is good enough," said Magruder.

Thagobar blinked. "Good enough for what?"

"For calling me."

Thagobar turned to the psychologist and mumbled something. Zandoplith mumbled back. Thagobar spoke to the specimen.

"Is your name Ed?"

"Strictly speaking, no," said Magruder.

"Then why should I call you that?"

"Why not? Everyone else does," Magruder informed him.

Thagobar consulted further with Zandoplith and finally said: "We will come back to that point later. Now . . . uh . . . Ed, what do you call your home planet?"

"Earth."

"Good. And what does your race call itself?"

"Homo sapiens."

"And the significance of that, if any?"

Magruder considered. "It's just a name," he said, after a moment.

The needle waggled.

"Another lie," said Thagobar.

Magruder grinned. "Just testing. That really *is* a whizzer of a machine."

Thagobar's throat and face darkened a little as his copper-bearing blue blood surged to the surface in suppressed anger. "You said that once," he reminded blackly.

"I know. Well, if you really want to know, *Homo sapiens* means 'wise man.' "

Actually, he hadn't said "wise man"; the language of the Dal didn't quite have that exact concept, so Magruder had to do the best he could. Translated back into English, it would have come out something like "beings with vast powers of mind."

When Thagobar heard this, his eyes opened a little wider, and he turned his head to look at Zandoplith. The psychologist spread his horny hands; the needle hadn't moved.

"You seem to have high opinions of yourselves," said Thagobar, looking back at Magruder.

"That's possible," agreed the Earthman.

Thagobar shrugged, looked back at his list, and the questioning went on. Some of the questions didn't make too much sense to Magruder; others were obviously psychological testing.

But one thing was quite clear; the lie detector was indeed quite a whizzer. If Magruder told the exact truth, it didn't indicate. But if he lied just the least tiny bit, the needle on the machine hit the ceiling—and, eventually, so did Thagobar.

Magruder had gotten away with his first few lies—they were unimportant, anyway—but finally, Thagobar said: "You have lied enough, Ed."

He pressed a button, and a nerve-shattering wave of pain swept over the Earthman. When it finally faded, Magruder found his belly muscles tied in knots, his fists and teeth clenched and tears running down his cheeks. Then nausea overtook him, and he lost the contents of his stomach.

Thagobar Verf turned distastefully away. "Put him back in his cell and clean up the interrogation chamber. Is he badly hurt?"

Zandoplith had already checked his instruments. "I think not, Your Splendor; it is probably only slight shock and nothing more. However, we will have to retest him in the next session anyhow. We'll know then."

Magruder sat on the edge of a shelflike thing that doubled as a low table and a high bed. It wasn't the most comfortable seat in the world, but it was all he had in the room; the floor was even harder.

It had been several hours since he had been brought here, and he still didn't feel good. That stinking machine had *hurt!* He clenched his fists; he could still feel the knot in his stomach and—

And then he realized that the knot in his stomach hadn't been caused by the machine; he had thrown that off a long time back.

The knot was caused by a towering, thundering-great, ice-cold rage.

He thought about it for a minute and then broke out laughing. Here he was, like a stupid fool, so angry that he was making himself sick! And that wasn't going to do him *or* the colony any good.

It was obvious that the aliens were up to no good, to say the least. The colony at New Hilo numbered 6,000 souls—the only humans on New Hawaii, except for a couple of bush expeditions. If this ship tried to take over the planet, there wouldn't be a devil of a lot the colonists could do about it. And what if the aliens found Earth itself? He had no idea what kind of armament this spaceship carried nor how big it was—but it seemed to have plenty of room inside it.

He knew it was up to him. He was going to have to do something, somehow. What? Could he get out of his cell and try to smash the ship?

Nope. A naked man inside a bare cell was about as helpless as a human being can get. What, then?

Magruder lay on his back and thought about it for a long time.

Presently, a panel opened in the door and a red-violet

face appeared on the other side of a transparent square in the door.

"You are doubtless hungry," it said solemnly. "An analysis of your bodily processes has indicated what you need in the way of sustenance. Here."

The quart-size mug that slid out of a niche in the wall had an odd aroma drifting up from it. Magruder picked it up and looked inside. It was a grayish-tan, semitranslucent liquid about the consistency of thin gravy. He touched the surface with his finger and then touched the finger with his tongue. Its palate appeal was definitely on the negative side of zero.

He could guess what it contained: a score, more or less, of various amino acids, a dozen vitamins, a handful of carbohydrates and a few percent of other necessities. A sort of psuedoprotoplasmic soup; an overbalanced meal.

He wondered whether it contained anything that would do him harm, decided it probably didn't. If the aliens wanted to dope him, they didn't need to resort to subterfuge, and besides, this was probably the gunk they had fed him while he was learning the language.

Pretending to himself that it was beef stew, he drank it down. Maybe he could think better on a full stomach. And, as it turned out, he was right.

Less than an hour later, he was back in the interrogation chamber. This time, he was resolved to keep Thagobar's finger off that little button.

After all, he reasoned to himself, I might want to lie to someone, when and if I get out of this. There's no point in getting a conditioned reflex against it.

And the way the machine had hurt him, there was a strong possibility that he just might get conditioned if he took very many jolts like that.

He had a plan. It was highly nebulous—little more than a principle, really, and it was highly flexible. He would simply have to take what came, depend on luck and hope for the best.

He sat down in the chair and waited for the wall to become transparent again. He had thought there might be a way to get out as he was led from his cell to the interrogation chamber, but he didn't feel like tackling six heavily armored aliens all at once. He wasn't even sure he could do much with just one of them. Where do you slug a guy whose nervous system you know nothing about, and whose body is plated like a boiler?

The wall became transparent, and the alien was standing on the other side of it. Magruder wondered whether it was the same being who had questioned him before, and after looking at the design on the plastron, decided that it was.

He leaned back in his chair, folded his arms and waited for the first question.

Thagobar Verf was a very troubled Dal. He had very carefully checked the psychological data with General Orders after the psychologists had correlated it according to the Handbook. He definitely did not like the looks of his results.

General Orders merely said: "No race of this type has ever been found in the galaxy before. In this case, the commander will act according to GO 234,511,006-R-g, Ch. MMCDX, Par. 666."

After looking up the reference, he had consulted with Zandoplith. "What do you think of it?" he asked. "And why doesn't your science have any answers?"

"Science, Your Splendor," said Zandoplith, "is a process of obtaining and correlating data. We haven't enough data yet, true, but we'll get it. We absolutely must not panic at this point; we must be objective, purely objective." He handed Thagobar another printed sheet. "These are the next questions to be asked, according to the Handbook of Psychology."

Thagobar felt a sense of relief. General Orders had said that in a case like this, the authority of action was all dependent on his own decision; it was nice to know that the scientist knew what he was doing, and had authority to back it.

He cut off the wall polarizer and faced the specimen on the other side.

"You will answer the next several questions in the negative," Thagobar said. "It doesn't matter what the real and truthful answer may be, you will say "No"; is that perfectly clear?"

"No," said Magruder.

Thagobar frowned. The instructions seemed perfectly lucid to him; what was the matter with the specimen? Was he possibly more stupid than they had at first believed?

"He's lying," said Zandoplith.

It took Thagobar the better part of half a minute to realize what had happened, and when he did, his face

119

became unpleasantly dark. But there was nothing else he could do; the specimen had obeyed orders.

His Splendor took a deep breath, held it for a moment, eased it out and began reading the questions in a mild voice.

"Is your name Edwin?"

"No."

"Do you live on the planet beneath us?"

"No."

"Do you have six eyes?"

"No."

After five minutes of that sort of thing, Zandoplith said: "That's enough, Your Splendor; it checks out; his nervous system wasn't affected by the pain. You may proceed to the next list."

"From now on, you will answer truthfully," Thagobar said. "Otherwise, you will be punished again. Is *that* clear?"

"Perfectly clear," said Magruder.

Although his voice sounded perfectly calm, Magruder, on the other side of the transparent wall, felt just a trifle shaky. He would have to think quickly and carefully from now on. He didn't believe he'd care to take too much time in answering, either.

"How many *Homo sapiens* are there?"

"Several billion." There were actually about four billion, but the Dal equivalent of "several" was vaguely representative of numbers larger than five, although not necessarily so.

"Don't you know the actual number?"

"No," said Magruder. *Not right down to the man, I don't.*

The needle didn't quiver. Naturally not—he was telling the truth, wasn't he?

"All of your people surely aren't on Earth, then?" Thagobar asked, deviating slightly from the script. "In only one city?"

With a sudden flash of pure joy, Magruder saw the beautifully monstrous mistake the alien had made. He had not suspected until now that Earthmen had developed space travel. Therefore, when he had asked the name of Magruder's home planet, the answer he'd gotten was "Earth." But the alien had been thinking of New Hawaii! *Wheeee!*

"Oh, no," said Magruder truthfully. "We have only a few thousand down there." Meaning, of course, New Hawaii, which was "down there."

120

"Then most of your people have deserted Earth?"

"Deserted Earth?" Magruder sounded scandalized. "Heavens to Betsy, no! We have merely colonized; we're all under one central government."

"How many are there in each colony?" Thagobar had completely abandoned the script now.

"I don't know exactly," Magruder told him, "but not one of our colonized planets has any more occupants on it than Earth."

Thagobar looked flabbergasted and flicked off the sound transmission to the prisoner with a swift movement of his finger.

Zandoplith looked pained. "You are not reading the questions from the handbook," he complained.

"I know, I know. But did you hear what he said?"

"I heard it." Zandoplith's voice sounded morose.

"It wasn't true, was it?"

Zandoplith drew himself up to his full five feet one. "Your Splendor, you have taken it upon yourself to deviate from the Handbook, but I will not permit you to question the operation of the Reality Detector. Reality is truth, and therefore truth is reality; the Detector hasn't erred since —since *ever!*"

"I know," Thagobar said hastily. "But do you realize the implications of what he said? There are a few thousand people on the home planet; all the colonies have less. And yet, there are *several billion* of his race! That means they have occupied around ten million planets!"

"I realize it sounds queer," admitted Zandoplith, "but the Detector never lies!" Then he realized whom he was addressing and added, "Your Splendor."

But Thagobar hadn't noticed the breach of etiquette. "That's perfectly true. But, as you said, there's something queer here. We must investigate further."

Magruder had already realized that his mathematics was off kilter; he was thinking at high speed.

Thagobar's voice said: "According to our estimates, there are not that many habitable planets in the galaxy. How do you account, then, for your statement?"

With a quick shift of viewpoint, Magruder thought of Mars, so many light-years away. There had been a scientific outpost on Mars for a long time, but it was a devil of a long way from being a habitable planet.

"My people," he said judiciously, "are capable of living

121

on planets with surface conditions which vary widely from those of Earth."

Before Thagobar could ask anything else, another thought occurred to the Earthman. The thousand-inch telescope on Luna had discovered, spectroscopically, the existence of large planets in the Andromedia Nebula. "In addition," he continued blandly, "we have found planets in other galaxies than this."

There! *That* ought to confuse them!

Again the sound was cut off, and Magruder could see the two aliens in hot discussion. When the sound came back again, Thagobar had shifted to another tack.

"How many spaceships do you have?"

Magruder thought that one over for a long second. There were about a dozen interstellar ships in the Earth fleet—not nearly enough to colonize ten million planets. He was in a jam!

No! Wait! A supply ship came to New Hawaii every six months. But there were no ships on New Hawaii.

"Spaceships?" Magruder looked innocent. "Why, we have no spaceships."

Thagobar Verf shut off the sound again, and this time, he made the wall opaque, too. "No spaceships? *No spaceships?* He lied . . . I hope?"

Zandoplith shook his head dolefully. "Absolute truth."

"But—but—but—"

Remember what he said his race called themselves?" the psychologist asked softly.

Thagobar blinked very slowly. When he spoke, his voice was a hoarse whisper. *"Beings with minds of vast power."*

"Exactly," said Zandoplith.

Magruder sat in the interrogation chamber for a long time without hearing or seeing a thing. Had they made sense out of his statements? Were they beginning to realize what he was doing? He wanted to chew his nails, bite his lips and tear his hair; instead, he forced himself to outward calm. There was a long way to go yet.

When the wall suddenly became transparent once more, he managed to keep from jumping.

"Is it true," asked Thagobar, "that your race has the ability to move through space by means of mental power alone?"

For a moment, Magruder was stunned. It was beyond his wildest expectations. But he rallied quickly.

How does a man walk? he thought.

"It is true that by using mental forces to control physical energy," he said carefully, "we are able to move from place to place without the aid of spaceships or other such machines."

Immediately, the wall blanked again.

Thagobar turned around slowly and looked at Zandoplith. Zandoplith's face looked a dirty crimson; the healthy violet had faded.

"I guess you'd best call in the officers," he said slowly; "we've got a monster on our hands."

It took three minutes for the 20 officers of the huge *Verf* to assemble in the Psychology Room. When they arrived, Thagobar asked them to relax and then outlined the situation.

"Now," he said, "are there any suggestions?"

They were definitely *not* relaxed now. They looked as tense as bowstrings.

Lieutenant Pelquesh was the first to speak. "What are the General Orders, Your Splendor?"

"The General Orders," Thagobar said, "are that we are to protect our ship and our race, if necessary. The methods for doing so are left up to the commander's discretion."

There was a rather awkward silence. Then a light seemed to come over Lieutenant Pelquesh's face. "Your Splendor, we could simply drop an annihilation bomb on the planet."

Thagobar shook his head. "I've already thought of that. If they can move themselves through space by means of thought alone, they would escape, and their race would surely take vengeance for the vaporization of one of their planets."

Gloom descended.

"Wait a minute," said Pelquesh. "If he can do that, *why hasn't he escaped from us?*"

Magruder watched the wall become transparent. The room was filled with aliens now. The big cheese, Thagobar, was at the pickup.

"We are curious," he said, "to know why, if you can go anywhere at will, you have stayed here. Why don't you escape?"

More fast thinking. "It is not polite," Magruder said, "for a guest to leave his host until the business at hand is finished."

"Even after we . . . ah . . . disciplined you?"

123

"Small discomforts can be overlooked, especially when the host is acting in abysmal ignorance."

There was a whispered question from one of Thagobar's underlings and a smattering of discussion, and then:

"Are we to presume, then, that you bear us no ill will?"

"Some," admitted Magruder candidly. "It is only because of your presumptuous behavior toward me, however, that I personally am piqued. I can assure you that my race as a whole bears no ill will whatever toward your race as a whole or any member of it."

Play it up big, Magruder, he told himself. *You've got 'em rocking—I hope.*

More discussion on the other side of the wall.

"You say," said Thagobar, "that your race holds no ill will toward us; how do you know?"

"I can say this," Magruder told him: "I know—beyond any shadow of a doubt—exactly what every person of my race thinks of you at this very moment.

"In addition, let me point out that I have not been harmed as yet; they would have no reason to be angry. After all, you haven't been destroyed yet."

Off went the sound. More heated discussion. On went the sound.

"It has been suggested," said Thagobar, "that, in spite of appearances, it was intended that we pick you, and you alone, as a specimen. It is suggested that you were sent to meet us."

Oh, brother! This one would have to be handled with *very* plush gloves.

"I am but a very humble member of my race," Magruder said as a prelude—mostly to gain time. But wait! He was an extraterrestrial biologist, wasn't he? "However," he continued with dignity, "my profession is that of meeting alien beings. I was, I must admit, appointed to the job."

Thagobar seemed to grow tenser. "That, in turn suggests that you knew we were coming."

Magruder thought for a second. It had been predicted for centuries that mankind would eventually meet an intelligent alien race.

"We have known you were coming for a long time," he said quite calmly.

Thagobar was visibly agitated now. "In that case, you must know where our race is located in the galaxy; you must know where our home base is."

Another tough one. Magruder looked through the wall

124

at Thagobar and his men standing nervously on the other side of it. "I know where you are," he said, "and I know exactly where every one of your fellows is."

There was sudden consternation on the other side of the wall, but Thagobar held his ground.

"What is our location then?"

For a second Magruder thought they'd pulled the rug out from under him at last. And then he saw that there was a perfect explanation. He'd been thinking of dodging so long that he almost hadn't seen the honest answer.

He looked at Thagobar pityingly. "Communication by voice is so inadequate. Our coordinate system would be completely unintelligible to you, and you did not teach me yours if you will recall." Which was perfectly true; the Dal would have been foolish to teach their coordinate system to a specimen—the clues might have led to their home base. Besides, General Orders forbade it.

More conversation on the other side.

Thagobar again: "If you are in telepathic communication with your fellows, can you read *our* minds?"

Magruder looked at him superciliously. "I have principles, as does my race; we do not enter any mind uninvited."

"Do the rest of your people know the location of our bases, then?" Thagobar asked plaintively.

Magruder's voice was placid. "I assure you, Thagobar Verf, that every one of my people, on every planet belonging to our race, knows as much about your home base and its location as I do."

Magruder was beginning to get tired of the on-and-off sound system, but he resigned himself to wait while the aliens argued among themselves.

"It has been pointed out," Thagobar said, after a few minutes, "that it is very odd that your race has never contacted us before. Ours is a very old and powerful race, and we have taken planets throughout a full half of the galaxy, and yet, your race has never been seen nor heard of before."

"We have a policy," said Magruder, "of not disclosing our presence to another race until it is to our advantage to do so. Besides, we have no quarrel with your race, and we have never had any desire to take your homes away from you. Only if a race becomes foolishly and insanely

125

belligerent do we trouble ourselves to show them our power."

It was a long speech—maybe too long. Had he stuck strictly to the truth? A glance at Zandoplith told him; the chief psychologist had kept his beady black eyes on the needle all through the long proceedings, and kept looking more and more worried as the instrument indicated a steady flow of truth.

Thagobar looked positively apprehensive. As Magruder had become accustomed to the aliens, it had become more and more automatic to read their expressions. After all, he held one great advantage: they had made the mistake of teaching him their language. He knew them, and they didn't know him.

Thagobar said: "Other races, then, have been . . . uh . . . punished by yours?"

"Not in my lifetime," Magruder told him. He thought of *Homo neanderthalensis* and said: "There was a race, before my time, which defied us. It no longer exists."

"Not in your lifetime? How old are you?"

"Look into your magniscreen at the planet below," said the Earthman in a solemn tone. "When I was born, not a single one of the plants you see existed on Earth. The continents of Earth were nothing like that; the seas were entirely different.

"The Earth on which I was born had extensive ice caps; look below you, and you will see none. And yet, we have done nothing to change the planet you see; any changes that have taken place have come by the long process of geologic evolution."

"Gleek!" It was a queer sound that came from Thagobar's throat just before a switch cut off the wall and the sound again.

Just like watching a movie on an old film, Magruder thought. *No sound half the time, and it breaks every so often.*

The wall never became transparent again. Instead, after about half an hour, it slid up silently to disclose the entire officer's corps of the *Verf* standing at rigid attention.

Only Thagobar Larnimisculus Verf, Borgax of Fenigwisnok, stood at ease, and even so, his face seemed less purple than usual.

"Edwin Peter St. John Magruder," he intoned, "as commander of this vessel, Noble of the Grand Empire, and representative of the Emperor himself, we wish to extend to you our most cordial hospitality.

"Laboring under the delusion that you represented a lower form of life, we have treated you ignominiously, and for that we offer our deepest apologies."

"Think nothing of it," said Magruder coolly. "The only thing that remains is for you to land your ship on our planet so that your race and mine can arrange things to our mutual happiness." He looked at all of them. "You may relax," he added imperiously. "And bring me my clothes."

The human race wasn't out of the hole yet; Magruder was perfectly well aware of that. Just what should be done with the ship and the aliens when they landed, he wasn't quite sure; it would have to be left up to the decision of the President of New Hawaii and the Government of Earth. But he didn't foresee any great difficulties.

As the *Verf* dropped toward the surface of New Hawaii, its commander sidled over to Magruder and said, in a troubled voice: "Do you think your people will like us?"

Magruder glanced at the lie detector. It was off.

"*Like* you? Why, they'll *love* you," he said.

He was sick and tired of being honest.

HOW RANDALL GARRETT
CHANGED WORLD HISTORY

Norman Spinrad

BAYCON, THE 1968 WORLDCON IN OAKLAND, California, was probably the most gonzo event in science-fiction history. Political riots in the streets around the University below, and high up on a hill, the world of science fiction took over the Victorian Claremont Hotel. Dope flowed like wine; wine flowed like water; weird drugs were everywhere; people were sleeping and even fucking in the halls. A heavy acid rock group played for a worldcon masquerade, and they and their groupies were wigged out and flying. Philip José Farmer gave his now-famous "REAP" Guest of Honor speech in which he outlined in great detail and enormous length all the coming crises of the 1970s. The fans had the whole hotel; the management was making money and didn't give a damn, and all in all it was a kind of reenactment of the fall of Rome.

Cast as Nero in this movie was none other than Randall (don't call me Randy!) Garrett. The banquet seemed to go on forever before it even got to Farmer's speech; the acoustics were dreadful, the food execrable; everyone was drinking himself blind in self defense, and there was only one toilet for about 500 people.

Just as Phil Farmer was about to go on before this audience of poisoned, bleary, bladder-bursting drunks, it was announced, to considerable groans, that Randall Garrett was coming on to sing a short song of his own composition. Out stepped Randall, rosy of cheek, a bit red of eye and dressed as a medieval troubador—to wit, stuffed into a flaming red union suit accoutred in cloak etc.

For a full hour (I clocked it) that seemed like a century, he sung a heroic ballad based upon a tale by Poul Anderson. Nobody could make out the words. Everyone was dying to take a piss. It was not what you would call a receptive audience. Nevertheless, Garrett pressed on to the bitter end even as Nero, amidst growing restlessness, catcalls and heckling.

The result was that when Phil Farmer finally came on to give his long prophetic speech in a nearly inaudible monotone, virtually no one was in any mood to pay attention. Thus we were not forewarned about the energy crisis, the coming series of recessions, the inflation, the loss of nerve, the whole mess of 1970s problems that was to beset the nation. Thus we did not heed Farmer's call to action.

And that's why Randall Garrett is directly responsible for the energy crisis, dollar-a-gallon gas, inflation, two recessions, the Ayatollah Khomeini, disco music and Roger Elwood. Garrett fiddled while we all burned.

Early Garrett again—neat, ingenious, chilling. When the story appeared it was the occasion for an accidental visual pun that Randall Garrett, that master of puns, did not at all applaud. The artist illustrating the little piece had done a drawing of a starship, an exploding sun and an electrical fuse. But to people who have dealt professionally with explosives —and Garrett is an ex-Marine—a fuse and a fuze are two quite different things. . . .

TIME FUZE

COMMANDER BENEDICT KEPT HIS EYES ON THE rear plate as he activated the intercom. "All right, cut the power. We ought to be safe enough here."

As he released the intercom, Dr. Leicher, of the astronomical staff, stepped up to his side. "Perfectly safe," he nodded, "although even at this distance a star going nova ought to be quite a display."

Benedict didn't shift his gaze from the plate. "Do you have your instruments set up?"

"Not quite. But we have plenty of time. The light won't reach us for several hours yet. Remember, we were outracing it at ten lights."

The commander finally turned, slowly letting his breath out in a soft sigh. "Dr. Leicher, I would say that this is just about the foulest coincidence that could happen to the first interstellar vessel ever to leave the Solar System."

Leicher shrugged. "In one way of thinking, yes. It is certainly true that we will never know, now, whether Alpha Centauri A ever had any planets. But, in another way, it is extremely fortunate that we should be so near a stellar explosion because of the wealth of scientific information we can obtain. As you say, it is a coincidence,

130

and probably one that happens only once in a billion years. The chances of any particular star going nova are small. That we should be so close when it happens is of a vanishingly small order of probability."

Commander Benedict took off his cap and looked at the damp stain in the sweatband. "Nevertheless, Doctor, it is damned unnerving to come out of ultradrive a couple of hundred million miles from the first star ever visited by man and have to turn tail and run because the damned thing practically blows up in your face."

Leicher could see that Benedict was upset; he rarely used the same profanity twice in one sentence.

They had been downright lucky, at that. If Leicher hadn't seen the star begin to swell and brighten, if he hadn't known what it meant, or if Commander Benedict hadn't been quick enough in shifting the ship back into ultradrive—Leicher had a vision of an incandescent cloud of gaseous metal that had once been a spaceship.

The intercom buzzed. The commander answered. "Yes?"

"Sir, would you tell Dr. Leicher that we have everything set up now?"

Leicher nodded and turned to leave. "I guess we have nothing to do now but wait."

When the light from the nova did come, Commander Benedict was back at the plate again—the forward one, this time, since the ship had been turned around in order to align the astronomy lab in the nose with the star.

Alpha Centauri A began to brighten and spread. It made Benedict think of a light bulb connected through a rheostat, with someone turning that rheostat, turning it until the circuit was well overloaded.

The light began to hurt Benedict's eyes even at that distance and he had to cut down the receptivity in order to watch. After a while, he turned away from the plate. Not because the show was over, but simply because it had slowed to a point beyond which no change seemed to take place to the human eye.

Five weeks later, much to Leicher's chagrin, Commander Benedict announced that they had to leave the vicinity. The ship had only been provisioned to go to Alpha Centauri, scout the system without landing on any of the planets and return. At ten lights, top speed for the ultradrive, it would take better than three months to get back.

"I know you'd like to watch it go through the com-

131

plete cycle," Benedict said, "but we can't go back home as a bunch of starved skeletons."

Leicher resigned himself to the necessity of leaving much of his work unfinished, and, although he knew it was a case of sour grapes, consoled himself with the thought that he could at least get most of the remaining information from the 500-inch telescope on Luna, four years from then.

As the ship slipped into the not-quite-space through which the ultradrive propelled it, Leicher began to consolidate the material he had already gathered.

Commander Benedict wrote in the log:

Fifty-four days out from Sol. Alpha Centauri has long since faded back into its pre-blowup state, since we have far outdistanced the light from its explosion. It now looks as it did two years ago. It—

"Pardon me, Commander," Leicher interrupted, "But I have something interesting to show you."

Benedict took his fingers off the keys and turned around in his chair. "What is it, Doctor?"

Leicher frowned at the papers in his hands. "I've been doing some work on the probability of that explosion happening just as it did, and I've come up with some rather frightening figures. As I said before, the probability was small. A little calculation has given us some information which makes it even smaller. For instance: with a possible error of plus or minus two seconds Alpha Centauri A began to explode the instant we came out of ultradrive!

"Now, the probability of that occuring comes out so small that it should happen only once in ten to the 467th seconds."

It was Commander Benedict's turn to frown. "So?"

"Commander, the entire universe is only about ten to the 17th seconds old. But to give you an idea, let's say that the chances of its happening are *once* in millions of trillions of years!"

Benedict blinked. The number, he realized, was totally beyond his comprehension—or anyone else's.

"Well, so what? Now it has happened that one time. That simply means that it will almost certainly never happen again!"

"True. But, Commander, when you buck odds like that

and win, the thing to do is look for some factor that is cheating in your favor. If you took a pair of dice and started throwing sevens, one right after another—*for the next couple of thousand years*—you'd begin to suspect they were loaded."

Benedict said nothing; he just waited expectantly.

"There is only one thing that could have done it. Our ship." Leicher said it quietly, without emphasis.

"What we know about the hyperspace, or superspace, or whatever it is we move through in ultradrive is almost nothing. Coming out of it so near to a star might set up some sort of shock wave in normal space which would completely disrupt that star's internal balance, resulting in the liberation of unimaginably vast amounts of energy, causing that star to go nova. We can only assume that we ourselves were the fuze that set off that nova."

Benedict stood up slowly. When he spoke, his voice was a choking whisper. "You mean the sun—Sol—might . . ."

Leicher nodded. "I don't say that it definitely would. But the probability is that we were the cause of the destruction of Alpha Centauri A, and therefore might cause the destruction of Sol in the same way."

Benedict's voice was steady again. "That means that we can't go back again, doesn't it? Even if we're not positive, we can't take the chance."

"Not necessarily. We can get fairly close before we cut out the drive, and come in the rest of the way at sublight speed. It'll take longer, and we'll have to go on half or one-third rations, but we *can* do it!"

"How far away?"

"I don't know what the minimum distance is, but I do know how we can gage a distance. Remember, neither Alpha Centauri B or C were detonated. We'll have to cut our drive at least as far away from Sol as they are from A."

"I see." The commander was silent for a moment, then: "Very well, Dr. Leicher. If that's the safest way, that's the only way."

Benedict issued the orders, while Leicher figured the exact point at which they must cut out the drive, and how long the trip would take. The rations would have to be cut down accordingly.

Commander Benedict's mind whirled around the monstrousness of the whole thing like some dizzy bee around a flower. What if there had been planets around Centauri

A? What if they had been inhabited? Had he, all unwittingly, killed entire races of living, intelligent beings?

But, how could he have known? The drive had never been tested before. It couldn't be tested inside the Solar System—it was too fast. He and his crew had been volunteers, knowing that they might die when the drive went on.

Suddenly, Benedict gasped and slammed his fist down on the desk before him.

Leicher looked up. "What's the matter, Commander?"

"Suppose," came the answer, "Just suppose, that we have the same effect on a star when we *go into* ultradrive as we do when we come out of it?"

Leicher was silent for a moment, stunned by the possibility. There was nothing to say, anyway. They could only wait. . . .

A little more than half a light year from Sol, when the ship reached the point where its occupants could see the light that had left their home sun more than seven months before, they watched it become suddenly, horribly brighter. *A hundred thousand times brighter!*

RANDALL GARRETT

Frank Herbert

IN THE SUNDAY *California Living* MAGAZINE for September 8, 1968, there is a beautiful color photograph taken beneath the oaks of the Marin County watershed near San Rafael. In the right foreground a bearded man uses an authentic reproduction of medieval cutlery to carve a roasted pig, complete with apple in its mouth. In the crowd of Creative Anachronists around this groaning board there is another bearded face with an impish smile. This is Randall Garrett waiting for his share of the good food—perhaps for more than his share because that was his way with many good things of life—including food and women.

This is not a sexist remark because Randall was not a sexist in the conventional sense; he was just completely sexual. You could follow his movements around this creative Anachronists' picnic by the squeals of women whose bottoms he had just pinched. This was one of Randall's mannerisms, fully in keeping with his other habit of leaning close to a well-developed woman and peering down her cleavage with a lascivious leer.

For this marvelous day, I remember, Randall wore the brown robe of a Friar Tuck. And I can recall thinking at the time a paraphrase from Dorothy Parker—"There but for a typographical error goes the story of his life."

There is no doubt that the merriment of that memorable occasion was amplified by Randall Garrett's presence. He was a bit of medieval humanity, openly ribald and earthy, temporarily in exactly the right setting. At a similar gathering in the proper setting between the years 900 and 1650 A.D., no one would have paid particular attention to his antics—no one, that is, except an outraged husband or two ... or three. ...

135

I began my magazine article about that picnic with these words:

"Did you awaken this morning fed up with the 20th century?"

That's the story of Randall Garrett's life. I suspect he has awakened every morning fed up with the 20th century.

One more thing: I recall that I went through that day exercising my prerogative which was to call Randall "Randy." He professed to hate this nickname and objected to it loudly. But I've always felt that it described him perfectly—at least on that day.

The best-known of the Garrett-and-Silverberg "Robert Randall" collaborations were the Belrogas stories from *Astounding*, written in 1955 and 1956 and subsequently collected in book form as *The Shrouded Panet* and *The Dawning Light*. But we had a secondary series going at about the same time, involving a mystery- solving Roman Catholic priest named Father Riley. Our hope was to sell the Father Riley stories to Anthony Boucher's *Magazine of Fantasy & Science Fiction*, for we knew that Boucher's passionate interests in life included (among others) Catholicism and science-fiction and mystery stories, and we felt that a hybrid mystery-science-fiction-story about a priest couldn't miss. But it did, for reasons I forget now, and the Father Riley stories wound up in Robert Lowndes' *Science Fiction Quarterly*.

A couple of years later—it was the last of all the Garrett-and-Silverberg collaborations—we tried again, doing a mix of mystery, science fiction and Catholicism. This time we replaced Father Riley with a nun, Sister Mary Magdalene, and built the story around yet another of Boucher's obsessions, cats. With the same result: Bob Lowndes published the story in *Science Fiction Quarterly*.

Boucher also had a deep interest in the opera. I think if we had managed to give him a story about a Catholic cat who sang tenor and solved science-fiction mysteries we would have sold it to him—but we'll never know.

A LITTLE INTELLIGENCE

Randall Garrett

SISTER MARY MAGDALENE FELT APPREHENSIVE. She glanced worriedly at the priest facing her and said, "But—I don't understand. Why quarter the aliens *here?*"

Her gesture took in her office, the monastery, the convent, the school, the Cathedral of the Blessed Sacrament. "Because," said Father Destry patronizingly, "there is nothing here for them to learn."

The nun eyed Father Destry uneasily. The single votive candle flickering before the statue of the Virgin in the wall niche beside him cast odd shadows over his craggy, unhandsome face. She said, "You mean that the beings of Capella IX are so well versed in the teachings of the Church that they couldn't even learn anything here?" She added with innocent sarcasm, "My, how wonderful for them!"

"Not quite, Sister. The Earth Government isn't worried about the chances of the Pogatha learning anything about the Church. But the Pogatha would be hard put to learn anything about Terrestrial science in a Cathedral."

"The walls are full of gadgets," she said, keeping her voice flat. "Vestment color controls, sound suppressor fields for the confessionals, illumination—"

"I know, I know," the priest interrupted testily. "I'm talking specifically about military information. And I don't expect them to tear down our walls to learn the secrets of the vestment color controls."

Sister Mary Magdalene shrugged. She had been deliberately baiting Father Destry, and she realized she was taking out on him her resentment against the government for having dumped a delegation of alien beings into her otherwise peaceful life.

138

"I see," she said. "While the—Pogatha?—Pogatha delegation is here, they're to be kept within the catedhral grounds. The Earth government is assuming they'll be safe here."

"Not only that, but the Pogatha themselves will feel safer here. They know Terrestrial feelings still run high since the war, and they know there could be no violence here. The Government wanted to keep them in a big hotel somewhere—a place that would be as secure as any. But the Pogatha would have none of it."

"And one last question, Father. Why does it fall to the Sisters of the Holy Nativity to put them up? Why can't the Holy Cross Fathers take care of them? I mean —really, I understand that they're alien beings, but they *are* humanoid—"

"Quite so. They are females."

The nun's eyebrows rose. "They are?"

Father Destry blushed faintly. "I won't go into the biology of Capella IX, partly because I don't completely understand it myself. But they do have a matriarchal society. They are oviparous mammals, but the rearing of children is always left to the males, the physically weaker sex. The fighters and diplomats are definitely female."

"In that case"—the nun shrugged in defeat—"if those are the Bishop's wishes, I'll see that they're carried out. I'll make the necessary arrangements." She glanced at her wristwatch and said curtly, "It's almost time for Vespers, Father."

The priest rose. "The Government is preparing a brochure on the—ah—physical needs of the Pogatha. I'll have it sent to you as soon as it arrives."

"Care and Feeding of Aliens, eh? Very well, Father. I'll do my best."

"I'm sure you will, Sister." He looked down at his hands as though suddenly unsure of himself. "I know this may be a hard job, Sister, but"—he looked up, smiling suddenly —"you'll make it. The prayers of everyone here will be with you."

"Thank you, Father."

The priest turned and walked out. Sister Mary Magdalene, unhappily conscious that though she respected Father Destry's learning and piety she could feel no warmth toward him as a person, watched him depart. As he reached the door a lithe coal-black shape padded over to him and rubbed itself lingeringly against the priest's legs.

Father Destry smiled at the cat, but it was a hollow, artificial smile. The priest did not enjoy the affections of Sister Mary Magdalene's pet. He closed the office door.

The cat leaped to the top of the nun's desk.

"Miaou," it said calmly.

"Exactly, Felicity," said Sister Mary Magdalene.

Sister Mary Magdalene spent the next two days reading the digests of the war news. She had not, she was forced to admit, kept up with the war as much as she might have. Granted, a nun was supposed to have renounced the devil, the flesh and the world, but it was sometimes a good idea to check up and see what all three were up to.

When the Government brochure came, she studied it carefully, trying to get a complete picture of the alien race that Earth was fighting. If she was going to have to coddle them, she was going to have to know them.

The beginning of the war was shrouded in mystery. Earth forces had landed on Capella IX 30 years before and had found a civilization two centuries behind that of Earth, technologically speaking. During the next 20 years, the Pogatha had managed to beg, borrow and steal enough technology from the Earth colonies to almost catch up. And then someone had blundered.

There had been an "incident"—and a shooting war had begun. The Pogatha feeling, late in arising, was that Earthmen had no right settling on Capella IX; they were aliens who must be driven off. The colonists refused to abandon 20 years' effort without a fight.

It was a queer war. The colonists, badly outnumbered, had the advantage of technological superiority. On the other hand, they were hindered by the necessity of maintaining a supply line 42 light-years long, which the Pogatha could and did disrupt. The colonists were still dependent on Earth for war material and certain supplies.

The war had waggled back and forth for nearly ten years without any definite advantage to either side. Thermonuclear weapons had not been used, since they would leave only a shattered planet of no use to anyone.

Both sides were weary; both sides wanted to quit, if it could be done without either side losing too much face. Human beings had an advantage in that Earth itself was still whole, but the Pogatha had an almost equal advantage in the length of the colonists' supply lines. Earth would win eventually; that seemed obvious. But at what cost? In the end, Earth would be forced to smash the entire Pogatha civilization. And they did not want to do that.

There was an element of pride in the Pogatha viewpoint. They asked themselves: would not suicide be better than ignominious slaughter at the hands of the alien Earthmen? Unless a peace with honor could be negotiated, the Pogatha would fight to the last Pogath, and would quite likely use thermonuclear bombs in a final blaze of self-destructive glory.

The four Pogatha who were coming to the little convent of the Cathedral Chapter of the Sisters of the Holy Nativity were negotiators that had to be handled with the utmost care. Sister Mary Magdalene was no military expert, and she was not an interstellar diplomat, but she knew that the final disposition of a world might rest with her. It was a heavy cross to bear for a woman who had spent 20 years of her life as a nun.

Sister Mary Magdalene turned her school duties over to Sister Angela. There was mild regret involved in this; one of Sister Mary Magdalene's joys had been teaching the dramatics class in the parochial high school. They had been preparing a performance of *Murder in the Cathedral* for the following month. Well, Sister Angela could handle it well enough.

The supplies necessary for the well-being of the Pogatha were sent by the government, and they consisted mostly of captured goods. A cookbook translated by government experts came with the food, along with a note: *"These foods are not for human consumption. Since they are canned, there is no need to season them. Under no circumstances try to mix them with Terrestrial foods. Where water is called for, use only distilled water, never tap water. For other liquids, use only those provided."*

There was also a book of etiquette and table settings for four. The Pogatha would eat alone. There would be no diplomatic banquets here. Sister Mary Magdalene found out why when she went, accompanied by Felicity, to talk to the sisters who prepared the meals for the convent.

Sister Elizabeth was a plumpish, smiling woman who loved cooking and good food and who ruled her domain with an almost queenly air. Looking like a contented plump *hausfrau* in her kitchen uniform, she smiled as Sister Mary Magdalene came in.

"Good morning, Sister."

"Have you opened any of the Pogatha food cans yet?" the sister-in-charge wanted to know.

"I didn't know whether I should," Sister Elizabeth said. Seeing Felicity prowling on the worktable in search of scraps of food, she goodnaturedly waved at the cat and said, "Stay away from there, Felicity! That's lunch!"

The cat glowered at her and leaped to the floor.

Sister Mary Magdalene said, "I'd like to have a look at the stuff they're going to eat. Suppose you pick a can at random and we'll open it up."

Sister Elizabeth nodded and went into the storeroom. She returned carrying an ordinary-looking can. Its label was covered with queer script, and it bore a picture of a repulsive-looking little animal. Above the label was pasted a smaller label which read, in Roman characters, VAGHA.

Sister Mary Magdalene flipped open the translated Pogatha cookbook and ran her finger along the "V" section of the index. Finding her reference, she turned the pages and read. After a moment she announced, "It's supposed to be something like rabbit stew. Go ahead and open it."

Sister Elizabeth put it in the opener and pressed the starter. The blade bit in. The top of the can lifted.

"Whoof!" said Sister Mary Magdalene.

"Ugh!" said Sister Elizabeth.

Even Felicity, who had been so interested that she had jumped up to the table to watch the proceedings, wrinkled her bewhiskered nose in disgust and backed away.

"It's spoiled," Sister Elizabeth said sadly.

But the odor was not quite that of decay. True, there was a background of Limburger cheese overlaid with musk, but this was punctuated pungently with something that smelled like a cross between butyl mercaptan and ammonia.

"No," said Sister Mary Magdalene unhappily. "It says in the book that the foods have distinctive odors."

"With the accent on the *stinc.* Do you mean I have to prepare stuff like that in my kitchen?"

"I'm afraid so," said Sister Mary Magdalene.

"But everything else will smell like that! It'll absolutely ruin everything!"

"You'll just have to keep our own food covered. And remember that ours smells just as bad to them."

Sister Elizabeth nodded, tightlipped, the joviality gone from her face. Now she, too, had her cross to bear.

The appearance of the Pogatha, when they finally arrived, did not shock Sister Mary Magdalene; she had been prepared for the sight of ugly caricatures of human beings by the photographs in the brochure. Nor was she bothered by the faint aroma, not after the much stronger smell of the can of stew. But to have one of them address her in nearly perfect English almost floored her. Somehow she had simply not prepared herself for intelligent speech from alien lips.

Father Destry had brought them in from the spaceport, along with the two Earthmen who were their honor escort. She had been watching the courtyard through the window of her office, and had thought she was quite prepared for them when Father Destry escorted them into the office.

"Sister Mary Magdalene, permit me to introduce our guests. This is Vor Nollig, chief diplomat, and her assistants: Vor Betla, Vor Gontakel and Vor Vun."

And Vor Nollig said, "I am honored, Sister."

The voice was deep, like that of a man's, and there was certainly nothing effeminate about these creatures. The nun, in her surprise, could only choke out a hasty: "Thank you." Then she stood back, trying to keep a pleasant smile on her face while the others spoke their pieces.

They were not tall—no taller than Sister Mary Magdalene's own five five—but they were massively built. Their clothing was full and bright-colored. And, in spite of their alienness, the nun could tell them apart with no difficulty. Vor Nollig and Vor Betla had skins of a vivid cobalt-blue color. Vor Gontakel was green, while Vor Vun was yellow.

The Government brochure, Sister Mary Magdalene recalled, had remarked that the Pogatha had races that differed from each other as did the races of Earth. The blue color was a pigment, while the yellow color was the color of their blood—thus giving the Pogatha a range of yellow-green-blue shades according to the varying amount of pigment in the skin.

In an odd parallel to Earth history, the Blues had long been the dominant race, holding the others in subjection. It had been less than a century ago that the Yellows had

143

been released from slavery, and the Greens were still poverty-stricken underdogs. Only the coming of the Earthmen had brought the three races together in a common cause.

Father Destry was introducing the two Earthmen.

". . . Secretary Masterson and Secretary Bass. They will be staying at the Holy Cross Monastery during the negotiations."

Sister Mary Magdalene had recovered her composure by now. Looking around with a sweeping gesture that took in Father Destry, the four aliens, the stocky Masterson and the elongated Bass, she said, "Won't you all sit down?"

"You are most gracious," said Vor Nollig brusquely, "but our trip has been a long one, and we are most anxious to —ah—the word—freshen up, is it?"

The nun nodded. "I'll show you to your rooms."

"You are most kind."

"I think you'll find everything prepared. If you don't, just ask for whatever you'll need."

She left the men in her office and escorted the four Pogatha outside, across to the part of the convent where they would be staying. When the aliens were installed in their rooms, Sister Mary Magdalene returned to her office and was surprised to find Father Destry and the two U.N. Secretaries still there. She had supposed that the priest would have taken the U.N. men over to the monastery.

"About the Pogatha," said Secretary Masterson with a nervous quirk of his fleshy lips. "Be rather careful with them, will you, Sister? They're rather—uh—prejudiced, you see."

"So am I. Against them, that is."

"No, no. I don't mean prejudiced against you or any other human. Naturally we don't expect much genuine warmth between peoples who are fighting. But I'm referring to the strong racial antipathy among themselves."

"Between the Blues, the Yellows and the Greens," Secretary Bass put in. "They try to be polite to each other, but there's no socializing. It's a different kind of prejudice entirely, Sister."

"Yes," Masterson said. "Any one of them might be willing to sit down to talk to you, but not while one of another color was around."

"I see," said the sister. "I'll keep that in mind. Is there anything else I should remember?"

Secretary Masterson smiled understandingly. "It's hard

144

to say. Handling an alien race isn't easy—but remember, they don't expect us to do everything right. They just want us to show that we're not purposely trying to offend them."

"I'll do my best," said Sister Mary Magdalene.

An hour later, Sister Mary Magdalene decided that she, in her capacity as a hostess here at the convent, had best go around to see how her guests were doing. Her robes swished softly as she went down the hallway. Behind her, Felicity padded silently along.

Sister Mary Magdalene paused outside Vor Nollig's door and rapped. After a moment it opened a little. The alien was dimly visible just inside the doorway.

"Yes, Sister?" said Vor Nollig.

Sister Mary Magdalene forced herself to smile ingratiatingly. "I hope everything's satisfactory."

"Oh, yes. Yes indeed." The door opened another few inches, far enough to let the nun see that Vor Betla stood behind Vor Nollig.

"Please you yes come in?" asked Vor Betla diffidently. There was something in the alien's tone that indicated that the invitation had been offered in an attempt at politeness, and that the Pogatha woman was not anxious to have it actually accepted.

Sister Mary Magdalene was still trying to decide what she should say when suddenly Vor Betla looked down and in a startled voice said, "What is?"

The nun's glance went to the floor. Felicity was standing there, her gleaming green eyes observing the Pogath woman intently. Sister Mary Magdalene scooped the cat up affectionately and held it against her. "This is Felicity. My cat."

"Gat?" said Vor Betla, puzzled.

"Cat," Vor Nollig corrected her. A babble of incomprehensible syllables followed. Finally Vor Nollig turned to the nun and said softly, "Pardon my breach of etiquette, but Vor Betla doesn't understand your language too well. She had never heard of a cat, and I was explaining that they are dumb animals kept as pets. We do not keep such animals on Pogathan."

"I see," said Sister Mary Magdalene, trying to keep the chill out of her voice. She was not pleased by the slighting reference to the cat. "If everything is fine, I'll look after my other guests. If you need anything, just ask."

"Of course, Sister," said Vor Nollig, closing the door.

The nun repressed what would have been an irrational and sinful current of anger. She swept on down the hall to the next apartment and knocked. "Poor Felicity," she murmured soothingly to the cat resting on her other arm. "Don't let their insults upset you. After all, they aren't humans, you know."

The door opened.

"I beg pardon?" said the green-skinned Vor Gontakel.

"Oh," Sister Mary Magdalene said, feeling awkward. "Sorry. I was talking to Felicity."

"Ah," said the green Pogatha.

"We came to see if everything was comfortable in your room. Didn't we, Felicity?"

"Meerorow," Felicity said.

"Oh, yes," said Vor Gontakel. "All is quite as should be. Quite."

"Meerowou," Felicity said. "Mrourr."

Vor Gontakel said, "This means what?"

Sister Mary Magdalene smiled. "Felicity says she hopes you'll call us if anything is not to your liking."

Vor Gontakel smiled broadly, showing her golden teeth. "I am quite comfortable, thank you, Sister. And thank you, Felicity."

The door closed. Sister Mary Magdalene felt more cheerful. Vor Gontakel had at least been pleasant.

One more trip to make. The last, thank Heaven. The nun rapped on the final door.

Vor Vun slowly opened her door, peered out, stepped back in alarmed distaste. "A cat!" she exclaimed.

"I'm sorry if I frightened you," Sister Mary Magdalene said quickly.

"Frightened? No. I just do not like cats. When I was a prisoner aboard one of your spaceships, they had a cat." The alien woman held out a saffron-skinned arm. Three furrows of scar tissue stood out darkly. "I was scratched. Infection set in, and none of the Earthmen's medicine could be used. It is a good thing that there was an exchange of prisoners, or I might have died."

The alien paused, as if realizing that her speech was not precisely diplomatic. "I am sorry," she said, forcing a smile. "But—you understand?"

"Certainly," the nun said. For the third time in ten minutes she went through the necessary ritual of asking after

146

her guest's comfort, and for the third time she was assured that all was well.

Sister Mary Magdalene returned to her office. "Come on, Felicity," she whispered soothingly. "Can't have you worrying our star boarders."

Father Destry was waiting for Sister Mary Magdalene when she came back from Mass the following morning. He was looking at her with a puzzled air.

"Where is everyone?"

Ignoring his question for the moment, Sister Mary Magdalene jabbed furiously at the air conditioner button. "Isn't this thing working?" she asked fretfully of no one in particular. "It seems as though I can still smell it." Then she realized that the priest had addressed her, and that he was still waiting with imperious patience for an answer.

"Father Pierce kindly invited us to use the monastery chapel this morning," she said, feeling a twinge of embarrassment at her own unintentional rudeness. "Our own is too close to the kitchen."

Father Destry's face showed his lack of comprehension. "You went over to the monastery? Kitchen?"

Sister Mary Magdalene sighed patiently. "Father Destry, I'm morally certain that it would have been impossible for anyone to have retained a properly reverent attitude at Mass if it was held in a chapel that smelled to high Heaven of long-dead fish!"

Her voice had risen in pitch during the last few words, and she cut off the crescendo with a sudden clamping together of her lips before her indignation distressed the priest. "The Pogatha rose early for breakfast. They wouldn't let Sister Elizabeth cook it. Vor Vun—that's the yellow one—did the honors, and each one ate in his—her—own room. That meant that those meals were carried from the kitchen to the rooms. You should have been here. We just barely made it through Lauds."

Father Destry was obviously trying to control a smile which inwardly pleased Sister Mary Magdalene. It was encouraging to know that even Father Destry could be amused by something.

"I imagine the air conditioners have taken care of it by now," he said carefully. "I didn't notice a thing when I came through the courtyard." He glanced at the big clock on the wall. "The first meeting between the official representatives of Pogathan and Earth begins in an hour. I want—"

There was a rap at the door.

"Yes?"

Sister Martha, one of the younger nuns, entered. There was a vaguely apprehensive look on her young face. "The Pogatha are here to see you, Sister."

She stood aside while the four aliens trooped in, led by the imposing Blue, Vor Nollig. Sister Mary Magdalene greeted them with as much heartiness as she could muster, considering the episode of breakfast.

Vor Nollig said, "If it is at all possible, we would like to stroll around the grounds, look at your buildings. Perhap you could take us on a tour?"

Hostess or not, the last thing Sister Mary Magdalene wanted to do now was shepherd the four aliens around the Cathedral grounds. She glanced meaningfully at Father Destry, who scowled faintly, then brightened and nodded.

"It would be a pleasure," the priest said. "I'll be glad to show you the Cathedral grounds."

And bless you for it, the nun thought as the little group left. After they had gone, she rubbed a finger speculatively across the tip of her nose. Was she wrong, or did there seem to be something peculiar in the actions of the aliens? They had seemed to be in a tremendous hurry to leave, and the expressions on their faces were strained. Or were they? It was hard to correlate any Pogatha expressions with their human equivalents. And, of course, Sister Mary Magdalene was no expert on extraterrestrial psychology.

Abruptly she ceased worrying about the behavior of the Pogatha. With her finger still on her nose, she caught the aroma of the morning's coffee drifting from the kitchen, where it was being prepared. She smiled. Then she indulged in the first, deep, joyous laugh she had had in two weeks.

That evening, after the Pogatha had returned to their quarters, Sister Mary Magdalene's private meditations were interrupted by a phone call from Secretary Masterson, the heavyset U.N. man. His fleshy face had a tense, worried look on it.

"Sister, I know this might be overstepping my authority, but I have the fate of a war to deal with."

"Just what's the trouble, Mr. Masterson?"

"At the meeting today, the Pogatha seemed—I don't

quite know how to put it—*offended,* I suppose. They were touchy and unreasonable, and they quarrelled among themselves during the conference—all in a strictly diplomatic way, of course. I'm afraid we got rather touchy ourselves."

"How sad," the nun said. "We all have such high hopes for the success of these negotiations."

"Was there some incident that might have irritated them, Sister? I don't mean to imply any carelessness, but was there anything that might have upset them?"

"The only thing I can think of is the smell of the morning coffee," said the nun. "They came to me asking to be taken on a tour of the Cathedral grounds, and they seemed in an awful hurry to get out of the building. When they were gone I smelled the coffee being prepared. It must have nauseated them as much as their foods bother us."

Masterson's face cleared a little. "That might be it. They *are* touchy people, and maybe they thought the coffee odor that they found so revolting had been generated for their benefit." He paused for a long moment before he said, "Well, that sort of thing is too much for you, and it's obviously too much for them. I'll speak to Bishop Courtland tonight. We'll have to make better arrangements. Meanwhile, do you think you could do something about supper tonight? Get them out of there somehow, and—"

"That might be a little difficult," said Sister Mary Magdalene. "I think it would be better if we ate out."

"Very well. And I'll talk to the bishop."

She waited a moment for the screen to clear after Secretary Masterson broke contact, then dialed the number of the Holy Cross Monastery on the far side of the Cathedral. The face of a monk appeared on the screen, the cowl of his white robe lying in graceful folds around his throat.

Sister Mary Magdalene said, "Father Pierce, you were gracious enough to ask us to your chapel this morning because of the alien aroma here. I wonder if you'd be good enough to ask us to dinner tonight? Our alien friends don't seem to like our odors any more than we like theirs, and so we can't cook here."

Father Pierce laughed cheerfully. "We'll have to use the public dining hall, of course. But I think we can manage it."

"It'll have to be in two shifts," the nun said. "We can't

leave this place deserted, much as we'd like to while they're eating."

"Don't worry, Sister. We'll arrange something. But what about tomorrow and the next day?"

Sister Mary Magdalene smiled. "We'll worry about that if we have to, but I think the Pogatha are on their way out of here. Secretary Masterson is going to make different arrangements with the bishop."

"You don't think they'll be transferred to *us?*"

"Hardly, Father Pierce. They'll have to leave the Cathedral entirely."

It was a pleasant, if ungracious thought. But Sister Mary Magdalene had taken no vows to put herself and her nuns into great inconvenience for the sake of unpleasant alien creatures. She would be glad to see them go.

Morning came. Sister Mary Magdalene sat in Choir, listening to the words of the Divine Office and wondering why the Church had been chosen as a meeting place for the two so alien races. It had not been a successful meeting thus far; but, she pondered, was there some deeper reason for the coming-together than mere political negotiation?

The soft, sweet voices of the women, singing alternately from opposite sides of the chapel in the *Domine, Dominus noster,* were like the ringing of crystal chimes rather than the deeper, bell-like ringing that resounded from the throats of the monks on the opposite sides of the great cathedral.

And, like crystal, their voices seemed to shatter under the impact of the hoarse, ugly, bellowing scream that suddenly filled the air.

A moment later, the singing resumed, uncertainly but gamely, as monks and nuns compelled themselves to continue the service regardless. Sister Mary Magdalene felt the unaccustomed tingle of fear within her. What had happened? Trouble with the aliens? Or merely an excitable visitor taken aback by a surprise encounter with one of the Pogatha?

It might be almost anything. Tension grew within the nun. She had to know.

She rose from her seat and slipped away down the aisle. Behind her, the singing continued with renewed vigor. But that ungodly scream still echoed in her ears.

* * *

150

God in Heaven, thought Sister Mary Magdalene an hour later. *What are You doing to Your servants and hand-maidens now? Whoever heard of a convent full of cops?*

She hadn't realized that she had spoken the last sentence half aloud until she saw Father Destry's astonished and reproachful expression. She reddened at once.

"Please, Sister!" the priest murmured. "They're not 'cops'—they're World Bureau of Criminal Investigation officers!"

Sister Mary Magdalene nodded contritely and glanced through the open door of her office at the trio of big, bulky men who were conferring in low tones in the corridor. The label, she thought glumly, made no difference. WBCI or not, they were still *cops.*

The nun felt dazed. Too much had happened in the past hour. Sister Mary Magdalene felt as though everything were twisted and broken around her, as the body of Vor Nollig had been twisted and broken.

Vor Nollig, the Blue; Vor Nollig, the female Pogath; Vor Nollig, the Chief Diplomat of Pogathan—dead, with a common carving knife plunged into her abdomen and her alien blood all over the floor of the room in which she had slept the night before.

She still slept there. She would sleep eternally. The WBCI men had not yet removed the body.

Vor Betla, the other Blue, had found her, and it had been the outraged scream of Vor Betla that had broken the peace of the convent. Sister Mary Magdalene wondered bleakly if that peace would ever be whole again.

First the scream, then the violence of the raging fight as the other two Pogatha had tried to subdue Vor Betla, who seemed to be intent on destroying the convent with her bare hands. And now, the quiet warmth of Sister Mary Magdalene's inviolate little world had suddenly and jarringly been defiled by the entrance of a dozen men, one right after another. But they had come too late. The blood had already been shed.

"You look ill, Sister," said Father Destry, suddenly solicitous. "Wouldn't you like to lie down for a while!"

Sister Mary Magdalene shook her head violently. "No! No, I'll be all right. It's just the—the shock."

"The bishop gave me strict orders to make sure that none of this disturbs you."

"I know what he said, and I appreciate it. But I'm afraid

151

we have already been disturbed." There was a touch of acid in her voice.

Bishop Courtland, his fine old face looking haggard and unhappy, had come and gone again. Sister Mary Magdalene wished he had not gone, but there was no help for it; the bishop had to deal with the stratoplane load of high officials who had rocketed in as soon as the news had reached the Capital.

One of the WBCI men removed his hat in a gesture of respect and stepped into the nun's office. She noticed out of the corner of her eye that the other WBCI men, belatedly remembering where they were, were taking their hats off, too.

"I'm Major Brock, Sister. Captain Lehmann told me that you're the sister-in-charge here."

Sister Mary Magdalene nodded wordlessly. Captain Lehmann had been in charge of the group that had come rushing in at Father Destry's call; they had been hidden outside the cathedral grounds, ostensibly to protect the alien visitors.

"I know this is—unpleasant," Major Brock said. He was a big man who was obviously finding it difficult to keep his voice at the soft level he believed was appropriate in here. "It's more than a matter of one life at stake, Sister. We have to find out who did this."

Sister Mary Magdalene nodded, thinking, *The sooner you find out, the sooner all of you will leave here.* "I'll do all I can to help," she told him.

"We'd like to question the sisters," he said apologetically. "We'd like to know if any of them saw or heard anything unusual during the night."

The nun frowned. "What time was the alien killed, Major?"

"We don't know. If she were human, we'd be able to pinpoint it within a matter of seconds. But we don't know how fast the blood—" He stopped suddenly on the "d" of "blood," as though he had realized that such gory subjects might not be proper conversation here.

Sister Mary Magdalene was amused at the WBCI man's exaggerated tact. "How fast the blood coagulates," she completed, a bit surprised at her own calmness. "Nor, I suppose, how soon *rigor mortis* sets in, nor how long it takes the body to cool."

"That's about it. We'll just have to check with everybody to see if anyone saw anything that might help us."

"Would you tell me one thing?" Sister Mary Magdalene said, glancing hesitantly at the silent, glowering figure of Father Destry. "Can you tell me who the suspects are? And please don't say 'everybody'—I mean the immediate suspects."

"Frankly," said Major Brock, "we think it might be one of the aliens. But I'm afraid that might just be prejudice. There are other possibilities."

"You don't suspect one of us!"

"Not now. But I can't overlook the possibility. If any of the sisters has a brother or a father in the Space Service—"

"I concede the possibility," said Sister Mary Magdalene reluctantly. "And I suppose the same thing might hold true for anyone else."

"It might, but conditions here pretty well confine the suspects to the sisters and the aliens. After all, you've been pretty closely guarded, and you're pretty secure here." The WBCI man smiled. "Except from invasion by cops." He won Sister Mary Magdalene's undying love with that last sentence.

Father Destry swallowed hard to maintain his composure and said, "I suppose I'll have to remain if the sisters are to be questioned. The bishop—"

"I understand, Father. I'll try not to take too long."

Sister Mary Magdalene sighed and checked the schedule of Masses in the Cathedral of the Blessed Sacrament. There would be little chance of her hearing Mass in the chapel here, with all this going on.

The nightmarish morning dragged slowly along. Sister Mary Magdalene phoned the Mother Superior of the order in Wisconsin to assure her that everything was under control; it was true, if not wholly accurate. Then it was the nun's task to interview each of her Sisters, one by one, to learn her story of the night before.

They knew nothing. None of them was lying, Sister Mary Magdalene knew, and none of them was capable of murder.

Not until the Major came to Sister Angela did anything new come up. Sister Angela was asked if she had noticed anything unusual.

"Yes," she said flatly. "There was someone in the courtyard last night. I saw him from my window."

153

"Him?" Sister Mary Magdalene repeated in astonishment, sitting bold upright in her chair. *"Him?"*

Sister Angela nodded nervously. "It—it looked like a monk."

"How do you know it was a monk?" asked the Major.

"Well, he was wearing a robe—with the cowl down. The moon was pretty bright. I could see him clearly."

"Did you recognize him?"

"It wasn't *that* bright, Major. But I'm sure it was—well, a man dressed in a monk's habit."

Major Brock frowned and chewed at the ends of his mustache. "We'll have to investigate this more fully."

Sister Mary Magdalene rose. A quick glance at the clock told her that it was her last chance to make it to Mass. For an instant, a niggling inward voice told her that missing Mass just this once would be excusable under the circumstances, but she fought it down.

"Would you excuse me?" she said to Brock. "I must attend Mass at this hour."

"Of course, Sister." Brock did not seem pleased at the prospect of having to carry on without her, but, as always, he maintained careful respect for the churchly activities going on about him.

Sister Mary Magdalene went out, headed for the cathedral. Outside, everything looked so normal that she could hardly believe anything had really happened. It was not until she reached the cathedral itself that depression again struck her.

The vestment radiations were off.

The vestments of the clergy were fluorescent; under the radiation from the projectors in the walls, the chasubles, tunics and dalmatics, the stoles, maniples and altar frontal, all glowed with color. The color depended on the wavelength of the radiation used. There was the somber violet of the penitential seasons of Lent and Advent, the restful green of Epiphany and the long weeks after Trinity, the joyous white of Christmas and Easter, and the blazing red of Pentecost. But without the radiations, the vestments were black—the somber black of the Requiem, the Mass of the Dead.

For a moment Sister Mary Magdalene's thoughts were as black as the hangings on the altar. And then she realized that, again, there was Reason behind whatever was going on here. There was no doubt in her own mind that the Pogatha were intelligent, reasoning beings, although

154

the question had never been settled on a theological level by the Church. She would pray for the repose of the soul of Vor Nollig.

Forty-five minutes later, she was walking back toward the convent, her own soul strangely at rest. For just a short time, there toward the end, she had felt oddly apprehensive about having had Vor Nollig in mind while the celebrant intoned the *Agnus Dei:* "O Lamb of God that takest away the sins of the world, grant them rest eternal." But then the words of the Last Gospel had come to reassure her: "All things were made by Him, and without Him was not anything made." Surely it could not be wrong to pray for the happiness of one of God's creatures, no matter how strangely made.

She was to think that thought again within the next five minutes.

Sister Elizabeth, round and chubby and looking almost comically penguinlike, was standing at the gate, tears rolling down her plump cheeks.

"Why, Sister Elizabeth—what's the trouble?"

"Oh, Sister, Sister!" She burst into real sobs and buried her head miserably in Sister Mary Magdalene's shoulder. "She's dead—*murdered!*"

For a wild moment, Sister Mary Magdalene thought that Sister Elizabeth was referring to the dead Pogatha, Vor Nollig, but then she knew it was not so, and her numbed mind refused to speculate any further. She could only shake Sister Elizabeth and say, "Who? Who is dead? Who?"

"Her—her little head's all burned off!" sobbed the tearful nun. She was becoming hysterical now, shaking convulsively. Sister Mary Magdalene gripped Sister Elizabeth's shoulders firmly.

"Who?"

Sister Elizabeth looked up. When she spoke it was in a shocked whisper. "Felicity, Sister. Your cat! She's dead!"

Sister Mary Magdalene remained quite still, letting the first tide of grief wash over her. A moment later she was calm again. The cat had been her beloved companion for years, but Sister Mary Magdalene felt no grief now. Merely pity for the unfortunate one who could have done such a brutal deed, and sorrow over the loss of a dear friend. A moment later the anger began, and Sister Mary Magdalene prayed for the strength to unravel the mystery of the sudden outbreak of violence in these peaceful precincts.

When she returned to her office a few moments later, the three living aliens were standing grouped together near one wall of the room. Secretary Masterson and Secretary Bass were not too far away. Major Brock was seated in the guest chair, with Father Destry standing behind him. Brock was speaking.

". . . and that's about it. Someone—we don't know who—came in here last night. One of the Sisters saw him heading toward the back gate of the courtyard, and another has told us that the back gate was unlocked this morning—and it shouldn't have been, because she's positive she locked it the night before." Brock looked up at Sister Mary Magdalene and his expression changed as he saw the frozen mask of her face. The nun was filled with hot anger, burning and righteous, but under complete and icy control.

"What is it, Sister?"

"Would you come with me, Major Brock? I have something to show you. And Father Destry, if you would. I would prefer that the rest of you remain here." She spoke crisply. This was, after all, her domain.

She led the two men, priest and policeman, to the courtyard and around to the rear of the convent. Then they went out to the broad park beyond. Fifteen yards from the gate lay the charred, pitiful remains of the cat.

Major Brock knelt to look at it. "A dead cat," he said in a blank voice.

"Felicity," said Father Destry. "I'm sorry, Sister." The nun knew the sorrow was for her; Father Destry had never felt much warmth for the little animal.

Major Brock rose and said, softly, "I'm afraid I don't quite see what this has to do with—"

"Look at her head," said the nun in a hot-cold voice. "Burned! That's the work of a Brymer beamgun. Close range; not more than ten feet, possibly less."

Brock knelt again, picking up the body and studying it closely for a silent moment. When he looked up, the cat still in his hands, there was new respect in his eyes. "You're right, Sister. There's the typical hardening of the tissues around the burn. This wasn't done with a torch."

Father Destry blinked confusedly. "Do you think the

156

killing of Sister Mary Magdalene's pet has something to do with the—uh—murder of Vor Nollig?"

"I don't know," Brock said slowly. "Sister? What do you think?"

"I think it does. But I'm not sure how. I think you'll find a connection."

"This brings something new into the picture, at least," said the Major. "Now we can look for a Brymer beam-gun."

Vor Betla, the second Blue, who had never been able to speak English well, had given it up completely. She was snarling and snapping at Vor Vun, who was translating as best she could. It appeared that all three of the aliens seemed to feel that they might be the next to get a carving knife in their insides.

Vor Vun said, "We feel that you are not doing as well as you might, Major Brock. We don't blame the government of Earth directly for this insult, but obviously the precautions that were taken to protect us were insufficient."

The Major shook his head. "The entire grounds around the Cathedral were patrolled and guarded by every detection instrument known to Earth. No one could have gotten in."

Vor Gontakel put the palms of her green hands together, almost as if she were praying. "It makes a sense. You would not want us to get out, of course, so you would have much of safeguards around."

"We grant that," agreed Vor Vun. "But someone nonetheless killed Vor Nollig, and her loss is great."

Vor Betla snarled and yapped.

Vor Vun translated: "You must turn the killer over to us. If you do not, there can be no further talk of peace."

"How do we know it wasn't one of you three?" asked Secretary Masterson suddenly.

Vor Betla barked something. Vor Vun said, "We would have no reason for it."

Major Brock sighed. "I know. That's what's bothered me all along. Where's the motive?"

Sister Mary Magdalene, watching silently, eyed the three aliens. Which one of them would have killed Vor Nollig? Which one might have killed Felicity?

Vor Vun? She hated cats; had she also hated Vor Nollig? Or had it been Vor Gontakel, the despised Green? But why would she kill Felicity? Had Vor Betla done it so she could be head of the delegation? That made even less sense.

Motive. What was the motive?

Had someone else done it? One of the secretaries, perhaps? Was there a political motive behind the crime?

And then—she had to force herself to think of it—there was the possibility that one of the monks, or, worse yet, one of her own sisters had done it.

If an Earthman had done it, it was either a political motive or one of hatred; there could be nothing personal in it. Vor Nollig, if she had been killed by an Earthman, had been killed for some deep, unknown or unknowable political machination, probably by order of the government itself, or else she had been killed because some Earthman just hated the enemy to such an extent that—

Sister Mary Magdalene did not want to think of blind hatred such as that.

On the other hand, if one of the three remaining Pogatha had done it, the motive could be any one of several. It could be personal, or political, or it might even have a basis in racial prejudice.

The nun thought it over for several minutes without reaching any conclusions. Motive would have to be abandoned as a way of finding the killer. For once, motive could not enter into the solution at all.

Method, then. What was the method?

Major Brock was saying: "Even the best of modern aids to crime detection can't reconstruct the past for us. But we do know part of the killer's actions. He—"

There was a rap on the door, and Captain Lehmann thrust his head inside. "Excuse me if I'm interrupting. See you a minute, Major?"

Brock frowned, rose, and went outside, closing the door behind him. Father Destry leaned over and whispered to the nun, "They may suspect me."

"Nonsense, Father!"

Father Destry pursed his lips suddenly and said nothing more. Major Brock put his head in the door. "Sister, would you come here a minute?"

She stepped into the hall to confront two very grim WBCI men. Captain Lehmann was holding a Brymer beamgun in one hand and a bundle of black cloth in the crook of his arm. A faint but decidedly foul stench was perceptible.

"This is the gun," Lehmann said, "that killed your cat. At least, as far as we know. An energy beam has no traceable ballistics characteristics. We found it wrapped in this—" He gestured toward the black bundle. "And shoved under one of the pews in the chapel."

With a sudden movement he flipped out the cloth so it was recognizable. Sister Mary Magdalene had no difficulties in recognizing it. It was the habit of a nun.

"The lab men have already gone over it," Major Brock said. "We can prove who the owner is by perspiration comparison, but there also happens to be an identification strip in it. The odor is the blood of Vor Nollig. It spurted out when she was stabbed through the heart."

Brock opened the habit so the ID tag became visible.

It said, *Sister Elizabeth, S.H.N.*

"We'll have to talk to her," said the Major.

"Of course," said Sister Mary Magdalene calmly. "I imagine you'll find it was stolen from her room. Tell me, why should Father Destry think you suspect him?"

The sudden, casual change of subject apparently puzzled Major Brock. He paused a moment before answering. "We don't, really. That is—" Again he paused. "He had a brother. A colonist on Pogathan. The Pogatha caught him. He died—not pleasantly, I'm afraid." He looked at the floor. "We have a similar bit of information on Sister Elizabeth. An uncle."

"You haven't mentioned my nephew yet," said Sister Mary Magdalene.

The Major looked surprised. "No. We hadn't."

"It's of no importance, anyway. Let's go check with Sister Elizabeth. I can tell you now that she knows nothing about it. She probably doesn't even know her spare habit is missing yet, because it was stolen from the laundry. The laundry room is right across from the aliens' quarters."

"Wait," Brock said. "You'd rather we didn't talk to her, don't you?"

"It would only upset her."

"How do you know she didn't do it?"

"For the same reason you don't think she did, Major. This thing is beginning to make sense. I'm beginning to understand the mind that did this awful thing."

He looked at her curiously. "You have a strange mind yourself, Sister. I didn't realize that nuns knew so much about crime."

"Major," she said evenly, "when I took my vows, I chose the name 'Mary Magdalene.' I didn't pick it out of the hat."

The Major nodded silently, and his gaze shifted to the closed door of the nun's office. "The thing is that the whole pattern *is* beginning to make sense. But I can't quite see it."

"It was a badly fumbled job, really," said Sister Mary Magdalene. "If an Earthman had done it, you'd have spotted him immediately."

Again the Major nodded. "I agree. That much of the picture is clear. It *was* one of those three. But unless we know which one, and know beyond any smidgen of doubt, we don't dare make any accusations."

The nun turned to Captain Lehmann. "Did your lab men find out where that gun was discharged?"

"Why, yes. We found faint burn marks on the floor near the door to Vor Nollig's room."

"In the corridor outside, about four or five feet away?"

"That's right."

"Now—and this is important—where were they in relation to the door? I mean, if a person were facing the door, looking at someone inside the room, would the burn marks be behind him or in front?"

"Well—let's see—the door opens in, so they'd have to stand at an angle—mmm. Behind."

"I thought so!" Sister Mary Magdalene exclaimed in triumph.

Major Brock frowned. "It almost makes sense, but I don't quite—"

"That's because I have a vital clue that you don't have, Major."

"Which is?"

She told him.

"We know what was done," said Major Brock levelly. "We know *how* it was done." He looked the three aliens over. "One of you will tell us *why* it was done."

"If you are going to accuse one of us," said Vor Gontakel, rubbing her green hands carefully, "I'm afraid we will have to resist arrest. Is it not called a 'frame'?"

"Is insult!" snapped Vor Betla. "Is stupid! Is lie!"

The Major leaned back in his chair and looked at the two Terran diplomats, Bass and Masterson. "What makes this so tough," he said, "is that we don't know the motive.

If the plot was hatched by all three of them, we're going to have a hell of a time—excuse me, Sister—proving it, or at least a rough time doing anything about it."

Masterson considered. "Do you think you could prove it to the satisfaction of an Earth court?"

"Maybe." Brock paused. "I *think* so. I'm a cop, not a prosecuting attorney."

Masterson and Bass conferred a moment. "All right— go ahead," Masterson said finally, "If it's a personal motive, then the other two will be sensible enough to see that the killer has greatly endangered the peace negotiations, besides murdering their leader. And I don't think it's a political motive on the part of all three."

"Though if it is," Bass interjected, "nothing we say will matter anyhow."

"Okay," Brock said. "Here's what happened. Sometime early this morning, around two—if Sister Angela's testimony is accurate—the killer went into the laundry room and picked up one of the nun's habits. Then the killer went to the kitchen, got a carving knife, came back and knocked on the door of Vor Nollig's room. Vor Nollig woke and came to the door. She opened the door a crack and saw what appeared to be a nun in the dim corridor. Not suspecting anything, Vor Nollig opened the door wider and stepped into full view. The killer stabbed her in the heart with the knife."

"Earthman," said Vor Betla positively.

"No. Where's your heart, Vor Betla?"

The Pogath patted the base of her throat.

"Ours is here," Brock said. "An Earthman would have instinctively stabbed much lower, you see."

Sister Mary Magdalene repressed a smile. The Major was bluffing there. Plenty of human beings had been stabbed in the throat by other human beings.

Brock said, "But now comes the puzzling part. You do not like cats, Vor Vun. What would you do if one came near you? Are you afraid of them?"

Vor Vun sniffed. "Afraid? No. They are harmless. They can be frightened easily. I would not pick one up, or allow it too close, but I am not afraid."

"How about you, Vor Betla?"

"Do? Don't know. Know nothing of cats, but that they harmless dumb animals. Maybe kick if came too close."

"Vor Gontakel?"

"I too know nothing of cats. I only saw one once."

161

"One of you," said the Major judiciously, "is telling an untruth. Let's go on with the story."

Sister Mary Magdalene watched their faces, trying to read emotion in those alien visages as the Major spoke.

"The killer did a strange thing. She turned around and saw Felicity, the cat. Possibly it had meowed from behind her and attracted her attention. And what does the killer do? She draws a Brymer beamgun and kills the cat! Why?"

The Pogatha looked at each other and then back at the Major. Their faces, thought Sister Mary Magdalene, were utterly unreadable.

"Then the killer picked up the cat, walked outdoors through the rear gate and threw it into the meadow. It was the killer that Sister Angela saw last night, but the killer had pushed the cowl back, so she didn't recognize the fact that it was a nun's habit, not a monk's. When the killer had disposed of the cat, she removed the habit, wrapped the beamgun in it and went into the chapel and put it under one of the pews."

"Very plausible," said Vor Vun. "But not proof that one of *us* did it."

"Not so far. But let's keep plugging. Why did the killer wear the nun's habit?"

"Because was nun!" said Vor Betla. She pointed an accusing blue finger at Sister Mary Magdalene.

"No," Brock said. "Because she wanted Vor Nollig to let her get close enough to stab her. You see, we've eliminated you, Vor Betla. You shared the room; you would have been allowed in without question. But Vor Nollig would never have allowed a Green or a Yellow into her room, would she?"

"No," admitted the Blue, looking troubledly at Vor Vun and Vor Gontakel.

"Another point in your favor is the fact that the killer looked like a monk to Sister Angela. There are no dark-skinned monks at this cathedral, and Sister Angela would have commented on it if the skin had looked as dark as your does. But colors are almost impossible to see in moonlight. A yellow or light green would have looked pretty much like human skin, and the features at a distance would be hard to recognize as belonging to a Pogath."

"You are playing on prejudices," said Vor Vun angrily. "This is an inexpensive trick!"

"A *cheap* trick," corrected Major Brock. "Except that it isn't. However, we must now prove that it was a Pogath. We've smelled each others' food, haven't we? Now, a burnt cat would smell no differently than, say, a broiled steak—except maybe a little more so. Why would the killer take the trouble to remove the cat from the building? Why not leave it where it was? If she expected to get away with one killing, she could have expected to get away with two. She took the cat out simply because she couldn't stand the overpowering odor! There was no other possible reason to expose herself that way to the possible spying eyes of Sister Angela or any other nun who happened to be looking out the window. It was clever of the killer to think of dropping the wimple back and disposing of the white part of the headdress so that she would appear to be a monk. I imagine it also took a lot of breath-holding to stand to carry that burnt cat that far."

The Pogatha were definitely eyeing each other now, but the final wedge remained to be driven.

"Vor Gontakel!" the Major said sharply. "What would you say if I told you that another cat at the far end of the corridor saw you stab Vor Nollig and burn down Felicity?"

Vor Gontakel looked perfectly unruffled and unperturbed. No Earthman's bluff was going to get by *her!* "I would say the cat was lying," she said.

"The other two Pogatha got a confession out of her," said Major Brock that evening. "They'll take her back to Pogathan to stand trial."

Father Destry folded his hands and smiled. "Sister, you seem to have all the makings of a first-class detective. How did you figure out that it was Vor Gontakel? I mean, what started you on that train of thought?"

"Sister Elizabeth," the nun said. "She told me that Felicity had been murdered. And she *had* been—murdered, I mean, not just 'killed.' Vor Gontakel saw me talking to the cat, and Felicity meowed back. How was she to know that the cat wasn't intelligent? She knew nothing about Terrestrial life. The other two did. Felicity was murdered because Vor Gontakel thought she was a witness. It was the only possible motive for Felicity's murder."

"What about the motive for Vor Nollig's murder?" Father Destry said to the Major.

163

"Political. There's a group of Greens, it seems, that has the idea the war should go on. Most of the war is being fought by Blues, and if they're wiped out the so-called minority groups could take over. I doubt if it would work that way, but that's what this bunch thinks. Vor Gontakel simply wanted to kill a Blue and have it blamed on the Earthmen in order to stop the peace talks. But there's one thing I think we left untied here, Sister. Have you stopped to wonder why she used a knife on Vor Nollig instead of the beamgun she was carrying?"

Sister Mary Magdalene nodded. "She didn't want every sister in the place coming out to catch her before she had a chance to cover up. She knew that burnt Pogatha would smell as bad to us as burnt cat did to her. But she didn't have a chance to use a knife on Felicity; the cat would have run away."

Major Brock nodded in appreciation. "A very neat summation, Sister. I bow to your fine deductive abilities. And now, I imagine, we can get our staff off the cathedral premises and leave you people to your devotions."

"It's unfortunate we had to meet under such unhappy circumstances, Major," the nun said.

"But you were marvelously helpful, Sister."

The Major smiled at the nun, shook Father Destry's hand tentatively, as if uncertain that such a gesture was appropriate, and left. Sister Mary Magdalene sighed gently in relief.

Police and aliens and all were leaving. The Cathedral was returning to its normal quietude. In the distance the big bell was tolling, and it was time for prayer. She was no longer a detective; she was simply Sister Mary Magdalene of the Sisters of the Holy Nativity.

It would be good to have peace here again. But, she admitted wryly to herself, the excitement had been a not altogether unwelcome change from normal routine. The thought brought up old memories of a life long buried and sealed away with vows. Sister Mary Magdalene frowned gently, dispelling the thoughts, and quietly began to pray.

RANDALL GARRETT

Anne McCaffrey

MY FIRST ENCOUNTER WITH THE EBULLIENT and irrepressible Randall Garrett was in print—thank goodness! Or I might have been detoured into another kind of life. Randall Garrett was at that time pseudonyming as Robert Randall with another young and struggling author (who shall be nameless but he was the Robert part of the name.) Little did I know then that both men would have such an effect on my life. I only know that I enjoyed *The Shrouded Planet* and its sequel, automatically read first anything by Robert Randall in the magazines I bought and hoarded. I envied this Robert Randall his easy style and good plotting, all the craft my own timidly submitted, and rejected, stories lacked. (Of course two heads *are* better than one.)

More to the point, McCaffrey. My first, in the flesh, real-life encounter with Randy occurred at my first Milford Science Fiction writers Conference to which Judy Merril had invited me in 1959: me and two other unknown women writers, Kate Wilhelm and the late Rosel George Brown.

I was with child—not great, but noticeably, and Randy was charm itself so that this pregnant lady felt much revived, if horrified, by his clever remarks and sly innuendos. (Randall Garrett has always approved of collaborations. Evidently he was very good at the literary ones—and I cannot judge by experience from the other sorts he suggested.)

Sometime after Gigi was born, Randall phoned me from Cleveland (I think it was). He wanted me to come join him and his then collaborator at the convention. He told me his partner approved. In some ways, I wished I had been free to go. But then, one always regrets sins of Omission.

165

Randall Garrett was at my first science-fiction convention in Washington, D.C., in 1963. I had the use of the family VW station wagon we'd brought back from Germany. As the model was new to the States, I had distinguished interest in it. Also rude advice about jumped-up beetles. However, I proved its capacity when I stuffed Isaac Asimov and Randy Garrett in the cargo boot, and accommodated Fritz Leiber, Gordy Dickson, Judy Merril and a redheaded girl after whom both Isaac and Randy lusted. We drove off to a Chinese restaurant of good fame and cheap price. This was how I learned that science-fiction writers who attend conventions are either in the bar or at the nearest Chinese or other ethnic eating place. (The hotel food was either too expensive or, by the gourmet standards of such a trencherman as Randall Garrett, inedible.) Such observation has stood me in very good stead in every convention city I've visited. One learned from Randall Garrett.

If I recall correctly events now two decades past, I do believe that Randall phoned me the odd time or two before he removed to the West Coast. It was very kind of him because, being a perceptive man behind all that bonhomie, he realized that I needed encouragement as an author, and good-natured sexy teasing as a woman. He was eager to supply more.

I also remember *Too Many Magicians*, and haunting the newsstands for the next installment in *Analog*—only I don't think it was "*Analog*" yet. Randy had once (or maybe more than once) mentioned that Isaac Asimov wasn't the only man who could write a science fiction mystery story. Randall compounded his felony with his usual wit and humour, and added magic to the mystery. And the story worked! Of course, Randy had superb help in his alter ego, Lord Darcy. Those two rogues must certainly be mental companions.

Randy was present at Baycon in 1968, in a helm I couldn't lift, much less wear. He was medievally accoutred, mail shirt and surcoat, for a broadsword fight with Poul Anderson on the lawn of the Convention hotel in Berkeley. John Campbell, Randy and Poul were ardently discussing medieval weaponry. John was of the opinion that the quarterstaff was the best all around, most easily procured and maintained hand weapon ever to be used. Over drinks—discussions with Randy were held invariably over drinks—the matter was thrashed until Randy and

Poul went to do battle. I'm sorry now that I didn't witness the dynamic duo "having at it." Probably I couldn't tear myself from the discussions at the bar—or maybe, I was scheduled in my capacity as secretary-treasurer of SFWA, an honorable office I had just assumed.

Later, Randy and Poul were back in the bar, dressed contemporarily (meaning Poul's plain-colored shirt didn't harmonize with Randy's Californian print), not particularly the worse for the wear and tear of the tourney, and discussing the student riots at Berkeley campus which had been vulgarly dispersed by the use of tear gas. (The stuff had also been endured by some of the convention attendees.)

Of course, it could have been the next day I saw them . . . you know how one day blends with another at a convention. And I was in the bar a lot, too, meeting the other authors—of course—and learning how to act like a science-fiction writer enjoying a convention. (It was only my third.)

I don't remember seeing Randy at St. Louiscon in 1969 and then matters got complicated for me and I ended up living here in Ireland. In 1978, when I was touring in the Midwest, someone told me that Randy had become a priest. I remember gawking like a loony since Randall Garrett did not, in my estimation, have the continence required for a man of the cloth. Some kind soul explained and then I could very well understand what Randall was doing! Bless his ever-expanding heart!

Does any one, except the two, know how much of Randall Garrett *is* Lord Darcy, and vice versa? By any road, they're a grand man, so they are!

Certainly Randall Garrett's most satisfying and enduring literary accomplishment is the Lord Darcy series. Into these elegant parallel-world stories he has poured his considerable erudition, his unapologetic love for imperial pomp and circumstance, and his skills as a teller of tales—and the readers have responded with resounding approval. The series began in 1964 with a sequence of novellas in *Analog* and reached a climax with the 1966 novel *Too Many Magicians*, published by Doubleday and recently reissued by Gregg Press. Then came a long silence in Garrett's writing career, but when he returned to the typewriter in the mid-1970s Lord Darcy returned with him, and we saw such stories as 1974's "A Matter of Gravity," 1976's "The Ipswich File," and 1979's "The Napoli Express"—with, one hopes, a good many more still to come.

The story reprinted here was the first of all the Lord Darcy items, which got the series off to a rousing start in the January 1964 *Analog*.

THE EYES HAVE IT

SIR PIERRE MORLAIX, CHEVALIER OF THE ANgevin Empire, Knight of the Golden Leopard and secretary-in-private to my lord, the Count D'Evreux, pushed back the lace at his cuff for a glance at his wristwatch—three minutes of seven. The Angelus had rung at six, as always, and my lord D'Evreux had been awakened by it, as always. At least, Sir Pierre could not remember any time in the past 17 years when my lord had not awakened at the Angelus. Once, he recalled, the sacristan had failed to ring the bell, and the Count had been furious for a week. Only the intercession of Father Bright, backed by the Bishop himself, had saved the sacristan from doing a turn in the dungeons of Castle D'Evreux.

Sir Pierre stepped out into the corridor, walked along the carpeted flagstones and cast a practiced eye around him as he walked. These old castles were difficult to keep clean, and my lord the Count was fussy about nitre collecting in the seams between the stones of the walls. All appeared quite in order, which was a good thing. My lord the Count had been making a night of it last evening, and that always made him the more peevish in the morning. Though he always woke at the Angelus, he did not always wake up sober.

Sir Pierre stopped before a heavy, polished, carved oak door, selected a key from one of the many at his belt and turned it in the lock. Then he went into the elevator and the door locked automatically behind him. He pressed the switch and waited in patient silence as he was lifted up four floors to the Count's personal suite.

By now, my lord the Count would have bathed, shaved and dressed. He would also have poured down an eye-opener consisting of half a water glass of fine Champagne brandy. He would not eat breakfast until eight. The Count had no valet in the strict sense of the term. Sir Reginald Beauvay held that title, but he was never called upon to exercise the more personal functions of his office. The Count did not like to be seen until he was thoroughly presentable.

The elevator stopped. Sir Pierre stepped out into the corridor and walked along it toward the door at the far end. At exactly seven o'clock, he rapped briskly on the great door which bore the gilt-and-polychrome arms of the House D'Evreux.

For the first time in 17 years, there was no answer.

Sir Pierre waited for the growled command to enter for a full minute, unable to believe his ears. Then, almost timidly, he rapped again.

There was still no answer.

Then, bracing himself for the verbal onslaught that would follow if he had erred, Sir Pierre turned the handle and opened the door just as if he had heard the Count's voice telling him to come in.

"Good morning, my lord," he said, as he always had for 17 years.

But the room was empty, and there was no answer.

He looked around the huge room. The morning sunlight streamed in through the high mullioned windows and spread a diamond-checkered pattern across the tapestry on the far wall, lighting up the brilliant hunting scene in a blaze of color.

"My lord?"

Nothing. Not a sound.

The bedroom door was open. Sir Pierre walked across to it and looked in.

He saw immediately why my lord the Count had not answered, and that, indeed, he would never answer again.

My lord the Count lay flat on his back, his arms spread wide, his eyes staring at the ceiling. He was still clad in his gold and scarlet evening clothes. But the great stain on the front of his coat was not the same shade of scarlet as the rest of the cloth, and the stain had a bullet hole in its center.

Sir Pierre looked at him without moving for a long moment. Then he stepped over, knelt and touched one of the Count's hands with the back of his own. It was quite cool. He had been dead for hours.

"I knew someone would do you in sooner or later, my lord," said Sir Pierre, almost regretfully.

Then he rose from his kneeling position and walked out without another look at his dead lord. He locked the door of the suite, pocketed the key and went back downstairs in the elevator.

Mary, Lady Duncan stared out of the window at the morning sunlight and wondered what to do. The Angelus bell had awakened her from a fitful sleep in her chair, and she knew that, as a guest at Castle D'Evreux, she would be expected to appear at Mass again this morning. But how could she? How could she face the Sacramental Lord on the altar—to say nothing of taking the Blessed Sacrament Itself.

Still, it would look all the more conspicuous if she did not show up this morning after having made it a point to attend every morning with Lady Alice during the first four days of this visit.

She turned and glanced at the locked and barred door of the bedroom. *He* would not be expected to come. Laird Duncan used his wheelchair as an excuse, but since he had taken up black magic as a hobby he had, she suspected, been actually afraid to go anywhere near a church.

If only she hadn't lied to him! But how could she have told the truth? That would have been worse—infinitely worse. And now, because of that lie, he was locked in his bedroom doing only God and the Devil knew what.

If only he would come out. If he would only stop whatever it was he had been doing for all these long hours—or at least finish it! Then they could leave Evreux, make some excuse—any excuse—to get away. One of them could feign sickness. Anything, anything to get them out of France, across the Channel and back to Scotland, where they would be safe!

She looked back out of the window, across the courtyard, at the towering stone walls of the Great Keep and at the high window that opened into the suite of Edouard, Count D'Evreux.

Last night she had hated him, but no longer. Now there was only room in her heart for fear.

She buried her face in her hands and cursed herself for a fool. There were no tears left for weeping—not after the long night.

Behind her, she heard the sudden noise of the door being unlocked, and she turned.

Laird Duncan of Duncan opened the door and wheeled himself out. He was followed by a malodorous gust of vapor from the room he had just left. Lady Duncan stared at him.

He looked older than he had last night, more haggard and worn, and there was something in his eyes she did not like. For a moment he said nothing. Then he wet his lips with the tip of his tongue. When he spoke, his voice sounded dazed.

"There is nothing to fear anymore," he said. "Nothing to fear at all."

The Reverend Father James Valois Bright, Vicar of the Chapel of Saint-Esprit, had as his flock the several hundred inhabitants of the Castle D'Evreux. As such, he was the ranking priest—socially, not hierarchically—in the country. Not counting the Bishop and the Chapter at the Cathedral, of course. But such knowledge did little good for the Father's peace of mind. The turnout of his flock was abominably small for its size—especially for weekday Masses. The Sunday Masses were well attended, of course; Count D'Evreux was there punctually at nine every Sunday, and he had a habit of counting the house. But he never showed up on weekdays, and his laxity had allowed a certain further laxity to filter down through the ranks.

The great consolation was Lady Alice D'Evreux. She was a plain, simple girl, nearly 20 years younger than her brother, the Count, and quite his opposite in every way. She was quiet where he was thundering, self-effacing where he was flamboyant, temperate where he was drunken, and chaste where he was—

Father Bright brought his thoughts to a full halt for a moment. He had, he reminded himself, no right to make judgments of that sort. He was not, after all, the Count's confessor; the Bishop was.

Besides, he should have his mind on his prayers just now.

He paused and was rather surprised to notice that he had already put on his alb, amice and girdle, and he was aware that his lips had formed the words of the prayer as he had donned each of them.

Habit, he thought, *can be destructive to the contemplative faculty.*

He glanced around the sacristy. His server, the young son of the Count of Saint Brieuc, sent here to complete his education as a gentleman who would some day be the King's Governor of one of the most important counties in Brittany, was pulling his surplice down over his head. The clock said 7:11.

Father Bright forced his mind heavenward and repeated silently the vesting prayers that his lips had formed meaninglessly, this time putting his full intentions behind them. Then he added a short mental prayer asking God to forgive him for allowing his thoughts to stray in such a manner.

He opened his eyes and reached for his chasuble just as the sacristy door opened and Sir Pierre, the Count's Privy Secretary, stepped in.

"I must speak to you, Father," he said in a low voice. And, glancing at the young De Saint-Brieuc, he added: "Alone."

Normally, Father Bright would have reprimanded anyone who presumed to break into the sacristy as he was vesting for Mass, but he knew that Sir Pierre would never interrupt without good reason. He nodded and went outside in the corridor that led to the altar.

"What is it, Pierre?" he asked.

"My lord the Count is dead. Murdered."

After the first momentary shock, Father Bright realized that the news was not, after all, totally unexpected. Somewhere in the back of his mind, it seemed he had always known that the Count would die by violence long before debauchery ruined his health.

"Tell me about it," he said quietly.

Sir Pierre reported exactly what he had done and what he had seen.

"Then I locked the door and came straight here," he told the priest.

"Who else has the key to the Count's suite?" Father Bright asked.

"No one but my lord himself," Sir Pierre answered, "at least as far as I know."

"Where is his key?"

"Still in the ring at his belt. I noticed that particularly."

"Very good. We'll leave it locked. You're certain the body was cold?"

"Cold and waxy, Father."

"Then he's been dead many hours."

"Lady Alice will have to be told," Sir Pierre said.

Father Bright nodded. "Yes. The Countess D'Evreux must be informed of her succession to the County Seat." He could tell by the sudden momentary blank look that came over Sir Pierre's face that the Privy Secretary had not yet realized fully the implications of the Count's death. "I'll tell her, Pierre. She should be in her pew by now. Just step into the church and tell her quietly that I want to speak to her. Don't tell her anything else."

"I understand, Father," said Sir Pierre.

There were only 25 or 30 people in the pews—most of them women—but Alice, Countess D'Evreux was not one of them. Sir Pierre walked quietly and unobtrusively down the side aisle and out into the narthex. She was standing there, just inside the main door, adjusting the black lace mantilla about her head, as though she had just come in from outside. Suddenly, Sir Pierre was very glad he would not have to be the one to break the news. She looked rather sad, as always, her plain face unsmil-

173

ing. The jutting nose and square chin which had given her brother the Count a look of aggressive handsomeness only made her look very solemn and rather sexless, although she had a magnificent figure.

"My lady," Sir Pierre said, stepping toward her, "the Reverend Father would like to speak to you before Mass. He's waiting at the sacristy door."

She held her rosary clutched tightly to her breast and gasped. Then she said, "Oh. Sir Pierre. I'm sorry; you quite surprised me. I didn't see you."

"My apologies, my lady."

"It's all right. My thoughts were elsewhere. Will you take me to the good Father?"

Father Bright heard their footsteps coming down the corridor before he saw them. He was a little fidgety because Mass was already a minute overdue. It should have started promptly at 7:15.

The new Countess D'Evreux took the news calmly, as he had known she would. After a pause, she crossed herself and said: "May his soul rest in peace. I will leave everything in your hands, Father, Sir Pierre. What are we to do?"

"Pierre must get on the teleson to Rouen immediately and report the matter to His Highness. I will announce your brother's death and ask for prayers for his soul—but I think I need say nothing about the manner of his death. There is no need to arouse any more speculation and fuss than necessary."

"Very well," said the Countess. "Come, Sir Pierre; I will speak to the Duke, my cousin, myself."

"Yes, my lady."

Father Bright returned to the sacristy, opened the missal, and changed the placement of the ribbons. Today was an ordinary Feria; a Votive Mass would not be forbidden by the rubrics. The clock said 7:17. He turned to young De Saint-Brieuc, who was waiting respectfully. "Quickly, my son—go and get the unbleached beeswax candles and put them on the altar. Be sure you light them before you put out the white ones. Hurry, now; I will be ready by the time you come back. Oh, yes—and change the altar frontal. Put on the black."

"Yes, Father." And the lad was gone.

Father Bright folded the green chasuble and returned it to the drawer, then took out the black one. He would say

174

a Requiem for the Souls of All the Faithful Departed—
and hope that the Count was among them.

His Royal Highness, the Duke of Normandy, looked
over the official letter his secretary had just typed for him.
It was addressed to *Serenissimo Domino Nostro Iohanni
Quarto, Dei Gratia, Angliae, Franciae, Scotiae, Hiberniae,
Novae Angliae et Novae Franciae Regi, Imperatori, Fidei
Defensori,* . . . "Our Most Serene Lord, John IV, by the
Grace of God King and Emperor of England, France,
Scotland, Ireland, New England and New France, De-
fender of the Faith, . . ."

It was a routine matter; simple notification to his
brother, the King, that His Majesty's most faithful servant,
Edouard, Count of Evreux, had departed this life, and
asking His Majesty's confirmation of the Count's heir-at-
law, Alice, Countess of Evreux as his lawful successor.

His Highness finished reading, nodded and scrawled his
signature at the bottom: *Ricardus Dux Normaniae.*

Then, on a separate piece of paper, he wrote: "Dear
John, May I suggest you hold up on this for a while?
Edouard was a lecher and a slob, and I have no doubt he
got everything he deserved, but we have no notion who
killed him. For any evidence I have to the contrary, it
might have been Alice who pulled the trigger. I will send
you full particulars as soon as I have them. With much
love, Your brother and servant, Richard."

He put both papers into a prepared envelope and sealed
it. He wished he could have called the King on the teleson, but no one had yet figured out how to get the wires
across the channel.

He looked absently at the sealed envelope, his handsome blond features thoughtful. The House of Plantagenet
had endured for eight centuries, and the blood of Henry
of Anjou ran thin in its veins, but the Norman strain was
as strong as ever, having been replenished over the centuries by fresh infusions from Norwegian and Danish
princesses. Richard's mother, Queen Helga, wife to His
late Majesty, Charles III, spoke very few words of Anglo-
French, and those with a heavy Norse accent.

Nevertheless, there was nothing Scandinavian in the
language, manner or bearing of Richard, Duke of Normandy. Not only was he a member of the oldest and most
powerful ruling family of Europe, but he bore a Christian
name that was distinguished even in that family. Seven

Kings of the Empire had borne the name, and most of them had been good Kings—if not always "good" men in the nicey-nicey sense of the word. Even old Richard I, who'd been pretty wild during the first 40-odd years of his life, had settled down to do a magnificent job of kinging for the next 20 years. The long and painful recovery from the wound he'd received at the Siege of Chaluz had made a change in him for the better.

There was a chance that Duke Richard might be called upon to uphold the honor of that name as King. By law, Parliament must elect a Plantagenet as King in the event of the death of the present sovereign, and while the election of one of the King's two sons, the Prince of Britain and the Duke of Lancaster, was more likely than the election of Richard, he was certainly not eliminated from the succession.

Meantime, he would uphold the honor of his name as Duke of Normandy.

Murder had been done; therefore justice must be done. The Count D'Evreux had been known for his stern but fair justice almost as well as he had been known for his profligacy. And, just as his pleasures had been without temperance, so his justice had been untempered by mercy. Whoever had killed him would find both justice and mercy —insofar as Richard had it within his power to give it.

Although he did not formulate it in so many words, even mentally, Richard was of the opinion that some debauched woman or cuckolded man had fired the fatal shot. Thus he found himself inclining toward mercy before he knew anything substantial about the case at all.

Richard dropped the letter he was holding into the special mail pouch that would be placed aboard the evening trans-Channel packet, and then turned in his chair to look at the lean, middle-aged man working at a desk across the room.

"My lord Marquis," he said thoughtfully.

"Yes, Your Highness?" said the Marquis of Rouen, looking up.

"How true are the stories one has heard about the late Count?"

"True, Your Highness?" the Marquis said thoughtfully. "I would hesitate to make any estimate of percentages. Once a man gets a reputation like that, the number of his reputed sins quickly surpasses the number of actual ones. Doubtless many of the stories one hears are of whole

176

cloth; others may have only a slight basis in fact. On the other hand, it is highly likely that there are many of which we have never heard. It is absolutely certain, however, that he has acknowledged seven illegitimate sons, and I daresay he has ignored a few daughters—and these, mind you, with unmarried women. His adulteries would be rather more difficult to establish, but I think your Highness can take it for granted that such escapades were far from uncommon."

He cleared his throat and then added. "If Your Highness is looking for motive, I fear there is a superabundance of persons with motive."

"I see," the Duke said. "Well, we will wait and see what sort of information Lord Darcy comes up with." He looked up at the clock. "They should be there by now."

Then, as if brushing further thoughts on that subject from his mind, he went back to work, picking up a new sheaf of state papers from his desk.

The Marquis watched him for a moment and smiled a little to himself. The young Duke took his work seriously, but was well-balanced about it. A little inclined to be romantic—but aren't we all at 19? There was no doubt of his ability, nor of his nobility. The Royal Blood of England always came through.

"My lady," said Sir Pierre gently, "the Duke's Investigators have arrived."

My Lady Alice, Countess D'Evreux, was seated in a gold-brocade upholstered chair in the small receiving room off the Great Hall. Standing near her, looking very grave, was Father Bright. Against the blaze of color on the walls of the room, the two of them stood out like ink blots. Father Bright wore his normal clerical black, unrelieved except for the pure white lace at collar and cuffs. The Countess wore unadorned black velvet, a dress which she had had to have altered hurriedly by her dressmaker; she had always hated black and owned only the mourning she had worn when her mother died eight years before. The somber looks on their faces seemed to make the black blacker.

"Show them in, Sir Pierre," the Countess said calmly.

Sir Pierre opened the door wider, and three men entered. One was dressed as one gently born; the other two wore the livery of the Duke of Normandy.

The gentleman bowed. "I am Lord Darcy, Chief Criminal Investigator for His Highness, the Duke, and your servant, my lady." He was a tall, brown-haired man with a rather handsome, lean face. He spoke Anglo-French with a definite English accent.

"My pleasure, Lord Darcy," said the Countess. "This is our vicar, Father Bright."

"Your servant, Reverend Sir." Then he presented the two men with him. The first was a scholarly-looking, graying man wearing pince-nez glasses with gold rims, Dr. Pateley, Physician. The second, a tubby, red-faced, smiling man, was Master Sean O Lochlainn, Sorcerer.

As soon as Master Sean was presented he removed a small, leather-bound folder from his belt pouch and proffered it to the priest. "My license, Reverend Father."

Father Bright took it and glanced over it. It was the usual thing, signed and sealed by the Archbishop of Rouen. The law was rather strict on that point; no sorcerer could practice without the permission of the Church, and a license was given only after careful examination for orthodoxy of practice.

"It seems to be quite in order, Master Sean," said the priest, handing the folder back. The tubby little sorcerer bowed his thanks and returned the folder to his belt pouch.

Lord Darcy had a notebook in his hand. "Now, unpleasant as it may be, we shall have to check on a few facts." He consulted his notes, then looked up at Sir Pierre. "You, I believe, discovered the body?"

"That is correct, your lordship."

"How long ago was this?"

Sir Pierre glanced at his wrist watch. It was 9:55. "Not quite three hours ago, your lordship."

"At what time, precisely?"

"I rapped on the door precisely at seven, and went in a minute or two later—say 7:01 or 7:02."

"How do you know the time so exactly?"

"My lord the Count," said Sir Pierre with some stiffness, "insisted upon exact punctuality. I have formed the habit of referring to my watch regularly."

"I see. Very good. Now, what did you do then?"

Sir Pierre described his actions briefly.

"The door to his suite was not locked, then?" Lord Darcy asked.

"No, sir."

"You did not expect it to be locked?"

"No, sir. It has not been for 17 years."

178

Lord Darcy raised one eyebrow in a polite query. "Never?"

"Not at seven o'clock, your lordship. My lord the Count always rose promptly at six and unlocked the door before seven."

"He did lock it at night, then?"

"Yes, sir."

Lord Darcy looked thoughtful and made a note, but he said nothing more on that subject. "When you left, you locked the door?"

"That is correct, your lordship."

"And it has remained locked ever since?"

Sir Pierre hesitated and glanced at Father Bright. The priest said: "At 8:15, Sir Pierre and I went in. I wished to view the body. We touched nothing. We left at 8:20."

Master Sean O Lochlainn looked agitated. "Er . . . excuse me, Reverend Sir. You didn't give him Holy Unction, I hope?"

"No," said Father Bright. "I thought it would be better to delay that until after the authorities had seen the . . . er . . . scene of the crime. I wouldn't want to make the gathering of evidence any more difficult than necessary."

"Quite right," murmured Lord Darcy.

"No blessings, I trust, Reverend Sir?" Master Sean persisted. "No exorcisms or—"

"Nothing," Father Bright interrupted somewhat testily. "I believe I crossed myself when I saw the body, but nothing more."

"Crossed *yourself,* sir. Nothing else?"

"No."

"Well, that's all right, then. Sorry to be so persistent, Reverend Sir, but any miasma of evil that may be left around is a very important clue, and it shouldn't be dispersed until it's been checked, you see."

"*Evil?*" My lady the Countess looked shocked.

"Sorry, my lady, but—" Master Sean began contritely.

But Father Bright interrupted by speaking to the Countess. "Don't distress yourself, my daughter; these men are only doing their duty."

"Of course. I understand. It's just that it's so—" She shuddered delicately.

Lord Darcy cast Master Sean a warning look, then asked politely, "Has my lady seen the deceased?"

"No," she said. "I will, however, if you wish."

179

"We'll see," said Lord Darcy. "Perhaps it won't be necessary. May we go up to the suite now?"

"Certainly," the Countess said. "Sir Pierre, if you will?"

"Yes, my lady."

As Sir Pierre unlocked the emblazoned door, Lord Darcy said: "Who else sleeps on this floor?"

"No one else, your lordship," Sir Pierre said. "The entire floor is . . . *was* . . . reserved for my lord the Count."

"Is there any way up besides that elevator?"

Sir Pierre turned and pointed toward the other end of the short hallway. "That leads to the staircase," he said, pointing to a massive oaken door, "but it's kept locked at all times. And, as you can see, there is a heavy bar across it. Except for moving furniture in and out or something like that, it's never used."

"No other way up or down, then?"

Sir Pierre hesitated. "Well, yes, your lordship, there is. I'll show you."

"A secret stairway?"

"Yes, your lordship."

"Very well. We'll look at it after we've seen the body."

Lord Darcy, having spent an hour on the train down from Rouen, was anxious to see the cause of all the trouble at last.

He lay in the bedroom, just as Sir Pierre and Father Bright had left him.

"If you please, Dr. Pateley," said his lordship.

He knelt on one side of the corpse and watched carefully while Pateley knelt on the other side and looked at the face of the dead man. Then he touched one of the hands and tried to move an arm. "Rigor has set in—even to the fingers. Single bullet hole. Rather small caliber—I should say a .28 or .34—hard to tell until I've probed out the bullet. Looks like it went right through the heart, though. Hard to tell about powder burns; the blood has soaked the clothing and dried. Still, these specks . . . hm-m-m. Yes. Hm-m-m."

Lord Darcy's eyes took in everything, but there was little enough to see on the body itself. Then his eye was caught by something that gave off a golden gleam. He stood up and walked over to the great canopied four-poster bed, then he was on his knees again, peering under it. A coin? No.

He picked it up carefully and looked at it. A button. Gold, intricately engraved in an Arabesque pattern, and set in the center with a single diamond. How long had it lain there? Where had it come from? Not from the Count's clothing, for his buttons were smaller, engraved with his arms, and had no gems. Had a man or a woman dropped it? There was no way of knowing at this stage of the game.

Darcy turned to Sir Pierre. "When was this room last cleaned?"

"Last evening, your lordship," the secretary said promptly. "My lord was always particular about that. The suite was always to be swept and cleaned during the dinner hour."

"Then this must have rolled under the bed at some time after dinner. Do you recognize it? The design is distinctive."

The Privy Secretary looked carefully at the button in the palm of Lord Darcy's hand without touching it. "I . . . I hesitate to say," he said at last. "It looks like . . . but I'm not sure—"

"Come, come, Chevalier! Where do you think you *might* have seen it? Or one like it." There was a sharpness in the tone of his voice.

"I'm not trying to conceal anything, your lordship," Sir Pierre said with equal sharpness. "I said I was not sure. I still am not, but it can be checked easily enough. If your lordship will permit me—" He turned and spoke to Dr. Pateley, who was still kneeling by the body. "May I have my lord the Count's keys, doctor?"

Pateley glanced up at Lord Darcy, who nodded silently. The physician detached the keys from the belt and handed them to Sir Pierre.

The Privy Secretary looked at them for a moment, then selected a small gold key. "This is it," he said, separating it from the others on the ring. "Come with me, your lordship."

Darcy followed him across the room to a broad wall covered with a great tapestry that must have dated back to the 16th century. Sir Pierre reached behind it and pulled a cord. The entire tapestry slid aside like a panel, and Lord Darcy saw that it was supported on a track some ten feet from the floor. Behind it was what looked at first like ordinary oak paneling, but Sir Pierre fitted the small key into an inconspicuous hole and turned. Or, rather, tried to turn.

"That's odd," said Sir Pierre. "It's not locked!"

He took the key out and pressed on the panel, shoving

181

sideways with his hand to move it aside. It slid open to reveal a closet.

The closet was filled with women's clothing of all kinds, and styles.

Lord Darcy whistled soundlessly.

"Try that blue robe, your lordship," the Privy Secretary said. "The one with the—yes, that's the one."

Lord Darcy took it off its hanger. The same buttons. They matched. And there was one missing from the front! Torn off! "Master Sean!" he called without turning.

Master Sean came with a rolling walk. He was holding an oddly-shaped bronze thing in his hand that Sir Pierre didn't quite recognize. The sorcerer was muttering. "Evil, that there is! Faith, and the vibrations are all over the place. Yes, my lord?"

"Check this dress and the button when you get round to it. I want to know when the two parted company."

"Yes, my lord." He draped the robe over one arm and dropped the button into a pouch at his belt. "I can tell you one thing, my lord. You talk about an evil miasma, this room has got it!" He held up the object in his hand. "There's an underlying background—something that has been here for years, just seeping in. But on top of that, there's a hellish big blast of it superimposed. Fresh it is, and very strong."

"I shouldn't be surprised, considering there was murder done here last night—or very early this morning," said Lord Darcy.

"Hm-m-m, yes. Yes, my lord, the death is there—but there's something else. Something I can't place."

"You can tell that just by holding that bronze cross in your hand?" Sir Pierre asked interestedly.

Master Sean gave him a friendly scowl. " 'Tisn't quite a cross, sir. This is what is known as a *crux ansata*. The ancient Egyptians called it an *ankh*. Notice the loop at the top instead of the straight piece your true cross has. Now, your true cross—if it were properly energized, blessed, d'ye see—your true cross would tend to dissipate the evil. The *ankh* merely vibrates to evil because of the closed loop at the top, which makes a return circuit. And it's not energized by blessing, but by another . . . um . . . spell."

"Master Sean, we have a murder to investigate," said Lord Darcy.

The sorcerer caught the tone of his voice and nodded quickly. "Yes, my lord." And he walked rollingly away.

"Now where's that secret stairway you mentioned, Sir Pierre?" Lord Darcy asked.

"This way, your lordship."

He led Lord Darcy to a wall at right angles to the outer wall and slid back another tapestry.

"Good Heavens," Darcy muttered, "does he have something concealed behind every arras in the place?" But he didn't say it loud enough for the Privy Secretary to hear.

This time, what greeted them was a solid-seeming stone wall. But Sir Pierre pressed in on one small stone, and a section of the wall swung back, exposing a stairway.

"Oh, yes," Darcy said. "I see what he did. This is the old spiral stairway that goes round the inside of the Keep. There are two doorways at the bottom. One opens into the courtyard, the other is a postern gate through the curtain wall to the outside—but that was closed up in the 16th century, so the only way out is into the courtyard."

"Your lordship knows Castle D'Evreux, then?" Sir Pierre said. Sir Pierre had no recollection of Darcy's having been in the Castle before.

"Only by the plans in the Royal Archives. But I have made it a point to—" He stopped. "Dear me," he interrupted himself mildly, "what is that?"

"That" was something that had been hidden by the arras until Sir Pierre had slid it aside, and was still showing only a part of itself. It lay on the floor a foot or so from the secret door.

Darcy knelt down and pulled the tapestry back from the object. "Well, well. A .28 two-shot pocket gun. Gold-chased, beautifully engraved, mother-of-pearl handle. A regular gem." He picked it up and examined it closely. "One shot fired."

He stood up and showed it to Sir Pierre. "Ever see it before?"

The Privy Secretary looked at the weapon closely. Then he shook his head. "Not that I recall, your lordship. It certainly isn't one of the Count's guns."

"You're certain?"

"Quite certain, your lordship. I'll show you the gun collection if you want. My lord the Count didn't like tiny guns like that; he preferred a larger caliber. He would never have owned what he considered a toy."

"Well, we'll have to look into it." He called over Master Sean again and gave the gun into his keeping. "And keep your eyes open for anything else of interest, Master Sean. So far, everything of interest besides the late Count himself has been hiding under beds or behind arrases. Check everything. Sir Pierre and I are going for a look down this stairway."

The stairway was gloomy, but enough light came in through the arrow slits spaced at intervals along the outer wall to illuminate the interior. It spiraled down between the inner and outer walls of the Great Keep, making four complete circuits before it reached ground level. Lord Darcy looked carefully at the steps, the walls and even the low, arched overhead as he and Sir Pierre went down.

After the first circuit, on the floor beneath the Count's suite, he stopped. "There was a door here," he said, pointing to a rectangular area in the inner wall.

"Yes, your lordship. There used to be an opening at every floor, but they were all sealed off. It's quite solid, as you can see."

"Where would they lead if they were open?"

"The county offices. My own office, the clerk's offices, the constabulary on the first floor. Below are the dungeons. My lord the Count was the only one who lived in the Keep itself. The rest of the household live above the Great Hall."

"What about guests?"

"They're usually housed in the east wing. We only have two house guests at the moment. Laird and Lady Duncan have been with us for four days."

"I see." They went down perhaps four more steps before Lord Darcy asked quietly, "Tell me, Sir Pierre, were you privy to *all* of Count D'Evreux's business?"

Another four steps down before Sir Pierre answered. "I understand what your lordship means," he said. Another two steps. "No, I was not. I was aware that my lord the Count engaged in certain . . . er . . . shall we say, liaisons with members of the opposite sex. However—"

He paused, and in the gloom Lord Darcy could see his lips tighten. "However," he continued, "I did not procure for my lord, if that is what you're driving at. I am not and never have been a pimp."

"I didn't intend to suggest that you had, good knight," said Lord Darcy in a tone that strongly implied that the thought had actually never crossed his mind. "Not at all. But certainly there is a difference between 'aiding and abetting' and simple knowledge of what is going on."

"Oh. Yes. Yes, of course. Well, one cannot, of course,

be the secretary-in-private of a gentleman such as my lord the Count for 17 years without knowing something of what is going on, you're right. Yes. Yes. Hm-m-m."

Lord Darcy smiled to himself. Not until this moment had Sir Pierre realized how much he actually *did* know. In loyalty to his lord, he had literally kept his eyes shut for 17 years.

"I realize," Lord Darcy said smoothly, "that a gentleman would never implicate a lady nor besmirch the reputation of another gentleman without due cause and careful consideration. However,"—like the knight, he paused a moment before going on—"although we are aware that he was not discreet, was he particular?"

"If you mean by that, did he confine his attentions to those of gentle birth, your lordship, then I can say, no he did not. If you mean did he confine his attentions to the gentler sex, then I can only say that, as far as I know, he did."

"I see. That explains the closet full of clothes."

"Beg pardon, your lordship?"

"I mean that if a girl or woman of the lower classes were to come here, he would have proper clothing for them to wear—in spite of the sumptuary laws to the contrary."

"Quite likely, your lordship. He was most particular about clothing. Couldn't stand a woman who was sloppily dressed or poorly dressed."

"In what way?"

"Well. Well, for instance, I recall once that he saw a very pretty peasant girl. She was dressed in the common style, of course, but she was dressed neatly and prettily. My lord took a fancy to her. He said, 'Now there's a lass who knows how to wear clothes. Put her in decent apparel, and she'd pass for a princess.' But a girl, who had a pretty face and a fine figure, made no impression on him unless she wore her clothing well, if you see what I mean, your lordship."

"Did you never know him to fancy a girl who dressed in an offhand manner?" Lord Darcy asked.

"Only among the gently born, your lordship. He'd say, 'Look at Lady So-and-so! Nice wench, if she'd let me teach her how to dress.' You might say, your lordship, that a woman could be dressed commonly or sloppily, but not both."

185

"Judging by the stuff in that closet," Lord Darcy said, "I should say that the late Count had excellent taste in feminine dress."

Sir Pierre considered. "H-m-m. Well, now, I wouldn't exactly say so, your lordship. He knew *how* clothes should be worn, yes. But he couldn't pick out a woman's gown of his accord. He could choose his own clothing with impeccable taste, but he'd not any real notion of how a woman's clothing should go, if you see what I mean. All he knew was how good clothing should be worn. But he knew nothing about design for women's clothing."

"Then how did he get that closet full of clothes?" Lord Darcy asked, puzzled.

Sir Pierre chuckled. "Very simply, your lordship. He knew that the Lady Alice had good taste, so he secretly instructed that each piece that Lady Alice ordered should be made in duplicate. With small variations, of course. I'm certain my lady wouldn't like it if she knew."

"I dare say not," said Lord Darcy thoughtfully.

"Here is the door to the courtyard," said Sir Pierre. "I doubt that it has been opened in broad daylight for many years." He selected a key from the ring of the late Count and inserted it into a keyhole. The door swung back, revealing a large crucifix attached to its outer surface. Lord Darcy crossed himself. "Lord in heaven," he said softly, "what is this?"

He looked out into a small shrine. It was walled off from the courtyard and had a single small entrance some ten feet from the doorway. There were four *prie-dieus*— small kneeling benches—ranged in front of the doorway.

"If I may explain, your lordship—" Sir Pierre began.

"No need to," Lord Darcy said in a hard voice. "It's rather obvious. My lord the Count was quite ingenious. This is a relatively newly-built shrine. Four walls and a crucifix against the castle wall. Anyone could come in here, day or night, for prayer. No one who came in would be suspected." He stepped out into the small enclosure and swung around to look at the door. "And when that door is closed, there is no sign that there is a door behind the crucifix. If a woman came in here, it would be assumed that she came for prayer. But if she knew of that door—" His voice trailed off.

"Yes, your lordship," said Sir Pierre. "I did not approve, but I was in no position to disapprove."

"I understand." Lord Darcy stepped out to the doorway

186

of the little shrine and took a quick glance about. "Then anyone within the castle walls could come in here," he said.

"Yes, your lordship."

"Very well. Let's go back up."

In the small office which Lord Darcy and his staff had been assigned while conducting the investigation, three men watched while a fourth conducted a demonstration on a table in the center of the room.

Master Sean O Lochlainn held up an intricately engraved gold button with an Arabesque pattern and a diamond set in the center.

He looked at the other three. "Now, my lord, your Reverence, and colleague Doctor, I call your attention to this button."

Dr. Pateley smiled and Father Bright looked stern. Lord Darcy merely stuffed tobacco—imported from the southern New England counties on the Gulf—into a German-made porcelain pipe. He allowed Master Sean a certain amount of flamboyance; good sorcerers were hard to come by.

"Will you hold the robe, Dr. Pateley? Thank you. Now, stand back. That's it. Thank you. Now, I place the button on the table, a good ten feet from the robe." Then he muttered something under his breath and dusted a bit of powder on the button. He made a few passes over it with his hands, paused, and looked up at Father Bright. "If you will, Reverend Sir?"

Father Bright solemnly raised his right hand, and, as he made the Sign of the Cross, said: "May this demonstration, O God, be in strict accord with the truth, and may the Evil One not in any way deceive us who are witnesses thereto. In the Name of the Father and of the Son and of the Holy Spirit. Amen."

"Amen," the other three chorused.

Master Sean crossed himself, then muttered something under his breath.

The button leaped from the table, slammed itself against the robe which Dr. Pateley held before him, and stuck there as though it had been sewed on by an expert.

"Ha!" said Master Sean. "As I thought!" He gave the other three men a broad, beaming smile. "The two were definitely connected!"

Lord Darcy looked bored. "Time?" he asked.

187

"In a moment, my lord," Master Sean said apologetically. "In a moment." While the other three watched, the sorcerer went through more spells with the button and the robe, although none were so spectacular as the first demonstration. Finally, Master Sean said: "About 11:30 last night they were torn apart, my lord. But I shouldn't like to make it any more definite than to say between eleven and midnight. The speed with which it returned to its place shows it was ripped off very rapidly, however."

"Very good," said Lord Darcy. "Now the bullet, if you please."

"Yes, my lord. This will have to be a bit different." He took more paraphernalia out of his large, symbol-decorated carpet bag. "The Law of Contagion, gently-born sirs, is a tricky thing to work with. If a man doesn't know how to handle it, he can get himself killed. We had an apprentice o' the Guild back in Cork who might have made a good sorcerer in time. He had the Talent—unfortunately, he didn't have the good sense to go with it. According to the Law of Contagion any two objects which have ever been in contact with each other have an affinity for each other which is directly proportional to the product of the degree of relevancy of the contact and the length of time they were in contact and inversely proportional to the length of time since they have ceased to be in contact." He gave a smiling glance to the priest. "That doesn't apply strictly to relics of the saints, Reverend Sir; there's another factor enters in there, as you know."

As he spoke, the sorcerer was carefully clamping the little handgun into a padded vise so that its barrel was parallel to the surface of the table.

"Anyhow," he went on, "this apprentice, all on his own, decided to get rid of the cockroaches in his house—a simple thing, if one knows how to go about it. So he collected dust from various cracks and crannies about the house, dust which contained, of course, the droppings of the pests. The dust, with the appropriate spells and ingredients, he boiled. It worked fine. The roaches all came down with a raging fever and died. Unfortunately, the clumsy lad had poor laboratory technique. He allowed three drops of his own perspiration to fall into the steaming pot over which he was working, and the resulting fever killed him, too."

By this time, he had put the bullet which Dr. Pateley had removed from the Count's body on a small pedestal

188

so that it was exactly in line with the muzzle of the gun. "There, now," he said softly.

Then he repeated the incantation and the powdering that he had used on the button. As the last syllable was formed by his lips, the bullet vanished with a *ping!* In its vise, the little gun vibrated.

"Ah!" said Master Sean. "No question there, eh? That's the death weapon, all right, my lord. Yes. Time's almost exactly the same as that of the removal of the button. Not more than a few seconds later. Forms a picture, don't it, my lord? His lordship the Count jerks a button off the girl's gown, she outs with a gun and plugs him."

Lord Darcy's handsome face scowled. "Let's not jump to any hasty conclusions, my good Sean. There is no evidence whatever that he was killed by a woman."

"Would a man be wearing that gown, my lord?"

"Possibly," said Lord Darcy. "But who says that anyone was wearing it when the button was removed?"

"Oh." Master Sean subsided into silence. Using a small ramrod, he forced the bullet out of the chamber of the little pistol.

"Father Bright," said Lord Darcy, "will the Countess be serving tea this afternoon?"

The priest looked suddenly contrite. "Good heavens! None of you has eaten yet! I'll see that something is sent up right away, Lord Darcy. In the confusion—"

Lord Darcy held up a hand. "I beg your pardon, Father; that wasn't what I meant. I'm sure Master Sean and Dr. Pateley would appreciate a little something, but I can wait until teatime. What I was thinking was that perhaps the Countess would ask her guests to tea. Does she know Laird and Lady Duncan well enough to ask for their sympathetic presence on such an afternoon as this?"

Father Bright's eyes narrowed a trifle. "I dare say it could be arranged, Lord Darcy. You will be there?"

"Yes—but I may be a trifle late. That will hardly matter at an informal tea."

The priest glanced at his watch. "Four o'clock?"

"I should think that would do it," said Lord Darcy.

Father Bright nodded wordlessly and left the room.

Dr. Pateley took off his pince-nez and polished the lenses carefully with a silk handkerchief. "How long will your spell keep the body incorrupt, Master Sean?" he asked.

"As long as it's relevant. As soon as the case is solved,

or we have enough data to solve the case—as the case may be, heh heh—he'll start to go. I'm not a saint, you know; it takes powerful motivation to keep a body incorrupt for years and years."

Sir Pierre was eyeing the gown that Pateley had put on the table. The button was still in place, as if held there by magnetism. He didn't touch it. "Master Sean, I don't know much about magic," he said, "but can't you find out who was wearing this robe just as easily as you found out that the button matched?"

Master Sean wagged his head in a firm negative. "No, sir. 'Tisn't relevant, sir. The relevancy of the integrated dress-as-a-whole is quite strong. So is that of the seamstress or tailor who made the garment, and that of the weaver who made the cloth. But, except in certain circumstances, the person who wears or wore the garment has little actual relevancy to the garment itself."

"I'm afraid I don't understand," said Sir Pierre, looking puzzled.

"Look at it like this, sir: That gown wouldn't be what it is if the weaver hadn't made the cloth in that particular way. It wouldn't be what it is if the seamstress hadn't cut it in a particular way and sewed it in a specific manner. You follow, sir? Yes. Well, then, the connections between garment-and-weaver and garment-and-seamstress are strongly relevant. But this dress would still be pretty much what it is if it had stayed in the closet instead of being worn. No relevance—or very little. Now, if it were a well-worn garment, that would be different—that is, if it had always been worn by the same person. Then, you see, sir, the garment-as-a-whole is what it is because of the wearing, and the wearer becomes relevant."

He pointed at the little handgun he was still holding in his hand. "Now you take your gun, here, sir. The—"

"It isn't *my* gun." Sir Pierre interrupted firmly.

"I was speaking rhetorically, sir," said Master Sean with infinite patience. "This gun or any other gun in general, if you see what I mean, sir. It's even harder to place the ownership of a gun. Most of the wear on a gun is purely mechanical. It don't matter *who* pulls the trigger, you see, the erosion by the gases produced in the chamber, and the wear caused by the bullet passing through the barrel will be the same. You see, sir, 'tisn't relevant *to the gun* who pulled its trigger or what it's fired at. The bullet's a slightly different matter. To the bullet, it *is* relevant

190

which gun it was fired from and what it hit. All these things simply have to be taken into account, Sir Pierre."

"I see," said the knight. "Very interesting, Master Sean." Then he turned to Lord Darcy. "Is there anything else, your lordship? There's a great deal of county business to be attended to."

Lord Darcy waved a hand. "Not at the moment, Sir Pierre. I understand the pressures of government. Go right ahead."

"Thank you, your lordship. If anything further should be required, I shall be in my office."

As soon as Sir Pierre had closed the door, Lord Darcy held out his hand toward the sorcerer. "Master Sean; the gun."

Master Sean handed it to him. "Ever see one like it before?" he asked, turning it over in his hands.

"Not *exactly* like it, my lord."

"Come, come, Sean; don't be so cautious. I am no sorcerer, but I don't need to know the Laws of Similiarity to be able to recognize an *obvious* similiarity."

"Edinburgh," said Master Sean flatly.

"Exactly. Scottish work. The typical Scot gold work; remarkable beauty. And look at that lock. It has 'Scots' written all over it—and more, 'Edinburgh,' as you said."

Dr. Pateley, having replaced his carefully polished glasses, leaned over and peered at the weapon in Lord Darcy's hand. "Couldn't it be Italian, my lord? Or Moorish? In Moorish Spain, they do work like that."

"No Moorish gunsmith would put a hunting scene on the butt," Lord Darcy said flatly, "and the Italians wouldn't have put heather and thistles in the field surrounding the huntsman."

"But the *FdM* engraved on the barrel," said Dr. Pateley, "indicates the—"

"Ferrari of Milano," said Lord Darcy. "Exactly. But the barrel is of much newer work than the rest. So are the chambers. This is a fairly old gun—50 years old, I'd say. The lock and the butt are still in excellent condition, indicating that it has been well cared for, but frequent usage —or a single accident—could ruin the barrel and require the owner to get a replacement. It was replaced by Ferrari."

"I see," said Dr. Pateley, somewhat humbled.

"If we open the lock . . . Master Sean, hand me your small screwdriver. Thank you. If we open the lock, we will find the name of one of the finest gunsmiths of half a century ago—a man whose name has not yet been forgotten—Hamish Graw of Edinburgh. Ah! There! You see?" They did.

Having satisfied himself on that point, Lord Darcy closed the lock again. "Now, men, we have the gun located. We also know that a guest in this very castle is Laird Duncan of Duncan. The Duncan of Duncan himself. A Scot's laird who was, 15 years ago, His Majesty's Minister Plenipotentiary to the Grand Duchy of Milano. That suggests to me that it would be indeed odd if there were not some connection between Laird Duncan and this gun. Eh?"

"Come, come, Master Sean," said Lord Darcy rather impatiently, "We haven't all the time in the world."

"Patience, my lord; patience," said the little sorcerer calmly. "Can't hurry these things, you know." He was kneeling in front of a large, heavy traveling chest in the bedroom of the guest apartment occupied temporarily by Laird and Lady Duncan, working with the lock. "One position of a lock is just as relevant as the other so you can't work with the bolt. But the pin-tumblers in the cylinder, now, that's a different matter. A lock's built so that the breaks in the tumblers are not related to the surface of the cylinder when the key is out, but there *is* a relation when the key's *in*, so by taking advantage of that relevancy—Ah!"

The lock clicked open.

Lord Darcy raised the lid gently.

"Carefully, my lord!" Master Sean said in a warning voice. "He's got a spell on the thing! Let me do it." He made Lord Darcy stand back and then lifted the lid of the heavy trunk himself. When it was leaning back against the wall, gaping open widely on its hinges, Master Sean took a long look at the trunk and its lid without touching either of them. There was a second lid on the trunk, a thin one obviously operated by a simple bolt.

Master Sean took his sorcerer's staff, a five-foot, heavy rod made of the wood of the quicken tree or mountain ash, and touched the inner lid. Nothing happened. He touched the bolt. Nothing.

"Hm-m-m." Master Sean murmured thoughtfully. He glanced around the room, and his eyes fell on a heavy stone doorstop. "That ought to do it." He walked over, picked it up, and carried it back to the chest. Then he put

192

it on the rim of the chest in such a position that if the lid were to fall it would be stopped by the doorstop.

Then he put his hand in as if to lift the inner lid.

The heavy outer lid swung forward and down of its own accord, moving with blurring speed, and slammed viciously against the doorstop.

Lord Darcy massaged his right wrist gently, as if he felt where the lid would have hit if he had tried to open the inner lid. "Triggered to slam if a human being sticks a hand in there, eh?"

"Or a head, my lord. Not very effectual if you know what to look for. There are better spells than that for guarding things. Now we'll see what his lordship wants to protect so badly that he practices sorcery without a license." He lifted the lid again, and then opened the inner lid. "It's safe now, my lord. *Look at this!*"

Lord Darcy had already seen. Both men looked in silence at the collection of paraphernalia on the first tray of the chest. Master Sean's busy fingers carefully opened the tissue paper packing of one after another of the objects. "A human skull," he said. "Bottles of graveyard earth. Hm-m-m—this one is labeled 'virgin's blood.' And this! A Hand of Glory!"

It was a mummified human hand, stiff and dry and brown, with the fingers partially curled, as though they were holding an invisible ball three inches or so in diameter. On each of the fingertips was a short candlestub. When the hand was placed on its back, it would act as a candelabra.

"That pretty much settles it, eh, Master Sean?" Lord Darcy said.

"Indeed, my lord. At the very least, we can get him for possession of materials. Black magic is a matter of symbolism and intent."

"Very well. I want a complete list of the contents of that chest. Be sure to replace everything as it was and relock the trunk." He tugged thoughtfully at an earlobe. "So Laird Duncan has the Talent, eh? Interesting."

"Aye. But not surprising, my lord," said Master Sean without looking up from his work. "It's in the blood. Some attribute it to the Dedannans, who passed through Scotland before they conquered Ireland 3000 years ago, but, however that may be, the Talent runs strong in the Sons of Gael. It makes me boil to see it misused."

While Master Sean talked, Lord Darcy was prowling

around the room, reminding one of a lean tomcat who was certain that there was a mouse concealed somewhere.

"It'll make Laird Duncan boil if he isn't stopped." Lord Darcy murmured absently.

"Aye, my lord," said Master Sean. "The mental state necessary to use the Talent for black sorcery is such that it invariably destroys the user—but, if he knows what he's doing, a lot of other people are hurt before he finally gets his."

Lord Darcy opened the jewel box on the dresser. The usual traveling jewelry—enough, but not a great choice.

"A man's mind turns in on itself when he's taken up with hatred and thoughts of revenge," Master Sean droned on. "Or, if he's the type who *enjoys* watching others suffer, or the type who doesn't care but is willing to do anything for gain, then his mind is already warped and the misuse of the Talent just makes it worse."

Lord Darcy found what he was looking for in a drawer, just underneath some neatly folded lingerie. A small holster, beautifully made of Florentine leather, gilded and tooled. He didn't need Master Sean's sorcery to tell him that the little pistol fit it like a glove.

Father Bright felt as though he had been walking a tightrope for hours. Laird and Lady Duncan had been talking in low, controlled voices that betrayed an inner nervousness, but Father Bright realized that he and the Countess had been doing the same thing. The Duncan of Duncan had offered his condolences on the death of the late Count with the proper air of suppressed sorrow, as had Mary, Lady Duncan. The Countess had accepted them solemnly and with gratitude. But Father Bright was well aware that no one in the room—possibly, he thought, no one in the world—regretted the Count's passing.

Laird Duncan sat in his wheelchair, his sharp Scots features set in a sad smile that showed an intent to be affable even though great sorrow weighed heavily upon him. Father Bright noticed it and realized that his own face had the same sort of expression. No one was fooling anyone else, of that the priest was certain—but for anyone to admit it would be the most boorish breach of etiquette. But there was a haggardness, a look of increased age about the Laird's countenance that Father Bright did not like. His priestly intuition told him clearly that there was a turmoil of emotion in the Scotsman's mind that was . . . well, *evil* was the only word for it.

Lady Duncan was, for the most part, silent. In the past 15 minutes, since she and her husband had come to the informal tea, she had spoken scarcely a dozen words. Her face was masklike, but there was the same look of haggardness about her eyes as there was in her husband's face. But the priest's empathic sense told him that the emotion here was fear, simple and direct. His keen eyes had noticed that she wore a shade too much make-up. She had almost succeeded in covering up the faint bruise on her right cheek, but not completely.

My lady the Countess D'Evreux was all sadness and unhappiness, but there was neither fear nor evil there. She smiled politely and talked quietly. Father Bright would have been willing to bet that not one of the four of them would remember a word that had been spoken.

Father Bright had placed his chair so that he could keep an eye on the open doorway and the long hall that led in from the Great Keep. He hoped Lord Darcy would hurry. Neither of the guests had been told that the Duke's Investigator was here, and Father Bright was just a little apprehensive about the meeting. The Duncans had not even been told that the Count's death had been murder, but he was certain that they knew.

Father Bright saw Lord Darcy come in through the door at the far end of the hall. He murmured a polite excuse and rose. The other three accepted his excuses with the same politeness and went on with their talk. Father Bright met Lord Darcy in the hall.

"Did you find what you were looking for, Lord Darcy?" the priest asked in a low tone.

"Yes," Lord Darcy said. "I'm afraid we shall have to arrest Laird Duncan."

"Murder?"

"Perhaps. I'm not yet certain of that. But the charge will be black magic. He has all the paraphernalia in a chest in his room. Master Sean reports that a ritual was enacted in the bedroom last night. Of course, that's out of my jurisdiction. You, as a representative of the Church, will have to be the arresting officer." He paused. "You don't seem surprised, Reverence."

"I'm not," Father Bright admitted. "I felt it. You and Master Sean will have to make out a sworn deposition before I can act."

"I understand. Can you do me a favor?"

"If I can."

"Get my lady the Countess out of the room on some pretext or other. Leave me alone with her guests. I do not wish to upset my lady any more than absolutely necessary."

"I think I can do that. Shall we go in together?"

"Why not? But don't mention why I am here. Let them assume I am just another guest."

"Very well."

All three occupants of the room glanced up as Father Bright came in with Lord Darcy. The introductions were made: Lord Darcy humbly begged the pardon of his hostess for his lateness. Father Bright noticed the same sad smile on Lord Darcy's handsome face as the others were wearing.

Lord Darcy helped himself from the buffet table and allowed the Countess to pour him a large cup of hot tea. He mentioned nothing about the recent death. Instead, he turned the conversation toward the wild beauty of Scotland and the excellence of the grouse shooting there.

Father Bright had not sat down again. Instead, he left the room once more. When he returned, he went directly to the Countess and said, in a low, but clearly audible voice: "My lady, Sir Pierre Morlaix has informed me that there are a few matters that require your attention immediately. It will require only a few moments."

My lady the Countess did not hesitate, but made her excuses immediately. "Do finish your tea," she added. "I don't think I shall be long."

Lord Darcy knew the priest would not lie, and he wondered what sort of arrangement had been made with Sir Pierre. Not that it mattered except that Lord Darcy had hoped it would be sufficiently involved for it to keep the Countess busy for at least ten minutes.

The conversation, interrupted but momentarily, returned to grouse.

"I haven't done any shooting since my accident," said Laird Duncan, "but I used to enjoy it immensely. I still have friends up every year for the season."

"What sort of weapon do you prefer for grouse?" Lord Darcy asked.

"A one-inch bore with a modified choke," said the Scot. "I have a pair that I favor. Excellent weapons."

196

"Of Scottish make?"

"No, no. English. Your London gunsmiths can't be beat for shotguns."

"Oh. I thought perhaps your lordship had had all your guns made in Scotland." As he spoke, he took the little pistol out of his coat pocket and put it carefully on the table.

There was a sudden silence, then Laird Duncan said in an angry voice: "What is this? Where did you get that?"

Lord Darcy glanced at Lady Duncan, who had turned suddenly pale. "Perhaps," he said coolly, "Lady Duncan can tell us."

She shook her head and gasped. For a moment, she had trouble in forming words or finding her voice. Finally: "No. No. I know nothing. Nothing."

But Laird Duncan looked at her oddly.

"You do not deny that it is your gun, my lord?" Lord Darcy asked. "Or your wife's, as the case may be."

"*Where did you get it?*" There was a dangerous quality in the Scotsman's voice. He had once been a powerful man, and Lord Darcy could see his shoulder muscles bunching.

"From the late Count D'Evreux's bedroom."

"What was it doing there?" There was a snarl in the Scot's voice, but Lord Darcy had the feeling that the question was as much directed toward Lady Duncan as it was to himself.

"One of the things it was doing there was shooting Count D'Evreux through the heart."

Lady Duncan slumped forward in a dead faint, overturning her teacup. Laird Duncan made a grab at the gun, ignoring his wife. Lord Darcy's hand snaked out and picked up the weapon before the Scot could touch it. "No, no, my lord," he said mildly. "This is evidence in a murder case. We mustn't tamper with King's Evidence."

He wasn't prepared for what happened next. Laird Duncan roared something obscene in Scots Gaelic, put his hands on the arms of his wheelchair, and, with a great thrust of his powerful arms and shoulders, shoved himself up and forward, toward Lord Darcy, across the table from him. His arms swung up toward Lord Darcy's throat as the momentum of his body carried him toward the investigator.

He might have made it, but the weakness of his legs betrayed him. His waist struck the edge of the massive oaken table, and most of his forward momentum was lost. He collapsed forward, his hands still grasping toward the surprised Englishman. His chin came down hard on the table top. Then he slid back, taking the tablecloth and the china and silverware with him. He lay unmoving on the floor. His wife did not even stir except when the tablecloth tugged at her head.

Lord Darcy had jumped back, overturning his chair. He stood on his feet, looking at the two unconscious forms. He hoped he didn't look too much like King MacBeth.

"I don't think there's any permanent damage done to either," said Dr. Pateley an hour later. "Lady Duncan was suffering from shock, of course, but Father Bright brought her around in a hurry. She's a devout woman, I think, even if a sinful one."

"What about Laird Duncan?" Lord Darcy asked.

"Well, that's a different matter. I'm afraid that his back injury was aggravated, and that crack on the chin didn't do him any good. I don't know whether Father Bright can help him or not. Healing takes the cooperation of the patient. I did all I could for him, but I'm just a chirurgeon, not a practitioner of the Healing Art. Father Bright has quite a good reputation in that line, however, and he may be able to do his lordship some good."

Master Sean shook his head dolefully. "His Reverence has the Talent, there's no doubt of that, but now he's pitted against another man who has it—a man whose mind is bent on self-destruction in the long run."

"Well, that's none of my affair," said Dr. Pateley. "I'm just a technician. I'll leave healing up to the Church, where it belongs."

"Master Sean," said Lord Darcy, "there is still a mystery here. We need more evidence. What about the eyes?"

Master Sean blinked. "You mean the picture test, my lord?"

"I do."

"It won't stand up in court, my lord," said the sorcerer.

"I'm aware of that," said Lord Darcy testily.

"Eye test?" Dr. Pateley asked blankly. "I don't believe I understand."

"It's not often used," said Master Sean. "It is a psychic phenomenon that sometimes occurs at the moment of death—especially a violent death. The violent emotional stress causes a sort of backfiring of the mind, if you see

198

what I mean. As a result, the image in the mind of the dying person is returned to the retina. By using the proper sorcery, this image can be developed and the last thing the dead man saw can be brought out.

"But it's a difficult process even under the best of circumstances, and usually the conditions aren't right. In the first place, it doesn't always occur. It never occurs, for instance, when the person is expecting the attack. A man who is killed in a duel, or who is shot after facing the gun for several seconds, has time to adjust to the situation. Also, death must occur almost instantly. If he lingers, even for a few minutes, the effect is lost. And, naturally if the person's eyes are closed at the instant of death, nothing shows up."

"Count D'Evreux's eyes were open," Dr. Pateley said. "They were still open when we found him. How long after death does the image remain?"

"Until the cells of the retina die and lose their identity. Rarely more than 24 hours, usually much less."

"It hasn't been 24 hours yet," said Lord Darcy, "and there is a chance that the Count was taken completely by surprise."

"I must admit, my lord," Master Sean said thoughtfully, "that the conditions seem favorable. I shall attempt it. But don't put any hopes on it, my lord."

"I shan't. Just do your best, Master Sean. If there is a sorcerer in practice who can do the job, it is you."

"Thank you, my lord. I'll get busy on it right away," said the sorcerer with a subdued glow of pride.

Two hours later, Lord Darcy was striding down the corridor of the Great Hall, Master Sean following up as best he could, his *caorthainn*-wood staff in one hand and his big carpet bag in the other. He had asked Father Bright and the Countess D'Evreux to meet him in one of the smaller guest rooms. But the Countess came to meet him.

"My Lord Darcy," she said, her plain face looking worried and unhappy, "is it true that you suspect Laird and Lady Duncan of this murder? Because, if so, I must—"

"No longer, my lady," Lord Darcy cut her off quickly. "I think we can show that neither is guilty of murder —although, of course, the black magic charge must still be held against Laird Duncan."

"I understand," she said, "but—"

"Please, my lady," Lord Darcy interrupted again, "let me explain everything. Come."

Without another word, she turned and led the way to the room where Father Bright was waiting.

The priest stood waiting, his face showing tenseness.

"Please," said Lord Darcy. "Sit down, both of you. This won't take long. My lady, may Master Sean make use of that table over there?"

"Certainly, my lord," the Countess said softly, "certainly."

"Thank you, my lady. Please, please—sit down. This won't take long. Please."

With apparent reluctance, Father Bright and my lady the Countess sat down in two chairs facing Lord Darcy. They paid little attention to what Master Sean O Lochlainn was doing; their eyes were on Lord Darcy.

"Conducting an investigation of this sort is not an easy thing," he began carefully. "Most murder cases could be easily solved by your Chief Man-at-Arms. We find that well-trained county Armsmen, in by far the majority of cases, can solve the mystery easily—and in most cases there is very little mystery. But, by His Imperial Majesty's law, the Chief Man-at-Arms *must* call in a Duke's Investigator if the crime is insoluble or if it involves a member of the aristocracy. For that reason, you were perfectly correct to call His Highness the Duke as soon as murder had been discovered." He leaned back in his chair. "And it has been clear from the first that my lord the late Count was murdered."

Father Bright started to say something, but Lord Darcy cut him off before he could speak. "By 'murder', Reverend Father, I mean that he did not die a natural death—by disease or heart trouble or accident or what-have-you. I should, perhaps, use the word 'homicide.'

"Now the question we have been called upon to answer is simply this: Who was responsible for the homicide?"

The priest and the countess remained silent, looking at Lord Darcy as though he were some sort of divinely inspired oracle.

"As you know . . . pardon me, my lady, if I am blunt . . . the late Count was somewhat of a playboy. No. I will make that stronger. He was a satyr, a lecher; he was a man with a sexual obsession.

"For such a man, if he indulges in his passions—which the late Count most certainly did—there is usually but one end. Unless he is a man who has a winsome personality—which he did not—there will be someone who will hate him enough to kill him. Such a man inevitably leaves behind him a trail of wronged women and wronged men.

"One such person may kill him.

"One such person did.

"But we must find the person who did and determine the extent of his or her guilt. That is my purpose.

"Now, as to the facts. We know that Edouard had a secret stairway which led directly to his suite. Actually, the secret was poorly kept. There were many women—common and noble—who knew of the existence of that stairway and knew how to enter it. If Edouard left the lower door unlocked, anyone could come up that stairway. He had another lock in the door of his bedroom, so only someone who was invited could come in, even if she . . . or he . . . could get into the stairway. He was protected.

"Now here is what actually happened last night. I have evidence, by the way, and I have the confessions of both Laird and Lady Duncan. I will explain how I got those confessions in a moment.

"Primus: Lady Duncan had an assignation with Count D'Evreux last night. She went up the stairway to his room. She was carrying with her a small pistol. She had had an affair with Edouard, and she had been rebuffed. She was furious. But she went to his room.

"He was drunk when she arrived—in one of the nasty moods with which both of you are familiar. She pleaded with him to accept her again as his mistress. He refused. According to Lady Duncan, he said: 'I don't want you! You're not fit to be in the same room with *her!*'

"The emphasis is Lady Duncan's, not my own.

"Furious, she drew a gun—the little pistol which killed him."

The Countess gasped. "But Mary *couldn't* have—"

"Please!" Lord Darcy slammed the palm of his hand on the arm of his chair with an explosive sound. "My lady, you *will* listen to what I have to say!"

He was taking a devil of a chance, he knew. The Countess was his hostess and had every right to exercise her prerogatives. But Lord Darcy was counting on the fact that she had been under Count D'Evreux's influence so long that it would take her a little time to realize that she no longer had to knuckle under to the will of a man who shouted at her. He was right. She became silent.

201

Father Bright turned to her quickly and said: "Please, my daughter. Wait."

"Your pardon, my lady," Lord Darcy continued smoothly. "I was about to explain to you why I know Lady Duncan could not have killed your brother. There is the matter of the dress. We are certain that the gown that was found in Edouard's closet was worn by the killer. *And that gown could not possibly have fit Lady Duncan!* She's much too . . . er . . .hefty.

"She had told me her story, and, for reasons I will give you later, I believe it. When she pointed the gun at your brother, she really had no intention of killing him. She had no intention of pulling the trigger. Your brother knew this. He lashed out and slapped the side of her head. She dropped the pistol and fell, sobbing, to the floor. He took her roughly by the arm and 'escorted' her down the stairway. He threw her out.

"Lady Duncan, hysterical, ran to her husband.

"And then, when he had succeeded in calming her down a bit, she realized the position she was in. She knew that Laird Duncan was a violent, a warped man—very similar to Edouard, Count D'Evreux. She dared not tell him the truth, but she had to tell him something. So she lied.

"She told him that Edouard had asked her up in order to tell her something of importance; that that 'something of importance' concerned Laird Duncan's safety; that the Count told her that he knew of Laird Duncan's dabbling in black magic; that he threatened to inform Church authorities on Laird Duncan unless she submitted to his desires; that she had struggled with him and run away."

Lord Darcy spread his hands. "This was, of course, a tissue of lies. But Laird Duncan believed everything. So great was his ego that he could not believe in her infidelity, although he has been paralyzed for five years."

"How can you be certain that Lady Duncan told the truth?" Father Bright asked warily.

"Aside from the matter of the gown—which Count D'Evreux kept only for women of the common class, *not* the aristocracy—we have the testimony of the actions of Laird Duncan himself. We come then to—

"*Secundus:* Laird Duncan could not have committed the murder physically. *How could a man who was confined to a wheelchair go up that flight of stairs?* I submit to you that it would have been physically impossible.

"The possibility that he has been pretending all these

202

years, and that he is actually capable of walking, was disproved three hours ago, when he actually injured himself by trying to throttle me. His legs are incapable of carrying him even one step—much less carrying him to the top of that stairway."

Lord Darcy folded his hands complacently.

"There remains," said Father Bright, "the possibility that Laird Duncan killed Count D'Evreux by psychical, by magical means."

Lord Darcy nodded. "That is indeed possible, Reverend Sir, as we both know. But not in this instance. Master Sean assures me, and I am certain that you will concur, that a man killed by sorcery, by black magic, dies of internal malfunction, not of a bullet through the heart.

"In effect, the Black Sorcerer induces his enemy to kill himself by psychosomatic means. He dies by what is technically known as psychic induction. Master Sean informs me that the commonest—and crudest—method of doing this is by the so-called 'simulacrum induction' method. That is, by the making of an image—usually, but not necessarily, of wax—and, using the Law of Similarity, inducing death. The Law of Contagion is also used, since the fingernails, hair, spittle, and so on, of the victim are usually incorporated into the image. Am I correct, Father?"

The priest nodded. "Yes. And, contrary to the heresies of certain materialists, it is not at all necessary that the victim be informed of the operation—although, admittedly, it can, in certain circumstances, aid the process."

"Exactly," said Lord Darcy. "But it is well known that material objects can be moved by a competent sorcerer— 'black' or 'white.' Would you explain to my lady the Countess why her brother could not have been killed in that manner?"

Father Bright touched his lips with the tip of his tongue and then turned to the girl sitting next to him. "There is a lack of relevancy. In this case, the bullet must have been relevant either to the heart or to the gun. To have traveled with a velocity great enough to penetrate, the relevancy to the heart must have been much greater than the relevancy to the gun. Yet the test, witnessed by myself, that was performed by Master Sean indicates that this was not so. The bullet returned to the gun, not to your brother's heart. The evidence, my dear, is conclusive that the bullet was propelled by purely physical means, and was propelled from the gun."

"Then what was it Laird Duncan did?" the Countess asked.

"*Tertius:*" said Lord Darcy. "Believing what his wife had told him, Laird Duncan flew into a rage. He determined to kill your brother. He used an induction spell. But the spell backfired and almost killed him.

"There are analogies on a material plane. If one adds mineral spirits and air to a fire, the fire will be increased. But if one adds ash, the fire will be put out.

"In a similar manner, if one attacks a living being psychically it will die—but if one attacks a dead thing in such a manner, the psychic energy will be absorbed, to the detriment of the person who has used it.

"In theory, we could charge Laird Duncan with attempted murder, for there is no doubt that he did attempt to kill your brother, my lady. *But your brother was already dead at the time!*

"The resultant dissipation of psychic energy rendered Laird Duncan unconscious for several hours, during which Lady Duncan waited in suspenseful fear.

"Finally, when Laird Duncan regained consciousness, he realized what had happened. He knew that your brother was already dead when he attempted the spell. He thought, therefore, that Lady Duncan had killed the Count.

"On the other hand, Lady Duncan was perfectly well aware that she had left Edouard alive and well. So she thought the black magic of her husband had killed her erstwhile lover."

"Each was trying to protect the other," Father Bright said. "Neither is completely evil, then. There may be something we can do for Laird Duncan."

"I wouldn't know about that, Father." Lord Darcy said. "The Healing Art is the Church's business, not mine." He realized with some amusement that he was paraphrasing Dr. Pateley. "What Laird Duncan had not known," he went on quickly, "was that his wife had taken a gun up to the Count's bedroom. That put a rather different light on her visit, you see. That's why he flew into such a towering rage at me—not because I was accusing him or his wife of murder, but because I had cast doubt on his wife's behavior."

He turned his head to look at the table where the Irish sorcerer was working. "Ready, Master Sean?"

"Aye, my lord. All I have to do is set up the screen and light the lantern in the projector."

"Go ahead, then." He looked back at Father Bright and the Countess. "Master Sean has a rather interesting lantern slide I want you to look at."

"The most successful development I've ever made, if I may say so, my lord," the sorcerer said.

"Proceed."

Master Sean opened the shutter on the projector, and a picture sprang into being on the screen.

There were gasps from Father Bright and the Countess.

It was a woman. She was wearing the gown that had hung in the Count's closet. A button had been torn off, and the gown gaped open. Her right hand was almost completely obscured by a dense cloud of smoke. Obviously she had just fired a pistol directly at the onlooker.

But that was not what had caused the gasps.

The girl was beautiful. Gloriously, ravishingly beautiful. It was not a delicate beauty. There was nothing flower-like or peaceful in it. It was a beauty that could have but one effect on a normal human male. She was the most physically desirable woman one could imagine.

Retro me, Sathanas, Father Bright thought wryly. *She's almost obscenely beautiful.*

Only the Countess was unaffected by the desirability of the image. She saw only the startling beauty.

"Has neither of you seen that woman before? I thought not," said Lord Darcy. "Nor had Laird or Lady Duncan. Nor Sir Pierre.

"Who is she? We don't know. But we can make a few deductions. She must have come to the Count's room by appointment. This is quite obviously the woman Edouard mentioned to Lady Duncan—the woman, the 'she' that the Scots noblewoman could not compare with. It is almost certain she is a commoner; otherwise she would not be wearing a robe from the Count's collection. She must have changed right there in the bedroom. Then she and the Count quarreled—about what, we do not know. The Count had previously taken Lady Duncan's pistol away from her and had evidently carelessly let it lay on that table you see behind the girl. She grabbed it and shot him. Then she changed clothes again, hung up the robe, and ran away. No one saw her come or go. The Count had designed his stairway for just that purpose.

"Oh, we'll find her, never fear—now that we know what she looks like.

"At any rate," Lord Darcy concluded, "the mystery is now solved to my complete satisfaction, and I shall so report to His Highness."

Richard, Duke of Normandy, poured two liberal portions of excellent brandy into a pair of crystal goblets. There was a smile of satisfaction on his youthful face as he handed one of the goblets to Lord Darcy. "Very well done, my lord," he said. "Very well done."

"I am gratified to hear Your Highness say so," said Lord Darcy, accepting the brandy.

"But how were you so certain that it was *not* someone from outside the castle? Anyone could have come in through the main gate. That's always open."

"True, Your Highness. But the door at the foot of the stairway was *locked*. Count D'Evreux locked it after he threw Lady Duncan out. There is no way of locking or unlocking it from the outside; the door had not been forced. No one could have come in that way, nor left that way, after Lady Duncan was so forcibly ejected. The only other way into the Count's suite was by the other door, and that door was unlocked."

"I see," said Duke Richard. "I wonder why she went up there in the first place?"

"Probably because he asked her to. Any other woman would have known what she was getting into if she accepted an invitation to Count D'Evreux's suite."

The Duke's handsome face darkened. "No. One would hardly expect that sort of thing from one's own brother. She was perfectly justified in shooting him."

"Perfectly, Your Highness. And had she been anyone but the heiress, she would undoubtedly have confessed immediately. Indeed, it was all I could do to keep her from confessing to me when she thought I was going to charge the Duncans with the killing. But she knew that it was necessary to preserve the reputations of her brother and herself. Not as private persons, but as Count and Countess, as officers of the Government of His Imperial Majesty the King. For a man to be known as a rake is one thing. Most people don't care about that sort of thing in a public official so long as he does his duty and does it well—which, as Your Highness knows, the Count did.

"But to be shot to death while attempting to assault his own sister—that is quite another thing. She was perfectly justified in attempting to cover it up. And she will remain silent unless someone else is accused of the crime."

"Which, of course, will not happen," said Duke Richard. He sipped at the brandy, then said: "She will make a good Countess. She has judgment and she can keep cool under duress. After she had shot her own brother, she might have panicked, but she didn't. How many women would have thought of simply taking off the damaged gown and putting on its duplicate from the closet?"

"Very few," Lord Darcy agreed. "That's why I never mentioned that I knew the Count's wardrobe contained dresses identical to her own. By the way, Your Highness, if any good Healer, like Father Bright, had known of those duplicate dresses, he would have realized that the Count had a sexual obsession about his sister. He would have known that all the other women the Count went after were sister substitutes."

"Yes; of course. And none of them could measure up." He put his goblet on the table. "I shall inform the King my brother that I recommend the new Countess wholeheartedly. No word of this must be put down in writing, of course. You know and I know and the King must know. No one else must know."

"One other knows," said Lord Darcy.

"Who?" The Duke looked startled.

"Father Bright."

Duke Richard looked relieved. "Naturally. He won't tell her that *we* know, will he?"

"I think Father Bright's discretion can be relied upon."

In the dimness of the confessional, Alice, Countess D'Evreux knelt and listened to the voice of Father Bright.

"I shall not give you any penance, my child, for you have committed no sin—that is, insofar as the death of your brother is concerned. For the rest of your sins, you must read and memorize the third chapter of 'The Soul and The World,' by St. James Huntington."

He started to pronounce the absolution, but the Countess said:

"I don't understand one thing. That picture. That wasn't me. I never saw such a gorgeously beautiful girl in my life. And I'm so plain. I don't understand."

"Had you looked more closely, my child, you would have seen that the face did look like yours—only it was idealized. When a subjective reality is made objective, distortions invariably show up; that is why such things cannot be accepted as evidence of objective reality in court." He paused. "To put it another way, my child: Beauty is in the eye of the beholder."

RANDALL, HARRY AND JOHN

Harry Harrison

A GOOD FEW YEARS AGO I WAS A REGULAR contributor to *Astounding,* so regular in fact that a serial of mine began in *Astounding* and ended in *Analog.* (The name of the magazine was changed while the three-part serial was running.) I did not visit New York very often— I was living in Denmark at the time—but when I did I of course visited John Campbell and usually had lunch with him. The Campbell editorial lunches were well known for their intellectual fireworks as ideas were discussed, explored, dissected and developed. Stories were born here, as were ulcers. It was never an easy thing, for Campbell made writers work the mental muscle and sweat hard at the task.

So there I was, barely recovered from a 24-hour flight on Icelandic Airways (the only airline that goes northeast from Copenhagen to get to New York—which is almost due west) and on the phone to John, getting the usual luncheon invitation and steeling myself for the ordeal. However, this was different from the one I had expected. We were about to leave John's office when another writer arrived. "Join us for lunch," John said. No writer born could refuse that invitation. Randall Garrett certainly did not.

I had known Randy for years, in and out of the Hydra club, but it had been a long time since I had seen him. We chortled hellos and dutifully followed John to the elevator and down to the German restaurant situated in the same building. Advantageous location was about all that could be said for it. I steeled myself for the ordeal. Intellectual battle unsupported by the balm of alcohol. John Campbell did not drink. Starving young writer that I was I did not offend the Master by drinking booze with the meal. Perhaps a beer to "wash down the food."

No sooner had we sat down than John began a quick 30-minute lecture on the physical details of atomic energy. I made notes on my napkin—then gazed with horror as Randy signaled a passing waitress and ordered a double martini with a twist, no olive. The heavens did not fall, the lecture continued unabated—and I had made a remarkable discovery. While John did not drink, he did not care a gnat's whisker if his guests did. "Make that two!" I heard a hoarse voice call out: my own.

A certain amount of work got done during lunch. I think. But I am sure that a lot of alcohol flowed freely. So freely that when John went back to work the free-as-birds writers managed to make the 30 feet across Lexington Avenue to a low bar where the discussion, and the drinking, continued. There is something decadent and hideously attractive about getting blotto during the workday when everyone else is slaving away. Randy and I exchanged many a good idea that afternoon, sealed our friendship and emerged blinking at the setting sun, arms about each other. And we had a wonderful idea.

We had given the editor of *Astounding* the benefit of our genius. Should we not be generous and share the wealth also with Fred Pohl, the editor of *Galaxy?* We could! Our generosity was perhaps explained by our knowledge that Fred's publisher, Bob Guinn, kept half-gallon bottles of booze in his office. To Hudson Street!

As might be imagined Fred was less than enthusiastic at the sight of two staggering writers at his doorstop. He smiled insincerely and invited us in, poured scotch into papercups and passed them over in the hopes that we would pass out or vanish or something.

This subtle ploy worked, for the rest of the day is hazy in memory. I do know that A. J. Budrys appeared at one point and I was miffed at him because he refused to shake hands with me. A quick round of fisticuffs was averted when Randy kindly pointed out to me that I was holding a lit cigar in my right hand—lit end facing inward. The last thing I do remember is Fred showing us a couple of covers he had bought and assigning each of us a cover to write a story around. Feeling very pleased with ourselves, Randy and I clutched photos of the covers to our bosoms as we were convinced we should leave. Mercifully, a curtain falls at this point.

I wrote my story, which was duly published in *Galaxy*, and I assume Randy wrote his. It was a pleasant day, a warm memory, one that has stayed with me a long time. And I will be forever grateful for Randy's example of how to deal with an editorial lunch. I have stopped many a waitress many times since.

Many thanks!

And this, too, is a Lord Darcy story—though it lacks, by conscious intent, the flamboyant trappings of quasimedieval splendor that the other ones have. For it is important not to forget that Lord Darcy is a man of the 20th century, and the 20th century has been a time of terrible warfare—as Garrett reminds us in this tale of Lord Darcy's earlier years.

THE SPELL OF WAR

THE LIEUTENANT LAY ON HIS BELLY IN THE middle of a broad clearing in the Bavarian Forest, on the eastern side of the Danau, in a hell of warfare many miles from Dagendorf.

He was 18 years old, and his fingers, clawlike, had dug into and were holding onto the damp earth on which he lay.

Ahead of him, far out of sight beyond the trees, the Polish artillery thundered and roared. It had begun only 30 seconds before, and already it seemed as though it had been going on forever.

Next to him, lying equally flat, was Superior Sergeant Kelleigh. The sergeant was more than twice the lieutenant's age, and had seen long service in the Imperial Army.

"What do you think, sir?" he asked in a hushed voice.

The lieutenant swallowed. "Damned if I know," he said evenly. He was surprised at how calm his voice sounded. It betrayed nothing of what was inside him. "Where are those damned shells going?"

"Over our heads, sir. Hear that whistling burble?"

"I do indeed, Sergeant. Thank you."

"Pleasure, sir. Never been in an artillery barrage before, sir?"

"No, I haven't. I'm learning."

212

Kelleigh grinned. "We all learn, sir. You faster than most."

"Thank you again, Sergeant." The lieutenant put his field glasses to his eyes and did a quick survey of the surrounding terrain. Too many trees.

A hundred yards to their rear, the shells from the big guns were exploding, making a syncopated counterpoint to the roar of the artillery pieces.

"I hope Red Company got out of that," the sergeant muttered. He was looking back toward the area where the shells were landing. "Damn, that's good shooting!" He touched his chest, where his bronze identification sigil rested beneath his combat jacket. "I'd think they were using a clairvoyant, except I believe our sorcerers are better than theirs."

"Don't worry, Sergeant; as long as you've got your sigil on you, you can't be seen psychically." The lieutenant was still looking through his field glasses. "If there are any infantry in that wood, I don't see them. I wonder if—"

Spang-ng-ng-ng!

The bullet sang off a rock not ten inches from the lieutenant's head.

"That's the Polish infantry, sir. Let's move it."

"Right you are, Sergeant. Roll."

Staying low and moving fast, the two men performed that maneuver known to the science of military tactics as *Getting The Hell Out*. In the 25 yards they had to move, several more bullets came close, but none hit anything but earth.

They rolled down the sharp declivity that was protecting the rest of Blue Company, and hit bottom hard enough to take the breath from them.

The lieutenant gasped twice, then said: "Where the hell were they firing from?"

"Damned if I know, sir. Couldn't tell."

"Well, they're out there in the woods somewhere. That's why all the artillery shells are going over our heads."

There was no more small-arms fire, though the big guns kept up their intermittent roar.

"We seem to be safe enough for the moment," the lieutenant said. Further down the ravine, they could see the rest of Blue Company.

"Aye, sir." The sergeant was silent for a moment, then said: "Been meanin' to ask you, sir, if you'll not consider it an impertinence . . ." He paused.

"Go ahead, Sergeant. The worst I'll do is refuse to answer if it's too personal."

"Thank you, sir. Been meanin' to ask if you were any kin to Coronel Lord Darcy."

"He's my father," said Lieutenant Darcy.

"It's a pleasure knowin' you, sir. I remember you as a kid—I served under the coronel ten years ago. A great officer, sir."

Lieutenant Darcy suddenly found tears in his eyes. He brushed them away with a sleeve and said: "Then you're Sergeant *Brendon* Kelleigh? My father has spoken of you often. Says you're the finest NCO in His Imperial Majesty's forces. If I ever see him again, I'll tell him of your compliment. He'll be honored."

"*I'm* the one who's honored, sir." The sergeant's voice was a little choked. "And you'll see him again, sir. You've only been with Blue Company for a week, but I've seen enough of you in action to know you're the survivor type."

"That's as may be," said the lieutenant, "but even if I make it through this mess, I may not see him again. You were with him in Sudan, I believe."

"When he got the bullet through his chest? I was, sir."

"It clipped his heart. Now his condition is deteriorating, and the Healers can do nothing. He'll not live out the year."

After a short silence, Superior Sergeant Kelleigh said: "I'm sorry to hear that, sir. Very sorry. He was a fine officer."

The lieutenant nodded wordlessly. Then he said: "Let's move south, Sergeant, back to Blue Company. Keep low."

"Aye, sir."

They moved down the ravine.

Thirty yards or so down, the two men met Captain Rimbaud, commander of Blue Company.

"I saw you two move back," he said harshly. "What the hell happened? None of that artillery is hitting around us."

He was a big man, two inches taller than Lieutenant Darcy's six feet, and a good stone heavier. He had a blocky face and hard eyes.

"Small-arms fire, sir," the lieutenant said. "From somewhere out in those woods."

The captain's hard eyes shifted to the sergeant. "That right, Kelleigh?"

Lieutenant Darcy let his young face go wooden. He said nothing.

214

"Aye, sir," the sergeant said stiffly. He, too, had recognized the slight on the young lieutenant. "They're out there, sir; no question of it. First shot came within a foot of us."

Captain Rimbaud looked back at the lieutenant. "Did you see any of them?"

"No, sir." No excuses. He didn't explain about the woods. Rimbaud should be able to figure that out for himself.

The artillery was still thundering.

The captain turned and climbed carefully up the eastern slope of the ravine. A quick peek over the edge, then he slid back down. "No wonder. This slight breeze is bringing the smoke in from those cannon. You two were in the clear. I hope they choke."

"Agreed, sir," said Lieutenant Darcy.

"I think—" began the captain. He didn't finish. There was a noise and a tumble of earth and small stones, and a man came rolling down the western slope of the ravine. Both officers and the noncom had spun around and had their .44 Morleys out and ready for action before the man hit the bottom of the ravine and splashed into the water.

Then they relaxed. The man was wearing the uniform of their own outfit, the Duke of Burgundy's 18th Infantry.

As the square-jawed, tough-looking little man came to his feet, Captain Rimbaud said: "You almost got yourself shot, coming in that way, Sergeant. Who the Hell are you?"

The little sergeant threw him a salute, which the captain returned. "Junior Sergeant Sean O Lochlainn, sir, commanding what is left of Red Company." His Irish brogue was thick.

After a moment, Captain Rimbaud found his voice. *"What is left of Red Company?"*

"Aye, sir. The artillery got us. Wiped out the captain, the lieutenant and both senior sergeants. Out of 80 men, there's at most 15 left." He paused. "I don't know if they'll all make it here, sir. There's small-arms fire out there, too."

"Mary, Mother of God," the captain said softly. Then: "All right, let's move down. If one of their observers can get word to their artillery, there will be shells dropping in here pretty soon."

Blue Company was another 35 yards down the ravine. They were warned to watch for Red Company, and during

215

the next few minutes 11 more of them came in. Then there were no more.

There were 75 men of Blue Company, and 12 of Red in that ravine now, all of them wondering what in Hell was going on out in those woods. For some reason, no artillery fire fell in the ravine. Either Blue and Red hadn't been spotted, or the observer couldn't get through to the guns.

While Captain Rimbaud and Sergeant Kelleigh checked out the troops, the young lieutenant sat down next to Sergeant O Lochlainn for a breathing space.

"Queer war it is," said Sean O Lochlainn. "Queer war, indeed."

Soldiers love to talk, if they have the time and opportunity. In combat, it is the only form of entertainment they have. In a hard firefight, their minds are on their precious lives, but as soon as there is a lull, and they are sure the enemy cannot hear them, they will talk. About anything. Family, wives, sweethearts, women in general, booze, beer, parties, bar fights, history, philosophy, clean and dirty jokes—

You name it, and a soldier will talk about it if he can find a buddy interested in the same subject. If he can't, he'll change the subject. But he'll talk, because it's almost the only release he has from the nervous tension of the threat of sudden dismemberment or death.

"All wars are queer, Sergeant," said Lieutenant Darcy. "What's so exceptional about this one?"

"I'd say, sir, because it is exceptionally stupid, even for a war." He glanced at the lieutenant. "Aye, sir; all wars are stupid. But this one is stupider than most. And for once, most of the stupidity is on the other side."

The lieutenant was beginning to like the stout little Irishman. "You think, then, that King Casimir is stupid?"

"Not as an overall thing, no sir," the sergeant said thoughtfully. "But His Slavonic Majesty has done a few stupid things. Wants to be a soldier, like his late father, and can't cope with it, if you see what I mean, sir."

"I do, indeed, Sergeant. Your analysis is cogent."

Sigismund III, from 1922 to 1937, had expanded the Polish Hegemony into Russia, and Poland now controlled it from Minsk to Kiev. But now the Russians showed signs of banding together, and the notion of a United Russia was one that nobody wanted to face, so Sigismund III had wisely abandoned Polish expansion toward the east. Had he remained king, it might well be that the present war would never have taken place, for that cagey old fox had known better than to attempt an attack westward against the Anglo-French Empire. But his son, Casimir IX, who had ascended the throne in 1937, knew no such wisdom. He saw the threat of the Russias and decided to move west into the Germanies, not realizing, apparently, that Charles III, by the grace of God King of England, France, Scotland and Ireland, Lord Protector of the New World, King of the Romans and the Germans, and Emperor of the Holy Roman Empire, would have to protect the Germanies. When Polish troops entered Bavaria, Prince Hermann of Bavaria had called to his liege lord for help, and King Charles had sent it.

Casimir IX wanted to be the military leader his father was, but he was simply not up to it.

Lieutenant Darcy wondered for a moment if that was the flaw in his own character. Coronel Lord Darcy had been a fine soldier and had won many honors in the field. *Am I,* the young lieutenant thought, *trying to be the soldier my father was?* Then: *Hell, no, I never wanted to be a soldier in the first place! I'm out here because the King needs me. And as soon as he doesn't need me anymore, I'm shucking this uniform and getting the Hell back home.*

"It's like Captain Rimbaud," said Sergeant O Lochlainn.

Lieutenant Darcy blinked, bringing his mind back to the conversation. "Beg your pardon, Sergeant? *What's* like Captain Rimbaud?"

"Meanin' no disrespect, sir," said the stout little Irishman, "but Captain Rimbaud's father was General Ambrose Rimbaud, of whom ye have no doubt heard, sir."

"I have," said the lieutenant. "I didn't know that Captain Rimbaud was his son."

"Oh, that he is, sir. Again meanin' no disrespect, sir, but the captain is well known throughout the battalion as a glory hunter."

"I'll reserve judgment on that, Sergeant," said the lieutenant.

"Aye, sir. I'll say no more about it."

The lieutenant edged his way up the slope of the ravine and took a quick look over the top.

He said: "Good God!" very softly.

"What is it, sir?" asked the tough little Irish sergeant.

"Take a look for yourself, Sergeant," Lieutenant Darcy said. "The place is alive with Polish soldiers."

A bullet from a Polish .28 Kosciusco rifle sang across the edge of the ravine, splattering earth over the two men. Then another.

Lieutenant Darcy slid back down the slope.

"With your permission, sir," said the stout little Irishman, "I'd just as soon not take a look now."

Lieutenant Darcy couldn't help but grin. "Excused, Sergeant. They've got us spotted." The grin faded. "There must be at least 30 of them up there in those woods. Probably more, since that smoke is obscuring a lot of them. And there must be even more, up and down the line." He frowned. "There's more smoke out there than one would think, considering how far back the artillery must be."

"I've seen it before, sir," said the Irishman. "It's more fog than smoke. On a cold, damp day like this, the smoke particles seem to make a fog condense out of the air."

The lieutenant nodded. "That accounts for the fact that the Polish infantry can stay inside that cloud and still breathe." He paused, then: "The cloud is getting denser, and it's moving this way. It will be drifting over this ravine in a minute or two. Get down to the captain and tell him what I saw. I'll stay here and make them think there's still a large force in this part of the ravine."

"Aye, sir." The sergeant moved south.

Lieutenant Darcy found an 18-inch piece of broken branch half in the rivulet that ran down the center of the ravine, and moved north about ten yards. Then he climbed up the bank again.

He took off his helmet, put it on the end of the branch, and drew his .44 Morley. Lifting the helmet with his left hand, he fired over the edge with the pistol in his right. He didn't care what his aim was; all he wanted to do was attract attention.

He did.

The bullet whanged off the crown of his helmet, knocking it off the stick into the brooklet.

Damn good shot, the lieutenant thought as he slid back down the embankment.

He retrieved his helmet. There was a shiny streak on the top but no dent. He put the helmet back on in spite of the wetness. By then, the smoky fog was drifting over the top of the ravine.

The lieutenant found himself a little jittery. *Have a smoke,* he told himself. *Relax.* The cloud over the ravine would mask the smoke from his pipe.

He took the stubby little briar from his backpack. It was already filled with tobacco, for emergencies just such as this. It took three flicks of his thumb to get his pipelighter aflame.

And then he found that his hand was shaking so badly that he could not light the pipe. He almost threw the lighter into the stream a few feet away.

He put out the flame and shoved both pipe and lighter back into his backpack.

Get hold of yourself, dammit! he thought. He was thankful that no one had seen him betray his fear that way. He was particularly thankful that Coronel Everard, the battalion commander and an old friend of his father's, hadn't seen him.

He was suddenly aware of the silence. The artillery had stopped. Now there was only the sporadic *crack!* of small-arms fire. He got to his feet and moved quickly south, toward the rest of Blue Company. The sun overhead shone sickly through the yellow-brown haze.

He almost tripped over the body that lay sprawled on the slope. The rivulet gurgled over the dead man's boots. The soldier was face-down, but the bullet hole in the small of his back showed that the slug had gone right through him. The lieutenant stepped over him, choking, and went on.

Blue Company, and what was left of Red, were up on the eastern slope of the ravine. They had scooped out toe-holds in the bank in order to stay near the top, but were keeping their heads down.

Captain Rimbaud saw Lieutenant Darcy and said: "Your diversion didn't work, Darcy. They know where we are. How they can see us through this smoke, I don't know."

"Nor do I, sir. Can you see anything?"

"Not a damn thing. I can see them moving occasionally, but not for long enough to get a shot at any one of them. Have you any ideas?"

Lieutenant Darcy tried to ignore the three bodies lying at the bottom of the ravine. "Can we move farther south, sir? That would put us closer to where the rest of the battalion is."

The captain shook his head. "The terrain slopes off rather rapidly, and this ravine gets shallow and disappears. The stream flows out into a flat meadow and makes a bog of it. They'd still have us in their sights, and we'd never make it across that bog."

219

The lieutenant nodded. "Yes, sir. I can see that."

The troops were firing sporadically into the fog, not with the hope of hitting the occasional flitting shadow that was visible behind the rolling fogbank, but with the hope that they could keep the Polish troops back.

Sergeant Arthur Lyon, second ranking noncom of Blue Company, came running up from the right. He stood six-two, and was solidly built. He was usually smiling, and the lines in his face showed it, but there was no smile on his face now.

"Sir," he said, addressing the captain, "They're moving in to the north of us. If they get into this ravine, we'll have enfilade fire raking us."

"Mary, Mother of God," the captain said with a growl in his voice. He looked at Darcy. "Any suggestions, Lieutenant?"

The lieutenant knew this was a test. Captain Rimbaud had been testing him ever since he had joined Blue Company. "Yes, sir. Apparently, they have us outnumbered. And the cessation of the artillery fire seems ominous to me."

Rimbaud narrowed his eyes. He did not like damp-behind-the-ears lieutenants who used words like "cessation" and "ominous."

"In what way?" he asked.

"They've been lobbing those shells over the woods, sir. They hit Red Company's line and nearly wiped them out. Why haven't they shelled us? I think it's because we're too close, sir. They can't elevate their guns enough to get over those trees and drop shells on us. An observer's messenger has been sent back to tell the Poles to pull their artillery back a hundred yards so they can get at us. In that case, sir, their infantry is merely trying to scare us; they won't come down this far for fear of their own artillery."

"What would you do, Lieutenant?" Rimbaud asked.

"Do we know the characteristics of the cannon they're using, sir?" Lieutenant Darcy asked.

"The six-inch Gornicki? I don't, personally; I'm not an artilleryman."

"But our artillery officers would?"

"Certainly."

"Very well, sir," the lieutenant said decisively. "Our artillery is southwest of here. If we go to the southern end of this ravine and head back that way, we can report what we know. The Polish guns won't go back any farther than they have to in order to lob shells into us. Knowing the characteristics of the Gornicki, the artillery officers can figure out where the guns *must* be when the shells start hitting this ravine, and they can lay down a barrage on the Poles."

The captain's eyes narrowed. When he spoke, his voice was heavy with a mixture of sarcasm and scorn. "I see. On the basis of pure guesswork, you would have us *retreat?* Not while *I* am captain of this company, we won't." He turned his head to look up and eastward, though he could see nothing but the sky and the upper portions of trees. "If they haven't come here after us in exactly ten minutes, this company is going over the edge of this damned ravine and straight through them. Got that?"

"Yes, sir," said the lieutenant. Such a charge would be suicide, and the lieutenant knew it.

"Lieutenant, north of here this ravine narrows down for a few yards, then it makes a slight curve to the east. Three men could hold off anyone coming down through there. Take Sergeant Lyon and Sergeant O Lochlainn with you. Grab some rifles from the dead; they won't be needing them, and a rifle is better for that sort of work than a handgun. Don't forget to take ammo. Now, get moving. Be back here in five minutes."

Silently, the three men obeyed.

They stayed low, and as close to the eastern bank of the ravine as possible.

It was autumn now, and the dry summer had left little water running down the ravine, but it was obvious that, come spring, when the winter snows melted, the water would be much higher. What was now a trickle would become a flood.

Now, the banks were six to eight feet above the water level, but in spring the ravine would be close to full.

"The captain has a lot of nerve," Sergeant O Lochlainn said quietly. There was a touch of sarcasm in his whispered voice.

"That's not nerve," said Sergeant Lyon. "Charging through that line is idiocy."

" 'Tis not what I meant, Sergeant," Sean O Lochlainn said. "What I meant was, he'd got a lot of nerve ordering me around; I didn't relinquish command of Red Company to him, but he assumes it."

"Then why did you obey?" Lyon asked.

"Habit, I guess. Habit." Sergeant O Lochlainn sounded as though he were unhappy with himself.

They came to the narrow part of the ravine. Here, the clay walls had been eroded back to uncover two huge slabs of rock, one on each side. They were almost perpendicular to the bottom, giving sheer walls seven feet high on the eastern side and nearly eight feet on the western. The gap between them was only three feet.

"I think the captain was right about this, sir," said Sergeant Lyon. "Three men with rifles can hold off anything that tries to come through there."

Lieutenant Darcy glanced at his wristwatch, then looked down the narrow corridor. It was straight for some thirty yards, then swerved northwest as the banks became clay again. "We can do it, I think," he said. "But watch out for grenades. I doubt if they have anyone who can lob a grenade that far up and over, but they might. Let's back up to that last bend. We can still pick them off if they try to come down that narrow gap, and there'll be less chance of anyone dropping a fistful of high explosive on us."

When they got into position, Lieutenant Darcy said: "If you would, Sergeant O Lochlainn, guard our rear and keep an eye on the eastern parapet, just in case the Poles try to cut us off from the rest."

"Aye, sir."

They waited. The minutes passed slowly.

"You're not a career man, are you, sir?" Sergeant Lyon asked.

"No. I saw enough of the Army when I was a boy. My father was a career man."

"Would that be the Coronel Lord Darcy that Sergeant Kelleigh always talks about?"

"Yes. Kelleigh was my father's top-kick in the old days. Are you career?"

"No, sir. When this mess is over, I'm taking my discharge as soon as I can get it."

Behind them, Sergeant O Lochlainn's voice said: "What're ye goin' to do, once ye get out, Sergeant?"

"Well, I used to think I had a call for the priesthood," Lyon said, "but I'm not sure of it, and as long as one isn't sure, one oughtn't to try it. I think I'll try out for Armsman. Being an Officer of the King's Peace is a job I think I can handle and one I *am* sure of. What about you, O Lochlainn?"

"Well, now, that's a thing I'm sure as sure of," the stout little Irishman said. "I'm going to be a Master Sorcerer."

"Indeed?" said Lieutenant Darcy. "Have you been tested for the Talent, then?"

"Why, sir, I already have me Journeyman's ticket in the Guild."

"You do? Then what 'the Hell are you doing in the Army? You could have got a deferment easily enough."

"So could you have, sir, I dare say. But *somebody's* got to fight this bloody war, sir. I volunteered for the same reason you did, sir." He paused. Then: "The Empire expects every man to do his duty, sir."

The lieutenant glanced at his wristwatch. Two minutes to go, and no sign of enemy activity. *Yes,* he thought, *the Empire* does *expect every man to do his duty.*

The Anglo-French Empire had already lasted longer than the ancient Roman Empire. The first Plantagenet, Henry of Anjou, had become King of England in 1154, taking the title of Henry II. His son, Richard the Lion-Hearted, had become King upon the death of Henry II in 1189. Richard I had been absent from England during most of the first ten years of his reign, establishing a reputation as a fighter in the Holy Land. Even today, Islamic mothers threaten their children with *Al Rik,* a most horrendous *afreet.*

Richard had been hit by a crossbow bolt at the Siege of Chaluz in 1199, and after a long bout with infection and fever, had survived to become a wise and powerful ruler. His younger brother, John, died in exile in 1216, so when Richard died in 1219 the crown had gone to Richard's nephew, Arthur, son of Geoffrey of Brittany. Known as "Good King Arthur," he was often confused in the popular mind with King Arthur Pendragon, of ancient Kymric legend.

During Arthur's reign, St. Hilary of Walsingham had produced his monumental works which outlined the theory and mathematics of Magic. But only those with the Talent could utilize St. Hilary's Laws of Magic.

Even today, such people were rare, and Lieutenant Darcy felt that it was a waste to allow Sean O Lochlainn to expose his God-given Talent to the sudden death that could come from combat.

Every man must do his duty, yes. But what was the duty of a Sorcerer?

"Someone comin' from the rear," said Sergeant O Lochlainn.

"Watch ahead, Lyon," the lieutenant said sharply. He turned to see what was coming from behind.

It was Senior Sergeant Kelleigh.

"What is it, Sergeant?" the lieutenant asked.

Kelleigh swallowed. "Sir, you are in command. Captain Rimbaud is dead."

The lieutenant looked at his wristwatch. One minute left, and no one had come down that corridor. "Let's move," he said in a quiet, calm voice. "Back to the company. Keep down."

It was not true calmness, the lieutenant knew; it was numbness, overlying and masking his fear. Fear of the artillery, fear of death and dismemberment, had been suddenly supplemented by a fear that was akin to, but vastly greater than, stage fright.

He? *He?* In command?

Mary, Mother of God, pray for me!

He was younger than any other man in the outfit, and he had less combat experience than most of them. And yet the burden of command had fallen on *him*.

He knew he dared not show his inner self; he dared not crack. Not for fear of showing himself a coward, but because of what it would do to the men. In a properly trained army, when the officers are taken out of action, the noncoms can carry on. Death is expected; it may come as a shock, but not as a surprise.

But for a commander to go into a panic of fear, to show the yellow, is more demoralizing than sudden death.

A soldier, consciously or subconsciously, rightly or wrongly, always feels that his superiors know more about what is going on than he does. Therefore, if an officer cracks up, it must be because he knows something that the men don't.

And fear of the unknown can cause more despair than fear of the known.

So the fear of causing catastrophe to his troops (*his* troops!) overrode all the other fears as he led the three sergeants back to the rest of the men while the irregular *crack!* of small-arms fire punctuated the air.

The captain's body lay a few feet from the rivulet that ran down the ravine. It was covered by a blanket. Lieutenant Darcy knelt down, gently lifted the covering and looked at his late commander. There was a bullet wound in his chest, just to the left of the lower tip of the sternum.

"Went right through 'im, it did, sir," said a nearby corporal. Whittaker? Yes; Whittaker.

The lieutenant carefully turned the body on its side. The exit wound near the spine, between the fifth and sixth ribs, was larger than the entrance wound, as might be expected. From the trajectory, the lieutenant judged it must have gone right through the heart. *Probably died before he knew he'd been hit,* he thought. He replaced the blanket and stood up.

"How long do you think it will be before the Poles get their guns back in position, Sergeant?" he asked Kelleigh.

Kelleigh looked at his wristwatch. "Another five minutes is all we can depend on, sir." He looked at the lieutenant and stood expectantly, awaiting his orders. So were the other two sergeants.

Without saying anything, the lieutenant went over to where the late captain had dropped his pack. He opened it and took out the little collapsing periscope. Then he climbed up the slope of the ravine wall and eased the upper end of the periscope over the top. The captain had carried the device because regulations said he should, but he never used it because he thought it a coward's gadget. Lieutenant Darcy believed there was a difference between caution and cowardice.

After half a minute, he said: "Sergeant Kelleigh, what are the men shooting at?" Most of the foggy smoke had cleared away, and the lieutenant could see nothing but woods out there. There wasn't a Polish soldier in sight.

Kelleigh climbed up the slope and took a quick look over the top. "Why—at those Polish troops out there, sir. They're behind those trees, shootin' at us." His voice had a touch of bewilderment in it, as though he were afraid the young lieutenant had lost his reason.

The lieutenant moved up and looked over the edge. He could see them now. Some were lying prone, some standing behind trees, and now and then one would move from one tree to another in the background. He slid down a little and used the periscope again. No one. The woods were empty.

"Sergeant O Lochlainn!" he snapped.

"Aye, sir!"

"Come up here for a minute. Sergeant Kelleigh, tell the men to cease fire and get ready to move out."

"Yes, sir." He slid down and was gone.

The stout little Irish sergeant clambered up to where the lieutenant was. "Aye, sir?"

"Take a look at those woods through the periscope. Then take a look over the top. And don't think like a soldier; think like a Sorcerer."

Sergeant O Lochlainn did as he was told without saying a word until he was done. But when he brought his head down, he looked at Lieutenant Darcy. "Shades o' S'n Padraeg! You're right, sir. 'Tis an illusion. There's no troops out there. It's a psychic effect that registers on the mind, not on the eye, so it isn't visible in a mirror."

"And it's being projected through that haze?"

"Aye, sir; it's needed for a big illusion like that."

Lieutenant Darcy frowned. "We can't say there isn't *anybody* out there. Someone is shooting at us."

"Aye, sir. And a pretty good shot, too."

"Can you dispel that illusion, Sergeant?"

"No, sir; not with the equipment I've got with me. Not in a minute or two." He paused. "If we could locate the sniper—"

Lieutenant Darcy was back at the periscope. "He must have us spotted here by now. Three of us have looked over that edge, but he can't know if it's the same man or not, so—" He stopped suddenly. "I think I see him. No wonder he's so good at spotting us."

"Where, sir?"

"Up in that big tree to the northwest. About 35 feet off the ground. Here; take the periscope."

The sergeant took it and, after a moment said: "Aye, sir. I see him. I wonder if there's any more about."

"I don't think so. Have you noticed the wounds of the men who have been hit were always high on the left side of the body?"

"Now that I think of it, sir. But I thought nothing of it."

"Neither did I until I saw that those Polish troops are illusions. Then I realized that whoever was doing the shooting was high up and to the northeast. Then everything was obvious."

"That's how you knew which tree to look at, sir?"

"Yes, I—" He stopped, listening to the silence. The order to cease fire had been relayed to his troops.

Sergeant Kelleigh approached and looked up the slope at his new commander. "Sir, the troops are ready to

226

march. We'd best get started if we're going to get out of here; sir; that artillery can start any minute now."

The lieutenant slid down the bank of the ravine. "Who are your two best riflemen, Sergeant? Your best shots."

"Corporal Whittaker and Senior Private Martinne, sir."

"Let's go. Come along, Sergeant O Lochlainn."

The remainders of Blue and Red Companies were waiting for them, packs on, rifles at the ready.

The lieutenant said "At ease" before they could come to attention, then said: "I want all of you to listen very carefully because we only have time for me to say it once. Sergeant Kelleigh, take this periscope and get up there and tell me what you see. Don't stick your head up; use the 'scope. While he's doing that, the rest of you pay attention.

"Sergeant O Lochlainn, here, has a ticket as a Journeyman Sorcerer. He and I have discovered that sorcery is being used against us. Not, I think, strictly Black Magic, eh, Sergeant?"

"Not at all, sir," said the Irishman. "An illusion is meant to confuse, but it does no direct harm. Not Black Magic at all."

"Very well, then," the lieutenant continued. "But we've been pinned down here by—"

Senior Sergeant Kelleigh came back down the slope, his eyes wide, his face white. "There's nobody up there," he said softly.

"Almost nobody. We've been pinned down by a lone sniper. All those Polish troops we've been firing at are illusions produced by sorcery. But you can't see them in a mirror.

"The sniper is in that big tree to the northeast, about 35 feet up. Corporal Whittaker, Private Martinne, the Senior Sergeant tells me you're crack shots. Take the periscope and spot that sniper. Then both of you keep up a steady fire. Kill him if you can, but at least make sure he stays down. The rest of us are going to go over the top and head for those woods while you keep up cover fire for us. As soon as we get there, we'll all cover for you, and you come running. Everybody got all that?"

"Yes, sir," came the ragged chorus.

"Now, I want you to realize one important thing: the Poles haven't got much infantry around. If they did, they'd use them, instead of relying on one man and a set

227

of illusions. They have damned few men to move, fire and protect those field pieces.

"So we, lads, are going through that woods and take those field pieces away from them."

Grins broke out on the soldiers' faces.

"It's going to be hard, but I want you to keep in mind that the soldiers you'll see when you get out there are only illusions. They can't hurt you. All the firing for the past quarter hour has been done by us and that sniper. Notice how quiet it is now. It has been so noisy in this ravine that we didn't realize *we* were making all the noise. But now we'll have to get out of here before the real noise starts."

Whittaker and Martinne were already up at the lip of the ravine. After a moment, the corporal said: "We've got him spotted, sir."

"Fire when ready."

The two men cut loose.

"Let's go, men," said the lieutenant.

And up and over they went.

Lieutenant Darcy, in the lead, threw a swift glance at the tall tree that held the sniper. Bullets from the rifles of Whittaker and Martinne were splashing bark off the trunk and the limb where the sniper was hiding. Good enough.

They moved fast, keeping low and spread out. It was possible that there might be more than one sniper around, though the lieutenant didn't think so, and playing it cautiously was the order of the day.

Ahead of them, the illusory Polish infantrymen still moved about, but they no longer seemed real. They were flickering phantoms that receded and faded as the Imperial troops moved toward them.

"Where's Kelleigh goin', sir?" Sergeant O Lochlainn's voice came from a few yards to Lieutenant Darcy's left. The lieutenant took a quick glance.

Instead of going straight for the woods, Kelleigh had cut off to the left at an angle. Covered by the rifle fire from Whittaker and Martinne, he was headed straight for the sniper's tree!

"He's going to get that sniper," Lieutenant Darcy said sharply. *The damned fool!* he added to himself. He hadn't ordered Kelleigh to do that. On the other hand, he hadn't ordered him not to—simply because it hadn't occurred to him that Kelleigh would do anything like that. *And it should have,* he told himself. *It* should *have!*

228

But now was no time to say anything.

The remains of Blue and Red Companies reached the woods.

"Get down!" the lieutenant snapped. "Lay some covering fire on that tree so that Whittaker and Martinne can get over here!"

The order was obeyed, and the two men came up and over just as the Polish Gornickis exploded into thunder, launching their six-inch shells toward the ravine.

Whittaker and Martinne were only a few yards from the edge of the ravine when the first salvo exploded at the bottom of it. If the shells had landed that close on level ground, the men would have died then and there, but the walls of the ravine directed most of the blast upward. Both men were knocked flat, but they were up again and running within seconds.

Then there was the crack of a rifle shot from the sniper's tree, and Martinne fell sprawling, his left eye and temple a smashed ruin. Whittaker kept coming.

The lieutenant snapped his head around to look at the tree.

Sergeant Kelleigh was still a few yards from it. The sniper hadn't seen Kelleigh yet; he had moved around to the north side of the tree, to another branch, and had seen the two men running. One shot, and Martinne was dead.

Then the sniper saw Superior Sergeant Kelleigh. He had to make a snap decision and a snap shot. Kelleigh, obviously hit, stumbled, fell and rolled.

But he was behind that tree, and the sniper couldn't adjust his precarious position fast enough to get his rifle to bear a second time. Kelleigh, flat on his back, had his .44 MMP out and firing. Two shots.

Even as the sniper fell, Kelleigh hit him with one more shot in midair.

Seeing all this from a distance, Lieutenant Darcy gave the order to cease fire. Then: "Sergeant Lyon, you are senior NCO now. Send someone out to look at Martinne. I think he's dead, but make sure. Sergeant O Lochlainn, will you come with me?"

The thunder of the guns went on, the shells fell screaming into the ravine to spend their explosions uselessly against the clay of the walls and other, equally lifeless clay.

The lieutenant and Sergeant O Lochlainn ran northward to where Sergeant Kelleigh lay.

He was still flat on his back, eyes closed, right hand

clasping his .44 Morley to his chest. It rose and fell with his chest. Beneath it, blood flowed steadily.

The lieutenant knelt down. "Kelleigh?"

The sergeant opened his eyes, focusing them unsteadily on the young face. "You know," he said distinctly.

The lieutenant nodded.

"Don't tell the coronel."

And then, very quietly, he died.

With his thumbs, the lieutenant pulled the eyelids down, held them for a few seconds. Sergeant O Lochlainn made the Sign of the Cross and murmured an almost inaudible prayer. The lieutenant made the same Sign in silence, letting the stout little Irishman's prayer do for both of them.

Then Sergeant O Lochlainn went to the body of the sniper. The Pole had fallen on his face and was very definitely dead. The Irishman opened the sniper's backback and began rummaging through it.

"Here! What are you doing?" Lieutenant Darcy asked. Robbing the dead was not a part of civilized warfare—if such a thing existed.

"Well, sir," said Sergeant O Lochlainn without looking up from what he was doing, "this man here was a sorcerer of some small ability, and he might have the paraphernalia I need. Ah! Just the thing! Here we are!"

"What do you mean?" the lieutenant asked.

"Well, sir," the sergeant said, looking up with a grin, "if we're going to take those field pieces away from the Poles, it might be better if they're attacked by a batallion instead of the bob ends of two companies. And believe me, sir, I'm a better sorcerer than he was."

Lieutenant Darcy tried to return the grin. "I see. Very well, Sergeant; carry on."

The artillery thundered on.

Lieutenant Darcy picked up his small group of men and moved eastward with them. The soft breeze brought the smoke and stench of the thundering guns directly toward them, but it drifted slowly, and it was not dense enough to make the men cough.

There was a grim smile on Sergeant O Lochlainn's face as they neared the eastern edge of the woods. Beyond was a clear space of half a mile or so square.

Sergeants Lyon and O Lochlainn and Lieutenant Darcy lay flat on their bellies watching the battery of eight Gornickis blast away. The lieutenant watched through his field glasses for a full minute, then said: "Fifteen, maybe sixteen infantrymen with rifles. The rest are all gun crews. Range about 800 yards." He took the binoculars from his eyes and looked at the Irish sergeant. "Where do you have to be to set up our phantom batallion, Sergeant?"

"I'll have to set it up right about here, sir. But I can establish my focal point, and then get out, leaving it to operate by itself."

"Good. Because when they see your illusions coming, those gunners are going to depress their barrels and fire point blank. Can you set up the illusion so that some of them will fall when shells explode around them?"

"Nothin' to it, sir."

"Fine. The rest of us will move south to those woods flanking them. Give us ten minutes to get there before you start the phantoms moving in. Then run like Hell to get down with us before they start firing straight in here instead of over our heads. From their flank, we can enfilade them and wipe them out before they know what's happening."

"It's goin' to tear Hell out of these trees," was all the sergeant said.

The lieutenant and Sergeant Lyon led the men south through the woods and then turned eastward again, well south of the clearing where the Polish artillery blasted away.

"All right now, lads," the lieutenant said, "set your sights for 350 yards. Keep low and try to make every shot count. We won't see the phantoms, but the Poles will. We will be able to tell when they see the illusion by the way they behave; their infantry will start firing their rifles toward those trees to our left, and the gunnery crews will stop their barrage and frantically start depressing the muzzles of their pieces. As soon as their infantry begins to fire, so do we. But—mark this!—*no volleys!*

"If we all fire at once, they'll spot us. Now, I'm going to count you off and I want you to remember your number. Whatever your number is, I want you to listen for that many shots from here before you fire. After that, you may fire at will, slow and steady. We're getting low on ammo, so don't be wasteful. Got it?"

They did. The lieutenant counted them off.

For a minute or two, nothing happened. Then everything happened. There were shouts and sounds of excitement from the Polish lines. The infantrymen threw themselves prone and began firing at nothing the Imperial forces

231

could see. The gunners began frantically spinning the wheels that would lower the aim of their guns.

The lieutenant, who had given himself no number and was therefore automatically Number Zero, took careful aim and fired. A man dropped limply and the lieutenant swallowed a sudden blockage in his throat. It was the first time he had ever deliberately fired at and killed a man.

The rest of the men, in order, began firing steadily.

Very rarely do battles go as one expects them to, but this was one of the rare ones. The Poles, to the very end, never did figure out where that death-dealing fire was coming from. The distraction of the phantoms advancing toward them in numberless hordes kept them from even thinking about their left flank. The action was over in minutes.

"Now what, sir?" asked Sergeant Lyon. "Shall we go out and take over those guns?"

"Not yet. Batallion can't be over a couple of miles south of here. Send a couple of runners. We'll wait here, just in case more Poles come. We'll be safer here in these woods than out there, standing around those field pieces. Have the runners report directly to Coronel Everard and get his orders on what to do with those things. Move."

"Yes, sir." Sergeant Lyon obeyed.

Lieutenant Darcy sat down on a nearby fallen log, took out his pipe, tamped it lightly and fired it up. Sergeant O Lochlainn came up and sat beside him. "Mind if I join you, sir?"

"Not at all. Welcome."

"Nice piece of work, sir."

"Same to you, Sergeant. I don't know what those Poles saw, but it must have been something to see. Panicked the Hell out of them. Congratulations."

"Thank you, sir." After a pause, the sergeant said: "Sir, may I ask a question? Maybe it's none of me business, and if so ye've but to tell me and I'll never think of it again."

"Go ahead, Sergeant."

"What was it Sergeant Kelleigh didn't want you to tell Coronel Everard?"

The young lieutenant frowned and puffed solemnly at his pipe for nearly half a minute before he said: "To be perfectly honest, Sergeant, I don't know of anything he would want me to keep from Coronel Everard. Not a thing."

No, he thought. *Nothing he had wanted to keep from Coronel Everard. He didn't want me to tell Coronel Darcy. And I shan't. Kelleigh made a terrible mistake, but he paid for it, and that's an end of it.*

"I see, sir," the Irishman said slowly. "He was dying and likely didn't know what he was saying. Or who he was talkin' to."

"That could be," Lieutenant Darcy said.

But he knew it wasn't so. He had known since he saw the captain's body that Kelleigh had shot him. The bullet had gone straight through, parallel to the ground, not from a high angle. And the hole had been made by a .44 Morley, not by a .28 Kosciusko.

It would have been simple. Men in a firefight don't pay any attention to what is going on to their right or left, and what is one more shot among so many?

Kelleigh had felt that the captain's decision to charge the Polish line was suicidal, and that Darcy's planned retreat was the wiser course.

When he found that the Polish troops were an illusion, he had paid for his crime in the best way he knew how. Captain Rimbaud had been going to do the right thing for the wrong reason, and Kelleigh could no longer live with himself.

There would be no point in telling anyone. Kelleigh was dead, and the only evidence—Rimbaud's body—had been blown to bits in the first Polish salvo to hit the ravine.

But—however wrongly, Kelleigh had given Lieutenant Darcy his first command. The lieutenant would never forget that, but he would always wonder whether it had been worth it.

The Hell with it, he thought. And knocked the dottle from his pipe.

MORGEN ROT

≈≈≈≈≈≈≈≈≈≈≈≈≈≈≈≈≈≈≈≈≈≈≈≈

Gordon R. Dickson

"*Morgen Rot*" (RED MORNING) IS A GRIM old German cavalry song. I have had a lifelong interest
Gordon R. Dickson
in songs and ballads and this was one that I had never really expected to hear sung by anyone to whom the German cavalry was more than a historic name. Thanks to Randall, I did hear it—once.

Back in the days before the Science Fiction Writers of America was invented, there was a publication by Theodore R. Cogswell, one of our fellow wizards, called *The Publications of the Twenty-First Century Institute*. In its pages was found the first large epistolatory gathering of professional science-fiction writers. Willy Ley, who was a grand old man of the field, was very appreciative of what this journal had done for us all, and had wanted to take Ted to dinner when he was in New York as a gesture of that appreciation.

As it happened, the dinner developed to include four of us—Willy, Randall, Ted and myself. Willy, Randall and I ended up going directly to the German restaurant Willy had chosen for the dinner. Ted was to meet us there later, having various other things to do.

On the walk to the restaurant, I remembered "*Morgen Rot*," and in a moment when we were temporarily out of Willy's hearing, I asked Randall about it.

"Do you suppose," I said, "that Willy knows the tune?"

"Why don't you ask him?" Randall said.

A sensible suggestion; and one that presumably had some justification. Like Ted, I was headquartered outside New York City. Randall, like Willy, lived there, and saw Willy a great deal more frequently than I did. The assumption was that Willy would not mind being asked.

Nonetheless, I hesitated. I had lived through the time of World War II. So, of course, had Willy. Possibly there might be some reason he might not like to be asked about an old cavalry song? I left the thought of asking him on hold, hanging it up in the sky, as it were.

We sat down at our table in the restaurant, and the waiter came around. It was not merely a German restaurant, it was a very Germanic restaurant. The waiter wanted our orders for drinks; Randall, following his friendly custom at the time, spoke up without hesitation.

"Double martini," he said.

So of course Willy also ordered a double martini, and, of course, so did I. This was in the good old days when it you did not specify that your cocktail should be served on-the-rocks, it came to you correctly and undiluted, except for the small, inevitable dilution involved in the mixing process, in a wide-mouthed cocktail glass. The martinis we were served were large, excellent and properly chilled. We chatted and waited for Ted to show up. In due course, the waiter came around again.

"Double martini," said Randall. And so said we all.

We continued talking and drinking double martinis, while the restaurant filled up around us with good folk intent on having dinner. Time went by but Ted did not show up. As a matter of fact, as we were to discover later, a minor accident had occupied him and he was not to join us at all. But at the time all we knew was that we were still waiting; and while Randall had had a good idea in the first place and we were all gentlemen who could drink more than two or three martinis at a sitting, there was a reasonable point of terminus to such activity.

I also thought that our waiter was becoming more and more restive under our failure to order dinner. In this, as it turned out, I was wrong—but I'm getting ahead of the story.

As time went on, the thought of the tune to *"Morgen Rot"* kept coming back to me, more and more temptingly. It was true that all it would take would be a relatively small amount of library research to turn up the sheet music; but the fact that I had Willy right there was going to my head. To hear the tune directly from him would bear the same relationship to getting it from sheet music that an authentic 18th century coin would bear to a modern museum facsimile.

About this time, we had started to talk seriously of

dinner. Randall, like all good angels, having planted the seed of the idea and generously watered it with orders of martinis, went off to the men's room; and, emboldened by our momentary privacy, I broached the matter to Willy.

"Willy," I said. "I've never heard the tune to *'Morgen Rot.'* Do you happen to know how it was sung?"

"Certainly," he said.

It is necessary at this point to mention once more the Germanic quality of the restaurant: the white table cloths, the polite, low murmur of voices, the stern visage of the waiter and the sterner visage of the maitre d', who had been glancing our way with increasing frequency in the last hour or so. Willy sat back in his chair.

I had expected him to hum me the tune—perhaps just a bar or two of it, but with that to guide me and the sheet music in hand . . .

He did no such thing. He sat back in his chair, as I just said, opened his mouth and proceeded to sing me four verses.

Willy Ley was a large man with a large voice. At this time it was a resonant, if slightly flat, bass. It is no exaggeration to say that it rattled at least the tableware of the surrounding dozen tables, and must have been clearly audible beyond the swinging doors leading to the kitchen at the restaurant's far end.

With the first line, I braced myself for the onslaught—the flying wedge of waiters who would discharge us into the street, probably calling the police at the same time. I remember thinking briefly that at least Randall, safely off the scene in the men's room, might escape the retribution that was sure to descend on the other two of us. I waited . . . but nothing happened.

I looked around, as Willy began the second verse. At the adjoining tables the diners were still dining and murmuring. Waiters were still going sedately back and forth with food and drink orders. Our own waiter and the maitre d' were individually staring at the ceiling and showing a party of three, just arrived, to a corner table. Willy and I might as well have been 40 miles away on a mountaintop for all the remark that was being made of Willy's singing.

It was then I realized—just as Randall came back to sit down with us, also paying no apparent attention to the rendition of *"Morgen Rot"* proceeding four feet from his right ear—the true nature of the difference that made

"Morgen Rot" the song it was, Randall and I the sort of people we were, and Willy, Willy.

It became perfectly clear to me that had Randall or I sung *"Morgen Rot,"* even under our breaths, that flying wedge of waiters would without question have arrived. But not when Willy sang it—not even if the ceiling had cracked.

Willy sounded right. He and *"Morgen Rot"* made an acceptable pair under any conditions in that restaurant. He knew this without having to think about it; and Randall—as I finally perceived when I caught his eye across the table—had also known it all along and counted on it.

One of the most recent Garrett stories—a delicious mixture of fantasy and science fiction that would have been quite at home in that famous and unique magazine of long ago, *Unknown Worlds*.

FROST AND THUNDER

ULGLOSSEN WAS DABBLING IN POLYDIMEN-sional energy flows again.

Do not try to understand Ulglossen. Ulglossen's time was—is—will be—three million years after Homo sapiens ruled Earth, and Ulglossen's species is no more to be understood by us that we could be understood by Australo-pithecus.

To say, then, that Ulglossen built a "time machine" is as erroneus—and as truthful—as saying that a big indus-trial computer of the late 20th century is a device for counting with pebbles.

Doing polydimensional vector analysis mentally was, for Ulglossen, too simple and automatic to be called child's play. Actually constructing the mechanism was somewhat more difficult, but Ulglossen went about it with the same toilsome joy that a racing buff goes about rebuilding his Ferrari. When it was finished, Ulglossen viewed it with the equivalent of pride. In doing the mental math, Ulglossen had rounded off at the 19th decimal place, for no greater accuracy than that was needed. But, as a result, Ulglossen's "machine" caused slight eddy currents in the time flow as it passed. The resulting effect was much the same as that of an automobile going down a freeway and passing a wadded ball of paper. The paper is picked up and carried a few yards down the freeway before it falls out of the eddy currents and is dropped again.

Ulglossen was not unaware of that fact; it was simply that Ulglossen ignored it.

The device, you see, was merely a side effect of Ulglossen's real work, which was the study of the attenuation of the universal gravitational constant over a period of millions of millenia. Ulglossen happened to be on Earth, and had some experiments to perform in the very early pre-Cambrian. Ulglossen went back to do so.

I'll try to tell this the best I can. I don't expect you to believe it because, in the first place, I haven't a shred of proof, and, in the second place, I wouldn't believe it myself if I hadn't actually experienced it.

Sure, I *might* have dreamed it. But it was too solid, too detailed, too logical, too *real* to have been a dream. So it happened, and I'm stuck with it.

It begins, I suppose, when I got the letter from Sten Ömfeld. I've known Sten for years. We've fought together in some pretty odd places, argued with each other about the damnedest things, and once even quarreled over the same woman. (He won.) He's a good drinking buddy, and he'll back a friend in a pinch. What more do you want?

A few years back, Sten and I got interested in what was then the relatively new sport of combat pistol, down in southern California. It's a game that requires fast draw, fast shooting, fast reloading and accuracy to make points. One of the rules is that you *must* use full-charge service cartridges. No half-charge wadcutters allowed.

We both enjoyed it.

Then, I didn't see Sten for some time. I didn't think much about it. Sten does a lot of traveling, but, basically, he's a Swede, and he has to go home every so often. I'm only half Swede, and I was born in the United States. Sweden is a lovely country, but it just isn't home to me.

Anyway, I got this letter addressed to me, Theodore Sorenson, with a Stockholm postmark. Sten, so he claimed, had introduced combat pistol shooting to Sweden, and had built a range on his property. He was holding a match in September, and would I come? There would be plenty of *akvavit.*

He hadn't needed to add that last, but it helped. I made plane reservations and other arrangements.

You would not believe how hard it is to get a handgun into Sweden legally. (I don't know how hard it would be to do it illegally; I've never tried.) Even though Sten Ömfeld had all kinds of connections in high places and had filed a declaration of intent or something, informing the government of his shooting match, and had gotten the government's permission, it was rough sledding. I had to produce all kinds of papers identifying the weapon, and papers showing that I had never been convicted of a felony, and on and on. Fortunately, Sten's letter had warned me about all that. Still, just filling out papers and signing my name must have used up a good liter of ink.

Eventually, they decided I could take my .45 Colt Commander into Sweden. Provided, of course, that I brought it back out again; I couldn't sell it, give it away, or, presumably, lose it, under dire penalties.

Mine isn't an ordinary, off-the-shelf Colt Commander. I had it rebuilt by Pachmayr of Los Angeles. It has a 4½-inch barrel, a BoMar adjustable combat rear sight, a precision-fit slide with a special Micro barrel-bushing, a special trigger assembly that lets me fire the first shot double action, and a lot of other extra goodies. It's hardchromed all over, which means it can stand up to a lot of weather without rusting. In a machine rest, I can get a three-inch group at a hundred yards with a hundred shots. When Frank Pachmayr finishes with a Colt Commander, you can damn well bet you've got one of the finest, hardest-hitting handguns in the world.

So I had no intention of selling, giving away or losing that weapon.

Sten Ömfeld met me at Arlanda Airport and helped me get through the paperwork. My Swedish is as good as his, just as his English is as good as mine—but he knows the ins-and-outs of the local ways better than I do. Then we got in his plane, and he flew me to his little place in the woods.

Not so little, and more of a forest than woods. It was on the Österdalälven—the Österdal River—on the western slope of the Kjölen, that great ridge of mountains whose peaks separate Norway from Sweden. It was some miles northeast of a little town callen Älvadalen, well away from everything.

Sten landed us in a little clearing, and said: "Theodore, we are here."

Sten always called me Theodore, another reason why he was a friend. I have never liked "Ted." My mother was an O'Malley, with red-auburn hair; my father was a blond Swede. Mine came out flaming red-orange. So I was "Ted the Red"—and worse—in school. Like the guy named Sue, it taught me to fight, but I hated it.

Of course, if Sten was speaking Swedish at the time, it came out something like "Taydor" but I didn't mind that.

He showed me through his house, an old-fashioned, sturdy place with the typical high-pitched, snow-shedding roof.

"You're the first one in," he told me. "Sit down and have a little *akvavit*. Unless you're hungry?"

I wasn't; I'd eaten pretty well on the plane. We had *akvavit* and coffee, and some *rågkakor* his mother had sent him.

"Tonight," he said, "I'll fix up the spices and the orange rind and the almonds and the raisins, and let 'em soak in the booze overnight for hot *glögg* tomorrow. And I've fixed it up for some people to drive up from Älvadalen with a *julskinka* we'll serve 14 weeks early."

"So I'm the only one here so far?" I said.

"First arrival," he said. "Which poses a problem."

I sipped more *akvavit*. "Which is?"

"I *think*—I say I *think*—you're going to outshoot the whole lot of 'em. Now, I've got this special course laid out, and a lot of 'friend-and-foe' pop-up targets. I was going to let each of you guys run it cold. But there are some of these hard-nosed skvareheads who'd secretly think I took you over the course early so you'd be prepared. They wouldn't say anything, but they'd think it."

"So what do you figure on doing?"

"Well, I haven't set the pop-ups yet; I was going to set 'em in the morning. Instead, I'm going to take all of you over the course before the targets are set, then set 'em up while you guys watch each other here." He roared with laughter. "That will keep you all honest!"

Sten isn't your big Swede; he's a little guy, five-six or so, and I stand six-four. I must outweigh him by 36 kilos. I could probably whip him in a fight, but I would be in damn sad condition for a while afterward. I have seen what has happened to a couple of large galoots who thought he'd be an easy pushover. He was standing over them, begging them to get up for more fun, but they couldn't hear him.

"Hey!" he said, "How about checking me out on that fancy piece of artillery, now that we've managed to get it into the country?"

I was willing. I showed him the Pachmayr conversion of

the Colt Commander, and he was fascinated. His final comment was: "God*damn,* what a gun!"

When we were glowing nicely warm inside the *akvavit,* and I could taste caraway clear back to my tonsils, Sten put the bottle away. "Got to keep the shootin' eye clear and the shootin' hand steady for tomorrow," he said. "Besides, I've got to do the *glögg* fixin's."

"Need any help?"

"Nope."

"Is there anyplace I could go hose a few rounds through the tube, just to get the feel in this climate?"

"Sure. There's a dead pine about 80 yards due south. I'm going to cut it down for winter fuel later, but I've put a few slugs in it, myself. Make damn heavy logs, I'll bet." He laughed again. Then: "Hey, you got a name for that blaster of yours yet?"

"No. Not yet." Sten had a habit of naming his weapons, but I'd never gone in for the custom much.

"Shame. Good gun should have a name. Never mind; you'll think of one. It's beginning to get late. Dark in an hour and a half. Dress warm. Good shooting."

Dressing warm was no problem. I was ready for it; I knew that the weather can get pretty chilly in the highlands of Sweden in September. Walking from Sten's little plane hangar to his lodge had told me that I wasn't properly dressed for afternoon; I knew good and well that the clothes I was wearing wouldn't be warm enough for dusk.

"What's the forecast for tomorrow, Sten?" I yelled at him in the kitchen.

"Cold and clear!" he yelled back. "Below freezing!"

"I should have known! You call me out of warm California so I can freeze my ass off trying to fire a handgun in Sweden!"

"Damn right! You got to have *some* sort of handicap! Shut up and go shoot!"

It really wasn't cold enough yet, but I decided I'd have a little practice in full insulation. I put on my Scandinavian net long johns, and an aluminized close-weave over that. I get my outdoor clothing from Herter's, in Minnesota; there's no one like them for quality and price. I wore a Guide Association Chamois Cloth tan shirt, Down Arctic pants, and Yukon Leather Pac boots. Over that went the Hudson Bay Down Artic parka with the frost-free, fur-trimmed hood.

For gloves, I had two choices: the pigskin shooting

242

gloves or the Hudson Bay buckskin one-finger mittens. I shoved the mittens in my parka pocket and put on the shooting gloves. *Try 'em both,* I told myself.

I'd had the parka specially cut for quick-draw work, with an opening on the right side for the pistol and holster. Before I sealed up the parka, I put on the gunbelt, a special job made for me by Don Hume, of Miami, Oklahoma. It has quick-release leather pockets, five of them, for holding extra magazines. The holster is a quick-draw job made for my sidearm. When Don Hume says, "Whatever the need," he means it.

"Carry on, bartender!" I yelled from the door. "I am off to the wars!"

"Be sure that old dead pine doesn't beat you to the draw!" he yelled back.

It was cold outside, but there wasn't much wind. I saw the dead pine, and headed for it.

Night comes on slowly in the north, but it comes early east of the Kjölen. Those mountains make for a high horizon.

Sten had, indeed, used that pine for target practice; he'd painted a six-inch white circle on it. I went up to the pine, then turned to pace off 25 yards.

I was at 20 paces when the wind hit.

I don't know how to describe what happened. It was like a wind, and yet it wasn't. It was as if everything whirled around, and *then* the wind came.

And I was in the middle of the goddamnedest blizzard I had seen since the time I nearly froze to death in Nebraska.

I stood still. Only a damn fool wanders around when he can't see where he's going. I knew I was only 50 yards from Sten's lodge, and I trusted the insulated clothing I was wearing. I wouldn't freeze, and I could wait out the storm until I got my bearings.

I put out my arms and turned slowly. My right hand touched a tree. I hadn't remembered a tree that near, but it gave me an anchor. I stepped over and stood the leeward side of it, away from the wind.

In those two steps, I noticed something impossible to believe.

The snow around my ankles was four inches deep.

There had been no snow on the ground when I started out.

And I don't believe there has *ever* been a storm which could deposit four inches of snow in less than two seconds.

243

I just stood there, wondering what the hell had happened. I couldn't see more than a couple of yards in front of me, and the dim light didn't help much. I waited. The howling of that sudden wind was far too loud for my voice to be heard over 50 yards. Sten would never hear me.

But he would know I was out in this mess, and he would know I would keep my head. I could wait. For a while, at least.

I looked at my watch to check the time. Very good. Then I leaned back against the relatively warm tree to wait.

My hands began to get cold. I stripped off the shooting gloves and put on the one-finger mittens. Better.

As sometimes happens in a snowstorm, the wind died down abruptly. It became a gentle breeze. Overhead, the clouds had cleared, and there came almost a dead calm as the last few snowflakes drifted down. My watch told me it had been 27 minutes since the storm had started.

The sun glittered off the fresh snow.

The sun?

By now, it should have been close to the peaks of the Kjölen. It wasn't. It was almost overhead.

I looked carefully around. I should have been able to see the dead pine, and I certainly should have been able to see Sten's lodge.

I could see neither. Around me was nothing but forest. Only the distant crest of the Kjölen looked the same.

The whole thing was impossible, and I knew it. I also knew that I was seeing what I was seeing.

My mother, bless her, had told me stories when I was a kid—old Irish stories about the Folk of Faerie and the Hollow Hills.

"If you're invited beneath a Hollow Hill by the Faerie Folk, don't ever touch a drop of their drink or a bite of their food, or when you come out after the night, 100 years will have passed."

Throw out that hypothesis. I hadn't been invited beneath any Hollow Hill, much less taken a drink or eaten a bite.

Unless Sten—

Oh, hell, *no!* That was silly.

But certainly *something* had gone wrong with time. Or with my mind. The sun was in the wrong place.

If you can't trust your own mind, what can you trust? As old Whatsisname—Descartes—said: *Cogito ergo sum.*

I think; therefore, I am.

244

I decided, therefore, that not only I *was,* but I was sane.

I had read about cryogenic experiments. Theoretically, if an organism is frozen properly, it can stay in a state of suspended animation for an indefinite time. Suppose that had happened to me. Suppose a sudden blizzard had frozen me stiff, and I had thawed out years later, without realizing that time had passed.

It didn't seem likely. Surely I would have been found by Sten. Or, if not, I'd have waked up flat on my back instead of standing up. No. Not likely.

But I decided to check it out. It would take a long time for Sten's lodge to deteriorate to the point where there were no traces left.

I walked over to where the lodge should have been, trudging through the ankle-deep snow. I'm a pretty good judge of distance and direction, and I checked the whole area where the lodge should have been.

Nothing. Pine needles under the snow; nothing under the pine needles but dirt. Nothing.

There was an old, broken tree stump about where Sten's living room should have been. I brushed the snow off it and sat down.

I don't think I thought for several minutes. Then I noticed that I was beginning to get a little chilled. Get some exercise and build a fire. I went out and gathered what broken bits of pine branches I could find, and built a small campfire near the stump. No rubbing two sticks together; my butane lighter still worked.

I sat there for an hour in a pale blue funk, wondering what had happened.

I know it was an hour, because I looked at my watch again. That was when I heard a quiet noise behind me.

I jerked my head around and looked. My hand went to my right hip. But I didn't draw.

Standing not ten paces from me were seven men.

They were quiet and unmoving, like frozen statues except for their eyes, which regarded me with interest, curiosity and caution.

They were heavily clad in dark furs, like Eskimos wearing black bearskins. Each one carried a long spear and a roundshield.

They weren't Eskimos. Eskimos don't have blue eyes and blond hair. Those blue eyes regarded me with suspicion.

I lifted my hands carefully, showing them empty. I

245

couldn't figure out the spears, but I didn't want to get in a hassle with the locals.

"Good afternoon, gentlemen," I said in Swedish. I kept my voice low and controlled. "Would you care to share the fire with me?"

There was a pause while all of them looked blank. Then one of them stepped forward and said something in an equally low and controlled voice. I couldn't understand a word of it.

Still, it sounded damned familiar.

I can speak—besides English—Swedish, Norwegian, Icelandic and Danish very well. I speak German with a weird accent, but I can make myself understood easily. Afrikaans is a language I can almost understand, but not quite. This was like that.

"I don't understand," I said.

The man who had stepped out—obviously the leader—turned and said something to the man next to him. The second man answered. Their voices were low and so soft I couldn't get the drift. I figured the second man was second in command.

The leader turned to me again and spoke in a louder voice, very slowly, syllable by syllable.

It took me a few seconds to get it.

I don't know if I can explain it to you. Look; suppose you were in that same situation, and some fur-clad character had come up to you and said: *"hwahn-thah-tah-pree-lah-wee-thiz-show-rez-so-tah-theh-drocht-ahv-mahrch-ath-peersed-tow-theh-row-tah. . . ."*

You might feel a little left out of it, right?

Then, suddenly, it comes to you that what he is doing is too-carefully pronouncing Chaucer's *"Whan that Aprillë with his shourës sootë/The droghte of March hath percëd to the rootë . . ."*

And then you have to translate that into modern English as: "When April, with his showers sweet, the drought of March has pierced to the root . . ."

It was like that to me. I got it, partly, but it was older than any Northman's tongue I had ever heard. It was more inflected and had more syllables per word than any I knew. It made Icelandic seem modern.

What he had said was: "You say you do not understand?"

I tried to copy his usage and inflection. It came out something like: "Yah. Me no understand."

246

I won't try to give you any more of my linguistic troubles. I'll just say that the conversation took a little longer than it should have.

"You must understand a little," he said.

"Yah. A little. Not well. I am sorry."

"Who are you, and what do you do here?"

"I called Theodore." But I pronounced it "Taydor".

"'What do you do here?" he repeated. Those spears weren't pointed at me, but they were at the ready. I didn't like the looks of the chipped flint points.

"I lost," I said. "I have hunger and suffer from cold."

"Where do you come from?"

"America. Across the western sea."

They looked at each other. Then the leader looked back at me. "You are alone?"

"I am alone." It was a dangerous admission to make. A lone man is easier prey than one who has friends. But I figured a bluff of having friends around wouldn't work, and I didn't want to be caught out as a liar right off the bat. Besides, if worse came to worst, I figured I could gun the seven of them down before they could touch me. But I didn't want to do that. Not unless they attacked me without provocation.

The spears remained at the ready, but the men seemed to relax a little.

"What is your station?" the leader asked.

It took me a second. He was asking my rank in life. Was I a thrall or a freeman or a noble?

"I am a freeman and a warrior," I answered honestly. The time I'd spent in the service ought to count for something. "But I have, as you see, no spear and no shield."

"Then how do we know you are a warrior? How did you lose your spear and shield?"

"I did not lose them. I have come in peace."

That flabbergasted them. There was a lot of low talk among them. I sat quietly.

I was taking the tide as it ran. I still had no idea of what had happened to me, but I was damned if I'd be a stupid tourist in someone else's country.

Finally, the leader said: "Tay'or, you will come with us. We will give you food and drink and we will talk over your oddness."

"I will come," I said. I stood up.

They gripped their spears more tightly, and their eyes widened.

I knew why. It was something none of us had realized while I was seated. I was bigger than any of them. Not a one of them was taller than Sten Ömfeld. But they looked just as tough.

I folded my hands on my chest. "I go where you lead."

They didn't all lead. The head cheese and his lieutenant went ahead; the other five were behind me, spears still at the ready.

It was about 20 minutes' walk, which made sense. The fire I had started had attracted their attention, and the wisp of smoke had led them to me. It had just taken them a little time to decide to investigate.

We ended up at a collection of log cabins. I was marched straight to the largest one and led inside, past a curtain of bearskin. I had to duck my head to get through the doorway. Just inside, the leader stopped and said: "You are in the mead-hall of Vigalaf Wolfslayer. Conduct yourself accordingly."

There was a fire in the middle of the earth-floored room, just below a hole in the roof which was supposed to let the smoke out. Maybe 80 percent of it went out, but the other 20 percent filled the air. Underneath the smell of pine smoke was an odor of rancid fat and cooked meat.

By the fire stood a man with a great gray-blond beard, and long hair to match. He was a giant of a man, compared to the others; he must have stood a full five-eight.

I took him to be Vigalaf Wolfslayer, and, as it turned out, I was right. He said two words: "Explain, Hrotokar."

Hrotokar was the leader of the squad who'd found me. He told his story straight, emphasizing the fact that I had given no trouble.

Vigalaf looked at me for the first time. "Doff your hood in my presence, Giant Tay'or," he said—not arrogantly, but merely as a statement of his due. I peeled back the hood of my parka.

"Truly, not one of *Them*, then," he said. "The Eaters-of-Men have no such hair, nor such eyes. Are you truly one of us, Giant?"

"A distant relative, Vigalaf Wolfslayer," I said. I thought I was telling the truth, but God knows how distant the relationship was.

"You will call me Father Wolfslayer," he said. Again, no arrogance—just his due.

"I ask pardon, Father Wolfslayer," I said. "I am not familiar with your customs. Forgive me if I err."

He nodded and eased himself down on a pile of furs near the fire. "Sit," he said.

I sat. My escort did not. Evidently, they knew his order had not been addressed to them. There were no furs for me, so I planted my rump on the bare earth of the floor, crossing my legs.

"Bring him mead," he said.

By this time, my eyes had grown accustomed to the gloom in the windowless mead-hall. I saw that there were other people back in the dark corners, all wearing furs. In spite of the fire, there was still a chill; most of the heat was going out the roof hole.

From one dark corner, there was a gurgling noise. Then a figure stepped forward, bearing a horn of mead. I mean it. An honest-to-God cow's horn, ten inches long, full of liquid.

I've done a lot of drinking in a lot of places, but the one drink I'd never tried until that moment was mead. I knew it was made from honey, so I had, somewhere in the back of my mind, the notion that it was sweet, like port or sweet sherry.

No such thing. This stuff tasted like flat beer. It had a certain amount of authority, however.

Before I drank, I thought I ought to say something. I lifted the horn and said: "I thank you for your hospitality, Father Wolfslayer." I drank.

It was evidently the right thing to say. I saw his beard and mustache curl in a smile. "Truly," he said again, "not one of *Them*."

I took the bit in my teeth. "Forgive my ignorance Father Wolfslayer, but you speak of *Them*. Who are *They?*"

His shaggy gray eyebrows lifted. "You know not? Truly, you are from afar. *They* are the demons, the Evil Ones, the Eaters-of-Men. *They* are from the Far North, and they come to slay and to eat. *They* speak as do animals. *They* are Giants!" He paused. "Not so great as you, but Giants, nonetheless." Another pause. "And they wear frost about them instead of furs, as decent folk do."

I couldn't make any sense out of that, but I filed it away for later reference.

"I know nothing of them, Father Wolfslayer," I said. "They are certainly no friends nor kin of mine."

An enemy of these people, obviously. But the "demon"

bit, and the "evil" and the "eaters-of-men" I figured as just so much propaganda.

"You speak well, Giant Tay'or," Vigalaf said. He raised a hand. "Bring him food."

The same person came out from the shadows, bearing a wooden bowl in one hand. This time, I looked more closely at who was serving me.

Me, I wear a beard. It's as red as the rest of my hair. I think shaving is a bore. The rest of the men there wore beards, too. My server was either a beardless boy or a woman. A people who use flint points on their spears find shaving more than a bore; they find it impossible. Besides, the lines around her eyes showed more character than a kid ever had. With those heavy furs on, it was hard to tell anything about her figure, but my instincts told me, more than anything else, that this was no teenage lad.

The glint in her eyes as they met mine confirmed my assessment of the situation. There was a slight smile on her lips as she handed me the bowl.

I automatically took it with my right hand. Then she held out her closed left hand toward mine. I opened my left hand, palm up. She dropped three nuts into it and turned away, going back to her dark corner.

I just sat there for a few seconds. The bowl contained some sort of porridge with a few chunks of meat in it. But there were no utensils to eat it with. And what about those nuts in my other hand?

I could feel every eye in the place on me. This was a test of some kind, but I didn't know what. What the hell should I do next?

Think, Sorenson! Think!

The mead-hall was utterly silent except for the crackling of the fire.

I don't know what sort of logic I used. All I knew was that if I failed this test I had better have my right hand free.

I closed my left hand on the nuts, put the bowl in my lap, and said: "Thank you again, Father Wolfslayer."

There was no answer. Carefully, I began to pick up the lumpy porridge with the thumb and first two fingers of my right hand, conveying the stuff to my mouth. No reaction from the audience. I ate it all. Then I put the bowl on the ground near me. Still no reaction.

It was those damn three nuts, then.

What was I supposed to do with them? Eat them? Give them back? Shove them up my nose? What?

I opened my hand slowly and looked at them. They were some kind of walnut, I guessed, but the shell on them was a lot thicker and harder than the walnuts I was used to.

I wiped my right hand off on my pantsleg. I didn't want a slick hand if I had to grab for my gun. Then I lifted my head slowly and looked at the Wolfslayer, holding his eyes.

He nodded silently and gestured with one hand.

The broad-shouldered blond woman brought me a flat rock, laying it on the ground in front of me before she retreated to her corner.

I got it then. Every man in the place—and the woman, too—carried a little stone-headed mallet cinched at the waist.

Well, what the hell. A chance is a chance.

Frank Pachmayr will supply you, if you want them, with magazines that have a quarter-inch of rubber on the bottom, which, according to some, makes it easier to slam the magazine home on the reload. I never cared for them. Mine are steel on the bottom—no rubber. A personal idiosyncrasy.

At that moment, I thanked God for my idiosyncrasy.

I put the three walnuts on the flat rock, and drew my weapon.

A gun should never be used that way. But, then, a gun should never be used in any way unless there's need for it. It saved my life that time. I took it out, grabbed it near the muzzle and carefully cracked nuts with the butt.

Call it instinct, call it intuition, call it what you will. It was the right thing to do. I found out later than the terrible Eaters-of-Men carried large stone axes, but not small ones. If they ever ate nuts, they cracked them by grabbing the nearest rock and slamming them. No delicacy.

The nuts, by the way, were very bitter.

As I ate the last one, there was a deep sigh that sounded all through the mead-hall. Wolfslayer said: "Giant Tay'or, will you be our guest?"

Searching back in my memory for what little I knew about the ancient history of the Northmen, I said: "I have no guest-gift for my host, Father Wolfslayer."

"Your guest-gift will be your strength, if you will give

it. Will you fight against *Them* when the Demons come again?"

That was a tough one. I only knew one side of the quarrel. But, what the hell, a man who can't choose sides, even if he's wrong, isn't worth a damn. "I have no spear or shield, Father Wolfslayer," I said. And realized I was hedging.

"They will be provided."

"Then I will fight for you."

"Then you are my guest!" Suddenly, he came out with a barrel-roll laugh. "Mead! Mead for all! Come, Giant, sit by me! Here is a skin!"

The party began.

After about the fourth horn of mead, the Wolfslayer leaned over and said: "Where did you come by such a strange mallet?"

"It was made by a friend in a distant country," I said. "It was made for my hands alone." I didn't want the old boy to ask to handle my Colt.

His bushy eyebrows went up again. "Of course. Are not all such, in all places?"

"Of course, Father Wolfslayer." More information. The nutcrackers were personal gear. Fine.

That night, I slept under a bearskin, still wearing my insulated outdoor clothing. I hadn't bathed, but nobody else around there had, either. You could tell.

When I woke up, I was sweating, but my nose was cold. Around me, I could hear thunderous snores, but somebody was moving around, too. I opened one eye a crack. I should have known. The men were still sleeping; the women were preparing breakfast. Women's lib had evidently not reached these people. Which reminded me—

Just who the hell *were* these people?

I was sleeping on my left side (A holstered .45 makes a very lumpy mattress), with my right hand on the butt of my pistol. I kept my eyes closed and checked for hangover. Nope. Whoever their brewmaster was, he made a good brew.

This was the first opportunity that I had had to really think since the squad of seven had found me in the forest. Since then, I had merely been doing my best to stay alive.

I realized that I had accepted one thing: Like Twain's Connecticut Yankee or de Camp's Martin Padway, I had slipped back in time. How far? I didn't know. I still don't. I probably never will. These people weren't Christians, by a long shot, and they'd never heard of Him; I'd got that much in my conversations the previous night.

They'd never heard of Rome, either, but that didn't mean anything. There were a lot of things they might not have heard of, way up here. Like Egypt.

Still, I think I must have been at least 1,500 years in my own past, and probably more. Their use of stone instead of metal certainly argued for great antiquity, and they didn't act at all like the bloodthirsty Vikings history records so vividly.

They were a hunting-and-gathering culture, with emphasis on hunting in the winter. Bear seemed to be their big game during the cold months. A hibernating bear, if you can find one, is fairly easy to kill if you can get it before it wakes up. The meat is good, and the skins are useful.

Snores were changing to snorts and snuffles; the men were waking up. I sat up and yawned prodigiously. Almost immediately, the broad-shouldered blonde of the night before was kneeling in front of me with a wooden bowl full of meat chunks and a horn of warm mead. She was really smiling this time, showing teeth. I noticed that the left upper lateral incisor was crooked. Charming. If only she'd had a bath.

"What's your name?" I asked, after thanking her for the food. As I said, I won't go into my linguistic difficulties. She didn't understand me at first, and we had to work it out.

"Brahenagenunda Vigalaf Wolfslayer's Daughter," she told me. "But you should not thank me for the food; you should thank Father Wolfslayer, for the food is his."

"I shall thank *him* for the food," I said. "I am thanking *you* for the preparing of it." After all, if she was the Wolfslayer's daughter, I was talking to a princess.

She blushed. "Excuse me. I must serve the others."

It occurred to me then that since everyone addressed the old man as "Father" maybe everyone called themselves his sons and daughters, whether they were biologically his children or not. I found out later that only his true children took the Wolfslayer's name. Brahenagenunda was his daughter, all right.

I saw a couple of the men going out, and I had a hunch I knew where they were going, so I followed them. I was right; they headed for the woods. When I returned, I felt much more comfortable. Snow is a poor substitute for toilet tissue, but it's better than nothing.

The cold was not too bitter. About minus two Celsius, I figured. The people from the other, smaller log cabins were going about their business, their breath, like mine, making white plumes in the air, as if everyone were puffing cigarettes. I was glad I'd never had the habit of smoking; I had the feeling tobacco would be hard to come by here-and-now.

Squad Leader Hrotokar was waiting for me just outside Vigalaf's mead-hall. "Hail, Tay'or."

"Hail, Hrotokar."

"We go to seek the bear, my men and I. Will you come?"

Another test, I decided. "I will come."

"There is spear and shield for you." Then he looked me over and became less formal. "Are you sure those funny clothes you're wearing will keep you warm enough?"

"They'll be fine," I assured him. I wasn't going to tell him that they were probably far better than the stuff he was wearing.

"Well, they'll have to do, I guess," he said. "I've got an extra jacket and trousers, but I doubt they'd fit."

"I think you're right. How do we go about this bear hunt?"

Primarily, it turned out, what we did was look for tiny wisps of vapor coming out of a crack in the snow. It indicated that a bear was holed away underneath, breathing slowly and shallowly in hibernation. Then we checked to see if the bear was a female with cubs. We only killed males.

I won't bother telling about that day's hunt, because that's all we did—hunt. Didn't find a damned thing. But Hrotokar and I got to know each other pretty well. Unlike most hunts, we could talk; there's not much danger of waking up a hibernating bear.

The thing was, I wasn't able to get in any practice with spear and shield that day. There's a Greek friend of mine in San José who is a nut on spear-and-shield work in the manner of the ancient Greek *hoplites*. He and a bunch of his buddies worked out the technique, and practiced it, using blunt, padded spears. I practiced with them, and got pretty good at it, but trying it for real is very different indeed. I've had lots of practice with bayonet-and-rifle, too, but I've never had to use it in combat. Or against a bear, even a sleeping one.

The sun shone most of the day, but the clouds came in in the afternoon, and it was snowing again by the time we reached the settlement.

We came in empty-handed, and so did all of the other squads but one. They had a bear, which caused great rejoicing and happiness throughout the community. (I never actually counted them, but I'd estimate there were between 55 and 60 people in the whole settlement.) One of the other squads had seen a deer, but that was the one that got away.

During the winter, most of the gathering done by the women is for firewood. Fallen branches, twigs, anything that will burn. If they find an occasional dead tree, or one that has fallen over, they mark the spot and tell the men about it. Then both sexes form a work party to bring it in.

I was not the guest of honor that night in the mead-hall. A guy named Woritigeren, who had killed the bear, got all the kudos—which he deserved. Father Wolfslayer stood up and made a speech about his bravery and prowess, and then a little guy with a limp—a bard, I guess—made up a chant about Woritigeren that made it sound as if he'd slain a two-ton Kodiak all by himself.

Then Father Wolfslayer shouted: "Mead! Bring mead!"

A woman came from the shadows and brought Woritigeren his horn of mead, but it wasn't Brahenagenunda. This one was older and a good deal more worn looking.

Another woman, even older, came out and whispered into Vigalaf Wolfslayer's ear. He scowled.

There was tension in the air; I could tell that. The mead for the hero was supposed to be served by the Wolfslayer's youngest and prettiest daughter, and that hadn't been done. Technically, Woritigeren had been given a social put-down.

Vigalaf Wolslayer rose with majestic dignity. "Woritigeren Hero," he said, looking at the hunter, who was still holding his mead-horn untasted, "neither I nor my women meant insult here. I have just been told that Vigalaf's Daughter Brahenagenunda has not returned from her wood-gathering. The sun has gone to his rest, and the blizzard is over all." He turned to the little guy with the limp. "Make us a prayer to the All-Father, Song Chanter."

He made us a prayer. I didn't understand a word of it; it

was in a language even older than the one they spoke. But it had a solemnity and dignity that made it a prayer.

One thing. I almost got caught out. I started to bow my head, but I saw what the others were doing in time, and looked upward, out the smoke-hole, toward the sky. I guess they believed in looking God in the face when they talked to Him.

When it was over, the Wolfslayer said: "It is her Wyrd. We shall look for her in the morning."

He was right, of course. I wanted to charge out right then and start searching, but in a blizzard, without lights, it would have been senseless. He—and we—had done all that was possible for the time being.

Wolfslayer lifted his mead horn. "Now, Woritigeren Hero, to your honor."

And the party was on again.

It may seem heartless, the way they behaved. Here was a woman—girl, really; she was only 16—out in the dark and the freezing cold, alone and without help, while her friends and relatives were having a merry time and getting all boozed up. But these were a practical people. When nothing can be done, do something else. She couldn't be rescued yet, so get on with the original schedule. When the time came, things would be done.

In the morning, the sky was clear again. The squads went out, this time both hunting and searching. Deer, bear or dear Brahenagenunda, whatever we could find.

We found nothing. The snow had covered everything. It was six inches deep on the level, and deeper in the drifts. She might have been lying under the snow somewhere, but you can't search every snowdrift.

There was no party in the mead-hall that evening. Neither game nor maid had been found. It was a gloomy night. I slept only because I was exhausted.

The next morning, I went out again with Hrotokar's squad. The gloom was still with us. We didn't talk much.

It was about noon when we came across the Death Sign. That's what Hrotokar called it.

"The Demons," he said very softly. "*They* are here."

I saw what he was pointing at. It was a human skull —the upper part, with the jawbone missing—impaled on a stake about 30 yards away.

"What does it mean?" I asked.

"War," he said simply. "*They,* too, want the bear and the deer. *They* come from the North, with their clothing

256

of frost. This is our hunting country, but *They* want to take it from us. Drive us away or kill us. Come, let us see."

He gave orders to the rest of the squad to be on the lookout, in case this was a trap of some kind. We went up to the Death Sign without seeing or hearing any living thing around.

The skull was a fresh one. There were still shreds of boiled flesh clinging to parts of it. The stake had been thrust through the opening where the spinal column had been. Footprints led to and from the grisly thing. It had been put there sometime that morning.

Hrotokar said in a low grating voice: "All-Father curse them. A man's skull they would have kept to drink from."

Then I saw the crooked left upper lateral incisor.

I know, now, what the word *berserker* means. A red haze of absolute hatred came over me. If there had been anyone to vent that hatred against, I damn well would have done it. I don't know how long that red haze lasted. It seemed eternal from inside, but the others were still standing in the same positions when I came out of it, so it couldn't have been too long.

I had not lost the hatred; it had merely become cold and calculating instead of hot and wild. "Hrotokar," I said calmly, "what do we do next?"

"We must tell the Wolfslayer," he said. From the sound of his voice, I could tell that the same cold hatred had come over him.

"And what will he do?"

"All the fighting men will follow these tracks until we find the Eaters-of-Men, and then we will slay them." He turned to one of the men. "Fleet-of-Foot, go and—"

"Hold, Hrotokar Squad-Leader," I said carefully. "This is a trap." Don't ask me how I knew; I just *knew*. "If Father Wolfslayer sends all the fighting men, that will leave the settlement unguarded. That is what *They* want us to do. Then, while we are following the trail, *They* will go to the settlement and butcher the women, the children and the old ones."

He frowned. "That very well may be, Tay'or. What, then, should we do?"

"How many of the Eaters-of-Men are there?" I asked.

"Half again as many as we have in the settlement. Maybe more. Perhaps we cannot win." He shrugged. "We must try."

"We can win. Do you trust me, Hrotokar?"

He looked at me for a long moment. "I trust you, Giant Fire-Hair."

"Good. Now, here's what you do: Send Fleet-of-Foot to warn Father Wolfslayer. But Father Wolfslayer is not to send more than another squad to us. The rest should stay at the settlement to hold off the Demons. Meanwhile, we and the new squad will loop around and come upon the Demons from behind. Do you understand?"

A wolfish grin came over his face, and he nodded. "I see. It shall be done."

It took an hour for the second squad to arrive. Then we started following the tracks. But not too far. Only one of the Demons had been needed to place that skull where it would be found, and it was his job to lead us off. As soon as the tracks in the snow began leading off in the wrong direction, Hrotokar and I led the men around in an arc, back toward the settlement.

Sure enough, the place was under siege.

The besiegers had the place surrounded. Hrotokar had been underestimating when he said that there were half again as many of the invaders as there were of Father Wolfslayer's people. There were over 50 males of the Demons surrounding the log cabins. That meant that their total numbers probably exceeded 100.

The Demons were human, of course. There was nothing supernatural about them. They came from the far east of Asia, I think. They were big, about six feet tall, and their faces were definitely Oriental. Mongols? Huns? I don't know. You name it, and you can have it. You wouldn't want it.

They weren't Eskimos; I knew that. But they wore "frost." Polar bear skins. White, you see. And they came from the North.

That makes sense, too. Look at a map of northern Europe. In order to get down into southern Sweden, they'd *have* to come from the North. From the East, they'd have had to come up through Finland and down south again.

Whoever they were, I did not like them.

They were closing in on the settlement when I and the 14 men with me came up behind them.

"Do we attack now, Fire-Hair?" Hrotokar asked softly. I don't know why, but he had evidently decided to give the leadership to me. He didn't sound very confident—after all, 15 men against 50?—but for some reason he trusted me.

"Friend," I asked gently, "how many of those could you kill in a charge?"

His eyes narrowed as he looked at me. "We come from behind. At least 15. Perhaps 30."

"Good. Kill me 15, and the rest I shall take care of."

I only had 50 rounds of ammo, and in a firefight you can't be sure every shot will count.

His eyes widened. "Do you swear?"

"I swear by the All-Father and by my life," I said. "Go, Friend Hrotokar. Kill the cannibal sons-of-bitches!" And I added: "When you go, scream like furies! I will be with you every hand of the way."

And I was.

When the two squads charged in, screaming war cries, I was with them. The Demons heard us and turned.

They came at us, spears at the ready. When there was 20 yards between the two opposing ranks, I tossed away my spear and shield, dropped to one knee and drew my pistol.

The thunder of that weapon echoed across the snowfield as I placed each shot. I think my own men hesitated when they heard that noise, but they charged on when they saw it was me doing the damage.

They didn't know what to make of it, but they saw the Demons, the Eaters-of-Men, fall one after another, and they knew I was doing my part, as I had promised.

Forty-five caliber hardball slugs from service ammo does more damage to living flesh than any other handgun ammo in existence. A man hit solidly with one of those bullets goes down and stays down.

I fired as if I were firing at pop-up targets, except that there was no 'friend-or-foe.' If it was wearing a polar-bear suit, it was a foe.

The cold hatred for these horrors burned in my brain. They were targets, nothing more. They were things to be shot down and obliterated. When one magazine was empty, I put in another without even thinking about it.

I still had half a magazine left when the fighting was over.

Forty-four of the no-good sons-of-bitches had fallen to me. Hrotokar and his squads had taken care of the rest.

I sat there on the ground, exhausted. Killing is not fun;

259

it is horrible. It is something you must do to preserve your own life, or that of your loved ones.

I don't know how long I sat there, with my pistol in my hand, but the next thing I knew, there was someone towering above me.

"Giant Tay'or Fire-Hair," he began. Then he stopped.

I looked up. It was Father Wolfslayer. He looked rather frightened. He cleared his throat.

I stood up to face him. I still couldn't talk.

All of of them backed away from me—not in fear, but in reverence. I didn't like that.

"We know you now for what you are," the Wolfslayer continued. "We will—"

And then something cut him off. The world spun again.

Ulglossen, having finished the experiments necessary, prepared to return to—

But wait! In the 21st decimal, there was an aberration. Some life-form had been dragged from its proper space-time. Poor thing. On the way back, Ulglossen would return the life-form to its proper era. More or less. After all, one should be kind, but one need not be overly solicitous toward life-forms of the past. Still, Ulglossen was a kindly being.

There was no snow on the ground. I was alone in the forest.

Before me was the dead pine that Sten Ömfeld had drawn a target on.

I turned. There was Sten's lodge, 50 yards away.

I went toward it. It didn't fade or go away. It was solid, as it should be. Somehow, some way, I was back in my own time.

I walked to the door. I think it took me at least two minutes to decide to open it.

"Sten?" I said.

"Yah? What do you want? I thought you were going out to shoot."

"Changed my mind," I said. "I'm short of ammo."

"Dumbbell," he said kindly. "Sit down and relax. We'll have a drink together when I'm finished."

"Sure, Sten; sure," I said. I sat down on the couch.

I think I know what happened. I remember hearing Hrotokar in the background saying: "His hammer smashed them! Killed them! And then came back to his hand!"

I can see how that illusion could come about. I hold the hammer in my hand and there is a thunderbolt and the foe falls dead—his head smashed in. And then the hammer is back in my hand. Sure.

Those folk had already shortened my name from "Teydor" to "Tey'or"; why not one syllable further?

My weapon has a name now, as Sten suggested. I looked up a man who knows Norse runes, and I had another man engrave those runes on my pistol, on the right, just above the trigger.

The engraving says: *Mjolnir.*

Yah.

The original.